"Don't taun[...]

Before Lacey could move or speak, his mouth mated with hers in a harsh, angry kiss. The solid wood door pressed against her back as unyielding as the solid length of his body fit itself to hers. His lips were savage, without gentleness, without tenderness. Lacey had to breathe, but his mouth captured her own so that she had to breathe with him and of him. The taste was bittersweet, possessive, and there was no way to escape the feverish pounding that spread through her whole body . . .

———————————
———————————

Praise for Theresa DiBenedetto's romantic masterpiece

SILVER MIST

"SIZZLING ROMANCE!
YOU'LL DEVOUR EVERY LINE."
—KAREN HARPER, author of *The Firelands*

"A RIVETING, COMPELLING LOVE STORY . . .
WITH *SILVER MIST*, THERESA DIBENEDETTO
ESTABLISHES HERSELF AS A POWERFUL AND
VERSATILE VOICE IN ROMANCE."
—*Romantic Times*

"COMPELLING . . . THIS IS CHOICE READING
WHERE YOU SINK INTO THE LUSCIOUS SPAR
AND PARRY BETWEEN A WOMAN BECOMING
AWARE OF HER SENSUALITY AND A MAN
BECOMING AWARE OF HIS HEART.
DON'T MISS IT!"
—*Rendezvous*

Diamond Books by Theresa DiBenedetto

SILVER MIST
WESTERN WINDS

WESTERN WINDS

THERESA DIBENEDETTO

DIAMOND BOOKS, NEW YORK

WESTERN WINDS

A Diamond Book / published by arrangement with
the author

PRINTING HISTORY
Diamond edition / September 1991

ISBN: 1-55773-577-8

Diamond Books are published by The Berkley Publishing Group,
200 Madison Avenue, New York, New York 10016.
The name "DIAMOND" and its logo
are trademarks belonging to Charter Communications, Inc.

PRINTED IN THE UNITED STATES OF AMERICA

10 9 8 7 6 5 4 3 2 1

To Tom and Libby
and their precious gifts of love,
Michael and Krysta.
And to my editor,
Hillary Cige,
whose caring and support
mean a great deal to me.

Chapter 1 ═══════════

"SO THAT'S THE Garrett princess."

"I warned you not to make condemning judgments," came the harsh reply, whispered as the graveside mourners raised their voices on the last notes of the hymn.

A slender, black-gowned young woman lifted her head, the absence of mourning hat and veil conspicuous among the somber crowd. Her gaze skimmed those who stood with heads respectfully bowed as they listened to the minister's words and targeted the two men standing well behind the mourners. The taller one, shabbily dressed, pulled his flat-crowned hat lower, hiding his eyes, but she felt the demand in them for her to look at him. Lacey Garrett no longer yielded to any man's command. She glanced away.

Coiled tension rode the man's hard body as the Texas morning sun spread its blanketing heat. When his elderly companion spoke, he listened but refused to shift his gaze away from her.

"We'll wait in Sy's office until everyone leaves. There won't be any awkwardness or unnecessary questions. I've already instructed Lacey and Curt Blaine to join us there."

"Us or you? You aren't gonna tell me that you spilled your precious secret." The laugh that followed was low but bitter. "This Blaine, her lawyer, isn't gonna take your news kindly. He's got her staked out, hog-tied, and ready for his branding iron."

1

"He'll accept it. They all will."

"And the princess? Will she meekly accept it?"

"Lacey will do whatever is necessary to keep the Reina. She knows her place. A bit spirited and prideful, I'll admit, but then, she's had to be. Ranching isn't easy for a woman."

"Woman? No. She's packaged skin and bone made up to look like one."

"That's enough! You don't know Lacey. You and the rest of them here don't understand how Sy raised her. Let's go. I want to be away from here before they're finished." The command in his voice brooked no refusal.

With a lazy stride the man sauntered after him, a smile curving his lips as he ignored the curious stares that followed them. The good judge had unwittingly provided him with weapons for the battle to come. Weapons, his hunter's instinct assured him, the Garrett princess wouldn't know how to counter.

"It's shocking, Hattie! She didn't shed one tear while your husband conducted that lovely service. Why, it was unnatural. And her disappearing like this is simply adding another disgrace," announced Mary Howard, a matron of some years and wife to one of Austin's most prominent bankers. A plain-faced daughter and a husband who quailed under her constant temper had left her with a bitter, jealous disposition. Thinking of the earlier rebuff that Lacey Garrett had given her, she was pleased to vent her anger.

"But then," she continued loudly, "what could anyone expect with the way she was raised. Breeches and guns! Even that name—Lacey—as fancy as the airs her mother gave herself. I declare to you, Hattie, that girl's a snip, marked for scandal. Wait and see if I'm not proven right." Without a thought to who might overhear her imperious voice, Mary was set to begin anew when the wrenlike woman at her side interrupted.

"Wouldn't you agree Lacey needs our charity now that her father is dead, too? The girl has no kinfolk to help her. It's a shame she was raised without a mother's gentle influence. And we all heard Tom Darcy declare his intent of forcing her to sell the Reina."

"Do you mean to tell me, Hattie Pearl Barnes, that you, a minister's wife, defend her? Could you possibly approve of the way she conducted herself today? Don't you agree that Sy Garrett raised her to be a hellion?"

"No. Dear me, no. That wasn't—"

"*No?*"

"Well, yes, I agree her upbringing—"

"Oh, hush! You haven't been in Sonora long enough to understand our ways. Until you do, I wouldn't put forth any of these foolish notions. Folks here, the important ones, that is, might take offense. And you do want them to contribute to the church's building fund, don't you?"

Faced with Mrs. Howard's imperious stare, Hattie bobbed her head in submissive agreement. After all, she consoled herself, Lacey Garrett had proved she could take care of herself, while Hattie and her husband were dependent on Mrs. Howard's good graces. Privately she felt sorry for the young woman, but she could not afford to antagonize her husband's staunchest supporter.

Seeking to remove herself from the opinionated woman, Hattie's squinting eyes focused on Maggie Olin, the Garretts' housekeeper, as she made her way to the once food-laden table. Hattie hurried to clear a space for the large bowl Maggie was carrying. A flush added a bit of color to her pale cheeks, and she hoped Maggie wouldn't hold her responsible for Mary Howard's opinions.

She need not have worried. Maggie would never give

anyone the satisfaction of acknowledging their criticism of Lacey. Privately she might agree with them, and the good Lord knew she verbally tore strips from Lacey's hide from time to time when she tried to flout every ladylike rule Maggie tried to instill in her. Fussing with positioning the large bowl of hot spicy chili she set down, Maggie frowned when she realized there was no sign of Lacey's black-garbed figure. It was foolish to think that for once she wouldn't have given them more to talk about.

Stepping aside to allow people access to the food, Maggie was annoyed by their greed. Platters that had been heaped with food bore only crumbs. Perhaps Lacey was being disrespectful by some people's standards, but Maggie thought of the mourners as a swarm of locusts who would come after the spoils of the Reina if Lacey was not strong.

"Ain't much left to eat, Maggie."

Hearing the familiar voice of Doc Culver, she smiled. "No, Doc, there ain't much, thank goodness. Maybe they'll soon leave." Maggie issued a reproving glance at the half-filled glass of whiskey he held, and Doc chuckled.

"Now, Maggie, don't take on so. I needed a bit of fortifyin' to listen to them."

"They hate Lacey. They hated Sy, too, but he was strong enough to make them respect him. I don't know what's goin' to happen to Lacey and—"

". . . and that gal has a temper that wants coolin'," Doc finished for her. "Seems to me Fletcher disappeared as well," he added with a searching glance over the men and the women he had tended for almost ten years.

"You didn't see Lacey?" Maggie wished he had, wished that he or someone Lacey respected had spoken to her. A building tension shimmered in the air, and Maggie felt ghostly fingers walk up her spine.

"No, not since we got back from the service. Don't worry

so, Maggie. Lacey can take care of herself. Here, let me help you carry these platters back."

"Thanks, Doc, but Annie McBride is tryin' to get your attention. She's due for her fourth soon. Go on," she urged.

Maggie was distracted by the men crowding the tables set with gallon jugs of homemade cider and rotgut whiskey. With a frown she noticed they had already emptied the crystal decanters of fine aged brandy that was once Sy Garrett's pride, since he had paid dearly to have it shipped from back East. Not even the Civil War tearing apart a country had interfered with Sy getting what he wanted. Lacey had won the argument to set the decanters out. A wry smile creased Maggie's lips. Few of the good ladies present had refused the sherry set aside for them, as evidenced by more than one flushed face.

Maggie stepped back from the table, rubbing the ache in the back of her neck. She had been up before dawn frying chickens and baking hams, although everyone attending the service had brought along baskets filled with foodstuffs, as was custom. She noticed that as the sun climbed to herald midday, people were beginning to seek shelter under the wide overhang of the roof that surrounded the open court-yard. Graceful arches allowed whatever breeze there was to reach the rooms that opened from the square. Maggie thought Sy had chosen well when he staked his claim to this land and reclaimed a burned-out shell of an old Spanish mission for his home. She shook her head, knowing Sy had taken pride in restoring its beauty, maybe too much so, just as he had taken pride in molding Lacey to what he had wanted.

Lost as Maggie was in her thoughts, it took a few moments for her to notice the sudden hush of voices. She turned, puzzled, and saw Lacey closing the door to her room. Gone was Lacey's high-necked gown of mourning.

Maggie watched her, disbelief forcing her to swallow a sigh of exasperation when she realized Lacey was dressed in her oldest working clothes. Lacey is deliberately trying to shock her guests, Maggie thought, as she focused on the look of defiance on Lacey's face.

The silence remained absolute as Maggie hurried to her side. "What devil rides you now to come out dressed like that in front of them?" she whispered, furious.

Lacey's warning look silenced her. Silenced her and those that stood gaping. One by one Lacey faced them down until a soft but steady murmur of voices began to hum once more. She knew Maggie was angry and rightly so about the worn twill pants that clung like a second skin to every curve. Lacey admitted that her faded blue shirt was tight, but she had worn a short black leather vest to hide the fullness of her breasts straining the fabric. She almost smiled recalling her father's warning when he handed her the vest for her fourteenth birthday. While she admired its supple softness, he had ordered her to wear it always. "Hide those curves," he said. "Keep the men in line that way. The less they remember you're female, the less trouble you'll have bossin' 'em." But Sy had been dead for six weeks. She was the undisputed boss of the Reina now, and that reminder made her lift her chin in an arrogant move.

Maggie could not understand what had made Lacey behave this way. It seemed to go beyond an act of defiance. Oh, she could recall times in the past when Lacey, with mule-headed stubbornness, had flouted Sy's laws and more than a few of Maggie's own rules, but never in such a disrespectful manner. With an abrupt move Lacey settled her flat-crowned hat firmly on her head, the few loose tendrils of hair that escaped it adding to her unladylike appearance. Her thick chestnut mane of hair was pulled back into the long single braid she favored, and Maggie thought of the time she had wasted trying to get Lacey to sit still long enough to pin it all into a decorous chignon.

"Well, now that you've all looked your fill, I'll leave." Lacey's silky voice held a challenge that carried across the courtyard. A few murmurs rose in disapproval, but she ignored them, walking with her head held high as people silently stepped aside to allow her passage.

Standing in the shadowed recess of an open doorway, one man's eyes followed her regal progress with a glint of admiration. He lifted his glass in silent salute before sipping the smooth-as-velvet whiskey. Summoned back into the room and ordered once again to close the door, he did so.

"There! That shows you, Hattie!" Mrs. Howard's voice, so unmistakable, rose above the others.

Lacey stopped and turned around slowly. With a cold smile that never reached her eyes, she stood there until she had once again gained their attention.

"Don't anyone leave on my account. I want you all to feel as welcome as you've been when Sy was alive. And just as welcome as you've always made me feel."

Lacey spun gracefully on booted heels, and her long strides carried her to the large imposing gates set in the back adobe wall. Two men crowded in on each side of her, but before they spoke to Lacey, the sly, sugared tones of April Darcy reached them.

"I told you she's afraid of dressing like a woman. Everyone knows she got to try an' be hard as a man, or she'll lose the Reina. Then who would want her even if she could pretend to be female?"

Janny Howard's timid voice hushed April as Lacey once again turned around. Her mocking gaze picked its insulting way over April's dark blue gown, lingering over each bit of abundant lace trim and the ruffles dancing with every heaving, furiously drawn breath. She knew she should ignore April's goading, just as Maggie and Sy had always cautioned her to do. But Sy was dead and Maggie was already angry with her. She had given these hard-bitten Texans enough to feed the gossips for a month of Sundays to come, but there was not a one of them who understood what she was feeling, April least of all.

When April couldn't stand another moment of Lacey's mocking look, she stood up. "Well, did a sidewinder get yore tongue?"

"No. I was just wondering what you knew about being a woman, April, wrapped up like some bit of fluff a man might set on his mantel to look at. 'Course, he could take you down now and again, dust you off, and show you about, but he wouldn't find much use beyond that for you, would he? You couldn't stand behind him, beside him, or up to him since you're so scared of soiling those precious lily-white hands. And that's the only thing that's lily-white about you."

"Lacey, that's enough!"

She glared at her lawyer, ready to answer him, but Doc Culver came between them, hustling Lacey off to one side.

With a last warning look at April's flushed face, Lacey looked beyond her to meet Tom Darcy's furious gaze. He wouldn't take the insult to his daughter lightly. Lacey smiled then and flipped one finger at her hat brim in salute, her stance indicating her readiness to do verbal battle with him, but Doc cut her off from their view.

"Just ignore the silly chit," he sagely advised. "She's not worth your gettin' riled over."

"I know I should have better sense than to listen to anything that spiteful witch has to say."

"April's never forgiven you for drivin' her brother away. You know how hard you were on Evan, even if I give you right not takin' him seriously. Sy wouldn't have let you marry him anyway, and that's a fact neither of the Darcys can accept."

"Sy would've chewed Evan up and spit him out in little bits. But Evan made his own decision about leaving. You'd think with him gone over a year that April and her father would let the past die."

"She's shown a definite bent toward having a malicious streak since she came back from that fancy girl's school back East. April enjoys baitin' you, Lacey, knowin' it wins her father's approval. What's more, you let her do it." His firm hands, belying his age, captured Lacey's. "Now, don't go gettin' your back up with me, girl. She's had a hard time of it, too, what with her pa thinkin' there ain't a man around good enough to court her. An' you both been raised motherless."

"Darcy will sell her to the highest bidder. He's made that as plain as his intentions of seeing me brought to heel and forced to give up the Reina. Much as I hate to say it, maybe it's a good thing Sy's sons never lived. Darcy would have April coiling like a snake around any man who could claim the Reina. I told him I'd see him in hell first." Her voice lent conviction to the fierce glitter in her eyes. "I'll fight that man any way I can with whatever it takes before I see him claim one blade of grass on Reina soil."

"Listen up, girl." Doc demanded her attention with a rough shake of her hands. "I knew when I warned Sy two years ago to ease up the brutal demands he made on that agin' body of his that this was gonna be. I'm surprised he lasted as long as he did. But then, he was a tough son of a gun. I want you to know I think you done a fine job in his place, and don't let anyone tell you otherwise."

Lacey nodded, impatient to leave him.

"You seen Judge Walker yet?"

"No, not yet. I'll see him after everyone leaves. Why?"

"Don't matter. Just you remember that Sy was a damn stubborn old fool," he stated gruffly, releasing her hands. "He was a bull of a man outwardly and a hard man to know. I called him friend, an' times were when it wasn't easy to do. His boots ain't gonna be easy to fill, girl, but he was a fool just the same."

Lacey found his remarks puzzling, but she was anxious to be gone. Leaving him, she came abreast of the open gates, annoyed to see that Curt Blaine and Ward Farel, the Reina's foreman, were waiting for her. She greeted them both with a curt nod.

"I'll ride out with you, Lacey," Ward said, pushing his wide-brimmed hat back on his head.

"I don't want anyone with me." His assumption that she wanted his company added to her annoyance. "I thought you were riding the north range to help Dex bring in that small bunch of yearlings."

"Ragweed's helping." The calm in his eyes belied the anger tightening his gut. "Wouldn't have stayed otherwise," he added, his tone low and respectful as always.

"And the extra men guarding the herd, is that taken care of?" When he hesitated in answering, Lacey clenched her hands into fists at her sides. "Ward, Sy hired you on, but you're kept on by me because I expected you to be able to follow all of my orders now." Lacey knew her tone insinuated that he was failing in that, for he lowered his gaze from hers.

"I'll see to it." Someday, he vowed, he would put that hellcat down where she belonged. But not even to satisfy the ache she caused in his loins would he jeopardize the soft spot he had on the Reina. He wasn't alone in his feelings. Curt Blaine stared hungrily at Lacey. Hell, Ward told himself, touching his brim respectfully and walking away, she was the kind of half-girl, half-woman a man ached to tame. But he had the advantage of time and place over the slick lawyer. Plenty of time to make his move.

"You were hard on him, Lacey," Curt pointed out, grabbing her arm to detain her. "You were going to stop and speak to me, weren't you?" Lacey's resentful look was his answer. "Well, you're going to hear me out. You can't talk to the men who work for you as if they haven't a bit of pride and then expect them to stay on now that Sy is dead." Softly then he coaxed, "Let me come with you. There's no need for you to ride out alone. We need to talk, and you can't keep me at arm's length now."

"Can't I?" His grip on her arm tightened, making her wish she had not goaded him. But she could not stand to see the pleading look in his brandy-warm eyes. "Curt, I'm grateful for your help these last few weeks. I couldn't have handled the paperwork and the ranch without you. But I need to get away from here—and I need to be alone. If I stay, I'll give them more to talk about."

Having no doubt that she would do just that, he released her arm. "Don't be long. The judge wants to see both of us before he leaves. And Lacey, stop being hard on these people. Most of them traveled a distance to pay their respects today. Sy was a man—"

". . . they hated and feared," she finished for him.

"Why do you goad them? Do you know the position you put me in by leaving? Wasn't waiting this long to hold a service to mark his passing enough?"

"You're judging me!"

"Me and everyone else here!"

Lacey bit her lower lip. She couldn't defend herself. She had given her word to Judge Walker that she wouldn't tell anyone he had asked her to wait until he returned.

Her silence stirred Curt's anger. "Do you care how hard I worked trying to smooth down the good ladies' ruffled feathers this morning? Even I'll be hard-pressed to keep this quiet. Can't you understand that you're not a child anymore?"

"I never was a child." Her voice was cool—low but cool. "And yes, I do understand exactly what I've done. You're the one who doesn't understand me if you think I give a hoot about gossipy old women."

"You should!" His hand thrust angrily through his hair, his slim body vibrating with tension. "How can we marry when you wouldn't be asked into one of their homes?"

With an abrupt move Lacey rushed through the gates, but Curt kept pace with her, crowding her against the adobe wall. "Hey, I'm sorry." He leaned close, attempting to take her into his arms, but Lacey neatly sidestepped him to avoid his embrace.

"All right. I'll wait. But just remember that although I'm a patient man when I want something, even I have my limit—and you're pushing me close to it."

One look at the flushed, set expression of his face told Lacey he was not finished yet. Resigned to listening to him, she leaned against the wall, careful to keep distance between them.

Her move brought a darker flush of resentment to his face. "I merely wanted to remind you—"

"What? That I'm not behaving like a lady? Or was it about marriage? I don't—"

"Stop it. It wasn't about us. I wanted to remind you that those same women you scorn so easily happen to number among them the wives of Austin's bankers. You'll need those men in the next few months for loans to tide you over until the herd is culled and sold. I can't believe you would forget that."

"You're too late with your warning. I already insulted Mrs. Howard."

"Howard! Her husband runs the largest Austin bank for the group of Eastern investors." There were times that he could shake her for her damn prideful foolishness.

"She dared to tell me that if I had an ounce of good sense like her sweet little Janny, I would marry the first man to have me."

"I asked. I'm still waiting."

"Don't start about marriage again," she snapped.

"Couldn't you control your temper long enough to listen and then walk away?"

"Listen? Walk away? Like I said, you don't know me. I don't need her reminder that I'm past the acceptable age of being choosy. Nor did I need to be told that with men so scarce around here for someone like me, I'd better take what I could. And don't bother cross-examining me. I don't remember exactly what I said that made her take off in a huff that should've burst her tight stays." Once again he blocked her forward move. "Please, I appreciate your concern, but—"

"Damn you, Lacey! Your appreciation isn't what I want."

"It's all I've got to give you now." She couldn't meet his gaze, which was filled with raw desire. Never again would she allow herself to be vulnerable to any man. Lacey knew her strengths and her weaknesses; she would not pay the demanded price for intimacy again. "Whatever else you want to talk about can wait until I get back."

"No. Not this time." His stance was aggressive, and Lacey was forced back against the wall. "I've had to put up with your insistence in having your own way about everything, including the wait to hold this memorial service—"

"How dare you!" she interrupted, her body rigid. "It was my decision to make. I own the Reina now, and I share my burdens and decisions with no one. Not even you, Curt. I had good reason for what I did. That's all you need to know. Besides, any show of weakness on my part when Sy died might have cost me the men I had hired. Darcy is just waiting for a chance to move in. I can't afford—"

"I know. I can't argue over that." A good lawyer knew when to admit defeat, and Curt considered himself one of the best. Lacey was headstrong, stubborn enough not to be swayed by any arguments he could voice that she was not capable of running the Reina. She already was.

"Before you go, did Judge Walker say why he had to see both of us before he leaves to ride circuit from here?"

"No. And I haven't seen him since the service. Do you know where he is?"

Lacey drew one leg up, resting her booted heel against the wall. Distracted by the seductive pose she innocently presented, Curt's gaze traveled the long length of her legs outlined by fitted pants. Raising his eyes to meet hers, he knew she was angry, but this time he didn't bother to soothe her.

"He's in Sy's office with that hard-faced saddle tramp he brought with him."

Lacey nodded, walking past him. She vaguely remembered the towering height of the shabbily dressed man standing alongside the judge at the gravesite. His face had been shadowed by the thick beginnings of a beard, his hat pulled low to hide his eyes. He had made her uncomfortable for a few moments with his intent staring, almost as if he were willing her to notice him.

She dismissed the notion as fanciful thinking.

What would a saddle tramp that the judge had in tow have to do with her or the Reina?

Chapter 2 ====

FROWNING AS SHE walked briskly toward the corral, Lacey knew she could not ignore Curt much longer. There had to be a way to make him understand that no man was going to rule her or the Reina.

Her horse, saddled and waiting, greeted her with a soft nicker. Restless, the stallion tossed his head, rattling the bridle bit as she mounted him. Wrapping the reins securely over her gloved hands, Lacey urged him into a long strided canter.

She deliberately ignored Ward standing with two of their hands in front of the bunkhouse. He was angry with her and had been since Sy died. Lacey knew their confrontations were obvious to the men. Ward was a good foreman, but he seemed to go out of his way to challenge her every chance that he could. If Fletcher Ross had not injured his leg breaking a mustang, he would still be foreman of the Reina. But Sy had known the pain his oldest and near only friend endured when he rode, so he had hired Ward to take his place.

As Lacey passed the last of the outbuildings, Fletcher hailed her, limping slightly. When Lacey rode up to him, he patted the sleek roan's neck. "Where'yer headin'?"

"Anywhere I don't have to listen to them."

"Ain't had time for yoreself since Sy passed on."

"I mourn him in my own way. It was just—well, I can't worry about what anyone thinks."

"Ain't got no call to tell me. I know. Seen Darcy?"

"Couldn't help it," she bitterly acknowledged. "His eyes rivaled a fire, they were so bright while he listened to the memorial service. I didn't want him on Reina land when we buried Sy six weeks ago, and if he's smart, Darcy'll be gone from my land before I get back."

"Don't know why the judge said to allow him to come," Fletcher remarked.

"I told you he insisted. I couldn't very well refuse him. After all, you and the judge were Sy's best friends. I wouldn't refuse you anything that you asked of me."

"The judge didn't seem much like hisself. Acted plumb nervous, like he had somethin' heavy on his mind."

"Well, when I get back I'll ask him. Funny that he made me promise not to let Curt read the will without him."

"You ain't worried? Ain't got a call to be. An' the judge bein' Sy's friend was most likely gonna tell you that if you needed him, he'll be there for you." With a last pat to the roan's neck he stepped back. "Go on with you. I'll mosey on up to the house and see if I can't get me some vittles. Maggie had me up and workin' in the kitchen with her afore dawn."

"Guess that platter of cold fried chicken and ham she stashed in the pantry must have your name on it. Maggie wouldn't let you go hungry, Fletcher."

"An' pie?" he called out. "Did she save me some pie?"

"Might have," Lacey returned, using the slight pressure of her knees to bring the horse into a canter. The moment she was out of sight, she felt the tension begin to ease.

An hour later she urged the horse up a steep rock climb, stopping before the edge of a slanted rock shelf that overlooked the Reina.

Beneath the shadow of her hat brim, her hazel eyes were a flash of light sweeping the vast expanse of undulating land that spread out before her and could only be compared in scope to the dominating blue sky above her.

Hooking one slender leg casually over the high pommel, she left the other to rest in the well-worn stirrup. She played with the ends of the reins, completely at ease with herself and her surroundings. Pride filled her.

"Mine." She whispered the word, understanding the pride that had been nurtured and instilled in her since she had been old enough for Sy to take her up before him and ride every foot of land. She dropped the reins, allowing the roan to nibble the short grass. Her touch was both admiring and affectionate to his sleek neck, for the stallion was her joy and the last gift Sy had given her, three months before on her twentieth birthday.

A thin silver haze of heat shimmered above the land, blending with the blue haze of distance as she turned to look behind her. East lay the swirling blue ribbon of the Colorado River winding its way toward the city of Austin. To the south her eyes tracked the beauty of the Blue Mountains, draped with an azure-blue light of the sky reflecting off their silver peaks. She twisted in the saddle, looking west, unable to see the Devil River but knowing it was there, and before it the small town of Sonora. Last, she gazed north, where the ranch boundary sprawled invisibly along the rugged foothills of the Bradys like a carelessly thrown blanket. Beyond them lay the unsettled lands that were home to the Comanche. The thought crossed her mind that many of the places in Texas had kept their Spanish or Indian names or reflected, as did her own home, the white-washed adobe buildings that foretold their Spanish origins.

It was a vast land, where there was room to think and

plan and dream, and she loved it. Loved the land, the heat, and the silence. Sy had known that. He had entrusted her to carry on with his dream.

It was here on the rock shelf that Sy had first stopped with Fletcher on his restless westward journey and made his decision that this was the land to claim.

Lacey found herself thinking of all the times she had questioned Sy why it was later that he named this spot the Queen's Rock and changed both the ranch's name and their brand to the Reina. Somehow he had managed to turn aside her questions. But Sy was a master at turning her aside.

The sound of cows lowing brought her attention to the cattle that spread like a russet tide in rich contrast to the lush grasses. Short-horned Durhams outnumbered the grand Texas longhorns munching contentedly on the newly curled spring grass. Cattle lay in the dappled shade of huge clumps of sagebrush, chewing quietly, waiting for sunset. They numbered close to four thousand head of prime stock that would bring her top dollar when the herd was sold. A few more weeks would see them sleek and fat enough to drive up to the newly completed railhead of the Kansas Pacific Railroad at Abilene. Lacey felt the same eager surge to get on with building the Reina, as did most of the people in the western territories. The Civil War had been over for nearly two years, and nothing could stop the tide of settlers searching for new land.

It was a fact she was aware of just as she had been forced to acknowledge that Sy's death, sudden as it was, could not interfere with the working of the ranch. With a shaken sigh she knew she could not allow anything to sidetrack her from her goal of keeping the Reina. Her lips trembled, her eyes held a stricken look of vulnerability, and her throat constricted tightly. A hoof striking stone startled her, and she turned to find a man watching her.

"Bo, you—"

"Figured you'd be up here."

"Yes. It somehow seemed the right place to come and mourn him."

He nodded, making no move to come closer or to talk. He had known she would come to the Queen's Rock, her place of solitude. And while most of the hands would stay away, he could not. His gaze lingered on the toll the last weeks had taken on Lacey. There were bruised shadows beneath her eyes, a hollowness to her cheeks, and a pale translucence to her lightly tanned skin. He gritted his teeth. It wasn't his place to comment. Lacey was driving herself as hard as she drove the men, and he wasn't sure who would break first.

"Want to talk?" he asked softly, making no move to dismount.

"In a bit."

"I got time. Always have for you."

Lacey acknowledged his words with a shy smile. Bo James always had time and patience for her, teaching her whatever she wanted to know, giving her, as Fletcher and Maggie did, the warmth and caring that Sy had no measure of for a motherless child.

"They still down there, waitin'?" he asked, motioning toward the sprawl of buildings far below them.

"Might be they're waiting to hear the terms of Sy's will. Why, I don't know." Her finely arched brows drew together in a frown.

"There ain't a question of who's gettin' the Reina?"

"No. Maybe they just want fodder for gossip."

"Hear tell you gave 'em plenty today and more'n enough in years past," he remarked with a grin.

Lacey returned it. Bo's face was rugged, lined with

spider-webbed creases. His eyes held the permanent squint of a man who spent too long in the sun.

"I'll stay, if you want."

"Sure." There was no need for her talk. Bo understood her silences. And she had to think of a way to make everyone, especially Curt, accustom themselves to the idea that she and she alone controlled her actions and the Reina. A gentle breeze blew a few stray tendrils of hair across her face, and her move was impatient to secure them beneath her hat. A small, impish grin touched her lips briefly, remembering the shocked looks her action had caused. She felt no guilt. Sy would have done the same. He had encouraged her to be independent.

Sy. Everything came back to him. Sometimes she felt frightened by the task he had left her.

Her sigh made Bo ask, "You ain't worried 'bout handlin' the Reina on your own? 'Cause if you are, don't. Me and the boys are all behind you."

"No, it's not that. But you're sweet to reassure me. I think I'm looking forward to the challenge. It's Curt's possessive behavior that bothers me. I don't want any man to clutter up my life. And Mrs. Howard—"

"That peacock hen?"

"Can't argue with you there. But she reminded me that I should think about marrying. If I don't, who will I leave the Reina to?"

"Curt offered for you more'n once. Seems to me he'd do right by you."

"He'll never love the Reina the way Sy did." Turning away, Lacey missed the tightening of Bo's lips. The breeze, slight as it was, died away, leaving a sultry heat to settle oppressively around her. Hunched over the pommel with her elbow resting on her knee, Lacey absently opened two more buttons on her shirt. She closed her eyes for a moment, murmuring, "Doc said Sy was a bull of a man and that his boots would be hard to fill. Even the minister said that Sy was a man among men. There isn't anyone that could deny it."

"Might be true," he answered with a grim tone. "All but Darcy, that is."

"Darcy? He's always hated Sy. Somehow I think their animosity went beyond a fight over water and land. You've been here the longest after Fletcher, Bo. Do you know—"

"Ain't had a call to pry."

"Sorry." She faced him, her smile widening as he nodded. Sometimes it was hard to remember not to question a man about his past as long as he did his work, even someone like Bo, who had been here nearly eighteen years.

"I'd best be gettin' back. Watch yoreself."

Lacey watched him ride away, her lips trembling. She would miss Sy, but even now that she was alone, there were no tears. There had been none when he died, and none this morning. She had heard their whispered comments about her unnatural behavior. But she couldn't defend herself. How could she explain to anyone that Sy never allowed her to cry?

She squeezed her eyes shut, trying and failing to shut out the sound of his harsh, contemptuous voice.

"Cryin' ain't nothin' more'n a damn silly female trick. Women think they'll get their own way by sheddin' tears. You ain't gonna cry. You ain't gonna be growin' up like some weak-kneed female."

And she had not. Blinking her eyes against the blinding rays of sun, Lacey could not recall the last time she had cried. A hard man, some called Sy, and she above all knew it was true. He had not been an easy man to please. There was no memory of his ever hugging or kissing her. Maggie had been there to tend real or imagined bruises, and there had been plenty of them in trying desperately to please Sy.

She had never called him Father. Strange that she should think of that now.

The roan's shift from a three-legged doze demanded her attention. His proud head lifted high, and Lacey hastened to reassure him, gathering up the reins. Two riders were heading in her direction. She squinted, trying to make out who they were, but they were too far away. The stallion communicated his sudden impatience for standing so long, and Lacey urged him down the steep grade.

Her musings clarified her belief that Sy had raised her to rule the Reina, and while she was saddened by his death, it would be dishonest to deny she was more than ready to take on the challenge.

The heat was intense. Sweat rolled down her face and neck. Lacey wiped it aside with the back of her hand. A sudden chill along with the desire to urge the roan away from home beset her. She dismissed it as being tiredness and was forced to bring her horse into a walk as Luke Hollis, one of her newer hands, rode toward her and the other rider veered off toward the milling cattle.

Easing his own dun-colored horse alongside, he briefly touched the brim of his hat. "Folks gone?"

"I hope so. I'm just heading back."

"Found nearly forty head up near the bluff. Got to give you right 'bout 'em bein' there."

Lacey merely nodded, but secretly she was pleased with his admission. Keeping the horses to a walk, they ambled along. One of the biggest obstacles Lacey had to overcome was having the men accept her as boss. There had been one or two incidents in town in the last few weeks where her hands had taken a ribbing because they worked for a woman. Luke's loyalty lent her additional courage.

"Ward tell you we got fewer calves?"

"No. We haven't had a chance to go over the count."

"Don't mean to butt in, him bein' foreman, but you're right to keep 'em bunched up for a while. Don't 'spect trouble, but none of us can be sure what Darcy'll do."

"I told Ward I wanted extra men guarding the herd at night." Lacey was watching him, saw him frown, and knew that Ward had not said anything about her order. "Guess I'll remind him when I get back."

"You do that. Miz Lacey, it ain't my place, bein' as how I'm new here, but we're all behind you. I jus' wanted you to know that if there's anythin' I can do, jus' ask."

Her gratitude filled her softly murmured thank-you as she rode off. There was one last place that Lacey had to go before she returned to the house.

The lone stand of pines marked the gravesites. She didn't dismount but stopped, staring at the four small headstones. There were names carved on each, for her brothers, who had all died before their first year had passed. It was the one thing that had marred Sy's dream for the Reina. He lacked a son, a living one, she reminded herself.

The thought no longer had the power to hurt her as it had when she was a child, too young to understand his rages that made him lock himself in his office and drink away the devil plaguing him. She had learned to stay away from him until he would emerge with bloodshot eyes and bellow his strident orders. Those times were best forgotten. Her mother's grave was set off from the others', and Lacey felt a deep regret that she had never known the woman who had given birth to her. She was the last born, the only survivor, the hated blot on Sy's manhood. Painful memories that belonged buried with him.

Lacey rode on. She had served her years of apprenticeship and learned the best each man had to offer. The earning of the men's respect had come hard, for Sy could not demand that from them, but she had earned it.

The Reina was hers.

When she reached the corral, Fletcher watched her dismount and waved her away with the reminder that the judge was still waiting for her. Whitewashed adobe walls seemed to shimmer in the afternoon's heat. The two oaken gates, their brass trim gleaming, stood open, revealing the empty courtyard.

Lacey heaved a sigh of relief to find everyone gone and the area clean. In the silence the serenity seeped into her. Open tiled archways framed lush, flowering plants, and an underground spring, necessary for survival against Indian attacks, filled a small stone pool in the courtyard's center. Wrought-iron benches were scattered around. It was a setting that Sy had provided for his bride, who longed for her home in New Orleans. And for the first time in a long time Lacey wondered if her mother's family still lived there.

"So, you decided to come back?"

Maggie's voice, filled with reproach, came from behind her. Lacey faced her, knowing she was in for a lecture.

"Goin' off like that! Makin' a—"

"Maggie, don't. Not now. What I need is a hot bath after I get done with Curt and the judge."

Staring up at her narrowed eyes, Maggie noticed yet again the hardness that was becoming more than a protective shell in Lacey.

Lacey saw Curt step out of the office, his stance indicating his impatience with her delay.

"You changin' 'fore you go in there?"

"No, Maggie. I don't want the surface trappings of a woman to impede me. Sy always said that wolves prey on the weak." Lacey was as startled as Maggie by her choice of words. "Don't mind me," she hastened to assure her.

"I'm just tired. Neither Curt nor Judge Walker would hurt me."

"Well, you know my feelings 'bout that one. He might be a good lawyer, folks seem to think so, but I never liked him. You be careful. He thinks he owns you and the Reina. You wouldn't be wantin' to repeat—"

"That's enough, Maggie!" There was pain in her eyes that she didn't bother to hide. Only Maggie knew she had suffered a miscarriage on the trail drive. Lacey knew that she had been lucky she was not far along, and so she was able to keep Sy from finding out. As it was, Sy had been out of sorts with her for taking on with her female complaints. Lacey bore his mutterings, all the while thinking that he would kill Curt if he knew the truth.

"I didn't mean to hurt you. Wasn't meanin' to stir up the past. I'm just warnin' you, that's all."

Lacey couldn't answer her. She walked toward Curt, who stepped aside as she entered the room. Her eyes blinked as she stood a few moments, letting them adjust to the dim interior.

Curt leaned close to ask, "Where were you so long?"

"Doesn't matter, I'm here now. And stop questioning me in that tone," she added, angry with his possessiveness. Still disturbed by the past Maggie had raked up, Lacey didn't bother to look at him. "Well, let's get this over with."

She headed directly to the desk dominating the far corner of the room. Lacey's hesitation was barely noticed before she sat in what she still considered to be Sy's chair. With a quick motion she removed her hat, carelessly tossing it on the desk.

"Judge Walker," she acknowledged with a quick nod. He stood with a drink in hand before the massive stone fireplace. Lacey half heard his murmurs of sympathy as she fought down the memory of her sixteenth summer, when

Curt had arrived in the small town of Sonora to set up his practice. He was young and brash, filled with charm, and Lacey thought herself in love with him. By summer's end she was no longer a girl. It took her a few moments to collect herself, and she glanced around the room.

It was the restless move of the man in the far shadowed corner that attracted her attention. Once again he was staring at her with a direct boldness that instantly infuriated her.

"Who are you?"

"Let me explain, Lacey," the judge solemnly intoned. "This isn't going to be easy, but—"

"With all due respect," she interrupted, "I asked him. But why is he here? This is a private matter that concerns no one else. If you're afraid of his trying to run, I'll have Fletcher keep watch over him."

"That won't be necessary, Lacey. You're right about this matter being private, and if you will let me finish–"

"Finish?" she snapped. "Why don't you try for plain and simple? Why is he allowed to be here?" She faced Curt, noted his silence and his shrug. "What's going on?" It was an instinctive move that forced Lacey to look again at the man sitting with a lazy ease in the far corner.

She really didn't expect him to answer her. He knew it and grinned. But neither of the two men she had appealed to were jumping in to answer her.

"They allowed me to stay here, Miss Garrett, because I belong here, same as you."

"What!" Lacey's shock tremored her voice. In mute appeal she glanced up to find Curt by her side.

"The judge was trying to explain to you that this is Rafe Parrish."

The name meant nothing to her. Lacey glanced at each

man in turn: the judge lowered his gaze, Curt stared at the floor, and the stranger boldly returned her look.

"Who the hell is he?"

Curt and the judge shared a despairing look. It was Curt who spoke first. "You wanted it this way, so tell her." He stepped closer and gave her shoulder a reassuring squeeze.

"Yes, do that." Lacey was beset by a coiling knot of fear snaking its way up from deep inside herself. Gripping the edge of the desk, she waited.

"There's no way to soften what I must reveal," Judge Walker stated, pulling a thick sheaf of papers from the inside pocket of his suit jacket.

"In view of the extraordinary circumstances, Lacey, I want you to listen to him," Curt ordered. "I've already looked over the papers he has and verified that it is Sy's signature."

"Papers?" she asked, tension flowing insidiously.

"There's a new will, dated three months ago. The one I had in my possession is void. I've read this new will, and while the terms shock me, I have no doubt that these are Sy's instructions the judge is carrying out."

At the sound of the judge clearing his throat, Curt spun around. "Neither Lacey nor I question your integrity, but what's at stake here can't be dismissed lightly."

"I accept that, Curt."

Lacey stared at the stately figure of the judge. His bushy eyebrows met over a wide beaked nose, giving prominence to his eyes. "Please, go on."

"Since the few smaller bequests remain the same, I'll wait to read them and, with your permission, proceed to that which concerns you."

She listened to his somber voice read of Sy's being of sound mind and his careful deliberation before setting down the new terms of his will. Her knuckles whitened in a death grip against the wooden desk. Feeling the stranger's eyes upon her, while she refused to glance at him, frightened her more than she cared to admit.

". . . and to Lacey Garrett, I must first ask her for her forgiveness. No man was more proud to call her daughter. I cannot with clear conscience leave her less than one half of the lands herein known as—"

"No! It can't be!" she shouted. Curt silenced her with a look so forbidding, it frightened her. Was that her meek whisper, apologizing to the judge? It had to be, for he continued.

"To the man known as Rafe Parrish, I humbly ask for forgiveness and bequest unto him an equal share of my ranch, the Reina. If for any reason he cannot or will not assume his half ownership, the ranch belongs in its entirety to Lacey Garrett, provided the additional terms I have set forth are met by either or both of them." The judge stopped, glanced at Curt and then at Lacey before he went on.

"Rafe Parrish must be a full working partner on the ranch for one year after my death before his name shall appear on its deed. Should he marry within that time, the term will be considered fulfilled. For the woman known to all as Lacey Garrett, I hereby set the following condition: If she marries within the year of my death she forfeits her claim unless she has title by default."

If the judge continued, Lacey didn't hear him. She was in shock. He could not have done this to her. Not Sy. But Judge Walker would have no reason to lie—he would never be a party to forging a phony document. Curt said he verified Sy's signature. Curt could be trusted, if anyone could. He was still in love with her. It had to be true that she had not paid the price to call the Reina her own. From the grave Sy was still making the laws she had to live by. But who was Rafe Parrish?

Mentioning his name silently filled her with a vile bitterness. Before she thought, she blurted out, "Who the hell are you that Sy would leave you half the Reina? Are you some bastard son coming to claim his share?"

Curt's startled "Lacey!" was followed by both men moving to block Rafe's rise from the chair.

"Get out," she demanded.

"But, Lacey," Judge Walker protested, "I haven't finished. There's the matter of a letter and other papers that Sy ordered me to give you personally. I want, no, need to explain to you how all this came about."

"I don't want to hear any more now. Leave me," she stated with the ring of authority that had been hers too long to be denied.

Chapter 3

WITH A CONSIDERING look that measured Lacey's temper, Curt motioned to the judge and then, without a word, to Parrish, urging them to leave.

Lacey heard the door close behind them, but she stared unseeing up at the ceiling. Her fingers clutched the wooden arms of the massive padded leather chair, and then, suddenly, she sagged back against it weakly.

Never, never before had she felt such loss and pain as she did at this moment. Not even Sy's death had brought about this sweeping desolation. Betrayal by the man she strove all her life to please speared her. And most damning of all, she thought with rising fury, she had gone to pieces like a female. For the first time she felt threatened and faced making a decision without facts to help her.

Hatred flared high inside her for the man who, with a look, made her feel so vulnerable. She shrank away from thinking of Sy Garrett's betrayal. But what else could she call it? Her deep, shuddering breaths kept time with the wood-and-brass ornamental clock sitting on the mantel. The sudden prickling short hairs on her neck forced her gaze from the ceiling down across the room.

The man whose name would be alongside her own as owner of the Reina sat there watching her as arrogantly as if it were his right.

A fresh surge of helpless rage flooded her. Right? He had no rights! Their gazes locked and Lacey shivered. How dare he stare at her like a hungry, predatory wolf?

He had no right to make her aware of herself as a woman. And how could he make her afraid of him without having uttered a word? His gaze remained steady, pinning her to the chair. She couldn't stand the tremors shaking her.

No man was going to make her feel cornered like prey. She would be damned in hell if she would let him get away with disregarding her orders!

Lacey drew a deep breath and released it. She had been a woman in a man's world long enough not to realize that if she backed down this time, it would give him an advantage over her. No one had ever had that. Nor, she vowed, glaring at him, was he going to be the first.

"You were included in my orders to get out, mister."

He heard the barely veiled fury in her voice. A corner of his hard mouth lifted in a taunting smile as he watched her grit her teeth in an effort to control her temper. There was no doubt she had one, none at all.

Lacey stared at him. He rose from the chair and walked with a stalking, catlike grace to stand before her. Straining her neck, she looked up at him, realizing he was every bit as tall as Sy had been, well over six feet. He leaned toward her, his broad shoulders filling her vision. She wanted to cringe under his gaze. Never had she been forced to encounter such obvious, crude arrogance in any man's eyes. It was, she decided, stricken with fear, as if he had stripped her naked and found her wanting.

"Get out," she grated from between clenched teeth.

There was no betraying flicker of emotion in his face to indicate that he heard her. Lacey studied him, hate vying with fury. His black hair, thick and softly waved, fell over the worn collar of his faded shirt. His face, with its growth of beard hiding the lower contours, gave him the appearance of wicked darkness. The rakish slant of his brows framed his eyes, boldly staring into her own and holding her immobile. They were of a jet-black coldness that chilled her even as his look changed to an animal-like wariness.

He smiled suddenly, wickedly. Softly then, he said, "Don't you ever dare order me in that tone of voice again, *princess*. I'm not one of your hirelings to be dismissed any way or any time you see fit. Understand?"

It was the dangerous fury in his gaze that held her silent.

"I've never had much truck with your kind of woman, but you push, I'll push back."

It was the steely threat in his voice, low timbered and husky, more than his look that brought her up out of the chair, leaning over the desk. Slamming both hands flat, her arms rigid, she brought her face to within inches of his.

"Your name isn't on the deed yet—if that damn will was true and—"

"You doubt it?" he cut in with a grin creasing the arrogant curve of his mouth.

"Yes! And don't you dare interrupt me again." Lacey fought for control. Fury seethed inside her. Their warm breaths mingled for a moment before she jerked her head back. Why she noticed how long his lashes were she never recalled later. Thick and black, their tips curled and the slant of them sweeping over his eyes called attention to the direction of his stare. His view was unobstructed to the exposed valley between her breasts. Her choice was to remain as she was, for she refused to make an admission that she feared him.

It was that exact moment, when neither moved, that Lacey knew she would fight him, not only for ownership of the Reina, but any other possession of hers he sought to take. No doubts clouded her mind that with the animal aura of danger exuding from him, as it had from Sy, she would be forced to fight him every step of the way.

"I don't give a damn about you or anything you claim. I want to be alone. I would also expect you to have some decency, if you are capable—"

"I don't. I choose to remain right here." He leaned closer over the desk, deliberately threatening her, his gaze shifting from hers to the thrust of her breasts. "Damn prettiest sight I've seen in a long time."

It was his mocking look that forced her palm up, the crack of flesh against flesh giving her the utmost satisfaction. He snagged her wrist before she could blink, dragging her close, their furious gazes locked together.

"You goddamned spoiled bitch! Don't ever dare that again."

He released her suddenly and sat on the corner of the desk. His move forced Lacey's gaze to the worn gunbelt strapped low on his hip. The rawhide ties seemed stretched to their limit to meet around his muscular thigh. Every little move of his body along with the intensity of his look said he could use that gun.

"I asked you to leave once. While I don't care what you find pleasing or not, this time I am asking—not ordering—you to get out."

"That's better, princess. But I ain't leaving, since you and me better get a few things straight right now."

Lacey recoiled from the knowing gleam in his eyes and the implacable note in his voice. He watched her from beneath hooded lids with a mocking tilt to his mouth that made her want to scream. Suddenly she realized he enjoyed baiting her. That knowledge made her assume a reasonable tone. "I'm not accustomed to having my requests ignored."

"Yeah. I know," he answered softly with a nod toward the closed door. Her hazel eyes narrowed, and her nostrils flared like a cornered animal scenting danger. He smiled. "By the way, princess, in case you missed hearing it, my name's Rafe Parrish. Use it when you talk to me. Where I hail from, we call it simple courtesy." Her hostile glare made him goad her. "Go on. Try it. Name rolls easy off the tongue."

Why was she, Lacey Garrett, letting him talk to her like this? He was rude, insolent, and nothing more than a drifter, by the shabby way he dressed. And he presumed to teach her courtesy?

Curt entered the room, distracting her. "Are you all right?" He scowled seeing Parrish sitting on the desk, leaning close to her. "In case you've forgotten, the judge is waiting and impatient to finish this."

"The lady's fine," Rafe answered without turning. "And this conversation hardly got started, much less finished."

Lacey drew a breath, furious with his arrogance, but she never had a chance to speak.

"You need to get your facts straight, Parrish. I am not only Lacey's attorney, which gives me the right to be here and question anything you do, but she is going to be my wife."

Neither man looked at Lacey or acknowledged her soft cry.

Rafe turned then, slowly, glanced at Curt and then back to her. "That true? You already promised to marry him?"

The contemptible tone of his voice made her close her eyes. Lacey was frightened, drawn back in time, hearing Sy's voice again. It was long minutes before she could regain a measure of control to look at both of them.

"Curt, please ask the judge to be patient a few minutes more. I'm sure whatever it is that this man feels he must say to me alone won't take long."

"I'll go," Curt said, feeling the tightening inside his gut

acknowledge Parrish as a threat to his plans. "But I'll be right outside if you need me."

Rafe ignored the warning look Curt shot him before he closed the door. He turned to Lacey, his gaze pinning her where she stood. "You didn't answer me, princess."

"Stop it! It's none of your business if I'm going to marry him or not. You have no right to ask." Lacey already hated the grin that twisted his lips before he spoke.

"But it is. You heard the terms of the will. You get hitched, I'll own it all. So everything on this ranch is now my business, partner. It's just one of the things I want to get straight between us."

"Oh?" Lacey made a supreme effort to control her temper. "What else did you want to get straight between us—*partner*? Tell me. I'm just adying to hear." To those who knew Lacey, there was warning in the honied tone.

But Rafe didn't know Lacey. He judged her by what he saw for himself. A spoiled princess, more than passably pretty, who played at being man-hard. Abruptly he slid off the desk, standing with his back toward her. No, he didn't know her any better than he had known Sy Garrett. When the judge found him rotting in that Mexican jail six weeks ago, he said they would all accept him, not easily, but eventually. He had no need to remind himself that nothing in his life had been easy. It was the hard lessons he had learned so early that served him now. The princess was not going to give him an inch of the Reina without a fight. But then, he had had to fight for whatever he wanted for twenty-six years.

"I don't expect my sudden intrusion into your life to be pleasing to you, but I'm here, princess, and I intend to stay." He reached the door when her demand stopped him.

"I'm not finished with you."

"Don't get riled," he countered softly. "Just calling the

judge and your lapdog, Blaine, to come in and get this over. We can settle what's between us later."

"Between us?" she sputtered. "If you intend to stay—"

"I am. Don't make the mistake of questioning my word."

Lacey decided to ignore his warning. "Leave that door closed, and don't ever, ever call Curt a lapdog. Mine or anyone's. He's a gentleman, something you wouldn't understand. He would never impose his will over my express wishes and—"

". . . and that's the kind of man you'll marry? One you can lead by rope and halter?"

"You are the damnedest, most rude, arrogant, and insufferable man to constantly interrupt me! Curt was Sy's good friend. He's a most capable attorney. He's—"

"Spare me a list of his virtues, princess. You forgot to call him a liar, 'cause I don't hear you saying you'll marry him."

Lacey found it almost impossible to draw breath for a moment. His look chilled her but forced her to speak.

"I can't marry him. If that will is true, I can't marry anyone, or I'll lose my share of the Reina."

"Yeah." He grinned, his eyes steady and direct on her. "I know."

"Shut up! Why don't you tell me what claim you have to the Reina? Did Sy owe you money?" she grated from between clenched teeth, her look scorning the possibility. "If he did, I'll buy you out."

Rafe didn't move but tension rode him. He glanced down at her fingers drumming impatiently on the desk.

"Well?" she goaded. "Don't you know? Where's that arrogant insolence that made you so bold?" Lacey stopped, realized how tensely he stood there, and took a few calming breaths. "You can't expect me to believe that you don't know why you are suddenly named heir to half of the Reina. Why the hell are you entitled to it?"

Familiar pain tightened his gut. Rafe targeted his gaze to her eyes, forcing himself to speak the words that he had not yet accepted.

"Sure I know. You already said it."

"Damn you! Stop talking in riddles and answer me. Why did my father leave you half the Reina?"

"Your father?" His fury flared high with another scornful look from her. His temper, never on a long lead, seemed ready to burst watching her gaze travel over him as if he were a saddle tramp begging for a handout. He pitied the man that did.

"You really don't know, do you?" he asked in a taut, barely controlled voice.

Lacey shook her head, a visible tremor shaking her.

"You said it, princess. I'm his bastard son come to claim his share."

"My father would never—"

"You're not his daughter. You're a bastard just like me."

Chapter 4 ═══════════

SHOCKED INTO SILENCE, Lacey stared at him. She could feel her mouth working, tried to speak, but no sound escaped. A constricting dryness gripped her throat, and she forced a swallow. There was no moisture left in her mouth. Rigidly poised, only her eyes moved to follow him across the room to the side table, where Sy's private stock of liquor was arranged in cut-glass decanters.

Her gaze targeted his large-boned hands on the fragile glass. If he gripped it hard, he would shatter it. Then he was at her side, holding out a glass of liquor, and when she didn't move, he raised it to her lips, ordering her to drink.

Lacey didn't move. She couldn't.

"Drink it now. It'll help."

Help? Nothing could rid her of this numbness stealing over her body.

Roughly taking hold of her chin, he forced her head up. Rafe stared at the bloodless lips before forcing the edge of the glass against them, tilting it with enough pressure that forced her to swallow. He refused to look into her eyes, but repeated his motion with the liquor until she gagged.

"Easy now," he whispered, holding the half-empty glass aside. He wanted to touch her but didn't. She suddenly appeared soft, small, and helpless, and he was afraid she would shatter. Once again he lifted the glass, and this time she finished it.

Lacey had tasted brandy, but never like this. Never with the taste of bitter bile souring her mouth as the liquid fire hurdled down her throat. She pushed the glass away, raising her eyes, like those of a wounded animal, to his.

It was that wounded, vulnerable look that shook Rafe to his core. Gone was the prideful, spoiled princess that defied a crowd with her gaze. He was suddenly aware of how small she really was. Her head would reach beneath his chin, her slight build, the delicate bone structure of her features all made her appear fragile. How could Sy Garrett let her believe she was his natural daughter? How could anyone?

A tiny whimper escaped her, and her eyes closed. The sound grated along his nerve endings, drawing him back into time, until he saw his mother make that same hopeless sound, that same despairing motion. Carefully then, he set the glass on the desk, holding his breath for a moment, afraid to make any abrupt move.

"Lacey?" he whispered just as she swayed toward him.

He swept her limp body into his arms, stunned by the emotional turmoil holding her caused him. Her long braid swung free, and he swore he could feel its brush against his knee down to his bone. With her head flung back over his arm, her arched throat was bare, and before he could stop himself, his lips brushed the tiny pulse beating there.

He lifted his head slowly, the scent of her filling him with every drawn breath. He had denied that she was a woman this morning, but it was not coy perfume that he breathed, but the essence of Lacey herself. Once again his lips rested against the delicate skin of her throat, his arms tightening as he cradled her close and headed for the door.

As he stepped out into the courtyard with his burden, Curt shot him a murderous look and ran to his side. "What the hell have you done to her?" he demanded.

"Where's her room?" Rafe asked, his gaze seeking the judge, a curt nod acknowledging his silently mouthed question.

"Give her to me, Parrish. It looks as if you've done enough."

"Get out of my way and show me her room. You'd better get that woman of hers to help."

One look at Lacey's ashen face, and Curt decided not to argue. He missed the flash of annoyance that Rafe wore as Curt went directly to Lacey's room, calling out for Maggie to come quickly as he stepped out of Rafe's way.

Rafe lowered her limp body onto the colorful counterpane covering her bed. He was angry with Curt's unerring knowledge of where her room was and his own reluctance to leave her. A quick glance around the room showed it to be starkly empty of feminine frills.

"Maggie's coming," Curt announced, standing at his side. "What did you tell Lacey?"

"The truth. Something her lawyer should've done."

Curt found himself stepping back from the cold glare in Parrish's eyes. He was suddenly aware that his height brought him level with the bridge of Rafe Parrish's straight, thin nose.

Maggie pushed the judge out of the way, coming into the room like a fury. "Land sakes! Get out! Both of you. Go on, right now." She barely glanced at the two men. All her attention was for Lacey. "It's all right, Maggie's here."

"Get out, Parrish. You've done enough," Curt ordered, grabbing his arm.

Rafe pulled free, his scowl forcing the judge to intervene.

"Curt, that's unnecessary. We must talk since Lacey's in no condition to hear the rest. 'Sides, I can't spend the rest of the afternoon here."

Rafe waited until Curt joined the judge before he crossed

back to the office, ignoring Judge Walker's demand that he wait. By the time he had tossed off two quick drinks and realized that this was whiskey to savor, Curt came into the room.

"Pour one for me, Parrish."

Rafe thought about disregarding his order, for it was that and not a request, before he turned. Beneath hooded lids his eyes appraised Curt's slick-heeled, dandified appearance. Instinct warned him there was more to this man than surface impression. Rafe sipped his drink, savoring the smoothest-aged whiskey he had ever tasted, and then poured half a glass for Curt. His survival had depended upon gut feelings and wits; Curt was branded enemy.

"Where's the judge?"

"He had to leave," Curt answered, moving toward the desk, where he sat on the corner.

"Look, Blaine, I know my showing up like this today shocked you and Lacey. It wasn't my idea. But you saw those papers he has, you know it's true. Did he give you the letter from Garrett to Lacey?"

Curt didn't answer immediately. He studied Rafe with a thoughtful look, sipped his drink, and then set it aside.

"I find it hard to believe that Sy Garrett didn't take me into his confidence. I've been handling all his legal matters for the past four years. Perhaps we both started off wrong. You must understand that my only interest is in protecting Lacey."

"And you figure I'll hurt her? I don't even know her."

"You've presented a threat to her ownership of the Reina—that's enough for Lacey."

"You aren't holding out hope that she'll work with me. Why? It can't be easy for her. Men won't work for a woman."

"The Reina hands do. They respect Lacey, Parrish. She has earned the right to boss them."

"Well, it's not right for a woman to act like a man."

Curt smiled, surprised to find himself agreeing with Rafe Parrish about anything. "No, but there you have it. Sy raised her to run the Reina, and she won't give over easy." Curt toyed with the glass a moment before he asked, "Where was it exactly that Judge Walker found you? I still don't understand how he became aware of your relationship with Sy."

"He claims that Garrett's been looking for me a long time." Rafe shrugged. "I was in Zaragoza, north—"

". . . of Morelos," Curt finished for him, pausing when he saw Rafe tense. No, he was mistaken, for Parrish was refilling his glass, raising it in silent toast before he drained it. "Better go easy with that, Parrish. It's smooth, but it kicks as hard as the bellywash you're most likely accustomed to drinking."

Rafe glanced down at his empty glass. He grinned, but there was no warmth or humor in it. "You think so? Well, that's a mite friendly kind of warning."

"I certainly hope we can be friends. It would be best for you and me to work out whatever differences we have until this matter with the Reina is resolved."

Friends? Rafe thought about what the word meant. Not that he knew, not really—he had called no man friend.

"So, finish telling me how the judge met you," Curt prompted, wondering what thoughts filled the man's mind. He was deep, no betraying emotions showed on his features, his moves all smooth, and Curt found himself growing nervous. Running his finger around the stiff edge of his starched linen collar, he knew he would call upon all his skills before Rafe Parrish betrayed a weakness he could use.

"Let's just say we had some, er . . . acquaintances in common and leave it go at that." His answer was truthful enough, although evasive, but it accomplished what he wanted. Curt relaxed, proving that he knew exactly where the judge had found him. "I guess that's what took him so long to find me," Rafe added. "I moved around a lot."

Curt refused his offer of a refill, but Rafe once again sipped appreciatively from his glass.

"I guess finding yourself half owner—"

"Not yet, Curt. There's the terms of the will to be met before that happens."

"Yes, well, yes, of course, but I don't see why they should present a problem to you. There are plenty of young women who would . . . well, with the prestige of owning the Reina, I'm sure—"

"Having trouble spitting it out? Then I'll say it for you. If I've got the Reina, I'll be considered worthy by the *good folk* 'round here to court their darlings."

Curt reacted to the bitterness in Rafe's voice. "You can't blame them, Parrish. You don't exactly look like a man who set down roots anywhere at any time."

"I haven't ever. I've traveled light, heading where I wanted and when."

"The judge said very little about your background, although he did mention that you had spent time in Mexico."

"It's been a second home for me. Got tired of running horses and cows up to Kansas and having some rancher rake in the profits of my sweat."

Curt jerked his head up, the solution he had been searching for handed to him by the very man he wanted to get rid of. His interest wasn't hard to feign. "Won't you find it impossible to settle in one place? Especially since you'll be one of those ranchers raking in profit from another man's sweat. In your position," he continued thoughtfully, glancing up at the massive portrait of Sy Garrett over the fireplace, "I would give serious thought to what running the Reina will entail. It's not a small ranch. The land area encompasses more than you can ride in a day from any one point. And while we have avoided any mention of Lacey, I think she is something we need to discuss. Sy Garrett, as the man who raised her, taught Lacey the value of ruling. She's young, I admit, but don't let her youth fool you into thinking she's one to back down. Threaten her in any way, and you'll have a fight on your hands."

"So you've said. I'll keep that advice in mind. We got off to a bad start, and I don't know how to fix that. She's had no time to get over her shock of finding out that I'm Garrett's natural son, much less that she's not his natural daughter."

"Lacey won't rest now until she knows who her real father is. But if I can help you in any way, just ask. Lacey has a temper, she's headstrong, too, but she will listen to reason." Curt watched Rafe's restless prowl around the room, touching objects that caught his eye but remaining silent. "You might think about making yourself scarce for a few days to give her time to adjust."

"Think that might help?"

"I am sure of it." Eagerly then, Curt went to Rafe's side. "I know it was foolish of me, Rafe, but I should have asked Judge Walker to leave those papers with me. If you had them and showed them to Lacey, it might ease what I'm afraid will turn into a confrontation with her."

"That makes sense. Where was he headed?"

"San Angela, then on to Sweetwater, before returning to Austin."

Rafe gazed at Curt, thinking, and what would it be? Bushwhacked on the trail, or once in Austin, if he reached

that far, having some gunman pick a fight with him? Curt
was so desperately transparent, Rafe almost laughed at him.

Maggie's entrance stopped Rafe from answering him.

"How is she?" Curt asked first.

"She's restin'. I had to give her some of that laudanum
Doc left for Sy. After what she told me, that judge is lucky
he left. As for you two, barkin' squirrels got more sense
than to lay that girl low today of all days. She had powerful
feelin's for Sy." Her gaze pinned itself on Rafe, and she
marched across the room to stand toe to toe with him.

"So you're his son." Maggie thought of what Lacey had
told her. There was a look about him reminding her of a
wolf, watchful, waiting, but it was the eyes that made her
own soften. His gaze was level, direct, never wavering
from her own until she passed judgment.

"Don't 'spect anyone made you feel welcome here on the
Reina. Guess it'll be left to me and Fletcher to remedy
that."

Rafe remained quiet, letting Maggie study her fill, asking
for nothing, expecting less.

"Can't doubt it none. You look like Sy—'specially
'round the eyes. I'm Maggie Olin, case you're wonderin'.
Been here nigh onto twenty years. I've been known to have
my say when I wants. And I'm sayin' my piece now. Your
pa was a man. Ain't no one give him nothin'. Ain't gonna
be easy for you to live up to him." She glanced down at his
boots and slowly raised her head. "There's a new pair of
boots of Sy's that'll fit you well enough." Abrupt as her
entrance, she left, without a look or word for Curt.

"So, you've just met Maggie," Curt remarked with a
tensing of his jaw.

"So I have," Rafe returned, grinning.

Curt found himself forced to take another look at Rafe
Parrish. Maggie's words caused something deeper than

curiosity. Something he didn't care to name. Obviously, he had missed quite a bit. Certainly, Rafe was at a height and build similar to Sy Garrett and bore a striking resemblance. It was the beginnings of his beard that had made him miss it. Rafe was staring back at him, his eyes hooded, much the way Sy's would look when he was weighing facts or scheming. But Rafe, he reminded himself, seemed to be open to his offer of friendship. That definitely was not a trait belonging to Sy Garrett. He had been a sly old fox. Changing the will without letting him know proved that Sy kept his own counsel. Could his son have the same trait?

The thought prompted him to ask, "Rafe, why don't you get your gear and settle in? I'll take you down to the bunkhouse and introduce you around. It might make it easier if I do, especially with Ward Farel."

"Who's he?"

"Foreman. Sy hired him on when old Fletcher Ross broke his leg on a broomtail four years ago. He's a big man, about your height. Lacey depends upon him. Heavily," he added. "Didn't you see him here this morning?"

"Can't say I recall him." How could he when he only had eyes for Lacey? It was one reason he had agreed with the judge and stayed in the office. But it wasn't something he could admit to this man, much less himself. Suddenly he was itching to get rid of Curt.

"It's a right kind offer, but I'll just sit here for a while. The whiskey," he said, holding up his glass, "is the best I've tasted. Guess it isn't hard for you to figure out I'm not used to such fine things. Never did have the money for them. Never figured I'd be wanting them. Take some getting used to, me having to change the way I've lived."

It was dismissal and Curt knew it. But he had to give it one more try. "If you have made up your mind not to give Lacey a few days to adjust, I will be forced to accept that.

But you should reconsider that decision. You could share my place in Sonora with me. You don't know the extent of Lacey's temper when she's goaded. That can be one hell-bent lady."

Rafe smiled and sipped his drink. "I figure it's best for me to begin as I mean to go." His voice grew hard, his eyes more so. "The sooner everyone understands that I mean to take my place as Sy Garrett's son the better. It would bode well for folks to accustom themselves to the idea that I'm staying. Especially Lacey."

"I'll return to town, but if you or Lacey need me to talk, or whatever, send a rider in."

"Sure thing, Curt." But Rafe wasn't looking at him, he was staring at golden whiskey. As soon as the door closed behind him, Rafe began rubbing the back of his neck, hoping to ease some of the tension that tightened his muscles. It had been harder than he would have believed. Damn the judge for leaving when he did! He needed that letter to face down anything Lacey could use against him. He frowned, thinking again of her face, the way her body seemed small and light in his arms, that cry that ruffled his nerve ends. But there was strength in her. She had stood like a princess, cool and regal, this morning at the service. Willow slender in that high-necked black gown, the sun glinting fire off her chestnut hair, and he couldn't take his eyes from her. He smiled, seeing her again, with that defiant lift of her chin, and that mouth . . . How would that mouth look swollen from a man's kisses, and those eyes fired with passion?

Fanciful thoughts that had no place being in his mind.

He eyed the big leather chair behind the desk and made his way toward it. His hesitation lasted longer than Lacey's had before she sat down, leaning back against the padded leather. Closing his eyes, he thought of what he had to learn about Lacey and about Sy Garrett, the bastard who had planted his seed and run. He supposed there was some justice in Sy's leaving him half the Reina.

"Reina," he whispered, squeezing his eyes tight. It was small consolation that Sy named his ranch for the young woman who had defied her family for his love. Hell, she had denied her traditions, her very life to be with him. But Garrett couldn't have wanted her, he warned himself, bitterness filling him. If he had, he would never have left her alone in Mexico.

Forcing his thoughts back away from the painful past, he opened his eyes, rubbing the thick stubble on his face. A bath, a shave, and clean clothes were first priorities.

Then he'd see about Lacey. She knew he was a threat and rightly so, but the passion she lavished on the land should belong to a man. She was not his type of woman. Slim-hipped, small breasted, spoiled . . . no, not his kind. But there was a coltish grace about her moves that drew him. And that temper . . . He smiled. She might tempt him to strip that pride quickly. Upon a bit of reflection, he thought better of it. She would expect that from him. He wanted her unaware, seeing him only as a threat to her hold on the Reina.

Patience, he warned himself, would bring all he wanted. And he wanted Lacey for the challenge she had issued without knowing today.

How hungry could he make her without taking her?

It was a question he pondered as he left the office to find Maggie.

Chapter 5 ═══════════

FROM THE TIME she had spit out the laudanum Maggie had given her, Lacey had one question.

Who was her father?

There was no denial of that man's word. She accepted what he said as fact. Judge Walker would not have brought him here, stating his claim, unless it was true.

Now she knew why he had asked her to wait until her return to hold a service for Sy. He had wanted Sy's son here, on the Reina, to see his father laid to rest.

Where did she start? Who did she ask questions of?

She lay flat on her back, dry-eyed, staring up at the ceiling. Oh, God, it hurt! Why had Sy Garrett raised her as his daughter? Never once had there been a hint, a whisper that she wasn't his own flesh.

Restless, she twisted to her side, staring at the yellowed abode wall. Her chest felt tight, and there was a slight burning sensation behind her eyes. By force of will she dismissed the threatened tears. Crying would not help. It never had.

She closed her eyes, fighting not to drag the past out of memory, but a shifting swirl of scenes came forth.

Maggie and her husband, Eric, Fletcher, Bo James, and Sy, tall as a god, scooping her up and holding her high on his shoulders. "Look," he said, "see what belongs to you."

Was she three, four? She didn't remember. Before that there were no images.

And Maggie, always Maggie, soft words soothing her, rocking her to sleep. Maggie, wrinkled face scowling, scolding her, and then offering a cookie and a smile.

Fletcher, Eric, and Bo, always having time for her, patience, never turning aside her questions, teaching and caring. All the things that Sy never had time to give.

Had he hated her? Was the woman buried in the grove her mother?

Questions and more questions. Sitting up, Lacey rubbed her temples against the headache forming. She would find out who her father was—no matter the cost—but now she had Rafe Parrish to contend with.

A squeaking noise brought her head up, and she glanced around, alert, not realizing she was holding her breath until she released it.

"God," she whispered, "I'm jumping like a prairie dog down his hole."

But she had a right to feel this way. That man had already proved he would take whatever he could.

Staring down at the wide, uneven planks of oak flooring, Lacey didn't really see the aged golden-brown shadings of the wood. She saw Sy Garrett's face fading, becoming Rafe's. It frightened her until she shivered. Yes, he resembled Sy physically, and the eyes, black and thick-fringed, and that taunting voice . . . *Stop it!*

He revealed his enjoyment in baiting her, and like Sy, his son would use any weakness against her. A weakness . . . that was what she needed. Well, she had a year before he took title to half the Reina. Something would—

"If he marries . . ." Damn Sy! Why had he put those terms in his will? He knew she didn't want to marry. He . . .

Lacey tensed. Had Sy believed that his son could take the Reina from her? Did he state that condition in the belief that she would marry his son to keep her share?

Fury propelled her from the bed. She stalked to the windows facing the back of the ranch. Clutching the crisp white curtain, she shoved it aside. Her eyes followed the slight curving slope to the stand of willows and cottonwood trees. Not a leaf stirred in the heat of the late afternoon.

Lacey stared at the graceful silver sweep of boughs leaning over the shimmer of water in the pond they surrounded. Pain eased slowly as she thought of learning to swim there, her mind eager to supply her with happier thoughts. She could see Sy, tanned as burnished copper, holding her small body in his strong arms, making her feel secure as they eased their way into the water. Within days he was encouraging her to strike out on her own. Since it was one of the few times he wore a look of pride, Lacey cherished the memory of the first time she called him to come and watch her swim across the pond.

But she had long since outgrown the pond, just as she believed she had outgrown the deep, driving need for Sy's grudgingly given approval.

Turning her back on more than the sight of the pond, Lacey began to prowl her room, touching the ancient wood mantel, bare of decorations, the high-backed cherry-wood rocker that had belonged to her mother. A push set it moving, and she remembered the nights Maggie had rocked her, and then the nights she sat alone.

"I have no right here." The trembling began and she could do nothing to stop it. The thought expanded like her pain. "I have no right to call any of this mine if Sy is not my father."

But why, then, did he leave her half the Reina? She could

not lose the land she loved. "And leave it all for him," she whispered with a violent shove at the rocking chair. "Never!"

Sounds intruded into her thoughts. Lacey spun around, facing the door in the opposite wall. The door led to a bathing room, a room Sy claimed her mother insisted upon, and beyond it was Sy's bedroom. Lacey was not thinking at all, but moving toward it, yet her walk was both soft and cautious.

She opened the door. The room appeared undisturbed. The woodstove fire was banked, its heat barely noticed as she glanced at the high-sided tub. Open shelves held linen towels and the harsh lye-ash soap that Sy favored. Lacey crossed the small room and stood before the other closed door that led to Sy's bedroom. The sounds were unmistakable. Someone was inside, moving around. Lacey wanted to deny what she would find if she opened the door, but even as she gripped the doorknob and turned it, easing the door open, she knew she would see him.

Rafe Parrish gave no indication that he had heard her. He stood with his back toward her as Lacey fought down the rise of fury. Her gaze slipped past him to a few meager possessions that she assumed were his lying on the blue and brown patchwork quilt of Sy's massive oak bed. On the straight-backed chair beside the bed hung saddlebags, worn and deeply scarred. Lacey gazed at the closed door leading to the courtyard, saw his gunbelt hanging next to Sy's fancy silver-trimmed one on the door pegs. He stood before the open wardrobe, fingering the cloth of Sy's suits hanging there, untouched since his death. Untouched by her order, and suddenly it did not matter who this man claimed to be, but only the need she had to assert her rights.

"Who dared to let you in here?" Glaring at him, she saw

his back muscles tense before he slowly turned around to face her. Tapping her foot impatiently when she received no reaction from him, Lacey crossed both arms beneath her breasts and demanded, "What are you doing in here?"

"Seems obvious." Rafe took two shirts from the bed and placed them on a shelf in the wardrobe. He took two steps toward her and stopped. "I'm stowing my gear. I didn't think I'd disturb you. Didn't know about that," he said, gesturing to the open doors behind her. "Maggie never said you were this close. You didn't bother to knock, either, but you're right welcome." Her stony countenance made him add, "You feeling better?"

"No thanks to you," she snapped.

"Reckon not. Curt left. And when I'm finished, I figured to—"

"Finished? You can't stow your gear in here. This is Sy's room."

Her tone was as incredulous as her look, but Rafe was pleased to see the hectic color flushing her cheeks. He met her glare with an inward sigh, knowing there was no way to get around their first battle place.

"The room is empty. I chose to fill it."

Rafe wondered if she heard him. Strangely silent, she stood still while he studied her, the thin shirt and tight pants revealing each curve and hollow of her body. She had none of the soft prettiness of a woman to attract him. But attract him she did. Her coldness or . . . Rafe found himself smiling. Lacey offered him a challenge with her slim-hipped stance. He turned and picked up two folded neckerchiefs, but her voice stopped him.

"You can't have this room. It's indecent! You can't stay in the house at all."

He faced her with a chilling glare. "Can't I?"

"No. And stop looking me over like some prize heifer

you're thinking of buying!" What did it take for him to understand how contemptuous his behavior appeared? What ever she had expected, it was not to hear him speak with a soft, almost measured patience.

"I wasn't thinking of a prize heifer. The will states that I own half, Lacey. Half of the ranch, half of the house, and half of all it contains. I've claimed this one room for my use."

"Sleep in the bunkhouse."

"I'm not your hired hand."

"Then take one of the back guest rooms," she raged, desperate to keep him as far from herself as possible.

"I'm no guest. Garrett's dead. You need a shrine to remember him, build one. It's my right to have what I want here, and you're having trouble accepting that." He stood tensed a moment before he stepped closer and then stopped. "Face it. Understand it now, before you squeeze yourself into a corner, Lacey."

"You dare to give me orders?" she grated from between clenched teeth, fighting to retain some control over her temper.

"Someone had better. You heard the terms of the will. A full working partner. That means I have a say in running the ranch and living here." He stopped, waited for her to deny him, and then found himself taunting her. "Have I got your coming in here all wrong? You want some other kind of arrangement? My bed's right there, but it wouldn't work. You're not hungry, princess. Not enough for me." His eyes targeted hers, his grin a wicked curve exposing a flash of white teeth. "No, you purely aren't woman enough to know hunger for a man."

"Hunger!" she screeched in feminine outrage, clenching her hands against the desire to physically attack him. Her eyes raked his body, filled with scorn. "And you think you are man enough to make me feel anything for you? I'd see you pushing up grass from the underside first."

"Threats, princess?" With a look of devilry he gave her tense figure a thorough assessment. "Maybe I figured you wrong. You've never been hungry for a man before, have you? Don't matter none if you admit it, but don't make childish threats against me."

He faced her with hands on his hips, the material of his shirt pulled taut across his shoulders, smiling impudently. Heat curled in her belly, sending a fine tremor down her legs. "What are you threatening me with?" she asked in a desperate whisper.

"You're one smart lady—figure it out. I warned you once that if you push me, I'll push back."

Her eyes darted around the room, anywhere but at the cool, appraising mockery of his eyes. She longed to tear that look from him, stepped farther into the room, but remembered his firm grasp on her wrist when she slapped him.

With a calm she was far from feeling, Lacey looked at him. "Any threats I make, I keep. If I promised someone a fight, I won't back down. You're baiting me into one, so you've had a warning." She watched a muscle tick angrily in his cheek, but his silence goaded her. "You try coming near me, you so much as threaten me that the only way I'll keep the Reina is in your bed, and I'll see you dead."

"I frighten you that much?" What the hell happened? He had only meant to taunt her a bit, and here she was forcing a confrontation.

Lacey's control had slipped, and she lashed out at him. "You wanted to get things straight between us. I will. Now. You stay out of my way, here, in this house, out on the range, and with the men, or I'll—" She stopped herself, gripped by a rage so intense, she could not finish.

"Go on. Finish. What are you going to do to stop me?"

Lacey smiled. It was a thin, mocking smile that was reflected in her eyes, widening now, a deadly feral gleam that made her look dangerous. "Are you a gambler, Parrish?"

Clearly puzzled, his answer was slow in coming. "I've been known to take a risk on the turn of a card."

"That's good." Lacey began looking at his scuffed boots, her gaze crawling up his legs, noting with satisfaction the tension in them. She rocked back on her heels, glanced at his hips, the cracked leather belt wrapped around a trim waist, and slowly counted every button up his shirt. Her breaths were even, so at odds with the pounding of her heart, but she kept at it, studying the cords standing out on each side of his neck as tension from her looks seemed to coil around and inside of him. When she finished inspecting the stubble on his face, she met his gaze unflinchingly.

And then she whispered softly, "Would you really risk your life?"

She could feel every nerve ending scream inside her, protesting the rigid control she was demanding of herself to stay and finish this.

"No, Lacey," he stated in a voice every bit as soft as hers. "With you alone as the stakes, the gamble isn't worth my life. And if you're done or not, get out. I want some privacy in my room."

He turned his back on her, every line of his hard body its own form of dismissal. With a sharp turn on her bootheels, Lacey left, slamming the door behind her. She waited a few seconds for the sound reverberating to stop and then turned the unused key in the lock, listening to it grate.

He'd have more privacy than he bargained for!

The splintering crash of wood came within seconds. She froze on the threshold to her room, terror holding her there.

His hand grabbed her arm painfully, spinning her around to face him. With that one-handed hold he shook her.

"Of all the damn stupid, childish things to do! Don't ever dare . . . do you hear me? Don't ever lock a door in this house against me again!"

His voice was a barely controlled throaty statement, but the tightness of his muscles straining his shirt made her realize he was somehow holding on to his fury. Lacey whimpered when his grip tightened, but she lifted her head.

"You never intended to leave me anything, did you?" Somehow she kept her features deceptively composed, keenly aware of his greater strength. "But I'm not part and parcel of the Reina that you reminded me you own half of." Pointedly dropping her gaze to his large hand encircling her upper arm, she added, "No man has ever handled me so roughly."

"Maybe it's time one did," he muttered.

Had she pulled her arm free, or had he let her go? She didn't know. She was admitting to herself it was an act of childish defiance to lock the door just as he claimed. But she never expected him to react this way. He was standing so close she could feel the pounding of his heart, every whiskey-tinged breath he released was inhaled as her own, and those eyes, dark and wary, staring into hers.

"I'll have someone fix the door," he said.

"You can't have anyone see this." She turned, the move allowing space between them, and gestured to the splintered door sagging against the frame. Two wood pieces were on the floor, torn from the other side. When he said nothing more, she looked back at him. His hand moved with an impatient gesture through the thickness of his black hair, until he pushed it back one last time and stopped.

"I'll fix it myself."

"I might have known you'd be able to fix a broken door.

What else can you do? What else do I expect from someone like you?" she demanded.

Rafe avoided looking at her. He had to strive to find a way to make a truce with this woman he had a feeling was going to take his life and change it in more ways than he cared to explore right now.

"And you?" he challenged. "What can I expect? More of this?"

Lacey had to get away from him and walked past him into her room. He followed her, but she knew it would be foolish to order him out. Maybe there was a possibility they could talk.

"I don't play at running this ranch," she began. "I put in as many hours as the men that hire on. There's damn little I can't do. Everything's been within my control since Sy had his first heart attack. I don't intend to give over one bit of it."

"That's not an answer. I asked what I could expect from you, not my ranch partner." Rafe found himself bewildered by his insistence for having an answer he knew she could not give him. As if she sensed that, her lashes, richly burnished with the same red-gold highlights as her hair, lowered over her eyes, effectively shutting him out.

"Well? What's it going to be, Lacey?"

"What do you want me to say? That I welcome you? That I'll make it easy for you to take over? I'm not a fool. That's one thing you can expect from me. The other is that I won't give over control to you or any man."

His laugh was bitter. "That's the first thing I've heard from you that is without question the damnedest truth." He walked to her bed, sat down, and boldly gazed around him. "We got off to a bad start. But I won't be pushed around by a woman. I'm not demanding you hand over control. But I'll share in all decisions made from here on in."

"Share? You wouldn't know—"

"Stop it! You don't give a man a chance to breathe before you jump all over him with that tongue sharp enough to slice ribbons in a steer's dry hide. All I'm getting at is . . . what the hell, you aren't listening, but it can't have been easy to handle this ranch alone."

"No, it hasn't been." Lacey crossed the room to her rocking chair, sat down, and felt both control and security return with the distance between them. Short of calling men to bodily haul him out, she made up her mind to listen.

"What about you? You haven't said much about yourself."

"Why ask? My past can't interest you one bit. You're the one that had the castle, princess, complete with king of all he owned."

"I didn't grow up like a delicate princess hidden away in a castle!" Her hands gripped the wood arms, muscles aching with the tension he called forth. "Sy was a hard man to please, to live with, and to work for. Just ask any of the men who have been with the Reina for years. Fletcher Ross or Bo James, even ask Maggie. They could tell—"

"I want to hear it from you," he insisted. "You're the Reina's princess."

"Oh, God, stop it! Stop calling me that." How cruel could he be? Didn't he understand the pain she felt?

Rafe couldn't understand why she would refuse to share memories of the man who fathered him. He stood up abruptly, started for the door, and then stopped. A devil rode his shoulder as he turned around. "What do the men call you?"

"Call me?" she repeated, her eyes targeted to his grin.

"Miz Garrett?" he prodded.

Lacey cringed at his sarcasm. Her throat seemed to close. Miss Garrett, she silently repeated. She had no right to that name. But then, whose name did she have a right to? The fight left her. Wearily she closed her eyes, her voice a defeated whisper. "It doesn't matter what you call me. The less you have to say to me, the better."

"Then princess it is."

Lacey's eyes opened. It was the mockery of his words that infuriated her once more; it was the sight of his submissive bow that made her jump up from the chair like a blue norther ready to strike. "What about the door? And what do I tell Maggie?"

"Don't tell her anything. You keep harping about being boss here. Or tell her the truth." He turned suddenly and found Lacey up against him. He stared down into stormy hazel eyes boldly meeting his. "You sure the hell aren't afraid of admitting the truth about anything, are you?"

For a moment Lacey swore he wasn't talking about the door at all. But his voice, harsh and angry, seemed to pit his will against hers.

"I'll think of something. Don't worry about it."

"Will you stop! I don't want you making up some tale to protect me. I don't need your help. I don't need you. No one wants to have everything destroyed. And that's what your coming has done. I curse the day Judge Walker found you. Do you hear me? I wish he had left you wherever it was. You're a bastard in the truest sense of the word! And what's more, you're a son of a bitch!"

She instinctively recoiled against the blaze of fury lighting his eyes. But only for an instant. Where there had been heat, now there was cold, a glacial chill that whipped her like his voice.

"You don't know when to stop, do you? Don't ever call me that again," he grated from a mouth whitened with rage. "Never, Lacey, never. Do you hear me?" His hand snaked out to grip her arm, dragging her against him, ignoring her

cry, her uncontrollable shaking. There was fear in her eyes
that silently begged release. His taut, low-voiced growl was
breathed against her lips. "I've killed men for saying it."

Hauled up against him, held by his punishing grip, Lacey
barely registered the shocked tremors passing through both
of them. From one breath to another his threat changed.

"But then, you're not a man."

Her breath was stifled in her throat, and to her shame, she
reacted instinctively to the male threat of him. Shaking her
head, her eyes seemed to widen, but nothing would free her
from his gaze.

"Oh, God, what are you doing . . . ?" The words were
torn from her, and his mouth curled into a slow, insidious
grin.

Chapter 6

"I COULD SHOW you how wild you make me with that savage little mouth." He released her with a shove. "But not now." Rafe softly closed her bedroom door behind him. Lacey was shocked into silence.

How could she stand living with him for a year?

There was no way she could stop the sudden sobs racking her body. "Why did Sy do this to me?" she cried in a hoarse whisper. Rafe Parrish was in her life to stay, and she admitted her fear of him. Wrapping her arms around her waist, she stood there, staring at the closed door. Her fear stemmed not from his unbridled rage, or his control, not even from the implied male threat of him. It was the ease with which he had broken her defenses and made her cry that spiked terror inside her.

She couldn't begin to think of the questions of her parentage that his coming here had raised. A fresh storm of weeping shattered what little control she had left.

Listening to her, Rafe stood in the middle of the bedroom. His anger needed time to simmer down. Never before had he faced a woman and found her infuriating scorn so apparent in every look and word she directed toward him. Never had he lost his temper so quickly. But then, he had never met anyone like Lacey. His women were bordertown drifters like himself. He cursed Sy Garrett, who had, with his will, turned his life into conflict.

Why had Garrett waited so long to find him? Why had the man tried to make right the empty promises he had offered to a woman he claimed to love? And why, Rafe asked himself, had he come to claim his share of the Reina?

Rafe gazed around the room as if the innate pieces of furniture could yield a clue to the man who held his life in a grip of precarious balance. By acknowledging him as his son, Garrett had set him to walk a knife's edge.

Turning toward the splintered doorway, Rafe no longer heard Lacey sobbing. He spared a thought to fetching the woman Maggie for Lacey, then dismissed it. Somehow he knew that Lacey's pride would make her hate him for exposing her now. She was just as much a victim of Garrett's manipulations as he was. Pity flared—then died. Lacey had her memories of love and a home to console her, while he had nothing but twenty-six years of hunger.

Hunger for a place to call home. Hunger for answers. Pain tightened his gut. He refused to allow it to take hold. He would find his own consolation in the thought that Garrett had not forgotten his mother. *Reina,* he had called his ranch, Spanish for *queen,* just like her name. Would that knowledge have added a measure of peace to her dying? It wasn't a question he could answer. Emotions that he had fought hard to keep buried began to surface. With a ruthlessness that governed his life, Rafe pushed them away.

He was here, half owner of the Reina, and he swore that no one would call him bastard again.

The room confined him, and he bolted from it.

In the act of opening her door, Lacey paused as she heard his bootheels strike against the bricks. She was not ready to face him. Her crying had ceased as abruptly as it had started. She controlled her fear of him, for nothing was as important as keeping the Reina. She would bargain with Rafe Parrish to keep it on any terms.

* * *

Maggie shot Rafe a quick look as he entered the kitchen.

"Coffee's hot," she said, kneading dough at one end of the table. "Supper's a mite late 'cause of the service an' all. Got your gear stowed?"

"Yeah. Seems you're the only one who's accepting my being here."

"But I don't count. Lacey's a horse of another color."

"I know." He met her direct gaze, somewhat surprised to find himself liking her. He did not take to people with ease, but there was something about Maggie that made him think he could trust her. He poured himself a cup of coffee and sat at the table.

" 'Fore you make yourself at home an' ask questions like you're dyin' to, best get that door fixed."

He almost choked on the black brew.

"Wasn't bein' nosy, if that's what you're thinkin'. Went to check on Lacey. Body be dead not to hear the ruckus. She got herself a temper, and you stroked her wrong." Maggie waited, punching and rolling the dough.

"It was over his room."

"Figures. Fletcher's down at the barn. He'll help. Don't want anyone else knowin'." She gazed at him and her smile was warm. "Lacey won't fight for long. Gal loves this ranch. Needs patience."

"Haven't had much truck with that." Rafe sipped and wondered why Maggie was on his side. The innate mistrust that governed him rose sharply. Sounds at the outside door distracted them.

"Wipe your boots 'fore you dirty my floor," Maggie ordered.

Rafe glanced at a thin, wiry man with sparse gray hair and a face the shade and texture of old leather.

"Fletcher Ross," Maggie announced. "Rode with your

pa a time. This here's Sy's boy they's talkin' 'bout. Goes by Rafe Parrish."

Fletcher wiped his boots on the flat strip of metal wedged by the doorway before he entered. "So, yore Sy's boy." Offering his hand without hesitation, he added, "Got a good grip, son. Maggie treatin' you right?"

Son. The word sent a shiver down Rafe's back. No man had ever called him son or cared how he was treated. Fletcher seemed to be of the same mold as Maggie; someone he might trust.

" 'Course I am," Maggie answered for Rafe. "He was plannin' to come see you. Needs some cut boards."

"Got a few," Fletcher replied, clearly confused. "Now, what in tarnation you plannin', son?"

"Has fixin' to do. Don't be askin', Fletcher."

Maggie's warning gaze meshed with Fletcher's. He was sure it had to do with Lacey. Rafe was staring into his cup, and Fletcher knew he wouldn't have it easy here. Not if what he had heard about his mother was true. For himself, he did not hold with judging a man on his beginnings, but this was Texas and memories were long. Hate ran hot against anyone that was not pure Anglo. Rafe stood up, and Fletcher's gaze tracked his height. He was a younger image of his father.

"Git, both of you," Maggie scolded.

"C'mon, son, we'll get what you need."

Maggie watched them leave, then quickly rolled and shaped her dough. Lacey had to learn to hog-tie her temper, or she would stir up trouble like a flash flood. Wiping her hands on her apron, Maggie frowned as she moved to the stove and began stirring a pot of stew. Rafe had a temper, too, and unless Lacey bent her stiff-necked pride and gave that man room, she would find herself losing ground.

* * *

At the same moment Lacey's thoughts parroted Maggie's. Short of murder, there was no way she could think of to get rid of Rafe Parrish. She stood in the open doorway to her room, gazing without seeing the lush serenity of the courtyard. She wasn't sure how much time had passed, but there was Rafe coming toward her, carrying an armload of wood.

Her first thought was to retreat, but she forced herself to face him. With her chin lifted to a defiant angle, she stared at him.

Rafe passed her without a glance or a word.

Crying did not set well on Lacey. Some women could appear dewy-eyed, but not her. Rafe had heard her gasp as he moved by, and he grinned, knowing he was not going to make it easy for her. He set the wood down in his room, removed a hammer and nails from his pocket, then studied the damage he had caused. A few pulls with the hammer freed the shattered wood of the doorframe. He tossed it aside and found Lacey watching him.

She ignored his scowl. "I see you're keeping your word to fix it."

"Always do."

"I'm sorry for what I called you," she began in an attempt to mend the breach between them. "I didn't mean it as a slur on your birth. It was . . ." She stopped as he deliberately disregarded her.

Rafe scooped up a few nails, grabbed the longest board, and hid his surprise at her attempt to apologize. It didn't add up as a move Lacey would make. He didn't question his certainty; he accepted it as truth.

Lacey simmered. He worked with a minimum of wasted motion. In short order he had nailed one board to brace the frame. The hammer blows were loud, and she hoped that

Maggie was not in the house, for the sound would carry. The thought of Maggie knowing what happened added a sullen note to her voice. "How did you get the wood without anyone seeing you?"

"Didn't," came his muffled answer as he hammered a short board across the top.

His rude abruptness goaded her. "Who saw you?" His silence, as he picked up the shattered wood and stacked it neatly, grated on frayed nerves. "Well?"

"Fletcher helped me. I can't replace the door till he cuts the slabs he's drying. I told him it can wait."

"You told him—"

". . . it can wait."

"Damn you! What am I supposed to do tonight?"

He leveled a mocking gaze at her. "I could think of a few things you could do, princess, but I don't believe you'd find them pleasing." Color flushed her cheeks. "Can't figure why you're all fired up. Close your door. I sure as hell won't come in without you inviting me. Maggie—"

"Maggie knows!" Lacey stepped closer to him. "And closing my door won't give me the privacy to bathe."

"Princess," he drawled, "ask nicely. I'll give you all the privacy you want."

She glared at him a moment, then spun around and stood, tapping her foot, her back rigid.

"Lacey," he began, distracted by the stray tendrils escaping her braid, which he couldn't resist touching. "So soft. My mother had hair like yours. Not in color—hers was dark, almost black, but just as soft and sweet smelling." He felt the fine tremor as he brushed her neck and withdrew his fingers. "Don't be stubborn, Lacey. I accept your apology and offer you a truce. Take it. I won't offer one again. Not for you or any woman."

The loud clanging of the old mission bell warned Lacey

that Maggie had supper ready. "Better wash up. Maggie doesn't like the food getting cold."

He gripped her shoulders, holding her in place. His grip wasn't tight, but Lacey could feel the strength in his hands.

"You didn't answer me," he grated.

"Accepted. Now, let me go."

"After supper I'll go down to the bunkhouse and—"

"You will not!" She pulled away from him. "I need to explain to the men what happened. You don't know how we work. You don't—"

"And left to you it'll stay that way."

Lacey felt pinned where she stood by his intense gaze. She couldn't deny what he said. Suddenly she was uncertain of how the men would react. Would they back her if she decided to fight Rafe?

He rubbed the back of his neck, glancing away from her. "We'll leave this till later."

Fletcher was already seated at the table when Lacey entered the kitchen. She stared at the four places and thought of Sy.

"You two gonna stand there or sit and eat?"

Lacey hadn't heard Rafe come up behind her. She motioned him to sit next to Fletcher.

Rafe pulled his hand back before Lacey saw he was about to hold her chair. Fletcher shook his head, silently warning him to let it go. Maggie set a heaping plate filled with a savory stew in front of him, smiled, and began to cut thick slices of bread. Once she sat, Rafe was embarrassed to find himself with a forkful halfway to his mouth when Lacey began to say grace.

Her blessing was brief, and although no one mentioned it, he felt a need to apologize. "I'm sorry. I didn't—"

"No big thing, son," Fletcher cut in. "Take you a bit to

get used to our ways. Eat up. Best stew you ever tasted. Maggie here"—he gestured with his fork—"jus' bakes the best durn apple pie, too. Lacey's almost as good," he bragged, trying to dispel the tension.

Rafe shot a look at Lacey. She pushed the food around on her plate. He felt guilty, knowing his presence was the cause. He envied her the warmth of home, the protective love of Maggie and Fletcher, and yet he was angry that she could take it all for granted. Her eyes rested on him with all the warmth of a prairie blizzard, making the food stick in his throat. But he finished his plate, and Maggie was quick to refill it.

"Guess you got a powerful appetite," Fletcher remarked with a grin. "Jus' like yore pa."

Lacey's fork clanged against the plate, her cry soft. She stood up, already whirling, her boots hammering out a staccato beat as she ran from the room.

"Talk without thinkin'," Fletcher muttered.

"No matter." Maggie offered the plate to Rafe. "You hit a raw spot. I'd better go to her."

"Leave her be." Fletcher patted her hand. "Best let her get it over with. Ain't that right, son?"

"Can't blame her for resenting me," Rafe answered. "Wish it wasn't so, but I wouldn't feel different."

"Good notion to use patience with a hard-nosed filly."

"Fletcher! Don't be calling her that."

"Don't get riled, Maggie. She don't come 'round easy. Rafe here'll do fine to ease his way with her."

"Obliged for your faith, but Lacey isn't what I want to talk about." He hesitated, but the questions plagued him. "Tell me about Garrett."

Maggie read the underlying hunger in his eyes, and a surge of pity welled up inside her. She just knew that he hadn't had an easy life and that asking for anything, from anyone, didn't come easy for him.

But it was Fletcher who answered him. "Hard man. We rode out here in spring of thirty-six to fight agin' Santa Ana. Figured to keep this territory under Mexican rule. Sy knew Stephen Austin from back East somewheres, and we'd been drivin' herds up near Missouri when we heard he needed help." He sipped his coffee, and seemed lost in thought for minutes. "Let's see now . . ."

"Land sakes, gettin' so old you can't remember."

"I remember, Maggie. Mighty rough times they was. Sy got wounded at the Battle of San Jacinto. We talked some, and when Houston offered up a thousand-acre parcel to any man that stayed to fight Mexico's claim, we figured we could do better comin' further West. Weren't nothin' here but a burned-out shell of an old mission. Sy never had much to call his, same as me. No folks to speak of. Set up on a high rock shelf and says this was his land as far as the eye could see. Wasn't called Reina, jus' home."

Maggie distracted both of them by refilling their cups and slicing pieces of apple pie. Rafe ate his quickly and then blew gently to cool the coffee as Fletcher spoke.

"Had us a heap of troubles, son. Fought Mexicans, Comanche, and Kiowa. Met up with Doshasan, a Kiowa chief, and found him a high-minded man. Took twenty head and left us alone after that first year. Came back, right regular, took his pick of the herd, and left. Shame he died last year. There's trouble stirrin' up north. An' then there's Darcy."

"That's right," Maggie said. "You watch him. He's been after water on the Reina from the first. Sy wouldn't sell him land, and Lacey flat turned him down, too. The man's slicker than clay after a rain."

"What I can't figure," Fletcher cut in, "is where you

been all this time, son. Don't seem right that Sy never told us 'bout you." He glanced up at Rafe. "Feelin' you ain't had it easy."

"Depends on who's measuring what's easy." Rafe shrugged. "Finish telling me about Garrett."

Maggie was watching Rafe and noticed the taut play of bunched muscles under his shirt. She reached out to pat his shoulder and said, "Don't mind him. You can't blame us for wantin' to know a little 'bout you. There ain't no rush." She rose and began clearing the table, stacking the dishes in a pan and working the hand pump.

"Don't need you steppin' in, Maggie. Been here nigh on to thirty years an' didn't know Sy had a son. Maggie's been with us close to twenty, give or take a few months. Her man got himself killed by a rattler near to ten years ago."

Maggie shook her head and continued. "Lacey found him. Much as I loved him, that girl carried on somethin' fierce." Rafe's puzzled look had her adding, "Sy wasn't one for givin' affection, and Eric, my man and me, well, we sorta loved Lacey like our own. Wasn't blessed with a child, an' she took to Eric."

"Don't take that to mean that Sy didn't care for her. He did," Fletcher explained. "Set a store by that girl."

Maggie poured herself a cup of coffee and joined them at the table. "Your pa raised Lacey to be hard. Weren't right, but that's the way of it. Her ma left him and went East to friends. He waited a bit, then went after her. She wasn't a strong woman, hated the heat and loneliness. Had to bury four boys that never made their first year. Her death left Sy with rage all tied up inside him."

She uttered a weary sigh, and Fletcher remarked, "It's a hard life for a woman. But he brought her back, an' two months later she birthed Lacey. Had us a high ole time."

"An' we all believed Lacey was his. Sy never once said different," Maggie added.

"Until now," Rafe murmured, staring at the table.

"That's right," Maggie agreed. "Her ma could hardly talk that night. Labored too long. Whispered 'Lacey' and passed on. We took it to mean she wanted that to be the baby's name. Now I ain't so sure. Shame the way she gave up, like all the fight and life jus' left her."

"That's something I can understand, Maggie." Rafe did not look at either of them. He thought of his own mother's death and realized that his envy of Lacey may have been misplaced.

Fletcher finished his coffee. "Sy Garrett was a blunt, straightforward cuss. His word was law on the Reina. Taught Lacey to be the same."

"Had her thinkin' she was a boy. A hard boy." Maggie rose and began to gather their cups.

Fletcher stood and placed his gnarled hand on Rafe's shoulder. "Folks called him ornery. But he was fair. Tried to right things with you, son. Remember that."

Rafe sauntered out into the courtyard, rubbing the back of his neck. He was bone weary but restless. He heard men shouting beyond the walls and turned to see Lacey running from her room.

"Stay here," she ordered, reaching the gates just as he did.

Rafe gritted his teeth and followed her outside.

A cluster of men made way for Lacey. "What happened, Cal?" she demanded as a rider stepped down from his lathered horse.

"Trouble. Just like you figured. Only Bo James been shot. Scanlon's with him. Ain't bad, but we need a wagon to bring him in. An' they ran off a few head."

Lacey spared a quick look around her. She had been

expecting trouble, and her men's faces told her they were of the same mind. A knot tightened inside her belly. This was the first incident of violence against the Reina since Sy's death, and they were waiting, reserving judgment on how she would measure up for them.

"We gonna ride?"

Lacey looked at Luke Hollis. He was a brushpopper who knew his business and a good tracker. His question was one every man wanted to ask. One of their own had been shot, and they wouldn't rest until the man who did it was caught. Before Lacey could answer him, Ward Farel joined them.

"What's all the ruckus?"

"Bo's been shot and a few head run off." Lacey barely controlled her fury. "Why didn't you follow my orders?"

"Don't get riled." He faced her, hating the way she lit into him in front of the men. "Ain't you got enough without takin' over my job?" His gaze picked out Rafe behind her. Hooking his thumbs in his belt, he added, "Let me handle this my way, Lacey."

"Pack your gear. You're finished. Cal, how many head did you say we lost?"

"Figure maybe ten. Can't be sure."

"You've got two months' wages owed, Ward. I'll have it ready less the loss of my cattle. And if you're ever found on Reina land, you're a dead man."

There wasn't even a whisper of protest as Lacey scanned the faces around her. She paid the wages, and any man who rode for a brand owed it his loyalty. It was a law that the raw Western lands had demanded, and one she had banked on. Fletcher came to her side with a lantern held high. Its glow revealed the rage in Ward's eyes. But Lacey refused to glance away or back down. She couldn't afford to keep on a man who refused to obey her orders and risked another man's life.

Rafe watched the two of them. Lacey's decision was swift, hard justice, but the only one she could have made. His move closer to her was an instinctive one to protect.

Ward noticed. "You ain't thinkin' clear, Lacey. We all know that." He gestured around him. "Right, boys?" His call for support was met with silence. "Know you had a shock today. Bo'll be fine. You head on back to the house, and I'll ride out myself." He reached for her arm. "Go on," he urged. "We'll have us a talk when I get back."

"Don't touch her." Rafe's order was a whisper, but Ward hesitated.

Lacey closed her eyes briefly, shaking her head. She wanted, no, needed time before confronting the problem of Rafe Parrish. His interference took away her choice.

In a curt voice she explained who he was for those who had not heard. She finished with "Rafe doesn't know the Reina or what problems we face, so I'm still the one giving orders. If anyone wants out now, speak up."

No one did. Rafe wanted to say something but had to content himself with her admission that he was half owner. He stood behind her, listening to Lacey's authoritative voice firing orders.

"We won't ride after them tonight," she said. "But if anyone sees something that's not right, shoot first."

Lacey spun on her heel and walked toward the house. Rafe met the curious glances the men shot at him, but no one approached him. Ward stood where she left him, his eyes narrowed, watching her.

"Ride out with me in the wagon, Rafe?" Fletcher asked, coming to his side.

"Yeah. Yeah, sure," he answered, unable to look away from Ward. There was something . . .

Ward went after Lacey suddenly, grabbing her arm and

spinning her around. Rafe was behind him in seconds, his big hand clamped on Ward's shoulder.

"I warned you not to touch her."

Ward dropped his hold on Lacey, the pressure of Rafe's hand forcing him around to face him.

"You driftin' greaser. I'll teach you to touch your betters." Ward's thick, hamlike fist shot up, catching Rafe solidly in his stomach. He stumbled back to the sound of Ward's laughter.

All the anger Rafe had held back came out, and Ward felt the brunt of it.

Lacey struggled against the hold Fletcher had on her, his warnings silencing her protest and orders for them to stop.

Rafe grabbed Ward's shirtfront in his left hand and landed a solid right to his jaw that sent Ward's head snapping back as Rafe released his hold on Ward's shirt and let his left fist connect with his jaw again. Ward raised his hands, instinctively protecting his face as Rafe drove sledging blows to his midsection with brutal efficiency. Ward tried to hit Rafe, but he moved easily to dodge him.

The men stood watching, eyes narrowed and judging, for most men would rather use their fists as a last resort in a fight. More than one whispered that Rafe's blows were measured to fall solidly where he aimed them.

Grabbing Ward's shirt again, Rafe flung him to one side. His breathing was labored, his voice harsh. "Lacey said you were finished. Since I'm half owner of the Reina, I'll back her orders with my own brand of talking." He spun around to face the men circling them, challenge glittering in his eyes. "Anyone else?"

Lacey pulled free of Fletcher's grip. She was both angry and frightened of Rafe, but anger won. "That's enough, Parrish. I don't need you to back up my orders. You had no right to beat him."

For a moment in the dark she could feel his hot gaze, and she had to force herself to stand still. Without a word he stalked off, his body rippling like a coiled whip.

Ward got to his feet painfully. "Someday that bastard is gonna pay for this." Wiping the blood from the corner of his mouth, he moved toward Lacey. "You'd better let me stay on. You can't control a greaser like that."

"He's not a greaser. He's a man, Ward." But she had already admitted to herself that she wouldn't be able to control him. "My orders stand. Meet me in the office."

Maggie waited for her at the back door. "How bad is Bo?"

"It's a leg wound. This is the beginning, Maggie. I know Darcy was behind this. I said I would fight him and I will, but Maggie, I hate the thought of the bloodshed."

"To keep the Reina, you'll do whatever needs doin'."

Lacey nodded and left her. Once in the office she stared at the little cash remaining in the strongbox. Curt was right. She would need to extend her credit with the bank and soon. If only she knew what Sy had done with the mortgage money he had received from the bank against the sale of the cattle. He had never told her, and she had never found the money. Rubbing her temples, Lacey knew that if the rustling continued, she wouldn't have enough cattle to sell. And the Reina already had notes against it.

Counting out the wages Ward had coming, she wondered if the judge had bothered to tell Rafe that they were land rich and cash poor. The new quarantine statutes, forbidding the import of Texas cattle into east Kansas, added problems.

Ward's entrance demanded her attention.

"You're gonna regret this, Lacey. That greaser's trouble. You got enough already. I'll stay on 'round Sonora or San Angela for a few days till you calm down. Sy wouldn't have handled it this way. You're a woman and need a strong man to stand for your rights with him as part owner."

"He won't stand in my way."

Ward took his money. "I ain't much of a bettin' man, but I'd gamble this—that afore the year is out, he'll have it all."

"You'd lose your money, Ward."

"Would I?" he countered. "You're ripe for a man's takin', woman. You got more snakes in the grass 'round you than you can count."

"But I shoot what I aim at. Don't forget, Ward."

"You ain't wearin' a gun. An' you never shot a man."

"But I could learn." Her hand cleared the desktop. She clicked back the gun's hammer. "Clear out."

Ward backed away. "Count your enemies, Lacey. But start on the Reina."

Chapter 7

LACEY WOKE TO a throbbing headache and exhaustion that she couldn't shake off as she dressed. The sun was full up, and she was annoyed that Maggie hadn't come to call her. Buttoning her calico shirt, she glanced at her closed bedroom door and wondered if Rafe was asleep. They had not exchanged more than ten words after he and Fletcher brought Bo James back to the house last night. His wound was not serious; the bullet had passed through the fleshy part of his upper thigh. She remembered how gentle Rafe had been in handling the older man, and that gentleness puzzled her.

After kicking her feet into an old pair of boots, Lacey left her room, checked on a sleeping Bo, and headed for the kitchen.

She stood with cup in hand as Maggie came in from the pantry. "Think we need to get Doc for Bo?"

"Don't 'spect we will. Rafe even said as much."

"Rafe? He saw Bo this morning?"

"Yep. An' if you're wonderin' where he is, he's gone. Rode out afore first light. Said to tell you he'll track those cattle." Maggie stared at the stormy expression in Lacey's eyes and set a bag of dried beans down on the table. She winced at the thud Lacey's cup made as she set it down. "Don't get riled," she cautioned. "You know I ain't never

78

told you nothin' that wouldn't do you some good, even if you ignore me at times. Girl, this isn't one of them."

"I won't be treated like some dim-witted child."

"Don't aim to lessen you act like one. Set down."

Lacey hesitated. Rafe had better than a four-hour start on her. She could never catch up with him. And she did have questions to ask Maggie. Questions that bittered the taste in her mouth.

"All right, we'll talk, Maggie. But I'll ask the questions. I need to know the truth about Sy and my mother."

With a weary sigh Maggie sat down across from her. "Honey, I know how hard you're takin' what your pa done."

"Don't call him that. He was not my father. But I swear that I'll find out who is."

Gripping Lacey's hand, Maggie's gaze softened. "I know you're upset 'bout that. Rafe figures that bothers you more'n anythin'."

"He does? And what else did you two talk about?"

Maggie had to ignore the bitterness in Lacey's voice. "You got questions, and that boy does, too. Listen and think, honey. I've never seen hunger like that boy's got in his eyes. Don't know all that much 'bout him, I admit it, but I'll tell you this, girl. Push him hard an' he's gonna shove right back. Might not like the direction his shoves are gonna take, either."

"What are you asking from me?" she snapped, pulling her hand free. "Should I welcome him? He's arrogant and insolent and—"

"An' jus' like his pa?"

"No. He'll never be the man Sy was."

Maggie thought back to the talk she had earlier with Rafe. He had revealed more than he knew about his feelings for Lacey, Sy, and the Reina, but Lacey wasn't ready to hear them.

"I don't want to talk about Rafe, Maggie. Tell me about Sy and my mother. Did you . . . well, did you know that I wasn't his daughter?"

"No. An' that's the truth. Your ma left here, oh, was summer's end. Sy let her go till he got a letter from her. An' then he lit out to find her. Sent us word near Christmas that he wouldn't risk travelin' till spring since she was with child. I figured she knew that when she left, maybe left 'cause she lost the others. An' then, come spring, they were back, an' soon after you were born. A tiny mite, too. Didn't figure you to make it, but you were a fighter even then. Sy never once said you wasn't his."

"My mother never mentioned someone else?"

"Not once. I ain't the type to pry. She was unhappy but kept to herself. Fletcher an' me didn't know 'bout Rafe, either. Sy was his own man. Don't know why he left half the ranch to Rafe, but he wouldn't have done it lessen the boy was his. Sy left Fletcher here when he'd go off for months to buy stock till he built up a herd. An' you ain't the only one hurt. Sy fooled us, too. Can't believe he kept so many secrets. Why, Bo was shocked. Got choked up an' angry when I told him. I'd swear that if Sy was alive, he might've gone after him for doin' this to you."

"Bo has always been there for me." Lacey's smile was bittersweet. At least someone was totally on her side.

"Rafe mentioned that the judge had papers you should see. You could—"

"I won't leave here now, Maggie. I can't."

"That boy ain't gonna run off with the Reina."

Lacey stood up abruptly, shoving her chair back. "You seem mighty fast to defend him."

"An' you're bitter." Maggie's patience was at an end.

"You ain't listenin'. Do what's best for the ranch, Lacey. Be the woman I know you can, an' the man won't hurt you, seein' as how you both want the same—"

"I have a ranch to work," she snapped.

"Do tell."

The pain of betrayal flared in Lacey's eyes, but Maggie knew her, and Lacey turned away. "I'm sorry for snapping, but I can't spend time mollycoddling him."

"Ain't asked you to, has he?"

"No. But he's a taker, Maggie. You're seeing him in need like a maverick bawling for its ma, but I can't give over a grassblade to him. He'll grab it all."

"That kind of talk'll tear the Reina apart! Is that what you want? War on the ranch? Got yourself a hide thicker than boot leather, but Rafe can help you. You remember Darcy—and he ain't alone in wantin' to slice the Reina into bits. All I'm tellin' you is do some clear thinkin' afore you make decisions you'll choke on."

Maggie had yelled at her before, but now there was an added harshness that Lacey had to listen to. She left her and walked down to the corral. When she noticed the big grulla gelding was gone, the throbbing in her head increased. It was Sy's favorite horse, and she knew without being told that Rafe had taken him for his own.

"Damn him to hell and beyond!" Lacey leaned against the pole rail fence, weary, fighting the knowledge that she would never control Rafe Parrish. She was tempted to remain at the home ranch today, but a need to know how the men felt about Rafe drove her to saddle a gray gelding for herself.

The sun was past midmark and Lacey had ridden for almost two hours before she reached the first golden-coated stragglers of cattle. She cut off toward a small stand of mesquite, where there was always water near, and dis-

mounted by the dying embers of a campfire. The coffeepot
was half full, and she poured out a cup just as Cal rode up.

"Didn't 'spect to see you, Miz Lacey. Rafe was here
before light and took Luke and Ragweed with him. It's been
quiet."

"That's what I came to find out."

"How's the old man?"

"Don't let him hear you call him that, Cal. He was
blaming himself for what happened last night. But Maggie
said he'll be fine."

Cal hunkered down by the fire, poking a few twigs into
the coals when Blewett Montell joined them. Both men had
worked for the Reina for as long as Lacey could remember.
Where Blewett was a big man, lantern-jawed and rawboned, Cal was lean, stoop-shouldered, and had a wry
twinkle in his eyes. Blewett accepted the coffee Cal handed
him and came to stand next to Lacey.

"Kinda hard to believe all hell broke loose last night.
Weren't need for you to ride up here. Rafe gave us orders.
You ain't to worry. It won't happen again. That Parrish is
young, but got to give him knowin' what's right."

Inside Lacey there was a surge of fury and resentment.
Rafe again. But there was hurt, too. Blewett did not give his
approval easily.

But he was waiting for her to say something. With an
angry toss of her head that sent her long chestnut braid
swinging, she faced him. "I'm here to find out how you and
the others feel about him, Blew. But I also wanted it clear
to everyone that I still own part of the Reina. Rafe Parrish
doesn't have the final say."

"Hold on, Miz Lacey," Cal said. "We figured you sent
him here. Like Blew said, man knows his business. Picked
up some dried blood spots near the ridge above where Bo
got shot."

"With Ward gone we'll need a ramrod," Blew pointed out in a soft voice. "Figure him for the job."

Lacey heard the underlying question and knew he was probing in his own way for what her feelings were about Rafe. The tension of having to choose her words carefully strained her voice.

"Rafe is Sy's son. But he must prove himself a full working partner to take title to his claim. I'll not stand in his way, but I won't be pushed out. Pass that on," she warned. "We didn't have time to get things straight last night, but we will. And when we do, there'll be no question of who is running what."

She tossed the last of her coffee out, set the cup down, and walked away. Mounted, she leaned over to adjust her stirrup and met their studied looks. "I don't want trouble."

Lacey kept her horse to a walk. Was this the way it would be? If Cal and Blew were an example, the men could feel that Rafe should be giving orders. All the years she strove to prove herself capable of running the ranch meant nothing. They were respectful, but she sensed an underlying feeling that men's business should be left to men. She wanted to be angry and felt a forbidding sense of loss.

Rafe was one of three mounted men overlooking the valley below. The high ridge where they stopped afforded them an unobstructed view of the sprawling ranch buildings.

"That's Darcy's spread," Luke Hollis informed him. "He had to be behind the rustlin' last night. There's been bad blood between him and Garrett long as I've ridden for the Reina. Bo James told me they used to make their gather with a few other small ranches, sort out the brands, and drive them together. Darcy claimed Garrett didn't keep an honest account for all. He refused to ride with him after the first time."

"It bothers me that it fits a mite too easy." Rafe pulled his hat brim lower, staring at the scene below.

"We tracked them this far. So, what're we gonna do?"

Rafe glanced at Ragweed, a lean, sallow-faced youngster who wasn't dry behind his ears. "We'll ride down and have a talk with Darcy."

"You plumb loco? That old man is mean and ornery, and he ain't one to stand and answer any questions." Luke shook his head. "He'll deny it. He always does. I told Bo that we was missin' calves. Even showed him where some Tumbling D riders cut them out. Didn't do no good. That Darcy chased him off. They find out we're this close, an' they'll do it to us."

"Let him try." Rafe pushed his hat back, wiped the beads of sweat from his brow, and hunched over the grulla's neck, watching the small figures below. He noticed one rider mount up and head out toward the ridge. A thin, merciless grin creased his lips. He knew they had been seen crossing Darcy land, he hadn't made any effort to hide, but he wasn't going to be chased off until he had some answers.

Luke had seen the rider, too. "Gonna wait?"

"Right here," Rafe answered, dismounting. He loosened the thong from his gun, caught the looks they exchanged, and said, "No sense in not being ready. While we wait, fill me in on Darcy, Luke."

Ragweed remained standing, but Luke came to sit beside him. "Darcy's spread is almost as large as the Reina's, but he ain't got enough water. He's been after Sy to sell him southeast acreage that has mountain-fed streams, but Garrett wouldn't consider it. Lacey don't let a blade of grass get touched lessen she says. Been with them almost three years and never heard tell of a harder man to ramrod for than Darcy."

"Any family?"

"A daughter and a son. Evan ain't around, but I heard aways back he was courtin' Lacey, and Garrett didn't take kindly to it. April's the daughter. There's bad feelings between her and Lacey. April figures herself the prettiest gal around and didn't like Ward and that lawyer fella sniffin' 'round Lacey like stallions after a prize mare. Not that Miz Lacey gave them a tumble. This here rustlin' has been going on for a while. Just a few head, but no one been shot at before."

"April ain't to blame," Ragweed cut in, drawing their attention.

"Boy," Luke said, "iffen you got yourself a hankerin' in that filly's direction, forget it. Darcy'll skin you alive for lookin'."

Digging one square-toed boot into the soft dirt, Ragweed hunched his shoulders. "Naw, Luke, you ain't got to tell me. Ain't got a chance with a lady like her."

There was more teasing between them, but Rafe wasn't listening. He thought about how to handle Darcy. He wouldn't ride in and demand their cattle back as well as whoever shot Bo. There was something that wasn't right about this. He had to admit that the last few miles of tracking they had done were blind: The rocky ground had not revealed hoofprints, just a few overturned rocks.

He just couldn't let Darcy slide by without knowing that he wasn't dealing with a woman alone. Rafe had no compunction about killing. His past had forced him into situations where a steady hand and clear thinking left no room for emotions. But he wanted peace, a chance to build something, not war. He stopped his musings when Luke shook his arm.

"You hear me?"

"No. Just thinking. What were you talking about?"

"How Darcy bought out the smaller spreads and figured the Reina would be his. Didn't reckon on havin' Sy laugh at him. Thought there would be gunplay 'tween them when that lawyer fella took April to a church supper in San Angela and then danced with Lacey most of the night. Darcy was riled like a rattler. He can't refuse April anything she wants. And she's just as bad, 'spectin' a man to come at a run fast as you could chuck down hot bear signs."

Rafe chuckled with him. "Bear signs" were fresh home-made doughnuts, and a man would travel far and fast for some. His hand picked up ground vibrations, but Ragweed still stood, shading his eyes to see who it was.

"Rider comin'," he muttered, "but it ain't a he."

A few minutes later Rafe found himself staring at a woman that had to be April Darcy. She reminded him of a delicate china figure, all blond, cream, and sultry blue eyes. Her stare was as bold as his as she walked a dainty-boned black mare close to where Rafe stood. But it wasn't Rafe she spoke to.

"Rather far from the Reina, Luke. Why?"

"Trackin' a few head that were stolen last night, Miz Darcy."

"And you?" she asked Rafe, gold-tipped lashes sweeping down to veil the sultry look that matched her voice.

"Rafe Parrish, and you don't seem concerned that we're looking for stolen cattle on your land."

Soft throaty laughter met his accusation. Rafe's eyes narrowed, and he grabbed for her horse's fancy silver-trimmed bridle.

"You're a stranger here, or you'd know that Darcy hands stay on Darcy land."

"I say different." Rafe heard her denial, but he never

expected her to take a cut at his face with her quirt. He grabbed it, pulling her forward, almost out of the saddle. The grip he had on the bridle stilled the frantic prancing of her horse. April's move was sudden to release the quirt, but she swept up the length of her reins. Rafe dodged the swing she made so that the leather brushed his shoulder.

"Seems to me your pa should dry behind your ears before he lets you out alone, ma'am. I've got no call to hurt you, but you swipe at me one more time, and I'll take you over my knee. Now, settle down. I really want to talk to your father."

"He doesn't bother with hired hands." April felt the heat color her cheeks at his smile. It was male and wicked and full of challenge. "Take your hands off my horse."

"Don't take orders too well, ma'am." Rafe knew he had not misread the curiosity in her bold gaze.

"Then you leave me no choice. Pandel! Dryen!" she called, grinning down at him. April watched his reaction to the sound of rifle hammers clicking, the spare turn he made to locate the two men above them, barrels pointed at him. When he looked up at her again, April barely managed to hold on to that grin under his furious gaze. "Now, Mister Hired Hand, back off."

Rafe spread his hands high and wide and stepped back. "I still want to talk to your father. Maybe it'll make a difference if you know that I own half the Reina now."

April verified the truth by the amused grins that Luke and Ragweed wore. Her own face flushed a deeper shade. "Lacey would never sell out."

"Didn't say she did." Rafe offered no other explanation. "You gonna order your boys to shoot or put their guns away?" he asked in a soft, warning voice.

April could not control a sudden shiver. He stood there, unperturbed, his legs slightly apart, his dark eyes gleaming, a reckless slant to his lips. If what he claimed was true, her father had to know. A blind panic rose, and she quickly dismissed it. There was something dangerous about him, something that went beyond his rough looks, the tied-down gun, and the disregard he showed for the rifles at his back. She refused to forget the debt she had long owed to Lacey.

"They won't shoot," she finally said. "But send Luke and the other one back to the Reina. We'll escort you to my father."

Rafe quelled Luke's muttered protest with a look.

"What'll I tell Miz Lacey?" Luke asked Rafe once he was mounted.

"Why, I'm paying a neighborly call with Miss Darcy's assurance that it will be a sociable one." Rafe glanced at the two Darcy riders that joined them. His hand rested on the butt of his gun, and he nudged his horse closer to April's. "That's the truth of it, right, boys?"

Neither man answered him. But then, neither missed his warning. April's laughter floated back to where Luke and Ragweed watched.

"Lacey won't like this," she said to Rafe.

"I don't account for my actions to Lacey or any woman," he answered. But there was no smile to soften his words. He didn't want to think about Lacey; he needed his wits sharp for this meeting with Darcy. Lacey had a way of clouding his thoughts. He shot a quick look at April, and for all her pretty lushness, he thought of a she-wolf, a hungry one. He had met her kind of woman in every town on the Texas border. She would consume a man if he let her. But he didn't want April. He wanted a chestnut-haired hellcat. Time was all he needed. Time and patience would give him everything he had hungered after for years. And after touching Lacey, he wanted it all.

Chapter 8

"ARE YOU SURE I can't get you anything else, Bo?"

"I'm fine, Lacey."

"Then I wish you a good night."

"Lacey, think about Maggie's idea. I know you're angry with her and Fletcher and now maybe me, but, honey, if you marry Rafe, you'll never lose the Reina."

"I don't want to hear—"

"I know. I know. Just a minute more. An' don't be givin' me that crazy-old-coot look. I'm hurtin' as is. I didn't speak up at supper, but what they said made sense. If he dies, you get it all. Fine. But if he marries someone else and there's a child, you'll be forced to share. It's a hard road Sy set you to walk. You've been battered like a windmill by a dust devil for weeks. Just don't let temper and pride blind you."

Lacey nodded and left him. How could she explain to him or Maggie and Fletcher that Rafe frightened her? She wasn't sure of the reasons why herself.

She stood in the courtyard, bathed in the feeble glow of a quarter moon, and wrapped her arms around her waist. Bo's advice weighed heavily, as did the feeling of being cornered by Maggie and Fletcher. She was being judged and found wanting by those she counted on for loyalty, by those very people she trusted.

Her soft leather slippers made whispers of sound as she

paced the length of courtyard. Rafe had earned the men's respect by taking action. She couldn't fault the orders he had given, even if she believed he behaved like a range-wild bull. Maggie wanted to mother him, Fletcher gloated with pride, and Bo thought he could offer her protection through marriage.

What had they seen in Rafe that assured them he was strong enough to hold the Reina?

The lone cry of a coyote broke the silence, and she paused, wondering if Rafe would return tonight. It was a fleeting thought, for she was unable to shake off the feeling of being betrayed. Rafe was simply a man. They knew nothing about him. Being male did not make him a better judge of how to deal with the threat Darcy presented.

Luke's version of what had happened between Rafe and April sent her instincts up in arms. Darcy would use any foothold to take the Reina. April was her father's daughter, willing to be bait to trap the right man.

And Rafe was a man.

Alone now, she admitted there was a compelling maleness in Rafe that challenged her. She both sensed and feared a wild recklessness in him that called to its mate inside her.

As suddenly as the thoughts came, she stopped them.

Once she had given in to that wildness. No man would ever again use it against her.

All she wanted, all she cared about, was protecting her land.

She couldn't fight April on her terms. April was soft and pampered and knew how to cater to men. Lacey valued her self-respect too much. A chilling shiver crept down her spine. That wasn't true.

She simply didn't know how.

"And I don't want to learn," she whispered.

The scrape of a bootheel made her spin around. Lean and dark, Rafe stood, staring at her.

"Waiting to tuck me in, princess?"

"No. No, I waited to talk with you."

He came toward her slowly, the dark of his clothes blending with the shadows. Lacey shivered again, staring at the soft buckskin chaps worn over his pants, defining his maleness. She backed away until she dragged her gaze up to his mouth. His smile mocked her fear.

"It's late. I'm dogged, princess, and you should be in bed. Whatever it is can wait till morning."

She brushed the loose hair from her face, stopping suddenly. His eyes watched her every move, every breath, like a predator.

Rafe clenched his hands. Freed from the braid, her hair was a thick, curled mass that enticed him to touch. She grabbed the knotted tie of her robe, a robe of some soft fabric that revealed more of her slender body than it concealed. His own body began a slow, delicious throb. She moved back, and the spare night breeze carried her scent to him. He lifted his head, nostrils flaring as if to catch and hold it. The slow throb surged into his blood, taunting him. Weariness disappeared. Every nerve tensed. And he stood there. Waiting. Watching her.

"Stop it," she demanded, sensing the change in him.

"Stop what, princess? Looking at you?" Rafe spread his hands from his sides and began stalking her. "I'm not touching you, am I? And that's what you're so afraid of, isn't it, princess?" His gaze clashed with hers, instant black lightning. "So afraid of me touching you. Why?" He shifted to block her darting move toward the center of the courtyard, leaving her no choice but to retreat toward her room, visibly shaken.

"Go to bed, Lacey."

His abrupt cessation of the game he started freed Lacey from her fear. "Don't give me orders. I am not afraid of you. I waited to talk to you, and what's more, you'll stand there and listen to me. You can't—"

"Christ, woman! You never learn," he muttered, coming at her fast to crowd her against her door, his fingers tangling in her hair, holding her head still. "Don't taunt a man when he's hungry, bright eyes."

Before Lacey could move or speak, his mouth mated with hers in a harsh, angry kiss. The solid wood door pressed against her back as unyielding as the solid length of his body fit itself to hers. His lips were savage, without gentleness, without tenderness. Lacey had to breathe, but his mouth captured her own so that she had to breathe with him and of him. The taste was bittersweet, possessive, and there was no way to escape the feverish pounding that spread through her whole body.

She was too conscious of the pressure of his long, hard-muscled legs against hers, the feel of his soft cotton shirt against her palms, the ruthless claim of his lips. His hand cupped her hip, levered her up a bit, then drove her pelvis into the cradle of his spread thighs, the hot length of his arousal buried between them. Lacey stilled.

An instinct of danger rushed through her bloodstream, her total awareness centered on the potent blend of darkness, the male rhythm of Rafe's body, and the growing weakness inside her.

His kiss offered no courting for her to open her mouth. His lips were greedy, impatient, as hungry as he claimed. Need, loneliness, and the feeling of being emotionally stranded these last weeks rushed into a response she could not control.

Her lips parted. His tongue took every dark secret like a conquering warrior. He demanded total dominion.

And to her shame, she gave it. Her arms rose, fingers testing the strength of his shoulders, and she arched up against him with a sob. His kiss would have her believe she was the first woman he had touched. The only woman he wanted.

A tiny sane corner of her mind whispered that he would not make a gentle lover. Rafe demanded too much. He took too much.

A sharp twist of her head brought a moment's respite. Once again the rough spear of his tongue pillaged her mouth. Taken. Branded his. And quickly incited to fight a sensual duel as his mouth softened, coaxing. Her breasts swelled against his chest, full and aching. Tiny whimpers forced themselves from her throat, and there was an instant stiffening of his body against hers.

Time hung suspended. She *was* afraid of him. His body clamored with need, but he lifted his head and eased the weight of his body from hers. Their breaths mingled, both labored, and through slitted eyes he watched Lacey, tempted to lick her bottom lip.

"You taste like warm, rich cream, princess." Her eyes, like those of a startled doe, lifted to his. He stroked the smooth arch of her throat, keeping her face turned up to him. "Since you don't kiss like a virgin, give me your mouth, Lacey. Give it like a woman. You know what I want," he whispered, sliding his hand inside her robe, one finger rubbing her neck. "Give it to me."

Her gaze flashed defiance at him. "No m-more." Annoyed with the quaver in her voice, she lifted her chin. "Stop demanding anything from me. And stop threatening." She prayed she had concealed feeling like an animal held at bay. The nearness of him, the male heat that lingered, and the raw desire in his voice were more than she knew how to handle.

Rafe frowned and suddenly released her to open the door. Gently pushing her into her room, he followed. The soft glow of the lamp caught the fire glints in her hair, but Rafe found he couldn't look at the swollen bruise of her mouth, nor could he meet her panicked look. Her cheeks were chafed from his night beard, and he rubbed his chin, sorry for abrading her skin. She could deny it all she wanted, but Lacey was woman soft. His body still ached to be buried in that softness.

"So talk," he said suddenly.

"Wh-what?" Helplessly, Lacey shook her head, pushing her hair back, watching him prowl around her room.

"You said you waited to talk to me. It's about me seeing Darcy, right? He denied having anything to do with Bo being shot and running off our cattle. You expected as much. And he's lost cattle, too. And I don't think he's lying. Everything would fit nicely if it was Darcy."

"You spent a few hours with him and cleared up years of trouble? You don't know him. And it couldn't have taken you this long to find that out." She could have bitten her tongue once the words were said, seeing the corner of his mouth lift tauntingly.

"That's not a question a lady would ask. I'm not accounting for my actions to you or anyone."

"But I'm not anyone. I'm your partner, remember?"

"Yeah. All right, I wasn't with him all this time. But he understands that he isn't dealing with you alone."

He was goading her and she knew it. They eyed each other warily. The thought of him coming to her from April set off a fierce desire to know that he had not been tempted to take what April could offer. Instinctively Lacey's gaze dropped downward to the blatant proof that he was still aroused.

Rafe grinned as she averted her gaze. "Remember, I

don't apologize. It's something I can't control around you.
And to keep things clear, April merely made me feel, shall
I say, welcome."

"Say what you want. It was all with her father's approval," she snapped, color flushing her cheeks. "You're a
fool!"

"Am I?" he taunted.

"If you weren't, you wouldn't have had to come back
here ready to . . ." She couldn't finish.

"Ready to what, Lacey? Take you? Maybe," he drawled,
"I'm just a hungry man."

Threads of tension coiled inside her, hearing the soft,
menacing note in his voice. She refused to acknowledge his
remark. She didn't want to think about what had happened
minutes ago. Lacey took refuge by attacking him. "Don't
flatter yourself about April's attentions. She wouldn't give
the likes of you a second look if you couldn't claim a piece
of the Reina."

"Would you?" he countered, soft and low.

An unreasoning blind panic made her turn away. She
stared at the fireplace, knowing she wouldn't answer him,
but she couldn't lie to herself. Lacey closed her eyes,
feeling him against her, an overpowering aura of sheer,
rugged male presence that dominated her senses. "How can
I trust you?" she whispered.

"You don't have a choice, princess," he whispered from
directly behind her.

"You'll lose all that Sy built and I'm trying to hold."

Rafe reached out, rubbing her arms, bunching up the soft
cotton sleeves of her robe. "Trembling, bright eyes? Why?
I haven't touched you . . . not the way I want to."

She was dizzy at the way he spun her around, gripping
her shoulders. The scent of him was male, sage and wind
and heat. Her lips were parched. She licked them and

looked up. His eyes were targeted on her mouth. "I want the Reina more than any man. Darcy and his daughter pose a threat to me. If you're with them, you're against me, Rafe. I'll prove that if you keep pushing me."

With a little jerk he pulled her closer. "The only thing you need to prove is that you're a woman."

She flinched at his soft, sarcastic tone. "I already have and found it painful."

His gut twisted at her frankness. His lips skimmed her temple, drifted down to her cheek, and then he let her turn away. "Who was he?"

"It doesn't matter. That's all in the past, but I won't forget the lesson I learned." Lacey freed herself and stepped back. "You're a taker, Parrish. I'm not for you."

He ached thinking of the ways he wanted to take her. His hand curled into a fist at his side. He would not touch her now. Not in a mood that was hot and savage when he didn't believe he would be gentle with her.

"Dream your dreams, princess. Soon I'll be the only man in your life and the only one in your bed."

Lacey vibrated with fury. She waited until he had reached the doorway. "Don't bet money on that. You'll lose, and what's more, you'll be disappointed." She had been goaded into the admission, and it hurt, but it seemed the only way to stop him.

"Is that what you believe, or is that what Evan Darcy told you before he left?"

"No." She was still shaking her head when he came back to her. Lacey raised her hand to stop him from touching her again. She didn't want to feel the thud of his heartbeat, but it pounded beneath her palm. She refused to measure the warmth of his flesh through his shirt, but that, too, seeped into her skin.

"Tell me who it was. Tell me, Lacey!"

"It wasn't Evan."

"Then I won't have to kill him."

"Stop this!" Her gaze locked with his. "No more. You can't make threats and—"

"Promises, princess. I make promises. I'll make you one now. I'll have you hot, wet, kitten soft, and wild with wanting me."

His voice was raw. Lacey couldn't breathe. His eyes held hers, daring her to deny him. Slowly she withdrew.

Rafe didn't stop her. He hadn't intended to warn her, but Lacey was like a thorn in his side, jabbing him with every move, drawing blood with every word. The taste of her lingered; like a fever it spread inside him, and only a thread of caution warned him what he risked to stay.

"Get out of my room, Rafe. And stay out."

"Sure, princess. But remember, I keep my promises."

"So do I, Rafe. So do I."

Chapter 9

BRAVADO AND PRIDE aside, Lacey avoided Rafe by riding out to each of the line shacks scattered over the Reina. For three days she took inventory of the supplies, made lists of needed repairs, and scouted for stray cattle. Through Maggie she learned that Rafe was line riding the herd at night. The raids had stopped, and Lacey wondered if Rafe's visit to Darcy was the cause. She couldn't deny being happy with the result.

The moment she walked into the kitchen this morning, she knew the uneasy peace was over. Rafe, lit by mottled streams of sunlight, sat at the table, talking softly to Maggie. He turned as Lacey hesitated in the doorway. His black hair was damp and tousled, his eyes pinning her.

"Well, well, don't you look the princess today."

"Don't be teasin' her, Rafe," Maggie chided, and to Lacey said, "You look really pretty, honey. It's nice seein' you dressed like a woman." When Lacey didn't answer, Maggie had to pay attention to the way she was glaring at Rafe's clothes. In an effort to forestall an outburst over his wearing a butternut-colored shirt and dark brown twill pants that had belonged to Sy, Maggie rose. She chattered on about the supplies she needed for the house as she bustled about the kitchen.

". . . Now, don't you think that's a fine notion, Lacey?"

"What? I'm sorry, Maggie, I wasn't listening." She ignored Rafe's grin and poured herself a cup of coffee. Damn him! If he stared any harder at her, he would begin counting the threads in her russet-colored skirt, or the stitches in every tuck of the cream cotton shirt, or measure the soft twists of the dark brown neckerchief tied around her neck.

"Lacey? You're takin' Rafe with you, honey."

"No!"

"No, princess?"

Her look warned him to keep quiet. Rafe stretched his arms and tucked them behind his head, leaning back in the chair. His grin was brazen.

"Can't see why not," Maggie continued, rummaging in one drawer, then another. "Can't seem to find my list. Must of put it in my room."

Rafe turned around the moment she left them, but Lacey spoke first. "You are not coming with me."

"Ain't I? But I was just going to ask if there's something wrong with the coffee. The way you're staring at the cup, bright eyes, makes me think you find it bitter."

"Your presence is bitter. And what are you doing here? I thought you were riding line at night."

"I live here. Just 'cause you've gone out of your way to avoid seeing me these last few days, doesn't mean I feel the same. I missed you. An' I've been doing my job. Came in at first light when Scanlon rode out to relieve me."

Lacey looked at him, lips pursed, eyes narrowed. He certainly didn't look like a man who had spent the better part of the night in a saddle. If anything, he was freshly shaven and appeared more rested than she felt. But he was not coming with her.

Maggie returned, waving her list. "Here it is. Now, I won't hold you two up. Jus' take care."

"Maggie, I told you he's not going with me. He needs to . . . to sleep, and I may not come back tonight. Someone—"

"That's all the more reason why I should come with you, Lacey. Can't have anything happen to *my* partner."

"Rafe can get to know folks an' the stores where we have accounts in San Angela, honey. An' don't forget the castor oil for Fletcher."

Lacey did not correct Maggie about where she was going. It was useless to continue to argue. Maggie could wind her down faster than a fifty-cent watch. "Hitch the wagon, Rafe. I'll be with you in a few minutes." She snatched the list from Maggie and left them to get her gun.

Once outside Lacey stood by the high-sided supply wagon and watched Rafe attach the harness straps on the team of horses to the wagon trace. He moved with a smooth, easy grace under the brassy sky. She refused to be caught staring and pushed her flat-crowned back to glance north. Thick clouds piled high, dark and gray, warning of rain.

He finished and stood gazing at her, one brow lifted in contemplation. *Feisty hellion*! He had a feeling she waited for him to remark about the holstered gun she now wore. A devil prompted him not to disappoint her. "You don't need a gun, Lacey. I'm with you."

She gritted her teeth, snapped the brim of her hat down, and climbed up onto the wagon seat. "Maybe I want to make sure nothing happens to you, *partner*."

"You know, bright eyes, you can tangle a man's breath up inside him every time he looks at you."

Her brow knitted in concentration. She sensed the loneliness in him, the darkness beyond his soul, and like the land she loved, knew Rafe could be harsh or beguiling by turns. Lacey had to look away from him toward the Bradys, rising tall and hard from the land. Thin clouds shimmered and swirled around the rocky peaks. She wondered what secrets they held, what secrets were hidden inside him, what warmth was concealed by his hard surface, and who, if anyone, had breached it. Since she wasn't a fool, she had to remind herself of the danger she sensed beneath his rugged surface.

"It's late, Rafe. We'd better leave."

His last words lingered in her mind as they rode for almost an hour in silence. Lacey was plagued by her unfair judgment of him. He had taken orders, put in more than his share of hours, and she found herself wanting his understanding for her anger over Darcy.

"Rafe, you haven't mentioned Darcy again, but I need to tell you why Sy hated him."

"I'm listening."

"When Darcy settled here, he had plenty of water, but his streams and a few water holes went dry. He bought out a few small ranches, but it didn't help him. Sy refused to sell him any land with water. He had faced droughts, and last year we faced the worst one. We lost three hundred head. Darcy ran his cows over our land, and Sy set men to guard the water holes with orders to shoot. It was horrible to see Darcy's cattle die, but we couldn't lose more of our own. This isn't a land where you can afford to indulge in pity to your own cost. Darcy swore to get even, and the raids started. Believe what you want, you won't change facts."

"None of that explains what's between you and April."

Lacey stared at his grim profile. She wanted to shake him and tried not to cringe when he returned her look, the smile on his mouth more than a little threatening.

"You won't say?"

"I won't say."

Silence reigned once again.

*   *   *

The four or five buildings could be called a town, Rafe decided. A trading post, a livery and blacksmith, a saloon, and a few cabins. "Ain't much," he remarked and set the pole brake. "Figured you would do your buying in San Angela not Sonora."

"I usually do."

"Then why . . ." He stopped himself when he noticed the wooden sign posted in front of an adobe house behind the trading post. *Curt Blaine*, he read and beneath it, *Attorney and Counselor At Law*. "When you see your lapdog, make sure he gives you those papers the judge had. There's a letter for you from Sy."

Irritated with Rafe for calling Curt a lapdog, Lacey was also relieved when he said nothing more. She got down without his help and entered Spanish Mike's trading post. It was dim and Lacey waited a moment, assaulted by the smell of newly tanned hides piled near the doorway. As she walked forward, she was forced to inhale the pungent odor of salt brine rising from large barrels that marked a path through the crowded store.

Spanish Mike was a strongly built man, missing the lobe of his right ear, and Lacey had no idea of his age. He was a reading man, always with a book or a months-old newspaper in hand. He glanced up from a ragged copy of one such paper now, acknowledging her with a smile.

"Miz Lacey, right sorry 'bout Sy. Couldn't get out to the service."

"Thank you, Mike." She knew his gaze had shifted to Rafe standing behind her, and Lacey didn't know how to introduce them. She glanced back at Rafe only to see his gaze fastened on something on the counter. She turned back and noticed the basket of fresh apples alongside a jar of peppermint sticks.

"New hand, Miz Lacey?"

"Partner," Rafe explained, reaching over to pluck an apple from the small pile.

His eyes closed in bliss as he bit into the juicy fruit, and Lacey stared at him. Fresh apples weren't available often, and when they were, their price was high, but something about the way he nibbled down to the core before taking another bite . . . Her thought stopped. She was arrested by the mischievous sparkle in his eyes when he opened them and looked at her.

"We'll take the whole basket."

"Rafe!"

"Now, that's a mite pricey, fella."

Rafe ignored Mike and held Lacey's gaze. "I've always wanted to taste a fresh apple."

His voice was gruff, his eyes defiant now, and Lacey felt her throat close. Her heart gave a lurch, for those few words told her so much about him. Hunger. Maggie had tried to explain the hunger Rafe had for so many things.

His white teeth sank into the apple again, and she suddenly didn't care if the basket cost the price of ten cows. "Put the whole basket on our account, Mike."

"And a jar of peppermint sticks," Rafe added.

Lacey bit her lip. She didn't know if she wanted to laugh or cry. "The whole jar, Rafe?"

"The whole jar," he confirmed, reaching out for another apple.

Lacey blinked back tears. Damn Rafe! He was twisting her emotions. A need to hold him, to promise he could have whatever he had longed for, whatever he wanted, swamped her.

"Hear they're building up at Permanent Camp again," Mike said. "Can't settle on who's commanding it. They've had a string of officers shifting through like prairie breezes."

"I didn't know." Lacey was thankful for the distraction Mike offered. She fumbled with the list, handed it to Rafe, and made her escape.

As she turned the corner of the store toward Curt's house, she heard the sound of riders but didn't bother to look back. Her thoughts were occupied by the confusion she was feeling over Rafe. She couldn't close her mind to the sight of him eating that apple. There had been no arrogance, no mockery from him, and a warm glow spread inside her that so simple a thing made him happy. But why should she care? She didn't like him. Shaking her head, Lacey knocked and greeted the widowed Mrs. Halsey, Curt's housekeeper.

Lacey accepted the woman's condolences, found out Curt had just returned from Austin that morning, and declined the woman's offer to announce her.

Curt's office at the back of the house was cool and sparsely furnished. He appeared visibly agitated as she entered and stood before his desk.

"Lacey, this is an unexpected pleasure. How did you know I was back?"

"I didn't—and this isn't a social call."

"Who rode in with you?"

"Rafe. I left him getting our supplies. Curt, I need your help."

"Blunt as always. And what about my needs?"

Lacey rested her palms against the desk. "Leave the past be. I want to know if you have those papers Judge Walker mentioned."

He toyed with his pen, shuffling the papers before him into an untidy pile. "I don't have them. Why?"

"Well, they belong to me. I wanted to read that letter Sy wrote. I need to understand what made him change his will and . . ." She stared down at the desk, rubbing one finger back and forth on the polished wood. "I was hoping that letter would mention who my father is."

"Then I will make it a point to see the judge when I return to Austin. Don't be upset. You know there is nothing I wouldn't do for you. Give me a few minutes. Mrs. Halsey was making fresh lemonade."

Lacey grew restless waiting for him to return. She couldn't stop thinking about Rafe and that look of bliss on his face.

Curt came back with a tray and set it on the desk, then poured out a glass for each of them. "Why don't you sit down and tell me how things are working out?"

Lacey refused to sit but sipped her drink and quickly filled him in on what happened with Bo. She stopped short of any mention of her own personal confrontations with Rafe. After explaining that she had fired Ward, she set her half-empty glass down. "And that's the other reason I came to see you. I know our credit is extended, but I need you to talk the bank into giving us a few more months."

He tilted his chair back, leaning against it, his grin wry. He wanted her so damn much. The brief affair he had had with her the summer she was sixteen had ended abruptly. Lacey's decision, and one he refused to accept.

"Marry me."

"What?" Her hazel eyes meshed with his. "Curt, did you listen to anything I've said? And you know I can't marry. I won't lose my share of the Reina."

"Just suppose I could promise that you won't lose it? What if you could own the Reina, without a partner, with no one to interfere?"

"What are you implying?" She watched the grim emotions flicker across his face, his eyes narrowed to thin, wary slits. Shocked, Lacey prayed for his denial.

Curt's chair came forward with a bang. He hunched forward over his desk, his gaze locked with hers. "I love you. You can't end a feeling like that. We had something special between us, Lacey, and I want it back. Marry me. I can offer you more than just the full ownership of the Reina."

"And what about Rafe Parrish?"

He had the grace to look away. "This is rough country. Accidents happen all the time. Men have been known to just disappear."

"No. No, Curt!" She backed away from the desk as he rose and came toward her. "You don't realize what you're saying. Don't even think about it. I would never condone murder."

"You wouldn't need to know, Lacey." He put his arms around her, fury held in check that she remained stiff and unyielding. "Can you ever forget that I was the first man to love you?"

She twisted her head to avoid his kiss, pressing her hands against his chest to keep some distance. "Curt, you're a special friend, but that's all I want or need you to be." His jealousy had helped her break off with him, and Lacey rationalized that his crazy idea of killing Rafe was just an extension of that feeling. His lips skimmed her cheek. "That summer," she whispered, "I thought I was all grown up and in love with you, but I didn't understand the . . ." "Consequences" was what she wanted to say, but didn't. It would be pointless to tell him that she had miscarried. "Oh, Curt, please, I don't want to hurt you." Her hand cupped his cheek, and she looked up at him.

"It's Parrish, isn't it? You'll take any man that can give you the Reina. Did he—"

"Don't you dare say such things to me!" She struggled free and stepped back.

"Can't you understand how strong my feelings are? The thought of another man touching you is enough to drive me insane. Please, Lacey, swear to me that he never touched you."

There was no need for words. He had his answer in the sudden flush tinting sun-gold cheeks, the lowered sweep of her lashes, and the defiant lift of her chin. "I'm sorry, Lacey. I shouldn't have asked. Just don't shut me out. Give us time. I'll ride to Austin as soon as I can to get those papers and bring them to you." Jamming his hands into his pants pockets, he turned his back on her. "I'll do my best to get the bank to extend you credit."

"Curt, I am sorry."

She left him, hurrying down the hall. It wasn't until she opened the front door that yells and gunshots reached her. Lacey ran, grabbing up her skirt and petticoats with one hand, drawing her gun with the other.

Flattened against the chinked logs of the trading post, Lacey cautiously peered around the corner. "Rafe!"

Pulled by a rope, his prone body was dragged past her in a cloud of dust. There was no time to take aim. Lacey got off two quick shots, but she couldn't identify the rider. She heard Spanish Mike yell over the drum of horses driven hard. A boom sounded and she knew it was Mike's buffalo gun going off. Horses whinnied and a man screamed. She couldn't stand not knowing what was going on.

"Get down!" Mike ordered, crouched behind their loaded wagon. Dust was settling in the street.

Frantic to find out where Rafe was, Lacey began to crawl toward Mike. Her skirt hem caught on the rough boards, and she tore it free.

"Where's Rafe?"

"I ain't sure. Maybe behind those cottonwoods."

"What happened? Who are they?"

"All hell broke when I went inside to get the last sack of flour. He was standing by the wagon when they rode by. Heard him yell, grabbed up blue lightning here, and scattered them quick."

They both became aware of the quiet at the same time. With his hand on her shoulder, Mike motioned her to stay put as he rose and inched his way around the wagon. Lacey couldn't wait and went around the other side. The street was empty.

"Lacey!"

She spun around to find Curt at her back, rifle in hand. "Are you all right?" he demanded, coming to her.

"I need to find Rafe."

She started off at a run toward the cluster of trees past the last cabin on the street. People milled about, but she neither looked nor answered their questions, calling Rafe's name when there was no sign of him.

She turned back, tears glistening in her eyes when she saw him stumble into the street from between the saloon and livery, jerking the rope off him.

"Rafe, are you hurt?" Her steps faltered. She couldn't believe he first turned to the woman at his side. It was April Darcy. Lacey's chin rose, her hand shaking as she holstered her gun, forcing herself to walk to him. His shirt was torn, his cheek bled, and April was already using her neckerchief to wipe it. Whatever desire Lacey felt to comfort him died.

"What happened, Rafe? I left you for a few minutes, and you couldn't stay out of trouble."

"Lord, Lacey!" April cried. "He almost got killed, and you act like a cold-blooded bitch. How could you blame him?"

Pride kept Lacey silent. People crowded her from behind, April clutched Rafe's arm, and both Spanish Mike and Curt fired questions at Rafe.

"Didn't see them," he muttered, accepting a drink from the bartender. He tossed it down, wiping his mouth. "It all happened too fast."

Curt drew Lacey to one side. "This could have been Farel's doing. You said he swore to get even with you. Rafe's dangerous, Lacey. He'll get you killed."

"Could be." But Lacey wasn't listening, not really. She watched April, using water someone had brought to her, wipe Rafe's face. A white-hot spear of jealousy pierced her. If Rafe got any closer to his angel of mercy, he'd be draped tighter than April's corset. She flashed Rafe a disgusted look. "If you're done being fussed over, I'm ready to leave."

"Lacey, wait. I'll ride back with you," Curt said.

Rubbing his shoulder, Rafe limped over to them. "No need." He dusted off his battered curled-brim hat, put it on, and eyed the bullet holes in the wagon. "My partner will *protect* me."

"Or kill you," April whispered from behind him.

"You keep that thought in mind, April." Lacey climbed onto the wagon seat, snapping the reins as Rafe settled next to her.

Chapter 10 ═══════════

ONCE THEY WERE well on their way, Lacey slowed the horses to a walk. "How bad are you hurt?" Her voice was gruff. She wouldn't look at him, and she prayed he wouldn't think she was soft for asking.

"I've been worse."

Well! So much for her trying to show concern. He certainly wouldn't get any sympathy from her again. "And you didn't recognize those men?"

"Like I said, it happened fast. I was standing by the wagon, waiting for Spanish Mike, and the next I knew someone tossed a rope over me and yanked me down."

Lacey gnawed her lip. She wanted an explanation of April's presence, but his tone did not lend itself to her asking. She knew he couldn't have arranged to meet April. He didn't know until they were away from the ranch that she wanted to go to Sonora. But April had no reason to be there. Unless Darcy was behind this attack on Rafe. Whatever Rafe thought, he was keeping it to himself.

The horses scented the rain seconds before the first drops fell. Lacey pulled up, scrambled over the seat, and began to pull the tarp over their supplies. Rafe joined her, but in moments a torrent hit them.

"Get underneath," he ordered, making a grab for the reins as the horses shied.

Lacey squirmed and wiggled herself backward to ensure that the canvas was tucked tight to keep their foodstuffs dry. Moving forward, she struggled to keep her skirt and petticoats from bunching up around her hips. Rafe was wedged in a crease between barrels and sacks. He extended his hand to her, his pain hidden by the darkness as he hauled her to him. Damp as she was, Lacey, with her back against his chest, found herself embarrassed as they fit together spoon fashion. Rafe's arm was locked around her waist; his breath curled over her ear, across her cheek, and mingled with her own. She inhaled the scents of whiskey, smoke, and peppermint.

"Ease up, princess," he whispered. "We'll be here a while. If you're hungry, I saved you an apple. Or did you satisfy your appetite with Curt?"

"What if I did? I don't account to you," she snapped, using his own words.

"I warned you that I'll be the only man in your bed. Don't lie to me."

"I'm not!" She ignored his threat. If she didn't, she knew Rafe would think she was challenging him.

"Did he give you the papers?"

"No. He didn't have them." She strained away from him, but he pulled her back. The intimacy of the dark, the rain, and their closeness made Lacey desperate to keep him talking. The cool damp had given way to the heat of their bodies. Rafe's breathing was slow and deep. Her own was erratic. "Curt thinks that Ward Farel was behind that attack on you. I didn't see who they were. But it bothers me that anyone knew—"

"Lacey, it's over. Stop worrying about it."

His heartbeat seemed to be pounding into her, his tone was dismissive, but Lacey valiantly tried again. "Rafe, how did Sy meet your mother? I . . . we haven't talked about—"

"And you think now is the right time?" She couldn't see the grin that went with his teasing, but he didn't miss her sincerity. She chose that moment to shift her weight. Her buttocks were snug against the cradle of his hips and the last thing Rafe wanted to do was talk. She was woman soft, woman-scented, and woman warm. He tilted his head, brushing his lips against her neck, pushing her hat off and then his own.

"Rafe, don't. We need to—"

"Talk," he murmured, inching his way up a bit so that he could reach her mouth. "There's another way to get to know each other, bright eyes."

Lacey buried her face against the rough burlap. It didn't stop him from trailing kisses alongside her neck, his laughter male and knowing when she trembled. Her mumblings were lost to him as he traced the shape and curl of her ear, then bit down gently on the sensitive lobe. She shivered, the echo of her own heartbeat pounding dully in her ears. Like the brush of a night breeze, his hand rose from her waist to cup her chin and turn her face.

"I've wondered if you tasted as good as I remembered." His mouth lowered to hers, fitted itself perfectly to the shape, and with a tenderness that he didn't know he was capable of giving, he kissed her.

Lacey was armed against aggression. She had no ready defense against the beguiling softness of his lips. Traces of whiskey and the sharp flavor of mint passed from his mouth to hers. He was not taking from her, but wooing her response in so delicate a fashion, she helplessly gave him what he wanted.

"So much woman hidden under that hard shell," he whispered, levering himself up and shifting her beneath him. He made a husky sound that was almost a groan, his arms tight around her. In a smooth motion he captured her mouth, sliding his tongue inside. His hand caressed her back, his fingers tangled in her braid. Rafe arched her body so that her breasts were pressed against his hard chest. He began rocking his hot, erect male flesh against her. His tongue moved in the same sensuous stroking as his powerful body, and slowly Lacey softened, giving those same rhythms back to him.

He winced as he moved his injured shoulder, but had to touch more of her. His hand caressed the length of her body, and half-wild cries fed his own desire. Her back arched in a reflex as old as passion, and he took what she offered, cupping his hand over one breast to find the sensitive tip. Her kittenlike cry stoked the fire that burned inside him to possess her, and he kneaded her soft heated flesh until her nipple hardened into a thrusting point.

Flooded by the wild sensations his touch and kisses brought, Lacey quivered in response. She opened her mouth wider beneath his, her fingers threaded through his hair. The drumming beat of the rain melded with the beat of her blood. Rafe offered a haven from the world where she had to be on guard, always strong. His kiss, the taut length of his body, his own husky sounds made her revel in being aroused, in being a woman. The hiss of his breath came swiftly, suddenly, and she opened her eyes to the intense gaze of his.

"Rafe?"

"It's all right, bright eyes," he said, his tone deep, gritty.

Lacey had no chance to ask what he meant. His mouth replaced his hand on her breast. Sweet and hot, the moist searching caress of his tongue made her cry out. Without knowing it, she held his head hard against her, filled with a wild pleasure. His urgent suckling made her breath come

quickly, raggedly. The savage race of her blood left her
defenseless, seething with a desire she had never known.
His knee wedged a space between her legs, their cramped
quarters hampering his move. When he lifted his head, she
reached for him, aching to feel his mouth loving her again.

"Rafe . . . please," she whispered huskily.

He took her mouth almost roughly. Hunger rode him. As
suddenly as the kiss began, he ended it. "You were right,
princess. It's not the right time or place." His lips brushed
hers, and he settled back. "But for both our sakes, don't
move. I want you so much, it's pulling me apart, and I want
you to trust me."

Lacey didn't move. Not by his order, but for being
stunned by his withdrawal. She hadn't tried to stop him.
The rain had eased to a gentle patter, but the tension
between them thickened like a coming storm.

"You don't understand, do you?" he asked in a tortured
voice. "I want you so bad right now, I hurt. But I can't take
you here . . . not like this." He took her silence as an
accusation. "I shouldn't have started anything. The wagon
is too cramped, but I could take you on the open ground like
some cheap *puta*. But even someone like me enjoys the
comfort of a clean bed. The first time—"

"First time!" she spat out with a sharp little laugh. "I told
you once that's not a gift I can give you." Raw, hot, and
aching, Lacey refused to lie.

"I remember," he muttered softly. "I was talking about
the first time for us. The rest doesn't matter. Whoever it was
didn't make you feel hot and wild. You wouldn't be here
with me like this if he had."

Rage for his assumption mingled with shame inside her.
She had no denial to offer him. How he knew what she felt,
Lacey didn't know. It was true, but it hurt. "Is that how it
was for your mother with Sy?"

"She loved him." Rafe grated the words from between clenched teeth.

"And Sy, did he love her?"

"She believed he did. Her family slaved for one of the *criolla* families that hold their pure Spanish blood to be a God-given treasure. Sy came in thirty-eight to buy cattle. That was when she met him. A rich *gringo*. He came again the year after, and the third time he came back in forty, they became lovers."

"I don't understand. He went East, met and married my mother the year after. Forty-one, Fletcher said. But Fletcher also told me Sy had gone back to Mexico several times. Maybe he was searching for her?"

"It didn't matter. Her family shamed her when she told them she was carrying his child. At first she believed he was coming back for her. When he didn't, she ran away. My mother wouldn't let her child be raised to slave for anyone."

Envy touched Lacey. "Then your mother was strong. Mine was so full of grief from burying an infant year after year that she ran away. Sy didn't even go after her. He waited and then wrote to Maggie that he wouldn't travel the winter roads with her because she was carrying a child. And now I know that she met the man who fathered me while she was back East."

"Maybe you're better off not knowing."

His voice was emotionless, but Lacey once again sensed underlying pain. "Why didn't she come to Sy? He was hard, but he was fair. I know he would have taken care of her. If he did love her, Rafe, Sy would have married her, and I would know who my father is."

"I guess it was her pride. She crossed the border and met Hilton Parrish, and married him to give me a name. That is the only thing he gave me. He was a gambler, and when he was winning, we lived good, but when he lost . . ."

Lacey groped for his hand, entwining her fingers with his. "Please, Rafe, don't stop. This is the first time you've told me anything, and you did ask me to trust you."

"And the past matters, princess? All ready to judge me by blood and background?"

She flinched from his hard, sarcastic tone. "No. I simply want to understand."

"We trekked all over . . . backwater mining camps, where he would scrounge up a stake most times by taking whatever money my mother earned by washing stinking clothes or cooking for miners. We lived in places they called towns 'cause they had a trading post and saloon. I guess I was about ten or so when we went back to Mexico."

Lacey didn't push him for more, but she felt a need to share with him. "Fletcher once told me that Sy thought my constant questions made him feel taller than God and smarter than the devil. I would have done anything to see warmth in his eyes when he looked at me." Her voice was flat with bitterness. "Now that I know I'm not his, I can understand why he held himself away from me. You call me princess, but I wasn't, Rafe." This time his fingers pressed hers. "I had to earn everything from him. When I proved myself to his satisfaction, he would give me a gift. Not the smile I longed for, or a hug, but something he could buy with money. I hated him for using money to control everything. I would hate any man that did the same."

Rafe listened and felt his gut twist. The rain had slackened to a mere drizzle, and he knew he had to stop her before she said more.

"It's time we started for home, Lacey."

The day had shaded down to gray dusk. Lacey didn't understand why he had once again withdrawn as they headed home.

She ached from the tension and thought longingly of a hot

bath. She wouldn't even mind a bit of Maggie's pampering to help soothe the emotional wringer Rafe had subjected her to. The first faint pinpoints of light were a welcome sight, and she sighed.

"Bet you're thinking of a hot soak," Rafe said. "I can act the gentleman and let you go first."

"I wasn't planning on giving you a choice," she snapped at his reminder of their having to share the same tub. Truth was, she hated being vulnerable to him.

The wagon wheels splashed through mud puddles, and Lacey sat forward anxiously. "Something's wrong."

Rafe had already noticed the bobbing lantern lights off toward one of the corrals. He urged the horses to a faster pace.

"Where in tarnation you two been?" Fletcher yelled. "Got to thinkin' I'd be forced to come lookin'. Luke rode hell-bent for leather aways back to find you. They hit us again. He sent Blew, Cal, and Mertson after them. Ran off close to sixty head this time. Got a good night horse saddled for you, Rafe."

"Was anyone hurt?" Lacey demanded to know, cursing her long skirt as she jumped down.

"Not this time."

"I'll use my roan, Fletcher."

"No, Lacey."

She glanced from Rafe's hand on her arm up to his face. "No?"

"Trust me, Lacey."

"You two gonna stand jawin'?"

"You were hurt once today, Rafe. And it might surprise you, but I do know this range."

He held her steady gaze with his own level one. "I'm not saying that you don't. I'm asking you again to trust me. Stay here where you'll be safe."

Be a woman, his eyes begged. *Let me protect you and what we claim*, they demanded. And Lacey, to her shock, agreed.

But it was a frustrated Rafe that returned late the next afternoon after another fruitless search. He was barely able to stand in the doorway of the office.

"We couldn't pick up a trail," he said to Lacey.

"Get some sleep, Rafe."

"What's all that on the desk?"

"Cattle counts, outstanding notes on the Reina. I don't know how much the judge told you about our debts. But they're heavy. We need every head to sell, or we could lose the land."

He couldn't meet her gaze. "Who knows?"

"Anyone that rides for us. Rafe," she whispered, appalled at his exhausted state, "we'll talk about this later. Get some rest."

He shoved his hat back, rubbing the back of his hand against his forehead. "You ever think that someone on the Reina might be working with the rustlers?"

Lacey rose from her chair, advancing on him like a fury. "No! And what's more, I never will. These men are loyal, and they've worked for us—"

"Spare me their defense, princess. Maggie already lit into me. Fletcher, now, he didn't think I was crazy."

He swayed where he stood, and Lacey moved without thought to brace him. "Will you go to bed and leave this be!"

Rafe locked his arms around her, inhaling the clean, sweet scent of her. "I smell like polecat." His head dropped to her shoulder. "You take me to bed, bright eyes."

"I'd like to take you—"

"Can't. I'm beat. Give me a few hours and make that offer again, princess."

"I'd like to take you by the ear and give you a good shaking," she continued as if he hadn't interrupted.

His lips nuzzled her neck, and he smiled. "If I wasn't dragging, I'd do more than that to get you to open your eyes."

She managed a half turn, slipped her arm around his waist, and led him out to the courtyard. "My eyes *are* open. Yours are closed."

But when she helped him to bed, deciding that he smelled more like a hardworking man than polecat, Rafe wouldn't let her go.

"Stay with me. I don't want to be alone."

His words were mumbled, and she stroked his bristled cheek, then smoothed his brow. What was he doing to her? She was angry one moment, exasperated the next, and in mere seconds he made her feel tender and protective toward him. When she lifted her hand, he held it to his lips, pressing a kiss against her palm. Lacey felt heat race down to her toes. His eyes closed, and she was helpless to move. With a boyish grin he tucked her hand beneath his cheek. In moments he was asleep, but it was a long while before Lacey slipped away.

For two days there was peace out on the range, war at the main house. Lacey couldn't shake Rafe of his pursuit that someone on the Reina was working with the rustlers.

She held her temper in check, tried to trust him, and grew desperate for him to understand he was wrong. When he began on Bo James, Lacey drew the line.

"No more of this pointless questioning. Bo watched me grow up. He was my teacher and friend just like Maggie and Fletcher and Blewett. Luke and Ragweed are the only new hands we have, and you said you were satisfied about them."

He towered over where she sat behind the desk. "And you keep harping it's Darcy."

"I've tried to explain to you that we face the same problems every rancher in Texas does. We count Darcy out. Fine. From there we have a carpetbag government whose actions to date have brought an escalation of Indian raids. Before Sy died, he got together with other ranchers, and they demanded that the army do something about them and the men that have drifted west still fighting a war that's been over for two years." She covered her face with both hands, rubbing the tension from her forehead.

Rafe came around the chair to stand behind her. His hand had barely settled on her shoulders when Lacey's head snapped up.

"Don't touch me. You sit down and listen."

"I get tired of fighting with you, princess." His hand slid around her neck, cupping her jaw and forcing her head back. "We can't seem to agree on much but this." His lips drank her unuttered protest for long moments.

Lacey's eyes closed the second his head lowered. The look in his eyes had been hot enough to light fires. Deep inside her, heat unfurled, and she wanted to be kissed and touched by him. But every time he ended their arguments like this, he left her frustrated . . . and afraid. She wished she could trust him completely, yet she was held back by the thought of his using the desire he stirred inside her to control her.

But the deepening thrust of his kiss, the heady scent of his warmth, even the callused tips of his fingers stroking her neck combined to heighten desire and cast aside fear.

Maggie screaming both their names put an end to her turmoil. Rafe broke their kiss and was at the door before Lacey managed to recover.

Luke, chest heaving, was trying to talk when Lacey joined them in the courtyard.

". . . fifteen head . . . by the creek."

"Take it easy, Luke," Rafe cautioned, meeting Lacey's eyes, forestalling her questions. "You heard. Only they didn't take them this time. They slit their throats and left them. You can't believe Darcy did that."

"This time I'm riding with you. Don't say a word, Rafe. I don't know or care who is behind it. But I swear I won't rest until I hang them."

"You're not riding with me!" he yelled at her back, for she was already running to her room.

Minutes later when Lacey came out of the house at a run, carrying her rifle, Rafe was waiting.

Lacey stopped short, glancing from him to Fletcher at his side. The significance of the big grulla, saddled and waiting, snapped her control.

"I wanted the roan, Fletcher, in case you weren't sure."

"You're not coming." Rafe stood, legs apart, slapping the reins of his horse against his palm. "Fletcher isn't hitching a mule for you."

"Fletcher doesn't take orders from you! Now, get out of my way."

"Your worst enemy is yourself, princess. Someone has got to have sense enough to curb—"

"Saddle my horse, Fletcher. Now."

Fletcher glanced from Rafe, looking like a thundercloud about to explode, back to Lacey, slowing raising her rifle, fury glinting in her eyes.

"I don't need curbing, Rafe. I know my enemies. Move out of my way, or you'll top the list." Late afternoon sunlight played shadows over his features. Lacey ignored the muscle twitching in his cheek, refusing to back down. She tightened her grip on the rifle. "Stop thinking like a man. I know this range. We can split up and cover more—"

"No. It's dangerous. They could still be out there."

Fletcher had heard enough. "Lacey can find a bee outta its hive, son. Best let her ride."

And ride they did until Lacey knew their search would again be hampered by the dark. She resisted every suggestion that Rafe offered to stop, driven by her fury over the senseless killing of cattle.

Rafe wouldn't admit it, but his thought paralleled hers. He knew Lacey was hoping to find something that would point guilt at Darcy, but Rafe couldn't buy that. His gut instinct said that someone on the Reina was betraying them, someone Lacey trusted. He had let her ride where she would to search, just as he let her order the men to bunch up the cattle and then ride out in teams to hunt for the killers.

They topped a small caprock rise, and Rafe pulled up, cursing the thick clouds that trickled moonlight to guide them. For once Lacey drew rein alongside without protest. The slump of her shoulders, the droop of her head, told of her own exhaustion.

"Go back, princess. We're not going to find anything more tonight."

She set her hat brim forward and without looking at him shook her head. "If you want to go back, I'm not going to stop you, Rafe." She lifted her canteen, drank deeply, and straightened her back. "I'm riding on."

It took him a few minutes to realize that Lacey veered north. The land leveled out as he followed, and Lacey took advantage of it. His grulla needed no urging to canter alongside the roan.

"Where the hell are you going!" he yelled, grabbing for the roan's bridle. He controlled his horse with his knees and viciously yanked to pull the roan's head down and around. "Looking to get yourself killed by riding to Darcy's now?"

The horses danced uneasily in place, and Rafe ignored her demands to let go. "Lacey, you don't have a lick of sense."

"That's how much you know," she snapped, grabbing for his handhold on the leather. "There are small canyons between the open range separating our lands. If anyone wanted to hide—"

"And you intended to ride there? I'm good with my gun, lady, maybe you are, too. But that's a fool's notion to try and corner—"

"Can't you trust me! Just for once let me prove that I know what I'm doing. Damn you! Let go!"

Rafe let go of the bridle, but he crowded the grulla next to the roan. "I told you once that you don't have to prove anything more to me. You want to go off and get yourself killed, do it. I won't stop you. Just remember, princess, that if anything happens to you, I'll own the Reina that much sooner."

Wispy clouds broke away from the moon, and its light revealed Rafe's granite-cut features that matched the mountains. Lacey stared into his cold black eyes. She hated him at this moment and thought of how easy it would be to shoot him.

As if Rafe read her thoughts, his gaze dropped to where her hand hovered over the holstered gun and rose slowly back to her eyes. "You'd never clear leather, Lacey."

"You've made me become a stranger to myself, Rafe. But you'll never—hear me—never control me."

He let her ride away, cursing her, damning her, and wanting her in the same moment. There was no way he could let her go without his protection, and he urged the grulla to follow at a walk. Damn the binding terms of Sy's will! He should have taken her when he had the chance. She'd be his, home where it was safe, not riding into who knew what danger. Lacey certainly wouldn't have the breath left to fight him.

Clouds banked the moon once again, and he lost sight of her. He sent the grulla into a lope, and when he caught up with her . . . Hairs prickled on the back of his neck. It was the grace of a second's warning.

Shots rang out ahead of him. He flattened out, his thoughts centered on Lacey. Two more shots split the night, a horse screamed, and then . . . silence.

Rafe hesitated to draw his gun or rifle until he knew where Lacey was positioned. Had she returned fire? It was the thought of her being pinned down, alone, that spurred him to ride, regardless of the danger to himself.

He veered around a small outcrop of rocks, crossed a shallow runoff, and came up out of the hollow at a run. The sudden bunching of muscled power beneath warned Rafe as the grulla jumped. Another shot echoed, and Rafe sawed on the reins, tearing the soft mouth of his horse, to hit the ground hard and running. In that brief moment he had seen the sprawled figures of Lacey and her horse.

His breath froze like winter's chill in his lungs as he crawled to her side. Her name was a croaking sound. He gathered her limp body up against him and listened to the night that was suddenly silent. His lips found the gash on her temple, and his breath left his body in an explosive rush. The grulla shied and snorted at the scent of blood. Rafe barely glanced at the dead roan.

Lacey's moan forced him into action regardless of the targets they both presented. He spoke softly to the grulla, lunging with one hand to grab the trailing reins. Lacey was dead weight as he lifted her into the saddle and swung himself up behind her. She cried out as he pushed his body over hers, keeping her bent over, his back exposed. At a walk, the grulla picked his way back down into the hollow.

Once across the stream Rafe switched the reins to his left hand, slid his right around her waist, and felt the seep of blood.

Guilt swamped him. His own words haunted him as he rode back toward the Reina. And for the first time since his mother died, Rafe prayed.

Coffee laced with whiskey sustained his wait until Maggie, her face drawn, joined him in the kitchen.

"I've done all I can, Rafe. Fletcher and Bo are gonna sit with her. No more than a bullet graze on her side, but that gash . . . well, I'd best send someone for Doc." Her eyes were as bleak as his. "Get some sleep, son. You're out on your feet."

He rubbed the back of his neck, finished his drink, and stood. "You do whatever you have to do, Maggie. Just make sure she's all right. Whatever you do, don't let her out of your sight. Put a guard on her if you have to."

"Where are you goin'?" she asked as he moved toward the door. "Blew or Scanlon can handle—"

"I know they can. That's why I'm leaving."

"Leavin'? Boy, what the—"

"Maggie! Lacey was shot from behind. I know how every head means the survival of the ranch, but someone tried to kill her. Or maybe the shots were meant for me. I need to know more than I can find out riding out day after day here."

Maggie had heard a similar tone of voice from his father too many times to continue arguing. "Be careful, son. The Reina needs you, but Lacey needs you more."

"I wish that was true, Maggie. More than you know."

Chapter 11 ═══════════════

"Is HE BACK yet?" Lacey winced as she raised herself up to a sitting position in bed.

Maggie shook her head, answering the same question that Lacey greeted her with for the past three mornings.

"Are you sure that no one knows where he—"

"Yes. Stop circlin' 'round like a cat chasin' tail. By your testy tone I'd guess you're feeling spry, but you didn't finish your food."

Lacey glanced at the tray beside her bed. "I can't eat, Maggie. I still feel sick, and besides, I'm worried about Rafe."

"Well, that's a change from all the snappin' an' bitin' you've been doin'. Does me good to hear you say it. Rafe was sure enough worried 'bout you."

"Sure. And he rode off to who knows where before he—"

"Hush! His face was white when he carried you to me. He was scared, Lacey. Scared. I ain't one to cry over burnt biscuits, but you should've listened to him an' not gone chasin' shadows. You've been carryin' a heavy load, honey," she said in a softened tone. "It's time you give over an' be what the good Lord made you . . . a woman. Stop tryin' to prove you're better than him at every turn."

"I wasn't trying to do that, Maggie."

126

"Well, that's a yarn of a different color." She spread open the curtains, faced Lacey, and beamed smiling approval. "Guess that knock on your head did some good. 'Bout time you trusted him."

Trust him? Lacey closed her eyes and rested her head against the pillows. She wanted to trust Rafe. There was a need inside her to do more than that. But the hard lessons she had learned from Sy Garrett held her back. He had always warned her never to give in to the soft instincts of a woman. It would make her weak . . . weak enough to lose the Reina. She glanced up as Maggie straightened the quilt.

"There's so much at stake, Maggie. More than you know. But until Rafe comes back, if he does, I guess I don't have a choice."

"He'll come back, never doubt it."

Impatient with the delay, Rafe paced in Judge Walker's office, waiting for him to return from court. Three days of hard riding, snatching sleep in the saddle, had brought him to Austin. Luck had ridden with him, for the day before, the judge had returned to the city.

This was the only man he could think of to shed light on the past. And then, there were a few things that he had uncovered, that he had shared with no one.

He glanced longingly at the soft leather chair, but knew that if he sat down, he wouldn't get up. Indecision over having made the right choice plagued him. Coming here to the judge smacked of asking for help, and as he had called no man friend, he had never asked anyone for help.

But stronger than his pride was his fear for Lacey's life.

Judge Walker entered, took one look at the thick black stubble on Rafe's face, met the haggard look in his eyes, and didn't waste time.

"You running or in trouble, Rafe?"

"I never run, but there's plenty of trouble."

Several decanters and glasses stood on a sideboard in the paneled office, and the judge, without asking, filled two glasses. "You look like you could use this first." He sipped his drink and settled himself in a leather wing chair in front of his massive oak desk. "Join me," he said, gesturing to the chair's empty mate.

Rafe tossed back his drink and sat down. Without mentioning his feelings for Lacey or the details of their personal confrontations, he told the judge all that had happened.

Silas Walker listened. He knew it had cost Rafe a measure of his pride to come to him. The weeks they had spent together, traveling from Mexico to the Reina, had revealed more about Rafe than he had realized. Silas understood pride. He had a healthy measure of it himself for his ability to judge men. Rafe's past would lead many to condemn him. Silas knew better. Rafe was a survivor under circumstances that would have broken another man.

"I'm glad to hear that Lacey's injuries were minor," he said as Rafe finished and leaned his head back wearily.

"I didn't say that. I left before Maggie was sure."

"Maggie's bandaged enough cuts and bruises to know. As for the rest, I can't say I'm surprised in view of what I've learned. Get the bottle, Rafe. I've news of my own to share."

Silas held out his glass to be filled. "I informed you that Sy was short of ready cash aside from that special bequest. I suspect that Lacey has made it plain your money is tied to the sale of cattle. We spoke of my checking into getting additional credit with the bank extended, and I did. But I'm afraid that my news isn't good. Every note against the sale of those cattle as well as the outstanding mortgages on the

Reina have been purchased." Frowning, he added, "As much as I hate to admit this, I have failed in my attempts to find out who bought them."

Rafe felt as if he had taken a blow to his gut. His plan had failed. Whoever held the notes would know that they needed every head sold at top price to buy them back. If there wasn't enough money, they could lose the Reina.

"There's more, Rafe."

"What the hell else matters?"

"There's talk that there's trouble between you and Lacey. Two bosses can't run a ranch efficiently. Men are reluctant as it is to lend money to a woman, especially one as young as Lacey."

"How did you hear about trouble between us?" Rafe's eyes were slitted as he stared at the judge, but he didn't give him a chance to answer. "The first few days were rough. Lacey fired Farel that very night I arrived. We had a fight, just like I told you. But things have been good between Lacey and me these last few weeks." He hunched forward in his chair. "We went into Sonora. Lacey saw Curt. She might have told him, but that doesn't make sense. Why would he want to spread word that we have any trouble?"

"I'd stake my own reputation that Curt isn't behind the rumors. The man's well respected, wants to marry Lacey, and wouldn't have anything to gain. As for Farel, I don't think he's smart enough to know the right people to talk to."

"What about Darcy?"

"He might have the right contacts, Rafe, but he's hard-pressed for cash, too. There is no way he could have bought up the notes. Not alone. Of course," he stressed, "we need to consider that rustling your cattle and selling them would ease his problem. But then, he wouldn't get much for them now. Not even from the army. They're buying whatever beef they can in an effort to keep the

Indians on the reservations and to prevent tempers from exploding again."

"You must have some idea of who could or would back him. Someone has money. I came here for answers, not more questions."

"Have another drink and calm down, Rafe. I'll try to explain that there is more involved than your immediate problems. The Republicans have money. But Darcy is a Southerner through and through. He and Sy were on opposite sides over the war. But Sy was against the South being placed under military rule as part of the Reconstruction Acts. Times are unsettled. Andy Johnson lacks the political wisdom and tact necessary to carry out the generous reconstruction terms that Lincoln intended. Throckmorton's out of the governor's seat, but Edward Pease hasn't made any decisive moves."

"What has all this to do with the Reina?"

Silas smiled. "The political climate of this country, of Texas, is important to you now that you own land. You should be aware, since it affects your taxes and your voting power. The Republican congressional leaders favor the radical extremes to retain their power in the federal government. Southern Democrats resent their loss of power. There are men who are desperate enough to force the military rule to end by whatever means they can." Silas poured himself another drink and sipped it slowly. "Rumors abound that they would supply the Indians with guns, stir what unrest and fear they can so that the army officers can't govern or keep the Indians in line."

"And you think that Darcy might be involved with these men?"

"I didn't say that. I wouldn't unless I was sure of the facts. It is a possibility to consider. Texans are fed up with having a scalawag government that turns its back on their problems." He rose abruptly and began to pace.

Rafe watched him, sat up straighter in his chair, and rubbed the back of his neck. The whiskey had hit him hard, and he shook his head to clear it.

"Aside from all this, word has come that Johnson is unstable. The Republicans want him out of office, and having met the man, I know him to be fearless but reckless. His term in office has been fraught with anger and sometimes senseless retaliation against Congress. All these political machinations will have a ruinous effect on our economy."

"Are you telling me that you can't help us at all?"

"I can arrange for private loans with some wealthy Northerners who are looking for sound investments. The Reina could be that."

Rafe's head snapped up. He heard the *but* at the end of the judge's words. "Tell me."

"If there was a stable union between you and Lacey—"

"A what?"

"Marriage, Rafe. If you married Lacey, you wouldn't need money from anyone."

"I know that," he mumbled, dropping his head into his palms.

"Is the idea distasteful to you?"

"No. I just don't want to tell her."

Silas wisely decided to let the matter rest. "I could get you some help to track down these rustlers."

"How?"

"The Rangers might be interested in what's going on. They're not overly fond of the army, but someone is stirring up trouble with the Comanche. They would have reason to scout around if they worked for you. Don't be looking at me like that. I know your feelings about anyone connected with the law. But after what happened to Lacey, no one would question you for hiring more men. You see, I agree with you that someone on the Reina is working with the rustlers."

Rafe made him wait while he gave careful thought to his suggestion. He couldn't fault it. And he could use the help. There was no way to oversee every man and keep a close watch on Lacey.

"I'll agree, but they take their orders from me. I don't want anyone else to know. Not even Lacey. And I want to take those papers you have back with me."

"What are you talking about?"

"Lacey needs to read that letter. I want her to know why Sy changed his will and gave me that special gift. I haven't lied to her, and I won't begin to. If she wants to marry me after she knows the truth, I'm more than willing."

"Rafe, I gave those papers and the letter to Curt before I left the ranch that day."

There was an instant blinding rage that forced Rafe to close his eyes. Curt had the papers. Lacey had been to see him. She knew what was in that letter from Sy. . . . What a damn fool he had been. His own words haunted him. He had asked her to trust him, to let him handle everything, and she had, leading him on, making him think she believed in him, cared . . .

"Rafe! Damn you, answer me! What's wrong?"

"You're right. I need outside help. Someone has set up the Reina for a fall—and from the inside."

"You know who it is?"

"You said it that first day. Lacey would do anything to keep the Reina. I told you she was shot from behind and it was dark. Maybe those bullets were meant for me." A deadly calm replaced the rage inside him. He stood up and faced the judge. "I'll meet you in the morning. I need to sleep. And judge," he added, stopping before the door, "tell those Rangers we'll be riding hard all the way. I've got an itch that won't be scratched until I get back to Lacey."

"Don't go off half-cocked without thinking this through. Seems to me that's what landed you in a Mexican jail. I promised Sy I would be a friend to you. We'll talk again."

Rafe merely glared at him and left. Silas slowly sat behind his desk, shaking his head. Lacey couldn't be behind this. She just couldn't. But Rafe had the dangerous look in his eyes of a man who had been betrayed.

As the fifth morning of Rafe's disappearance drew to a close, Lacey tried to cling to the fact that she still trusted Rafe. Tired of sitting in the courtyard, she was about to enter her room when the sound of voices arrested her attention. It was Maggie, wiping her hands on her apron, cautioning Curt to keep his visit brief.

Striding toward her, Curt's gaze lingered on her startled look, her pale skin, and the small bandage on her temple.

"I came as soon as I heard what happened, Lacey. But the stories were confused. Someone said you took a fall when your horse was shot out from under you, and then I met Doc Culver, and he said you were shot."

"I was shot and so was my horse. Please, sit down."

"I also found out that Rafe Parrish is gone. Did he do this to you?"

"No. Rafe was with me. If he hadn't been, I would never have made it back. Honestly, Curt, I can't believe you rode out here to accuse him."

"I came because I was worried about you." He tried to ignore the way she pulled back when he reached out to touch her cheek. "Do you know who did it?"

"No. It was too dark. I didn't see anything, and they were

behind me." Lacey winced as she turned to pour out a glass of lemonade. "Would you like some?"

"Sure." He ran his hand in a distracted manner through his hair. "Lacey, after what happened in town and this senseless shooting, won't you reconsider my offer of marriage? You need someone to protect you. Things are getting out of control. I heard about the cattle. That's the work of a sick, revengeful mind."

"On that point I agree, but I won't marry you, Curt."

"Where the hell did Parrish go? Is he out hunting for whoever shot you?"

Lacey didn't want to lie. The truth was, she didn't know if Rafe was indeed doing just that. "Curt, I was just about to rest for a while. Why don't you stay for supper? We'll talk afterward."

"All right. You rest. I'll ride out and find Parrish. I want some answers."

"Curt, he's not here. I don't know where he is. No one does. Just leave it be . . . please."

"Only if you will promise me to think carefully about my offer. Wait," he demanded when she tried to speak. "I'm afraid for you, Lacey. You can't expect me to stop caring about what happens to you. That's all. I'll tell Maggie I'm staying."

But Lacey found that she couldn't rest. Curt had voiced a question that nagged at her. Did others believe that Rafe had shot her? He had enough to gain by her death. And where had he gone? Was he hiding because he was guilty or hunting whoever shot her?

As she freshened up for supper, Lacey knew she would not have the answers to those questions until Rafe returned.

Bo James's leg was almost healed, and he joined them for supper. Fletcher was the first to hear the arrival of horses, and he rose to stand by the doorway.

"It's Captain Chase and—well, I'll be, he's got Evan Darcy with him. Want I should fetch 'em in to supper?"

"Please, Fletcher," Lacey answered. "Maggie, would you set two places? We can squeeze them in."

"Ain't jus' the two of 'em. Got a private, too," Fletcher announced. "I'll tell 'em to wash."

"I wonder why they're stopping here?" Lacey murmured.

"I was about to ask you why, Lacey." Curt didn't bother to hide his annoyance.

"Darcy's been sellin' horses to the army," Bo informed them. "Seems I heard talk aways back that he was doin' good goin' down to Mexico, buyin' stock, an' herdin' them up here."

"Don't surprise me any," Maggie said, placing folded linen napkins at the extra places. "Tom Darcy tried to keep his son under his thumb too long. Maybe the boy's got some backbone after all." She eyed the table, unconcerned about feeding three extra men. The two plump chickens, cut up and fried golden brown, would have been barely enough, but she had fried up beefsteaks along with ham slices swimming in redeye gravy to tempt Lacey's appetite. Pickled corn, new carrots, and a heaping platter of hot biscuits completed their supper. Nodding to herself, she placed another jug of fresh cider on the table.

"Good evening, Miss Garrett."

Lacey smiled as Captain Chase walked in. Of average height, and a rather slight build, he had a charming manner and smile that she responded to warmly. He stood holding his hat with one hand; the other pushed the damp locks of gray-streaked hair from his forehead.

He gestured behind him. "Private Cardeen. I speak for both of us in thanking you for your kindly invite to supper. We've been eating hardtack and jerky for days." His gaze rapidly took in the spread on the table. "Looks mighty good, ma'am."

It was Maggie who urged them to sit and began passing bowls to them. Lacey was staring at the door, where Evan Darcy stood.

It had been over a year since she had seen him, and the change was a startling one. Evan had filled out all the promise of his lanky frame. The buckskin shirt and pants he wore fitted his body snugly. His hair was a riot of brown and blond shades from the sun, thick and wavy, but longer than she remembered—it now reached the collar of his shirt. He had grown a mustache that gave his face a hard look. His blue eyes, the shade of a summer sky, were as thoroughly assessing her own appearance.

The captain coughed in embarrassment at their lengthy stares, but it was Curt who finally spoke.

"It's good to see you again, Evan. It's been a long time."

"Yeah," he answered softly. "It sure has."

No one was fooled into thinking he was answering Curt, for he had not taken his eyes from Lacey.

"You gonna stand there, boy, and let my cookin' get cold?"

"No, Maggie." He set his hat on a peg near the door. "Been too long since I ate home cooking."

Lacey quickly said grace and, when done, answered the captain's questions about her bandage.

"And you have no idea who shot you?" he asked.

"No. I explained that to Curt earlier. My partner and I were tracking, and it was dark. It could have been anyone. Even your father, Evan."

Since everyone knew how Evan felt about his father, no one was surprised when he offered no defense. "I heard this new partner of yours, Lacey, has greaser blood. That true?"

The insult to Rafe touched a raw place inside her, and

Lacey had to control her temper. She didn't think to ask how he knew anything about Rafe. But she cautioned herself not to answer immediately. Most Texans hated anyone with either Mexican or Indian blood in them. There was too much bitterness over the killing committed by all in the last thirty years of fighting over land for it to be forgotten. She had never considered it as a measure of judging a person. Neither had Sy. He couldn't have, if he had loved Rafe's mother so much that he left their son half the Reina. And there were her own feelings for Rafe to consider.

With eyes as unfriendly as two shotgun bores, she stared across the table into Evan's blue ones. "Rafe is not a 'greaser,' Evan. And that's your term, not mine. He's Sy Garrett's son, a fact you may not be aware of, but a true one. Never repeat that term in my hearing again. And tuck this warning away. Rafe wouldn't take kindly to hearing it."

"Just warning you, that's all. Man with greaser blood ain't to be trusted."

"I agree with Evan," Curt said. "I've tried to tell you that, Lacey. Not that it did me any good." He refused to look at her, his bitterness in his voice, for he had heard enough of her defending Rafe Parrish.

Maggie shot Curt a hard look. "You'd best eat your supper, *mister*, an' leave Lacey to judge for herself what kind of a man he is. There's some that don't like strangers pokin' in the Reina's business."

"Maggie, really, that was uncalled for." But Lacey lowered her head, hiding her smile and deciding it was time to do a little questioning of her own.

"So tell us, Captain, why are you so far south?"

"Evan's been helping us track a renegade band of Comanche. They've raided ranches up around the fort and farther west."

"You tracked them here? But we've never had trouble

with them. They took a few head of cattle, but Sy was always aware of that. We have never come under direct attack."

"Ain't only raiding but killing, ma'am," the private volunteered and swallowed whatever else he was about to say along with his food at the silent command his officer gave.

Lacey looked up at the captain, unable to hide her alarm. "I believe you should tell us what has been happening, Captain Chase."

He hesitated but knew that she had a right to know the danger they could be facing. "I know there's resentment for the army's control over the government. That's led us to believe that someone is stirring up the Indians by selling them guns. Permanent camp is being built. We can keep watch over the Butterfield, Goodnight, Comanche, and Chihuahua trails now. But our forces are scattered in the West. Satanta, a Kiowa chief, and the Comanche admitted they're raiding again. They want their lands and their buffalo back." He shook his head, and disgust colored his voice. "Officers like Sheridan and Custer are talking about the need for a harder stand with the Indians. Too many are leaving the reservations and looting north of here."

Lacey listened as he continued, hiding her horror at the tales of brutal murders of innocent children on both sides and of women too old to be used as slaves or sold into Mexico for guns. She didn't think to interrupt him when the thought rose that few, if any, scalps were taken. She recalled Sy telling her that the warlike Comanche took an enemy's scalp to count coup as a point of honor. The stories continued and the thought slipped away.

"I'm warning everyone. This is the first time, with Evan's help, that we've kept track of them."

"We appreciate the warning, Captain. I wish I had more information to offer."

"Are you sure, Lacey?" Curt asked. "Or are you afraid that whatever you say would cast a bad light on Rafe Parrish?"

She gave him her full attention, hazel eyes glaring. "Explain to me what you mean by that uncalled-for question!"

Curt grabbed her hands with his. His eyes, filled with love and concern, held her own. "I should have thought that was obvious, Lacey. Listening to the captain, you should realize that nothing bad happened on the Reina until Parrish came here. What do any of us know about him?"

Lacey opened her mouth to answer him but stopped herself. How could she offer her instincts about Rafe in defense of him? Her gaze was snagged by Fletcher's.

His eyes held a shrewd, cold look. He was not about to let it pass. "Ain't got a lick of sense to be sayin' that. Sy's boy can't be a part of this, I tell you. I'd stake my life on it. He jus' ain't got cause to, iffen you think on the facts. An' what gives you the right to come here an' eat his food, then be accusin' him?"

Curt sat with a thin semblance of a smile on his lips. He had proof of what kind of a man Rafe Parrish was, but he wasn't going to reveal it to anyone. Anyone, that is, but Lacey. And only when he deemed the timing to be right. Like a tinhorn gambler, this was his ace in the hole.

Satisfied that he had shut him up, Fletcher rose. "Wait, Maggie. I'll lend you a hand with dessert." He knew she couldn't stand looking at Curt one second more than he could.

Lacey turned to Evan to break the tension. "Are you going to continue scouting, or have you come home?" He confused her with the quick darting look he shot at Curt.

"I only rode this far with the captain. I guess I'll stop home, but I don't have plans. Heard that you were a bit shorthanded. Wouldn't offer a friend a job, would you?"

Since Lacey was gazing into his eyes, she missed the horrified looks that Bo, Fletcher, and Maggie exchanged. She knew Evan hated his father and for that reason could be trusted. Rafe might not like it, but after all, the Reina was still half hers.

"The pay is twenty dollars a month, board, and your pick of the remuda. But I warn you, Rafe is a boss. I don't want any trouble between you. We have enough."

"Won't get any from me. And I've got my own horses. As for this partner giving orders, we'll see. You're the boss of the Reina."

Once the words would have made her glow, but now Lacey found them unsettling. As soon as the pies were finished, she led the men into the front *sala* to enjoy their brandy and cigars. A restlessness overtook her, and she left the house.

Chapter 12 ===========

LACEY STARED AT the moon's brilliant reflection on the still waters of the pond. She leaned against the trunk of a cottonwood tree and felt the sultry air wrap itself around her. Captain Chase's warnings presented a new threat to the Reina, and she found herself wishing that Rafe were there to shoulder the burden of making decisions.

The admission was not an easy one for her to make. The enforced rest Maggie had insisted upon had left Lacey with too much time to think. Rafe centered in every thought she had. She missed him. She wanted him as a woman who knew this man was worthy of her love, of her trust.

But at what price would she have her desire? Rafe would demand total surrender, not only of herself but of the Reina. With a sharp sigh she sat upon the sparse grass and closed her eyes. Sy would call her weak for allowing herself the temptation to dream that Rafe could want both her strength and her softness.

But for these few peaceful moments she gave in to the clamor of memories that brought back the feel of Rafe's mouth taking hers. And she trembled to recall the flood of wild passion that exploded between them. The snap of dry twigs behind her brought her out of her reverie.

"I had a feeling you would be here, Lacey," Curt said, pushing aside the low-hanging branches.

She resented his intrusion, but more, resented his reminder that she had shared this spot with him on too many nights, first talking, then exploring her newly awakened senses. She shifted slightly when he sat down.

Curt didn't speak. His memories were carrying him back to the nights Lacey drove him wild with her innocence and half-promised surrender in this very spot. But he had claimed her for his own and would have kept her if she had not left on a trail drive. When she returned, she refused to resume their relationship. His hand clenched the earth when he recalled the begging desperation that made him threaten her into marrying him. It was a mistake, a bad one, for she had only laughed when he said he would tell Sy.

His teeth grated together, and his ears rang with her words: "Tell him, Curt. He won't force me to marry you. Sy taught me to think like a man, and they don't pay for their pleasures. Women do, but I can't be a woman and keep the Reina."

He forced himself to release the tension and the past and reached out for her hand.

Lacey couldn't help compare the smoothness of his hand with Rafe's callused ones. But she knew Curt never did anything without a reason. He had sought her out, so there was no point in waiting to find out why.

"You want something, Curt, so tell me."

"So cold. I remember how warm you can be. Lacey, I love you. I'm willing to wait for you to love me again, but I want to marry you now. Can you sit here and not remember what it was like between us?"

"I wasn't thinking about us. If you must know, I was thinking about Rafe."

For an instant he crushed her slender fingers in his grip, then released her hand. "He's a man who hasn't a shred of decency in him, Lacey. A man who's not worth a moment of your time."

Lacey rose to her knees and half turned toward him. "If you know something about Rafe, tell me. Either that or stop hinting at having secrets about him!"

He grabbed her arms, pulling her toward him. "I can't take any more of you defending him. I'm the one who loves you." His mouth closed over hers, demanding the passion that he once taught her. He had caught her off-balance, and she fell heavily against his chest, her cry muffled by his lips.

Lacey tore her mouth free. "Curt, stop! My side. You're hurting me."

"I never meant to hurt you, Lacey. Here, let me help you up." He came to his feet swiftly and lifted her to stand beside him. "You don't know how crazy you make me."

"I can't help that. You were going to tell me about Rafe. If not, I'll say good night."

"You want to know about him? Well, you will. Meet me in the office, Lacey."

She watched him stride away, and she was besieged by a sudden chill. She had never seen Curt in a rage before, but his voice had been that of a man ready to kill. But as she hurried to the office, her thoughts were not on Curt but on Rafe.

What was Curt going to tell her about him?

The lamps were out in the *sala*, so Lacey assumed that Maggie had seen to rooms for Captain Chase and his private. She left the office door open and lit the lamp on the desk and then several others so that the room was brightly lit. She wanted no intimate setting for whatever Curt had in mind.

He walked in and handed her a sheaf of papers. "Sit

down and read these and then tell me you will still defend Rafe Parrish."

Lacey sat behind the desk and had to pull the lamp closer as she labored over the cramped handwriting. Time slipped away, several pages had to be reread, and she forgot that Curt sat across from her, drinking and watching her.

And watch her he did. He saw the tears that raced down her cheeks and knew he had been right to make her read all the information that Sy Garrett had ordered to be gathered about his son. If Rafe Parrish had been here to face Lacey, Curt felt his triumph would have been complete. And when she was done, staring blindly across the room at him, he rose.

"You have questions?"

"Is all this true, Curt? Are you positive there's no mistake?"

He avoided her pleading gaze. His hate had built to a point where he wouldn't deny it if he could. Yet his voice betrayed nothing of his feelings. "I would spare you pain if I could, but I didn't make this up. I didn't take it upon myself to search this information out. Judge Walker had this report, ordered and paid for by Sy. The judge knew what kind of a man Parrish was before he brought him here." With his hands jammed into his pants pockets, he paced the floor in his best courtroom manner. "I will admit that I've withheld this from you, but I did it so that we could all give Parrish a chance. Every man deserves a fresh start, but Lacey," he pleaded, leaning over the desk, "I couldn't allow you to go on blindly trusting him without knowing his past."

Lacey was shaking as she stood up and pushed the chair back. She couldn't look at Curt. "Will you leave this with me? Rafe has a right to know about this. He has the right to explain it."

He came to her side, gently turning her toward him. "Lacey, just think what this means. I could use this to put him away so that he can never harm anyone. And you would have the Reina once I got rid of him."

She heard Curt but dismissed his words for those that were seared on her mind. Inside a raw ache spread into pain. She didn't want to believe what she had read—she didn't want to think that Rafe had been using her.

"Lacey, haven't you listened to me? Love, don't shut me out. Need me again, please. Let me help you."

Without thought she responded to his plea and rested her head against his shoulder. Her throat was dry, and tears blurred her eyes with a burning intensity. And a tiny voice whispered that she had to give Rafe a chance to tell his side. When Curt once again whispered his plea to let him help her, Lacey roused herself to push him away.

"I can't make a decision now. You'll have to wait. I need time, Curt."

He stood unmoving as she left him. Realization dawned that he had made a terrible mistake in underestimating her feelings for Rafe Parrish. She wasn't going to give him the satisfaction of being the man to rid her of a partner and hand the Reina to her. And he knew Lacey once her mind was set on a course of action. The last four years had taught him patience. He could only withdraw and rethink his plans.

Lacey never heard him leave. She stood in Rafe's room, crushing his shirt in her hands, willing Rafe's return to tell her his damning past was all a lie. The woman's softness that had begun to bloom inside her folded its tender petals inwardly, protecting all that made her vulnerable to Rafe.

Maggie greeted the overcast morning with a feeling of unease that Rafe had not yet returned. She managed a smile when Fletcher told her that Curt had not stayed the night.

"Gone for good, I hope," she grumbled, aware that the presence of Captain Chase and the private eating stacks of hotcakes kept her from talking. Evan joined them before they were finished, asking for Lacey.

"Plum tuckered out," Maggie answered. "Shouldn't have been out of bed so soon." Her bustling about did not encourage any further questions. Once they were gone, she checked on Lacey and quietly closed the door when she found her sleeping.

Bo James was waiting for her in the courtyard before the kitchen door. "How's she doin'?"

"Better. I'm glad to find her restin'."

"Maggie, maybe it ain't my business, but I had trouble sleepin' last night and came out here. Curt was in the office with Lacey for a long while. When she come out, I think she was cryin'. Don't know what's all goin' on, but I don't take a cotton to Blaine bein' 'round her."

"Well, you ain't the only one, Bo. I could've sliced his tongue to jerky-size strips when he started mouthin' off 'bout Rafe. He's a good man. Like Fletcher said."

"Ain't had much truck with him like you two, an' I got some doubts. Jus' don't want anythin' hurtin' Lacey. I feel like you and Fletcher, havin' watched her grow. Love that girl like she's mine."

"Don't need to be tellin' me that, Bo. But my bones tell me that Rafe and Lacey are gonna face trouble worse than we saw in the old days. You mark my words if it ain't so."

Bo remembered those very words when Luke rode in a few hours later with the news that Mertson had been pinned down by gunfire while the small gather he had made of yearlings were run off.

Fletcher had gone into town, and Maggie didn't have the heart to tell Lacey, so it was up to Bo.

He found her seated by the edge of the stone pool, trailing

her hand listlessly in the water. She was so lost in thought that Bo had to shake her shoulder to gain her attention. Her hazel eyes were dulled with pain, and he wondered again what had happened with Curt last night. For a lost moment Lacey reminded him of her mother, and his gut twisted.

But her eyes lost their dullness as he quickly told her what had happened. And the threat to the Reina made her cast aside her personal worries.

"Have the boys saddle me a horse, the black this time. I'll be a few minutes."

"You can't ride with your wound. Tell me what you want done and I'll go."

"You're leg isn't healed yet. Saddle my horse. I have to go."

There wasn't a man who faced Lacey Garrett, holding aloft a coiled rope in her gloved hand, that remembered she was a woman. Her voice was cold and her eyes spit fury as she offered a two hundred dollar bonus to the first man who hanged one of the rustlers. And when she was done, she motioned Luke to her side as she dismounted.

"Since Rafe isn't here, Luke, I want you to take over posting the men. Set them up on the highest land points around the herd. They're to keep a fire burning high all night, and if anyone spots these mangy bastards, they can smother their fire. One or two men can keep watch from below. Everyone is exhausted, but this way we might have a chance to catch them."

"It might work. God knows the men could use some rest."

"It better work, Luke. I don't want to hear of another hide touched on my range again!" She swung back into the saddle and was surprised when Luke stopped her.

"You're riding back to the house?"

"No. The night I was shot, there were things I wanted to check. I'm going there now."

Luke met the grim determination in her eyes with a hardened stare of his own. He had promised Rafe he would keep watch over her. "You can't ride out alone."

"Remember who you're talking to, Luke. I don't take orders, I give them."

"I ain't forgettin'. But that army captain told us what's happenin'. You ain't never been near Comanche. I have and that's why you ain't ridin' alone."

"Well, if that's true, then you should know that the good captain didn't realize that but for one raid, they didn't take scalps."

Lacey had caught him and caught him good, Luke admitted to himself. It had bothered him, too, but he hadn't thought to point it out. "Well, if it ain't the Indians, it's some renegade band. You can't go alone."

"Ragweed," she called out, raising herself high in the saddle. "Ragweed, you're riding with me." Glancing down at Luke, she added, "Satisfied?"

"Not much. Just be careful."

Rafe was bone-weary, pushing himself and his horse to the limit of their endurance. He glanced back at the two Rangers accompanying him, satisfied that the judge had been right; they both had the look of down-on-their-luck cowpunchers. Rafe also knew they were both skilled with their guns and neither man was a fool. Matt MaCabe, the older of the two, met his look with a grim smile.

"How much farther, Rafe?" he asked with a gruff voice that matched his face. There was a hardness to him, bore out by the scar that jagged down his cheek, the depth of his brown eyes that revealed nothing of his thoughts, and the rigid set of his body.

"We're on the edge of Darcy land now," he answered, drawing rein on the top of a small rise. He pushed his hat back and scanned the terrain below. If his memory served, he was near the canyons that Lacey had wanted to check out the night she was shot. A few hours more would not matter. "We'll take a look here before we ride on."

Hank Peters, the other Ranger, took a long swallow from his canteen. He was, Rafe decided, one of the most quiet men he had run across, but his eyes missed little. His slight build shifted in his saddle, and he pointed to the cloud of dust rising behind a lone rider heading for them.

They watched for a few moments, and then Rafe swore. He knew that black mare. And her rider. He wasn't about to answer questions about the two men with him and ordered them to wait while he rode down to April.

He urged his horse through a thick swatch of gramma grass, and his annoyance grew in light of April's warm smile. "Lose your way, Rafe? You're riding on Darcy land again. Or are you still looking for whoever shot Lacey?" She nudged her mare against his horse so that he was forced to move at a walk with her.

"In light of that, why are you riding alone? Or are you sure that they wouldn't shoot you?"

"Don't accuse my father of trying to kill a woman!" April slid from her saddle and dropped the reins as she stepped up to a flat rock shelf. She removed her hat and shook her hair until the blond curls tumbled like a cloud of gold dust around her shoulders. Determined to wipe that amused smile from Rafe's lips, she sat down and leaned back on her elbows, aware of the provocative pose she offered.

Rafe was no longer smiling. The soft blue cotton shirt pulled taut across her generous breasts, and her eyes glittered with invitation. He knew the moment she spotted the two men waiting above and dismounted to forestall her questions. The tip of his boot nudged her hip, and he leaned forward. "April, you're a lot of woman, but not for me."

Her eyes widened in shock. How dare he! Why only last night Ward Farel had told her she was a woman men would kill for. Since he now worked for her father, April knew she could use his hate for Rafe, but she wasn't about to let Rafe get away with insulting her! She lunged for his face.

Rafe grabbed her shoulders, shoving her flat against the rock. "Lacey's the only woman I want. If you're looking to cause trouble, I'll give you more'n you can handle. And tell your father that if he lied to me, I'll come gunning for him."

April barely swallowed her cry. Her gaze shifted past his broad shoulders and when she quickly looked back into his furious eyes, her smile was gloating. "Explain this to her."

"What?" But even as he asked, Rafe looked up. "Lacey."

She was up on the ridge above them. He could feel the heat of her gaze pinning him.

And for a moment Lacey did just that. She stared down at April sprawled beneath Rafe and felt the bile rise in her throat. With a cry she yanked her horse around and rode away.

For a stunned minute more Rafe remained as he was. He released April and backed away from her as if she were something vile. "I know you couldn't have planned this, that's all that's keeping you alive right now."

"You tore my shirt!"

"Don't be running to your father with any lies. I won't get railroaded by a woman again. Try it, April, and you'll wish to hell you'd never set eyes on me." He mounted and waved the two men down to join him. It was easy to believe that Lacey could be behind the rustlings when he was away from her. But he knew with a gut-wrenching certainty that Lacey would count what she saw as betrayal. And as if she had been next to him, touching him and looking into his eyes,

Rafe swore that feeling of betrayal had come not from his partner, but from a woman. His fury faded to be replaced by a sense of despair that he would be once again defending himself.

Defending him were words Lacey silently echoed as she rode with a mindless rage and outdistanced Ragweed. Sy had been right; thinking like a woman, feeling like one, left her weak, and Rafe had used that weakness. But he would never do it again.

She was still repeating that vow when morning came with a light cool breeze and sun-streaked shadows. Once dressed, Lacey checked on Rafe's room, but nothing had been touched.

"Damn coward!" she muttered. Absently rubbing her side, she joined Maggie and Fletcher for breakfast.

"You can march right back to bed, girl. Runnin' off, gone half the night, too. I swear, Lacey, you're lookin' to kill yourself tryin' to catch these polecats."

"Maggie, if I don't, who will? Rafe? We haven't been graced with his presence for almost a week. I believe that he found personal business more important than protecting the Reina. I *don't* want to hear one word about him."

Maggie exchanged a perplexed look with Fletcher, but both were silent.

Lacey eyed the stack of hotcakes and bacon that Maggie set in front of her. "I don't want—"

"Can you spare some of that for me?"

"Evan." Lacey forced a smile, wondering if he had overheard what she said and then dismissed it. "Don't stand there. Join us. Here," she offered, pushing her plate toward him. "Eat these." She shot a warning look at Maggie not to press her.

"Guess you're wondering what kind of a welcome I got at home," Evan began. "I'll spare you asking. With the exception of my sister, nothing's changed. Seems that no matter how much time I gave pa, he'll never bend. I 'spect he'll make sure everyone knows that he's disowned me for working here."

"Evan, I won't hold you—"

"Never mind, Lacey. It wouldn't do no good. But I want you to hear from me that Farel is workin' for him."

"Well, I hope he'll follow your father's orders better than he did mine. His disregard got Bo James shot. I hope that won't be a problem with you. If taking my orders rubs you wrong, don't stay."

"Wouldn't be here if I couldn't take your orders. I know that before you think like a woman, you put the Reina first. That's good enough for me to call you boss."

They both ignored Maggie's grumbling and Fletcher setting his cup down with a bang.

Lacey's smile warmed. A devil prompted her to say, "Thank you, Evan. Lately, I seem to need the reassurance that I can run things and not keep busy with homey tasks." Satisfied that she made her point, Lacey watched him eat, and when he was done, she carried their cups and his plate to the basin. "If you're ready, Evan, we'll ride out."

He flashed her a boyish grin, his eyes holding secret laughter. "I have something down at the corral for you."

Tied next to his rawboned paint was a white mare, and when Lacey couldn't resist running her hands over the velvet smoothness of her long-muscled neck, Evan whispered that the mare was for her.

"You can't mean that. She must be worth—"

"I drove her up with the last herd I ran up from Mexico. Pure-blooded stock, Lacey. From the Arabian horses the Spanish brought over. When I heard what happened to that roan Sy gave you for your birthday, well, I thought you'd like her."

Lacey was entranced with the horse, Evan with watching her. Neither noticed that Fletcher stood behind them. He frowned at hearing this, for he knew Evan had been gone for a year. He'd been pondering why Evan would take on a cowpuncher's wages when he made more money running horses for the army. But what set him to scratching his head, and prickled his neck hairs, was how Evan knew about Lacey's roan. Sy had given her that horse not more than six months ago. Fletcher backed away when Lacey gave Evan a quick hug and Evan took advantage, to his way of thinking, and kissed her.

Fletcher wasn't the only one watching them. Rafe sat on his horse, his lips thinned while the muscle in his cheek twitched. Who the hell was this son of a bitch? And why wasn't she stopping him? Rubbing her hands all over his shaggy hair . . . his own scalp warmed in memory of that same caress.

But Lacey wasn't caressing his hair, she tugged and then yanked at it to pull Evan's head back. "Don't read more than a thank-you into this, Evan. I don't want a man cluttering up my life."

"Is that warning just for me, or does it include that tough-looking *hombre* behind you?"

Lacey spun around, her body shielding Evan. At least it appeared that way to Rafe. His eyes pinned her. "Guess my killing myself to get back here was a waste of time."

"Killing yourself? If only you had, Rafe."

"Who the hell is this, Lacey?" Evan asked, moving aside.

"Rafe Parrish," she stated coldly, "this is Evan Darcy."

And Rafe's eyes were as cold, assessing him, then dismissing him. "Hire yourself a bodyguard, Lacey? Seems you should've found someone you could trust."

Evan's hand rose to his gun, but Lacey once again

stepped in front of him. "I can trust Evan. That's more than I can say for you." She couldn't quite meet Rafe's eyes. She gestured at the two men slightly behind him. "Hire a few bodyguards of your own?"

"Hank Peters. Matt McCabe. This is Lacey Garrett, my partner. I worked with them for an outfit northeast of here aways back. They're good hands."

Lacey heard the dare in his voice and found herself clenching her hands. "Evan, you know Blewett. Ride out and see him. My   and I need to talk." She gazed up at Rafe. "I'll wait for you in the office."

Evan waited until Rafe had sent the other two men off to the bunkhouse to get settled and then moved to his side when he dismounted. "I want to clear up any misunderstanding you might—"

"Save it. There's nothing I want to hear from you."

Evan grabbed his arm. "You got no call to—"

"Let . . . go."

Evan met the black fury in his eyes and released him. He was never one to tangle with a man unless he was sure to win. He was fast with his gun, but he knew Rafe was faster. Evan had to remind himself that he was not here to cause any trouble. But he swallowed gall as he offered his hand. "I don't aim for trouble. I just needed a job, and Lacey gave me one."

Rafe ignored his hand. "If you're here to work, best get to it. And stay the hell away from Lacey, or you'll have me to answer to." He strode away, furious that he acted like a damn stallion squaring off over a mare. But he couldn't wipe out the sight of her in another man's arms.

Maggie greeted him with a smile. "I'll whip up a fresh batch—"

"Not now, Maggie."

"Rafe," she cautioned as he reached the doorway, "you

need to wash that trail dust off and shave." Her gaze found no softening in his. "Please, don't go to her riled. At least let me fix you some coffee." Pity for his exhausted state filled her as she handed him a cup. "Things have been happening that you need to know about first." And she told him about Curt's visit, the army captain's warnings, and Evan.

Rafe didn't bother to ask questions, but he realized that Maggie was right. He would wait to see Lacey. God knew he wanted to strangle her and kiss her senseless, but if Curt had shown her those papers, he would have to answer for them. And the thought of a hot bath after days of riding sounded more appealing than another confrontation with Lacey.

Lacey had closed the door behind her and alternated between sitting and pacing as she waited for Rafe. Anger seethed inside her. She wasn't sure how much time had passed, but as she opened the door, she knew he had to be finished settling those men he had hired. Unless he was with Evan? The thought spurred her to leave the office, but she saw Maggie coming from his room. The bundle of clothing she held told Lacey exactly where Rafe was.

"He had to take a bath and keep me waiting!" she muttered as she entered her room. She grabbed up her pitcher and filled it with the icy cold springwater.

Humming softly to himself, Rafe had to admit that Maggie was right. The hot water had soaked some of the deep aches from his body. He had already shaved and washed the dust from his hair and sat thinking when the sudden shock of cold water hit him from behind.

Gasping and sputtering, he stood, shaking his head like an enraged bull, and grabbed hold of Lacey's arm. Another toss of his head splattered water all over her. His grin came as slowly as her head moved upward.

Lacey wanted to shock him, not be shocked herself. But Rafe in all his male glory held her still. She shivered and closed her eyes. Her breath was lodged in her throat. She could still see Rafe, muscles rippling, the short dark curling hairs on his chest arrowing down to his navel, the flat belly, lean hips tapering into ropey thighs, and she forced herself to stop.

Tugging against his grip, she managed to stretch her free arm back, blindly groping for the stack of linen cloths behind her. She grabbed one, slammed it forward against his body, and cried out when he pulled her close.

"You need—"

"I know exactly what I need, Lacey," he whispered, tilting her chin up. "Look at me."

Chapter 13 ════════

LACEY COULDN'T OPEN her eyes. It was enough for her to inhale the hint of spice from the soap he used, a scent that was body warm and male. She pushed against him, her fingers tangling his chest hair before sliding over his wet flesh, the same wetness that was soaking her shirt.

"Lacey."

It wasn't the soft murmur of her name, but his wicked chuckle that made her look up at him. His black eyes were dancing with glints of humor. She didn't have time to react to the shift of his grip on her so that one arm held her securely.

"You need cooling off, bright eyes." With his free hand he grabbed the bucket with clean water and poured it over her head.

Lacey shoved him. Water dripped from her hair, plastered her shirt and camisole to her skin, and soaked down her pant legs into her boots. "You damn savage!" She swung a fisted hand that he caught easily, the humor gone from his eyes.

"I warned you, princess, act like a child, and I'll treat you like one."

Lacey shrieked when he scooped her up into his arms, stepped over the rim of the tub, and carried her into his room. Her gaze fastened on his. She stopped her futile twisting. The dark grave look in his eyes was possessive, filled with strong emotions, far too complex for her to sort out. She felt the tension that tautened his body as his gaze shifted with her shaken breaths to the rise and fall of her breasts. The sudden memory of his mouth tugging on one sensitive tip made her nipples tighten, and a frisson of pleasure spiraled down to the pit of her stomach, making her want to moan. She wanted to feel his mouth on her again, to feel his need and heat, but she still feared being vulnerable to him.

"Put me down, Rafe."

"I like the feel of you right where you are, bright eyes. This way I won't worry what you're up to behind my back."

His taunting snapped her temper. "I know you're stronger. You humiliated me with your dousing. You've had your revenge. Now, put me down!"

"Just to show that I can be a gentleman." He lowered her to the bed slowly, watching her roll to her side, then scramble up toward the headboard. With one hand he snagged her boot, warning her with his look not to kick him.

"What's the matter, Rafe? Wasn't April enough for you? Stop manhandling me! I don't want you to touch me."

He could deal with her temper, but not with her contempt. He wanted her so badly, he could feel every nerve screaming a demand for him to take her. Rafe fought the rush of fear that came as swiftly, fear that the past would win and take everything he wanted, everything he needed.

He left her abruptly, totally unconcerned with his naked state. Slamming open the wardrobe door, he pulled out a blue cotton shirt, jamming his arms into the sleeves. He didn't button it but grabbed a pair of worn denims from the shelf below. He felt Lacey watching his every move to slide the cloth against his damp skin, and he cursed her while he struggled to button his fly.

Impatiently running his hands through his hair, he faced her. "What the hell were you doing out on the range yesterday? You had no business——"

"Stop attacking me!" She came to her knees, eyeing the doorway, but Rafe stepped between the bed and freedom.

"Why is Darcy working for us? And why the hell did Curt wait to give you those papers? Oh, don't look rabbit-snared, princess. I know he gave them to you."

"He wanted to give you a chance!"

"A chance to what? Hang myself?"

His voice held a hint of savagery, but it was the fury glittering in his eyes that made Lacey roll off the bed and flatten herself against the corner wall. Rafe moved at the same moment she did, lunging across the bed, coming to his feet, slamming his fist against the wall above her head.

"Don't . . . move." He closed his eyes, his chest heaved with every breath he dragged into his lungs, and he waited, not daring to speak or move until he had himself under control. When he finally looked at her again, she was holding tight to her side. "You hurt yourself." He had to make an effort to smooth the savage edge off his voice. "And you're wet."

His gaze slid down her body like a tangible caress, making Lacey aware of the wet cloth clinging to her breasts. She squeezed herself into the corner to avoid his hand. "I don't want you to touch me," she warned, feeling almost battered by the leashed violence she sensed in him.

Her warning went unheeded. His black eyes dared her to deny him again as he stripped her shirt and camisole without hurting her, but without a sign that he saw or responded to her nakedness. She stared at his hands, trembling but making no move to cover herself. His callused fingertip brushed her barely healed wound, and she winced, holding her breath until he muttered an oath and stepped back. Her shoulders sagged with the release of her breath, and she saw him fling her clothes to the floor.

Rafe grabbed one of his shirts from the wardrobe and threw it at her. "Put it on, princess, so I don't touch you."

Her fingers shook as she buttoned it under his watchful gaze. Her side throbbed, but bravado had fled, and she made no move to escape even when he came to stand in front of her once more.

"We'll stand here all night until you answer me, Lacey."

"I don't owe you answers. It's the other way around. Where have you been? Why did you hire those men? And why were you with . . ." She glanced down, her gilt-tipped lashes hiding the luminous sheen in her eyes.

"Don't stop. That's what's eating you, isn't it? Me being with April?"

"No! How dare you demand anything from me? You're a renegade, a thief. A cheat and a liar. I know all there is to know about you, Rafe." She was trembling from rage and had to stop, but Lacey knew she made a mistake to look up at him. His eyes were heavy-lidded, intent on her, his face a hard mass of angles filled with anger. When he said nothing, offered no defense, she found herself burning to know if it was all true.

"I know where the judge found you. You were in a Mexican jail. They were going to hang you for running guns to the outlaws down there who claim they're helping to fight for freedom. And it wasn't for any noble reasons. You did it for the money. Just like you've stolen horses on both sides of the border."

"That's not all you know. Finish it." His hand moved in a savage cutting gesture, and he towered over her. "What else has me condemned?"

Lacey swallowed. Her gaze dropped to his chest. The muscles beneath the flat mat of black chest hair were taut, but she couldn't look away. He prodded her again, softly whispering his fury, and she found the heat of him, this close, made it impossible for her to think, let alone speak.

"Tell me, Lacey. Tell me what you believe to be true."

"What did you expect me to do?" she cried softly. "You weren't here. Curt only showed me those papers to protect me. To stop me from getting myself tangled up with a man like you."

"You were getting feelings tangled up between us?"

"Yes."

"It wasn't fighting me for control of the Reina anymore, was it?"

"No! Damn you, no!" She pushed him, but he stood firm. Lacey gave vent to the frustrating storm of emotions with her fists, beating his chest. Rafe did nothing to stop her. "Let me go," she pleaded.

"I can't. I won't," came his denial. "I'll wipe every question from your—"

"And then what? Will you use me to get what you want and then discard me like *Señorita Martainez?* I told you I had read it all."

He spun around, and Lacey felt the strength drain from her. There was no emotion left in her voice. "Why, Rafe? Your own mother—"

"Leave her out of this! What the hell do you know?" he grated from between clenched teeth, facing her again. His hand flexed at his sides. "I didn't have anything to do with her. . . . I didn't leave her belly filled with my child."

Lacey stared at him. She raised her hand to touch him, but he spun away, grabbing his boots. "Are you always running? Can't you face up to what you've done? Would I be asking if I didn't want to hear your side?" Lacey pushed herself away from the wall, stepping toward him. "Run," she taunted, "you're good at it."

He moved so fast, Lacey wasn't sure what had happened, but in seconds she was sprawled beneath him on the bed.

"You've been trying to snap my leash since the day I got here, princess. I'm on the short end of a thread." He cursed his luck, which didn't run in any direction but away from him, and fought against the scent of her clouding his mind, softening the blunt edge of his anger. Her face was white, and he knew he had hurt her. Again. The word was enough to force him to roll to his side. "You want to hear it from me?"

She met his gaze, eyes bleak as the winter's icy darkness, and nodded.

"I told you we lived a day-to-day existence with Parrish after my mother married him," he stated flatly. "Sometimes she spoke of returning to the warmth of Mexico when she couldn't stand the damp cold of backwater mining camps. Hilton had himself a good week gambling. He won a small bag of gold nuggets. I stole his horse and his gold when he refused to give her half for food. My mother didn't argue. She couldn't. He had beat her and her health was already failing. My luck, if you could call it that, held all the way south. We had enough to rent a small place near Zaragoza right over the border."

Rafe rose abruptly and began to pace the room. He never once looked at Lacey, but she couldn't take her eyes from him. She listened to him tell of the days and weeks that followed, sometimes smiling with him, sometimes feeling the pain his voice revealed. She began to fully measure the depth of his hunger for a place of his own, the same hunger that Maggie and Fletcher told her he had. Inside herself she cried for a boy trying to eke out the barest form of existence, the likes of which she had never known. And she screamed in silence for a boy forced too soon to become a man.

". . . when there was no work, I took their offer. I was damn big for my age and already earned a name for brawling 'cause they hate mixed blood as much as Texans."

"No more, Rafe," she whispered, flushing under his harsh gaze.

"But there's more. It was easy to sneak across the border, steal a few horses or cattle or rob a *gringo* and then slip back to Mexico. Money was good, my mother better. She had food, as much as she wanted. That wasn't the only reason. I liked the excitement of outwitting the border patrols, both the Federale's and the Union soldiers'. I wasn't a helpless boy. I was a man when I came in from a raid, with money to spend on drink and women. And then I got caught."

His silence and still posture had Lacey moving to sit, ready to go to him. Instead, she asked, "You couldn't have been more than sixteen or so. Did they try to kill you?"

"Kill me?" he repeated with a soft, mocking laugh. "Better if they had. No, they locked me in a Federale jail and waited for the men I worked for to come and get me."

"They were so sure of that? Honor among thieves?"

"No honor, princess. I had the money from the sale of the horses. But I had buried it—instinct, whatever. I had bad feelings. And honor among the soldiers had nothing to do with it. They wanted it for themselves."

With a muttered curse he raked his hand through his hair, his voice suddenly low so that Lacey leaned forward, straining to hear him.

"For three weeks they kept me there. I had to force myself to eat the slop they called food after I had nothing left to trade but my pants. My belt brought me a hard roll free of maggots, my boots . . . Ah, what the hell am I bothering for! You can't understand."

"But I want to, Rafe. Please, look at me."

Again that bleak flatness met her level gaze, but he spoke. "I slept with one eye open to keep watch for the rats, and when the beatings and bribes didn't work, they threatened me." He slammed the wardrobe door closed, but stood there, seeing what she could not, his back toward her.

"Rafe? I don't understand. How much more could they threaten you?"

"I wasn't the only prisoner they had. There were men held in cells for years."

With a dawning horror her mind turned in the direction he pointed, but she didn't want to believe him. She gave a strangled cry and met the agony in his eyes. "No. No, they couldn't have done that to you. Tell me they didn't, Rafe! Tell me!" she screamed, wrapping her arms around her middle, desperate to contain both pain and nausea.

"No. It never happened. But the thought that it could, that I was helpless to stop it, was enough to keep me awake. Days on end, awake and alone, shivering in a cold sweat with every footstep that came near my cell. The days blurred one into another. There was some *fiesta* in town, and most of the soldiers were away. The four men I worked with came that day, but it was a trap. They were killed, and I was released."

"Released," she repeated, sighing with relief only to tense when he laughed.

"Yeah. And when I finally went for the money, it wasn't there. But I was branded a traitor on both sides of the border. There's your honor among thieves. So I turned to the one thing I had left. I sold my gun to whoever wanted to buy it. No questions asked and none invited."

Lacey jumped up and stopped when he shifted his stance to block her. "I'm not leaving. I just don't understand why you couldn't have moved north. No one would know about you. People opened the Western territories by running from their pasts or looking to start over."

"You think I didn't try! I punched cows for an outfit out of Kansas, wasn't there more'n three, maybe four weeks, and suddenly I was fired. I'm a greaser, Lacey—don't look at me like that! That's what they call me. And the same thing happened again and again till I couldn't take any more. My mother was dead. There wasn't enough money to buy the medicine she needed. I didn't . . . I couldn't even scrape up enough to pay the priest to say a mass for her."

She went to him then, wanting only to comfort, and he stepped away from her.

"I don't want your damn pity!"

"I don't pity you. But finish it. Get rid of all the hate bottled up inside you."

"What the hell does a princess know about hate? The only thing you claim Sy Garrett denied you was love. That's all you've ever been denied!"

"Wasn't that enough?"

Her voice was soft but laden with pain. Pain that twisted a knife inside him. "Yeah," he admitted, "maybe it was." He looked at her, then away. She still had questions in her eyes. "You want to know why I was in jail on that trumped-up charge of gun running?"

"That's almost the last of it, Rafe," she answered with an outward calm.

"It was because of Ana Louisa."

"Ana—"

"*Señorita* Martainez. Ana Louisa de Valdaiz y Martainez is her full name. The woman I supposedly got with child and then abandoned."

His voice was so bitter, Lacey could only nod for him to continue.

"I was hired by her father to be her bodyguard. Only *el*

patrón was too late. She already had her lover and was afraid he would be killed. She begged me to help her run away, and we were caught. When her father found out she was with child, he accused me of running guns to the *Juaristas* and sent her to a convent. That's when Judge Walker came."

"How did he get you out?"

"He bribed them. Any more questions, princess?"

Lacey buried her pity, but she couldn't rid herself of the sorrow that went bone deep. And it was from the sorrow she had caused him that she spoke. "Rafe, I'm sorry. I never meant to hurt you. I never meant for you to rake up a past that—"

"Is it all in the past now?"

Lacey looked up at him. He was watching her, his eyes intent, a pulse beating slowly in his neck, the slow, even rhythm of his breathing so at odds with the sense she had that her answer mattered. His mouth tautened into a flat line as the seconds ticked past. She either believed him or didn't. Her decision.

But Rafe wasn't waiting any longer. He planted himself in front of her, lifting his hands to cage her face between them. "I want you, Lacey. I want a fresh start. A home. A woman I can trust. One who trusts me." He closed her eyes with light kisses, stole a shimmering tear from her lashes, and brushed her mouth once. "God, I want to be so gentle with you, and I'm shaking. I'm shaking 'cause I don't know how. I don't want to hurt you."

He stole the whisper of his name from her lips, taking her mouth, and the wild, sweet taste of her exploded through him. Rafe claimed her lips, knowing he had never wanted a woman the way he wanted Lacey. He fought not to pull her down and bury his hard aching flesh deep within her.

Lacey wrapped her arms around his waist, wanting to

hold him and be held by him. The wildness awoke inside her, a wildness that Rafe encouraged with the molten intensity of his kiss until it melted with a sharp need to heal the raw wounds of the past. She knew the danger of risk, but desire shimmered in her blood, a desire that went beyond passion, for it was the desire of all that made her a woman who longed to give this one man everything he wanted.

His name was a cry of surrender from her lips, and his arms tightened around her. She fitted herself to him perfectly, hard to soft, heat matched with hunger. His tongue claimed her mouth, deeply, repeatedly, with a hot certainty that she was his. With barely restrained urgency he scattered kisses over her face and neck, his teeth dragging aside the shirt to bare her shoulder, and with that same restraint he savored the taste of her silken skin.

"*Mujer,*" he whispered. "*Siempre mujer,*" he added, feeling the shivers that coursed over her as his hair brushed against the rising curve of her breast. "Woman, always woman," he repeated, over and over, drinking her half-wild cries.

Lacey felt her knees give way and clung to his broad shoulders. Her head fell back under the sizzling kisses he pressed along her jawline and down her bared throat. He found the pulse beating in the fragile hollow of her throat, and his tongue slowly laved it until the beat was as frantic as his own. His hands slid down her body and lifted her up into him. Lacey began to move her hips against the hard evidence of his desire, and he took her mouth again with a husky groan.

"I've wanted you burning like this for me from the first time I saw you," he whispered, his fingers digging into her buttocks, rubbing her against him. And every tremor of need that he drew from her stoked the fire inside him higher.

"Do you want *me*, Rafe? Me, not just the Reina?"

He lifted his head slowly and gazed down at the luminous sheen of her hazel bright eyes. "I want you." His voice was savage, and he glared at her with a feral gleam in his black eyes. "*You*. Hear me? Understand? *I want you*."

"Yes . . . Rafe, yes," she said, closing her eyes, unable to look at his. His bruising kiss made her forget the tiny doubts. His was a primitive power barely leashed that invaded her every sense, and when she responded, his mouth began to gentle, coaxing not dominating.

Rafe stroked her slender hip, sliding his hand beneath the loose shirt to caress her back. Lacey stood on tiptoe, instinctively straining to ease the taut fullness in her breasts. He shifted his body slightly to one side, and Lacey held on to the firm muscled strength in his upper arms. His hand cupped her breast, the rough pads of his fingers finessing the hardened nipple, his groan deeply satisfied, sparking flame inside her.

"I want my mouth on you. On all of you, Lacey. I've never said that to another woman. I've never wanted," he murmured, his voice husky with longing, "just wanted a woman so much."

Her hands clung to his shirt, her lips tasting the tanned skin of his neck, her teeth delicately testing the resilience of the muscle beneath. He was warm and salty and male. His subtle move increased the pressure of her mouth, and she used her tongue to make tiny forays on his skin until his shirt stopped her. Rafe moved his leg between hers and Lacey bent one knee to slide her leg restlessly up and down his. She was empty and aching, twisting against him with silent entreaty.

He lifted her, his mouth locked to hers and moved toward the bed. Rafe eased her down, then followed, trapping her in heat.

He broke the kiss, and Lacey opened her eyes to look up at him. She was held by the burning intensity of the yearning in his eyes. Rafe tilted her head to one side, pressing kisses on her face, his fingers sure and steady as he unraveled her thick braid and spread her hair with deep stroking motions that revealed his pleasure.

His knee pressed her side as he rose slightly, and Lacey couldn't prevent a gasp of pain. Rafe froze, then rolled to his side, gathering her into his arms.

"What did I do? I hurt you, didn't I?"

"No. No, Rafe." But he wasn't listening to her. He unbuttoned her shirt impatiently, spread it open and lightly touched her side. Lacey drew in her breath. He lowered his head, his lips soft, tender, as he kissed her wound. "Rafe, don't . . . you didn't—"

"It should have been me." He was tormented by the thought that he had believed Lacey the guilty one. "I promise I won't hurt you again."

Lacey cradled his cheek, drawing his face up. "You didn't hurt me. You can't, not the way you mean. I've never been made to feel so precious."

"Lacey, God, Lacey, you don't know—"

She silenced him with her fingertip. In that same silence she offered herself to him. Rafe's face was flushed, his eyes glittering as he stared down at her satin-smooth breasts. Drawn tight, dusty rose nipples were velvet and waiting, inviting his touch. Lacey ached for him and skimmed the damp curling hair on his chest. She longed to touch him the way he had touched her, but fear that he wouldn't like it, wouldn't let her share with him, stopped her. "I want you, Rafe," she whispered. "I won't break. And you won't hurt me."

"Remember that," he said harshly, his fingers molding the shape of her breasts, his thumb slowly rubbing the

engorged tip. Lacey trembled and moaned his name,
closing her eyes. His lips courted hers, and she lost herself
in the wash of sensations that began to coil inside her,
tightening the moment his mouth kissed the quivering flesh
he held.

Her fingers dug into his arms. His mouth was hot. His
tongue teased, lashing then soothing, his warm breath
kindling a rising fever through her before he pulled her into
his mouth, suckling hungrily.

Lacey knew he wanted her, but he made her feel
cherished, too, as if she were the only woman who could
give him what he needed. Her pleasure sounds echoed his,
and she drew his head tight against her, feeling tension
snare her once again when he slid his thigh between her
legs.

Hampered by being held on her side, Lacey tried to free
her arm. Her fingertips brushed the soft cotton denim and
his erect flesh. Rafe stilled. His mouth slowly withdrew
from the glistening peak as he raised his head.

"If I take you now, I will hurt you."

His features were passion sharp, his cheekbones flushed,
but it was his eyes that held her. Lacey felt herself drawn
into the unsated black depth with a dizziness that would not
end. "Rafe?"

"It's all right," he soothed, searing a line of kisses from
her lips to her belly. The heat of his mouth, the velvet
roughness of his tongue made fire spread inside her. With a
lover's delicacy he bit her, rolling her onto her back, his
fingers stroking her other breast, coaxing the tip into
hardness. He smiled when she shuddered, taking her mouth
in a powerful, possessive kiss. His hand savored the sleek,
feminine curves and strength that twisted beneath him.

Lacey felt the same storm that tautened his body, the

warmth of his ragged breaths a lover's song over her skin, and her cry pleaded.

"I made you a promise, didn't I? Remember?" His mouth hovered over hers, his lips taunting hers between words. "I promised you'd be hot, wet, kitten soft, and wild with wanting me." He leaned away from her, his hand sketching the curve of her thigh, his thumb pressed to the veed joining, gentling and arousing her with the same motion.

"Which are you, bright eyes?"

Her eyes were fever-bright with flecks of gold, and her heartbeat was as erratic as her breathing. Shafts of sunlight and shadow banded them both, drawing Lacey's hand to touch the firm line of his jaw. The sun warmed the back of her hand, but his skin was hot. She could not look away from him.

"Tell me." Rafe rested his hand on her thigh, desire surging to a dangerous peak, and he fought to control it.

She swallowed and found there was no moisture left in her mouth. "All." His hand flexed, pressing down on her, and Lacey felt his touch like a brand. "Did you expect me to lie?" He shook his head slowly, his lashes sweeping down to conceal his gaze, but his smile deepened with distinct male satisfaction. Before she lost her courage, Lacey pushed his shirt off his shoulder. "I want to touch you, too."

"I'd like that." He rolled to his side, stripped off his shirt and came back to her. "Now you." Rafe lifted her carefully, slid her shirt off, but his lips couldn't resist tasting the skin he revealed. "I've never had a woman who wanted to touch me, really wanted to, without being paid for it."

Lacey felt the tears welling in her eyes—she couldn't stop them. Nor did she want to. Suddenly the fear of being a woman, of being vulnerable to Rafe, left her. How could she withhold anything of herself from him now? She couldn't. Not when he touched her as if she were delicate enough to break and then kissed her with a possessive hunger that knew no end.

And when she was aching, craving the blaze of his mouth on her breasts once more, he moved to satisfy that silent demand.

"Rafe? Rafe, you make me feel—"

"Show me. Show me," he repeated with a groan, kneading the flat plane of her belly while he stroked his tongue over the soft undercurve of her breast. His hand shook as he worked her belt buckle open. "Man's pants, but all woman warm," he whispered, lowering his head to kiss the small vee of skin each opened button revealed. Lacey tensed. "Don't you like that?" he asked, gazing up at her.

"I don't know. No one ever—"

"And no one will," he grated in a savage voice, working one callused fingertip beneath the open edge. "And don't ever let me catch you outside of this bed without drawers on."

"Rafe, I—"

"Oh, Christ, you're so kitten soft."

His eyes closed as he lowered his head to rest against her belly, and Lacey lost her moment's anger, threading one hand through the silky texture of his hair. She smiled at his sound of pleasure. The curve of his shoulder beckoned kisses, she scattered them fervently, then licked lingering spice scent from his skin. Rafe's breathing quickened, heating her flesh, and she caressed the length of his muscled back, her eyes drifting closed when she skimmed the small scars that marked his life.

His body seemed to coil and tighten in response to her touch, just as hers was flooded with the same growing tension.

Rafe slipped off the bed and kneeled in front of her.

Lacey raised herself up and flushed at the sight of her wanton sprawl. Her legs were spread on either side of his shoulders as he pulled off her boots and tossed them aside. He peeled off the damp socks, his smile boyish as he glanced up at her.

"Are you ticklish, bright eyes?"

But there was no answering smile on Lacey's mouth, or in her eyes. Her mouth was full with the promise of the passion that awaited him, and her eyes, her eyes darkened with a desire that stole his breath. His hands weren't steady as he tugged her pants off and rose quickly to remove his own.

"Be sure you want me, Lacey. There'll be no going back."

There was strength and power and a beauty uniquely male as Rafe stood, poised and waiting. Lacey lifted her arms in an age-old gesture of both feminine demand and longing that he come to her.

And when he did, she clung to him, almost frightened by the intensity of his wanting, even while she ached to return its measure to him. Their shared kisses were fervent, their bodies slick with sweat. Overtaken by the storm unleashed between them, tremors passed from one to the other.

Lacey cried out when he pressed his palm above the warm soft darkness unfolding at his urging. She wanted to incite him to hurry and yet never wanted the exquisite fevered strokes to stop.

Rafe turned her to her side, careful not to injure her wound. He shook with the force of his need to claim her for his own. His satisfaction came with a groan torn from deep inside him at finding her hotter than he had dreamed, satin damp and hungry for him. Her wild cries spiked his desire. Sweat gleamed on his body. With an unsteady hand he guided her thigh over his hip and demanded in a harsh, raw voice, "Open your eyes, Lacey. Watch me make you mine."

Face to face they lay, the glistening peaks of her breasts nestled against his hair-rough chest. Lacey had to force her eyes to remain open, to see his features drawn with a pleasure so strong, it almost seemed pain. Her own eyes reflected her moment's fear . . . it had been so long . . . but his mouth stole her moan as he came into her. With new sensitivity Rafe sensed her fear, stilled, waiting, until Lacey forced the tension to leave her.

She cradled his cheek, felt the storm that passed through him and knew an emptiness that only he could fill. He began to thrust inside her, and her breath caught, lost in the savagery of this kiss she offered him. Her fingers dug into his back. Need rushed through her. Emotions and feelings, hot and pounding, grew more intense, rioting until she could not bear another moment. Rafe gripped her buttock, lifting her with him as he rolled onto his back.

Her hair fell in a tangled curtain. Their joined lips whispered yearnings, then pleas. Lacey poised on a razor edge, then trembled as wildfire consumed her.

Rafe had waited for that first sweetly violent shiver to take her. He surged deeply into the silken heat of her. Burning now. Wanting the fire to never end. And when the flame of her became torment, rippling over him, grabbing at him, he was no longer gentle.

He knew from her cry that she burned with him and for him in that final untamed ecstasy.

Chapter 14 ══════════════

SWEETLY ACHING, LACEY dreamily watched the late afternoon shadows play across the adobe wall. Rafe lay beside her, stroking her cheek with the backs of his fingers, keeping her head nestled against his damp shoulder. For the first time in her life Lacey gloried in being a woman. A deep loving peace filled her, and she moved to gaze up to look at Rafe.

His eyes were closed, the passion-drawn features blunted with a lover's satiety, his breathing even, his lips molded with the hint of a smile. With one fingertip she teased the curl of his lashes, her heart swelling with love for him. She longed to whisper those words, but she was beset by an unease that forbade it. Lacey puzzled over why this feeling should come to her now. She didn't understand it, no more than she could understand why she obeyed it.

Sensitive to her stirring, Rafe lazily opened his eyes. A love-flush lingered on her cheeks. Suddenly shy, her lashes hid her gaze from him. He couldn't resist the beckoning pout of her mouth and leaned down to enjoy its soft giving. And he wanted her. Now. Yet again. His palm slid along the smooth skin of her thigh, her hip, and curved to fit the swell of her breast.

Their gazes met.

"Rafe? We can't."

His hips nudged her belly. "I don't seem to have much choice." She trembled against him, and he brushed aside the thick tangle of her hair. "Want me?"

Lacey moaned softly.

"Give me your mouth, Lacey. I want that first."

"First?"

He used his tongue to tease open the corner of her lips. "I never did get to taste all of you."

Rafe didn't know if the thought of having all he ever wanted or Lacey's whispered "yes, oh, yes" sent the near explosive lightning rush of need through him. It was a need so fierce that he shook from its force. She opened to him with heat and a blinding trust that he silently swore he would shelter. And when she touched him in a lover's gentle query, he knew it didn't matter what had spurred the force; it was simply a part of loving Lacey.

Slowly stirring awake in the early morning hours, Lacey turned and reached out for Rafe's warmth. He wasn't there.

Bewildered, she sat up, shoving her hair back. "Rafe?" His name was a whisper in the room. She gripped the quilt for a moment, then pushed it aside, forcing herself to move and light the lamp. It took her eyes a few seconds to adjust, and she scanned the room.

His clothes were gone.

Seized by panic that something had happened, Lacey ran from the bed. Surely he would have awakened her. Even as satiated as she had been, she could not have slept through anyone entering the room to wake him. They had fallen asleep entwined, unable to lose that final closeness.

She slid on the still-wet floor of the bathing room and opened her own bedroom door. Lacey hadn't expected him to be in here, but she hadn't expected to begin to cry.

How could he have left her alone? He couldn't have

pretended to be as deeply moved as she had been by what they shared. No . . . No!

Lacey dressed with almost frantic haste. But she had no strength to control the ragged sobs that tore from her. She cursed every tear. This was Sy's constant warning come to life. This is what being a woman meant. This clawing fear of being used, of being vulnerable.

She jerked her belt tight and froze. Rafe had trembled at her touch, she had heard him cry out—she could not believe that his loving had been a lie. There had to be a reason, a damned good reason why he had left her.

Quietly closing the door to her room, Lacey glanced up at the first pink streaks of dawn lighting the night sky, and then her gaze was drawn across from her. There was a thin stream of light coming from beneath the office door.

Lacey was drawn toward the stream of light as surely as she had been drawn by the silken savagery of Rafe's desire for her. She refused to allow one question to crowd her mind as she reached for the gleaming brass handle to open the door. To her shock, the door was locked.

Rafe jumped up from behind the desk at the first rattle at the door. He was there in moments, unlocking it, regret clouding his eyes as he looked at Lacey.

"What are you doing in here, Rafe?"

Confusion colored her voice, but her gaze was furious. And he found that he couldn't meet her eyes. He swore to himself for losing track of the time. The brilliant sheen of her eyes said more than any words. He moved to gather her into his arms, but Lacey took him by surprise, shoving him aside.

Shadowed corners of the room gave way to a bright circle of lamplight on the desk. She barely glanced at the half-empty decanter of liquor; her gaze targeted the papers scattered over the top.

"I asked you what you are doing in here, Rafe."

"Lacey, listen. I didn't mean to leave you. I—"

"That no longer matters," she snapped, dragging up the remnants of her pride.

He eyed her rigid back and clenched his teeth with a grating sound. "Don't put your pride up like a sodbuster's wall between us, princess. I warned you there would be no going back." He slammed the door closed and found satisfaction in the way she spun around toward him, her cry soft when he locked the door and pocketed the key.

"There's no need to lock it, Rafe. I'm not the one who runs."

"Don't goad me. I didn't want to have you wake up alone. I . . . Oh, hell! You're not listening to me."

"I haven't heard one word worth hearing." Her gaze and voice were bitter and cold, but she had to stifle a surge of compassion when he rubbed the back of his neck, a look of defeat in his eyes. "Tell me why you came in here."

"Where's my woman?"

With a defiant gaze Lacey's chin rose. "She's lost somewhere in the tangled sheets on your bed. Only don't rush out to find her. She wasn't real, Rafe. She wasn't . . . anything."

"*Ramera!*" he swore with a soft violence that made her flinch.

"From your tone I believe I'll thank you for whatever you called me. It has to be better than the lies you whispered. And I'm still waiting for an answer."

"How much do you know about the notes that Sy signed against the sale of the cattle?"

"As much as I need to. Worried, Rafe? Don't be. I'll make sure you get your fair share."

His stance tautened with deadly menace. "I warned you once, princess. I won't do it again."

Lacey retreated toward the massive stone fireplace to put distance between them. What had happened? Why was he doing this now? She stared at the man she had thought her lover, a man that held no secrets, and found that she looked into the chilling eyes of a stranger. It was as if the hours they had been together had never happened. Lacey trembled, but his gaze compelled her to answer.

"It wasn't for any special reason that he signed them. I mean, nothing happened that we needed the money. When I asked him about it, he refused to discuss it. Sy did not invite questions about money or his orders. When he extended the notes in the spring, I kept quiet. Even with the loss of a few hundred head, we should be able to pay them off." Nervously fingering her belt, Lacey gathered her courage. "Now that I've answered you . . . tell me why you have this sudden interest to know?"

"I went to Austin to see the judge. That's where I was, Lacey, not with April."

"Why? Were you trying to find a way to break the will or pull out?"

He wished he could believe that the flare in her eyes was hope that he would say no, but Rafe couldn't lie to himself. The thought that she wanted him to say yes set his teeth on edge. He had lost more ground than he first believed and didn't know how he was going to recover it.

"No," he finally answered. "I'm not pulling out. But the bank is no longer holding the notes. Someone bought them and no one knows who it is." He moved toward the desk, unable to tell her that he had had the same idea, for those notes would give him a hold on the Reina that Lacey couldn't buy her way out of. She avoided looking at him, and he knew he had hurt her. Gut instinct warned that this wasn't the time to tell her about the special bequest that Sy had left to him. Nothing would make him forget yesterday.

Whatever reasons Curt Blaine had for withholding that
letter Sy wrote to Lacey, he knew it bought him time. And
maybe she was right. Curt might have been trying to give
him a chance to start clean. God knew, Lacey wouldn't have
run like hot honey in his arms if she had read that letter.

Lacey stared at the floor, her hands shoved into her
pockets. If what Rafe said was true, it could mean disaster
for them unless every head reached the railhead at Kansas.

"I still don't understand what made you check on this."

"Call it a hunch I had after you were shot. With one of us
dead and the other blamed, whoever has those notes could
move in and take the Reina. It wasn't a secret that you
wanted me out. But then, with my past it would be damned
easy to prove I was the one that shot you."

"No! I never thought that!"

"I never said you did. But if you were killed, who could
prove I didn't do it? They know we're hard-pressed for
ready cash, and while it cost plenty to buy those notes, one
less partner—"

"They! What makes you think it's anyone but Darcy?
Does his daughter—"

"The judge," he cut in. "He had already ruled out Darcy
as not having the money. And just once, leave April out of
it." The wounded look in her eyes pierced him. He'd had
enough of talk that only served to drive them further apart.
Stalking her until she was cornered, Rafe ignored her
struggle to push him away. With a firm grip on her
shoulders he demanded, "Do you believe that April or any
woman could mean something to me after the way you gave
yourself to me? Doesn't this say it all . . . ?"

His kiss was brutal. A savage invasion that shook her.
His lips seem to devour her, making her weak, stripping her
defenses. Softly cruel, his mouth held hers captive, stealing
her breath, leaving her nothing as he claimed the dark

warmth of her mouth. Lacey ceased struggling when his thumbs pressed the soft sides of her breasts. His hands swept up, his fingers sinking into her hair, holding her head immobile as if he was afraid she would escape. And finally the hunger, the wildness he had shown her, rose up, blinding her to anger, to doubts, stilling her fears until she cried out, wanting him.

"Marry me," he whispered, lifting his head. Her eyes were lambent and glazed with longing, and he gave her no chance to refuse him. His mouth was at once predator taking hers prey and a lover's promise to cherish.

And when he released her, Lacey held him tight, her voice trembling. "I'm afraid of you. I'm afraid of what you make me feel, Rafe. If I marry you, I lose—"

"No. No one loses. The Reina will belong to both of us. It's what Sy would've wanted. When we have a child . . . Christ! Look at me. I'm shaking for want of you." He dropped his hand and splayed it across her flat stomach. Both their gazes looked down as he pressed lightly. "You could be carrying my seed now." With his other hand he tilted her face up. "Would you like that, Lacey? Would you have my baby?"

The depth of the desire in his eyes and something almost vulnerable broke Lacey's last defense. "A baby—"

"You first, a home, and then a baby," he murmured, pressing kisses to her bared throat.

"Rafe . . . I need—"

"I know."

". . . time," she finished. "And I can't think when you—"

"I know that, too." He pulled her tight against him, desperate to hear the words he needed. "Say yes, Lacey. Say that all this sweet hot fire is mine. Always."

"Yes. For always."

* * *

In the days that followed, days of hot golden sun that
melted away into nights of softly raging passion, Lacey and
Rafe were lost in a world of their own. As if the world were
at peace with their joy, nothing marred their happiness.

The rustlings had ceased, and the constant vigil was
eased while Lacey shared the beauty of the Reina with Rafe.
Each place was marked forever in her memory with their
abandoned lovemaking. Sometimes teasing laughter spread
from a fragrant grove of pine as long, spicy needles hanging
overhead lent protective boughs to shield the lovers entwined below. She led him to streams hidden in the
mountains, where they bathed in sun-warmed waters and
shared dreams whispered against the cascading flow of
turbulent mountain runoffs.

Lacey opened herself like the glory of a rose coming into
full bloom. Every exquisite joining was a reaffirmation of
her being a woman, in love and loved in return. There was
a feverish greed in her to see the proud set of Rafe's
shoulders as he worked or gave orders to the men. His slow
smile, the wicked teasing, the cherishing look in his eyes
made her give not only herself but almost complete control
of the ranch to him.

On this sun-drenched morning she dressed with a decided
anticipation, for Rafe had been gone for two nights. They
had made plans to meet this afternoon at one of the line
shacks. Lacey smiled, thinking of the picnic lunch she
intended to bring with her and the hunger Rafe would
satisfy afterward. Her hands stilled in the act of buttoning
her green cotton shirt. It was all so perfect—how could it
last? The desire between them was an ember set to flame by
the merest touch, the briefest meeting of gazes. She willed
the disturbing thought away and forced herself to finish
dressing. Once her braid was securely fastened, she hurried
to the kitchen.

Maggie beamed what was now a familiar indulgent smile, and they worked, Lacey frying chicken, Maggie shelling peas fresh from their garden, in companionable silence.

When Lacey set a platter of chicken on the table, Maggie said, "I've made fresh biscuits and saved pie for your lunch. Does my body good to see you two so happy, honey."

Lacey gave her a quick hug and sighed with contentment. If Maggie had told her weeks ago that she would be eager to please Rafe and share all she could with him, she would have rebelled with the very spirit of her being.

She grabbed a basket from the pantry and left Maggie to pack the lunch while she went down to the barn to saddle her horse.

"Ain't seen much of you lately," greeted Bo as she came out of the tack room.

Slinging the saddle over the end stall, Lacey saw that he was still limping. For a few moments they spoke of ranch business, and then Lacey asked, "Why haven't you been up to the house, Bo? Is your leg bothering you so much?"

"Ain't to worry yourself. Aches some, but it don't stop me from doin' what needs to get done." Bo watched her brush down the silvery hide of the horse Evan had given her. "You're real happy with Rafe, ain't you?"

"Yes, I am." She stopped and glanced at him. "Do you like him, Bo? I know how Maggie and Fletcher feel, but you've never said."

"He makes you smile like sunshine, Lacey. That's good enough for me. You ain't bothered 'bout Sy not being your pa anymore?"

For a moment her eyes darkened, but she smoothed the saddle blanket over the horse's back. "I still think about it, Bo. Maybe someday I'll find out the truth. I need this time with Rafe. Both of us need it," she added with a fierce note.

Bo slung the saddle on, and she cinched the belly strap tight while he bridled the horse. They parted in silence, but Bo stood watching her as Luke and Evan Darcy rode in.

"So Parrish let you keep my gift," Evan remarked, pushing his hat back as Lacey walked up to them holding the reins in one hand.

"It wasn't his decision, Evan," she answered with a cutting edge to her voice.

"Figured with him running things, it was."

"Well, you're wrong. You understand that, don't you, Luke?" But Lacey didn't give him a chance to answer her. "Rafe and I made the decision together that he would be giving the orders. But we talk about those orders first. I warned you, Evan, didn't I?"

"Heck, Lacey, Evan here don't mean nothing by it," Luke cut in. "We all heard 'bout you marrying him."

She studied each man's face, looking for signs of discontent. Evan turned away, but Luke's gaze never wavered. With a brisk nod she left them. There was no point in clashing with either of them over her choice. Marrying Rafe was the right decision. It had to be.

"Wonder what I said that made her riled?" Luke asked as Bo joined them by the corral.

"You set a spur under her cozy blanket about marrying Parrish," Evan said, "and like the half-tamed mare she is, Lacey ain't gonna ride smooth for any man."

Bo glared at Evan, wishing he had a good ten years lighter on his frame. He had no real liking for Rafe, but Evan wasn't his choice to replace him. He couldn't fight him, but he wasn't about to let his remark go unanswered.

"Boy, you better hope that spur don't come back and set your ass to pinchin' none. Parrish ain't a man to set back when his fence's been jumped if you're thinkin' fool thoughts."

Luke gazed from one to the other. There was a hard warning in Bo's voice, reflected in his eyes as he stared at Evan. Knowing how Evan felt about Lacey, Luke pitied him, but his loyalty lay with the Reina and her owners, so he added a softer warning to Evan.

"You'd better listen to him. Rafe ain't a man to fool with. If you want to hang on—"

"You think I'm afraid to lose this job?"

Luke listened a moment to the jeering laugh that followed. Evan stood watching him, tense now, waiting for his answer. "I ain't talkin' 'bout no job. I'm just tryin' to tell you plain out, Rafe'll kill any man that tries to take Lacey." He grabbed Evan's arm, shaking it. "You can't be blind. He loves her, Evan. Asked him right out and he said as much." Seeking confirmation, he turned to Bo. "Ain't I right? Tell him you heard Rafe, too."

Grinning from ear to ear, Bo spoke with a deadly calm.

"You heard him right, Evan. The man's gonna shoot first without wastin' time on fool questions if any man tries jumpin' his fence."

"I can take him, any time, any place." Evan stepped up into his saddle without another word and rode off.

Bo spat a mouthful of tobacco juice where Evan had stood. "Best thing to get rid of snake venom, Luke."

"Ah, don't take on so. Evan didn't really mean it."

"You'd best be right. If you ain't, that's one man that won't find himself an anthill to hide in if he goes near Lacey."

Luke didn't answer him, for Lacey chose that moment to come out of the house. She tied the basket to her pommel and mounted up, and Luke thought she looked as pretty as an ace high flush as she slowly rode away.

Lacey kept her horse to an easy canter. Craggy rocks marked the trail, scattered, then loomed with increasing

frequency as she headed up into the mountains. She thought
of the first time she had come this way. Sy had led her
packhorse, telling her she could change her mind and he
would send one of the men in her place. She had refused,
determined to prove to him and to the men that she was
capable of withstanding the loneliness of a four-week stay at
the line shack. And Lacey had learned what it meant to be
cooped up alone with only the wind, the snow, and a horse
for company.

Glancing back at the lowlands supporting the open
chaparral of fine-leaved mesquite, she realized how far up
the trail she had come. Ahead, prickly evergreen shrubs
were towered by live oaks that blanketed the hillside, and
her attention was drawn to the dotted color in the rock
crevices. Like vibrant gems, rose and purple blazing star
flowers bloomed in riotous profusion against their dull
shaded backdrop.

With an impish smile she stopped to pick a few. Her gaze
was dreamy as she stroked her cheek with one flower. The
first time she and Rafe had made love in the open, the field
had been covered with these flowers. She recalled the
almost solemn look of Rafe's eyes as he gathered a large
bouquet and, warning her to be still, had blanketed her body
with them. A heated flush stole through her, and she closed
her eyes, seeing the two of them. The sun-sheened darkness
of Rafe's hair as he bent to kiss her, the first flower he lifted
and the kisses that followed each bit of flesh he bared. Heat
spread inside her and she trembled, hearing again his husky
sigh, his whisper as he reached the soft inner skin of her
thigh . . . "This is the only flower I want for my own."

It was a memory among many to treasure, for he had
gently worshiped her with his lips beneath the blaze of the
sun in the midst of tall grasses and flowers until her soft cry
sang sweeter than any birdsong.

While Lacey was lost in her remembrances, two riders watched her from the ridge above. April Darcy turned to her brother. "I don't understand why you still want her after what she did to you. Where's your pride, Evan? She said you weren't man enough to rule her or the Reina. And now she has Rafe."

Evan's smile belied the hard glint of his eyes. "But you want him, don't you? Just do what I said. Leave Lacey and the Reina to me."

"You're sure he'll be up there?"

"He'll be there, and if you do it all right, he'll stay."

They both heard Lacey's humming and watched as she mounted.

"Will you follow her?" April asked, backing her horse down the slope.

"No. I'd best get back before I'm missed."

Lacey glanced up as a small shower of pebbles were dislodged above her. She shaded her eyes and then shrugged, thinking it was only a small animal. Further up the trail she stopped to watch a wild hare scamper through the tall grass, noting the climb of the sun, willing Rafe to be waiting for her.

But she lingered, knowing it was too early for him to have gotten to the line shack.

Waist-high needlegrass grew up around the old weathered shack, and April, with her mind set on what she was about to do, dismounted and led her mare into the lean-to. Foul-musty odors greeted her when she opened the cabin door, and she jumped back at the sound of mice scurrying to hide. Reminding herself that minutes might be all she had, she hurried to make good use of them.

With a wild, almost boyish yell, Rafe spurred his horse over the last flat run before the shack. He hoped that Lacey was waiting. Two days apart was far too long, he admitted to himself, much as he would admit, when asked, that he loved Lacey.

The past was finally behind him. He didn't care that Curt would ride out one day and give her the letter from Sy. She agreed to marry him. She loved him. Nothing could happen to change that.

The soft, greeting nicker of a horse from the shadowed interior of the lean-to sent his blood to simmer. He was down and running into the cabin's dim interior in seconds.

Running, straight into April's waiting arms.

Her lips clung to his mouth with a desperation he fought free of. Grabbing her shoulders, he shoved her away.

Speechless for a moment, he raked a flint-eyed gaze over her. April's blond curling hair was in total disarray, streaming wildly over her shoulders, spilling down the low bodice of her camisole. A flush of fury stained his cheeks. There were tears in the fragile fabric! Her shirt, boots, and hat were carelessly tossed on the bunk behind her.

He tried to speak and couldn't over the choking sensation filling him. If Lacey walked in and found her here with him . . . "You damn bitch!"

His hand snaked out and grabbed her hand roughly, dragging her to the doorway.

"Rafe! Wait. I didn't know you'd be here. I swear that. I like to come up here by myself and—"

"You picked today to come here! You're lying. Who put you up to this?"

"No one." April hung back, her eyes beseeching him. "What difference does it make? Just as no one put me up to this, no one but you knows I'm here."

With a frantic look outside Rafe let her go. "Get dressed and get out."

"Stop looking at me as if you can't stand the sight of me, Rafe. That night you came to our ranch, you didn't—"

"—Take what you offered. I kissed you a few times. It was a mistake. Hurry up." He stood with his back toward her, begging the powers that be to grant him time.

"Rafe," she whispered softly behind him. "I know I'm forward for a woman, but . . ."

"But what?" he demanded, spinning around.

April stepped back. "Please, don't be angry. Didn't you care for me a little? When you kissed me—"

"What the hell do you want from me?"

"It's Lacey, isn't it? I heard you were going to marry her, but I didn't believe it. I thought I meant something to you."

The forlorn tone of her voice and pleading gaze sent a rush of guilt through him. He swallowed his anger and forced himself to her side where he picked up her shirt.

"Put it on. I want you gone before Lacey gets here. If you thought there was more between us, April, I'm sorry. It's Lacey I love."

April flung her arms around his neck, twisting herself so that Rafe had to turn with her. His arm swept up around her waist to keep them both from falling. April clutched his shoulders, her gaze frantic toward the door. "Rafe," she moaned, her smile triumphant.

It was her smile that made him turn his head. Lacey stood framed in the doorway, her gaze bewildered, one hand clutching the wood, the other holding crushed flowers.

"Rafe?" Lacey heard the quiver in her voice, but it was merely the forerunner of the violent trembles that shook her body.

"It's not—"

"Tell her," April demanded, fighting to hang on to Rafe. "Tell Lacey where you spent the last two nights!"

Lacey listened to her, her mind registered April's lush

and tumbled appearance, but her gaze silently pleaded with Rafe for denial.

"You can't believe her! You said you trusted me. Lacey! You said you loved me." Beyond caring whether or not he hurt April, he savagely yanked her arms down.

"I did, didn't I?" she whispered in a dazed voice.

In those few frozen moments April played her wild card. "If Rafe wasn't with me, I couldn't know about the few scars on his back, could I? Or that he laughed about your being shy when he took you in an open field?"

Lacey flinched as if she had been hit. Her stricken gaze lowered to where she had dropped the bouquet of blazing stars. Slowly she backed away, staring at the vile flowers that mocked her with their soiled beauty.

Chapter 15 ══════════════

RAFE RAN, BUT Lacey was already mounted, yanking hard on the reins. Her horse reared, and he dived to grab the bridle. Lacey dug her heels into the horse's sides, and the mare responded with a prancing leap. Rafe barely managed to fall and roll out of the way. He was up and reaching for her stirrup when Lacey flung the basket at him. She kicked her boot free and caught him square in the belly. Rafe doubled over and for a tense moment looked at her eyes.

If Lacey had a gun, she would have shot him.

He was in a kneeling crouch in the trampled grass and knew she wouldn't believe him. He couldn't move as she rode off. He couldn't breathe. A harsh roar filled his ears and then another sound intruded its deadly warning.

On his left, just past his line of vision, was a rattlesnake. He drew a shallow breath, let it out slowly, not daring to move as the rattle sounded its warning again. Rafe knew it was too much to hope that the snake would slither away.

He almost smiled. Lacey had trampled the grass and likely disturbed it. That last look in her eyes wished him dead. Unless he was extremely careful now, he might grant her that wish.

Not a whisper of air stirred the tall needlegrass. His right arm strained with tension as he moved his hand by inches from the ground up toward his gun. Rafe strove to keep his balance in his awkward crouch. Sweat beads popped out over his face, and a few ran into his eyes, blinding him. The sun blazed down, but a cold shiver fingered his spine. His palm slid up and slowly curled around the butt of his gun. He was desperate to fill his lungs with one deep breath, but he knew he couldn't chance it.

The worn, wooden grip of his gun caught for a second and then was free. He inched it upward out of the holster. Rafe prayed for time. For one clean shot.

April came running toward him.

He had a second to make a choice. Warn her or fire. He moved too fast. The flat-head, diamond-backed rattler struck once, and then once again.

Rafe cried out to April, drew, and fired. He jumped up, grabbed the knife sheathed at his side and used the bowie's finely honed blade to cut through his worn denim pants. He had to ignore the skin he sliced with it. The bared fang marks were too high on his thigh for him to bite into them. He opened his flesh, forcing the blood to flow. As quickly as he had worked, Rafe knew he wasn't fast enough. Intense pain shot through his leg.

April swayed where she stood and then backed away. Rafe would kill her for what she did if she stayed. But the sight of him bleeding made her hesitate.

Dragging his leg, Rafe went past her as if she wasn't there and managed to get into the shack. He went straight for the wooden cupboard, where he hoped to find a bottle of whiskey. Even when the men wouldn't use the shack for months, they would leave a bottle behind. And he found one in the far corner.

Ignoring the dust, he pulled the cork free with his teeth, his other hand pressing the flesh of his leg open to keep it bleeding.

He tasted the liquor with the tip of his tongue. Rotgut, the

cheapest cactus juice that passed for whiskey. Damn good
for snakebite but not for drinking. Rafe knew he wouldn't
drink it now. Could not, when he remembered the warning
an old Mexican had given him when they had tried to save
a man who was snake bit. The fool in his ignorance had
finished off a bottle of whiskey before they had gotten to
him. He was dead within the hour, and the old man had
blamed it on the whiskey, claiming the liquor spread the
poison.

He was about to pour the liquor on his leg when he saw
the shadow across the floor. His heart slowed for a beat as
he looked up, hoping it was Lacey.

"Let me help you," April whispered, staring at the
blood-soaked pants.

"Help?" he grated from between clenched teeth. "You
looking to finish me off?"

April came to him, draping his arm over her shoulder.
"Get on the bunk, Rafe. There's water in my canteen, but
don't move around."

Rafe didn't have the strength left to argue. The poison
was spreading, and April was his only hope. He spared her
a quick look as she came back and began to build a fire.

Lifting the iron cookpot, April stripped off her shirt to
wipe out the cobwebs. Rafe moaned and she cut a few strips
to bandage his leg when she was finished even as he weakly
urged her to hurry.

"I am," she snapped, more frightened than she could
admit to him. Everyone knew what to do for a snakebite,
but she had never done it. Rafe groaned. "The water's
taking too long to heat."

He heard the panic in her voice and forced himself to
dredge up a measure of calm. "The hell with the water.
Stick the knife in the fire."

April glanced at him and blanched. He was twisting his

neckerchief with his gun barrel as a makeshift tourniquet, and the blood spurted.

Using her shirt, April grabbed the knife from the fire. The blade was hot and blackened. Ashen white, she stood at his side.

Rafe closed his eyes in despair. The sheen of sweat on her face told him she wouldn't be able to do it. He grabbed the knife from her hand. "Hold the gun. I'll cut. But you'll have to—"

"I know what to do." April dropped to her knees, forcing herself to watch him make the needed cuts deep into the bites. She swallowed bile and leaned forward. Sucking and then spitting out the blood, she lost track of time until his hand weakly pushed her away.

"I think . . . you got it all."

April doubled up, staggering to the door. She knew he could hear her retching, but she didn't care. When she was done, she leaned weakly against the cabin wall. Evan had what he wanted, and so, in a way, did she. If Rafe survived. . . .

Surviving was the one thought Lacey allowed herself in her headlong flight down the mountain trail. She had heard a single gunshot, but with the ripping pain of the betrayal she felt, she didn't care if April or Rafe was the target.

The pain was all encompassing, and when her mare was winded, Lacey dismounted and walked her home. With every step she took upon the land, she reaffirmed it was all that mattered. The earth would never betray her, and Rafe Parrish . . . She stumbled and squeezed her eyes closed, falling to her knees.

He never wanted her. Lies, all lies. The simple truth destroyed her. "Woman," he called her. Another name for a weak fool.

Never again would she let him use her, she vowed, and repeated when dusk fell, and she made her way home.

Ragweed was sitting on the high rail of the corral fence, and Lacey, exhausted, accepted his offer to help unsaddle the mare. She couldn't face Maggie, and lingered outside, the dejected set of Ragweed's shoulders cutting through her own misery. Although he was an orphan, Ragweed usually had a good sense of humor despite his harsh life. She was hit with the realization that she had lost touch with the men that worked for her. Because of . . . No, she would not say his name, even to herself.

"Looks like you lost your best gal or your pay to the men, Ragweed. I've got the time, if you want to talk."

"Ain't got a best gal, Miz Lacey. It's the races. I ain't gonna be able to ride in 'em."

"The races?"

"Independence Day in San Angela."

Bemused, Lacey shook her head. She had lost touch with not only what was happening around the Reina but with time. With all the wild hoopla the town could muster, the day would be celebrated for the Texans who had won independence from Mexico. There would be contests on just about everything, from how far a man could spit his tobacco juice to how long he could sit the meanest long-horn.

"I still don't understand why you can't ride in them. I know the men had to draw lots to take turns to go, but you all understand that the herd can't be left unprotected."

"I knowed that. An' I ain't complainin'. I jus' got stuck with goin' at night. Had myself set on winnin' that prize money."

"Have you been gambling away more than your wages in those card games at night? I know how easy it is to get carried away by a big pot and filling an inside straight."

"You played cards with the men?"

"When I could slip out from under Maggie's watchful eye. And it was Sy and Bo who taught me how."

"Ain't that, Miz Lacey. Got my eye on a fancy saddle old man Willis has for sale. Said he took it in on trade from some drifter down on his luck."

"The man must have been. I've heard of a horse or a rifle going but not a handgun or saddle."

"That's what Willis claimed. Wants a hundred dollars."

Lacey leaned against the railings, pulling off bits of dried bark. "Can't you trade places with someone?" She was beginning to lose the tension that had filled her, for she had truly missed this sort of talk with any of the men.

"Shouldn't be botherin' you with this. Already talked to Rafe. Said I had to take the breaks the way they came." He jumped down and stopped when Lacey grabbed his arm.

"He doesn't have the final say!"

"But he made it clear that you wasn't to be bothered—"

"I'm still an owner of the Reina!" Lacey hung on to her temper by a thread. This had to be the first step she took to reclaim what was hers. "I'll ride that day for you. I didn't plan on going to San Angela. So don't think I'm doing this just for you."

"Can't let you do that. Rafe'll—"

"Rafe can go to hell!" She wanted to shake him for mentioning his name again. Releasing his arm, Lacey stepped in front of him. "I hired you. I'm giving you an order. Me, Lacey G . . . Garrett." She almost choked calling herself Garrett, but thankfully, Ragweed didn't notice.

"Sure, but—"

"But nothing. The matter is settled. You ride with the other men in the morning." She started to walk away, and half turned back. "Ragweed, you'd better win that race."

"Miz Lacey, that's a promise! I've got a big, blanket-hipped Appaloosa from that last string I helped to break. He's fast, too. Sure to beat anythin' anyone puts up against him."

"Then I'll expect to see you come riding home with that fancy saddle."

With a high leap Ragweed tossed his hat, caught it, and shouted a wild yell as he ran for the bunkhouse. Here he was feeling sorry for himself, and Miz Lacey, who a body couldn't get near lately, made everything right for him.

Lacey wished his joy was contagious, but weariness settled heavily on her shoulders as she slipped in the gate, praying she would avoid seeing Maggie. Luck was with her, but once in her own room she restlessly paced its confines. There was no way she could avoid thinking about Rafe.

Painful as it was, Lacey knew there was some form of justice in having discovered his lies before she had married him.

The thought did not bring much needed solace. He was sure to return, and she had to be ready to face him. From the depths of the bitterness she felt at his betrayal, she knew she had the weapons to defeat any demand he would make to give him a chance to explain. Rafe had told her how he went crazy when she showed him scorn or contempt.

"And he means nothing to me," she whispered, staring at her reflection in the mirror. "He never did . . . and now he never will."

Recapturing her authority tested her temper in the days that followed as she worked until she was exhausted. She refused to answer any questions about Rafe, refused to hear his name mentioned. Daily she rode out, culling the weak cows, the calves that were not fattening, or those that had been injured by wolves prowling the outskirts of the herd.

Her sturdy little mustang that she had caught, broken, and trained herself could be seen all over the ranch, with a rigid Lacey in the saddle and Evan Darcy at her side.

Maggie was beside herself. Lacey's refusal to talk about what happened with Rafe left her feeling helpless. She had thought that Rafe loved Lacey, that the love they shared was the same enduring kind she had shared with her husband, Eric. Lacey was hurting, but she had outgrown the simple comfort Maggie could offer. The fine anger lines around Lacey's mouth, the feral glitter in her eyes, and the whip-sharp tongue spoke of a woman's pain. The pain a man had caused and only that man could heal.

Maggie wasn't alone in her feelings. Fletcher, standing with Bo in the shelter of the barn doors, watched Lacey ride past with Evan. He shook his head, spit out a wad of tobacco juice, and spoke to Bo.

"Jus' 'pears to me that understandin' she had with Rafe to marry ain't gonna happen. He up an' disappeared, an' I swear she'd just as soon kill him if he shows up."

"Nearly chewed my head off when I asked her yesterday if we should start lookin' for him. My gut says there's somethin' wrong 'bout his leavin'."

"I did the same. She give me this dark look an' swore she didn't give a hoot to hell where he was so long as he didn't come back."

"Been near a week that he's gone. Didn't seem that he would jus' take off. But maybe, jus' maybe, it's for the best that he's gone."

Fletcher shook his head, then rubbed his jaw. "Can't see as how you'd feel that way. She's hurtin', Bo. I just can't figure where in tarnation he took off to like a damn chaparral cock."

"If he comes back and hurts her more, I'm gonna skin

that thick-headed son of a bitch and use his hide to wipe my boots."

Fletcher was taken aback by the vehement tone of Bo's voice, but before he could say anything, Bo pushed past him into the sunlit yard.

"I'll be damned," Bo muttered as Fletcher joined him.

Shading his eyes with his hand, Fletcher gazed at the rider looming close. He'd know that big grulla of Sy's anywhere. Rafe had come home.

As one their glances moved to where Lacey waved Evan off and stood leaning against the corral fence.

"Seems we ain't the only ones that spotted him," Bo remarked. "An' it looks like I won't get a chance at his hide."

Lacey controlled the sudden harsh breaths she drew into tortured lungs. She fought down the impulse to run. Last night she had convinced herself that he had gone, for good this time. Only the hate that had time to fester held her rooted to where she stood.

Rafe's eyes seemed to bore into her as he came close enough for her to see the dark circles under his eyes. She had to remind herself that she could face him, face anything. She was strong enough to withstand the storm she sensed about to break. She had to be, or the choice would be for her to be the one to break, and that she would never do.

He was clean shaven, his skin pale. Time receded for a moment, and Lacey swayed where she stood. What had happened to give his eyes that haunted look? She couldn't ask. Her gaze drifted down, took note of the new shirt and pants. But once more she refused to question him. He brought the horse abreast of her, and Lacey lifted her chin in a challenging manner, her gaze direct but empty of emotion.

She could feel herself scream inside as he casually looped

the reins over the pommel, his black eyes narrowed, holding hers as he leaned down. "Lacey, I—"

"No. There's nothing you can say that I want to hear." His jaw tightened, the muscle in his cheek twitched, and still she refused to look away from him.

The second passed, neither willing to give the other quarter. The breeze swept suddenly down from the mountains, sounding to Lacey like a wild wounded animal's cry, very like the scream lodged in her throat. She bit her lip to keep it buried as he finally dismounted.

"Fletcher," he called, "grain him good. He's had nothing but grass." And to Lacey, "When you're ready to talk, I'll be waiting, princess." Without a look back he walked away before he lost control of himself.

Lacey sagged against the fence. Seeing him had been ten times easier and a hundred times worse than every nightmare. But he left her feeling he had won the hand without her ever seeing what cards were dealt. Her eyes tracked his moves toward the house and first noticed that he limped. Maggie came running from the doorway, but he brushed past her. Lacey involuntarily thought back to that day at the line shack. The gunshot . . . Had he been shot? She stifled the thought.

Feeling anything but the cold rage she had wrapped herself in would open the wound again. She couldn't survive a repeat of these last few days. But she had a right to know what he intended to do.

Behind her Fletcher forced Bo to remain with him. Their words were angry, and Bo stomped off to the barn.

Maggie glanced up from the dough she was kneading as Lacey came into the kitchen. "Where is he?"

"Inside. He didn't say much, Lacey." She watched helplessly as Lacey went into the courtyard. "Lord, the fur's gonna fly higher than a trapper's coon dog." With a wish that she dared to interfere between the two of them, Maggie punched down the dough with a vengeance.

The greenery and flowers in the courtyard mocked Lacey as she strode past without a glance. The echoing sound of her boots resounded emptily against the mud-brick tiles, reflecting the hollow feeling she had inside her.

The impulse to confront Rafe before he began challenging her orders directed her to his room. It came as no surprise to find him standing right inside the doorway as she abruptly entered. What did surprise her was his firm, biting grip on her arm as he pulled her farther inside and then slammed the door closed.

"It took you long enough to follow me," he growled by way of a greeting. "And hold back that tongue lashing you're itching to let fly. I'm in no damn mood to hear it."

"As sure as hell is coming, I don't care what you're in the mood for!" She yanked her arm free and rubbed it.

"You'll first listen to what I have to say. I didn't spend those nights with April. I didn't—"

"Shut up! If your conscience is bothering you, go see a priest for confession. I won't hear any more of your cold-blooded lies."

Rafe spun her around, leashing his temper. He forced her chin up so he could look into her eyes. Lacey defeated him by closing them. He fought down the desire to kiss her into submission, but knew he could not let her control this confrontation.

"You don't want to hear anything. Fine. I have no intention of explaining exactly what happened. You wouldn't believe me. But you're wrong . . . dead wrong."

Her body shook with a tremor, whether from her anger or his nearness, she didn't know. She stepped back and he let her go.

"What do you intend to do now, Rafe?"

"Intend? What the hell is that supposed to mean? I swear you're not making sense. Everything goes on just the way it's been."

"No."

"Nothing's changed!"

"It already has!" she yelled back, forgetting every vow to be calm.

"You stubborn witch. Don't make this harder than it has to be." He drew in a harsh breath and released it. "Lacey, you're mine. My woman, remember that. No matter what you believe, what you think, nothing will ever change that."

"Woman," she snarled. "*Fool* is what you mean."

Rafe had had enough. He grabbed her. "I'll keep you here until you admit you're mine."

"No!" She shoved against him, and all the rage bottled inside exploded. Like a fury she attacked him. Clawing and kicking, wildly twisting against his hold, Lacey tried to fight her way free.

But Rafe used his strength, kicking her feet out from under her and taking her down to the floor. He pressed his heavier weight on her body, letting her spend herself in a futile effort, willing her rage to end.

Lacey weakly turned her head aside. She couldn't even draw one calming breath. His body was molded to hers like a second skin. She shuddered, shocked at the warmth shimmering through her, an insidious heat that came to life in response to his body pressing hers.

There was no way to disguise his flesh, hard and hot against her. The desire she felt was mirrored in his eyes.

"I want you," he murmured, as if echoing her thought.

Lacey tensed and refused to answer.

His lips moved over the wild tumble of her hair, brushed

her cheek, and settled on the corner of her mouth. "I could easily make you want me, bright eyes."

She bit her lip, jerking her head away.

Rafe lowered his mouth to her bared throat and then whispered, "I told you there would be no going back." He could feel her shake beneath him and despaired of breaking the wall she had erected. Forcing her fingers to entwine with his, he raised her hands to lie flat on either side of her head. "You can lie to me with words, but you can't make your body lie."

He shifted his grip to hold both her hands with one of his and levered his body to the side. There was grim satisfaction in seeing her fight the desire that was beginning to consume her. Stroking her side, he cupped her breast, his thumb rasping over the already hardening nipple.

"You want me," he grated, and when she still refused to answer, he pulled the shirt free of her pants, sliding his hand beneath it.

Lacey was forced to look at him then. There was a savage glitter in his eyes, and she knew until she spoke he would go on torturing her.

"*Yes!* But you weren't the first man I wanted. Only the man that showed me I could want someone else. Maybe three times will prove lucky for me!"

He watched the rage and the pain flicker in her eyes. "I could make you want only me, but if I did, you'd never forgive me, would you? I don't want war in our marriage."

"There isn't going to be any marriage."

"I warned you not to make childish threats that would back you into a corner, bright eyes."

Lacey summoned the last reserves of her strength and anger. "And I warned you that you would be risking your life. Whatever was between us is dead. Leave it buried."

She stared at him, eyes cold, her voice flat. "There will never be any marriage between us."

He moved over her powerfully, letting her know the force of his body. "You're mine. No man will ever have you unless he's willing to lose his life. You believe you hate me. Hate's akin to love, Lacey. It's a lesson you need to learn."

Rafe let her go, rolled to his feet, and was out of the room before Lacey realized that she was free. She lay on the floor, fighting the shudders that came over her in waves. Her body still held his heat and hardness, an imprint that would never fully leave her. She didn't know if she wanted to scream or cry. How could she fight him? Hating him was destroying her, but she couldn't run. There was no place to go.

Chapter 16

VISIBLY SHAKEN, RAFE stood in the courtyard. He knew he should ride out and away from her, but his steps led him to the office. He wanted a drink. No, he wanted a bottle. Maybe then the raw ache inside him would cease tearing him apart. He slammed the door closed behind him. Taking a glass from the sideboard, he held it high before venting his rage and throwing it at the fireplace.

He grabbed a bottle and took a long swallow, his eyes targeted on the glittering shards of glass. The liquor burned as it went down his throat. But something had to warm the cold knot of fear in his belly. He was going to lose it all; Lacey, the Reina, and the money.

He had left April convinced that it was sheer chance she had come to the line shack that day. But short of killing her, she refused to tell him how she knew about him making love to Lacey in the open field. Someone had seen them, that was clear enough. But who?

Holding the bottle aloft, he knew he shouldn't give Lacey time to marshal strength to rebuild her walls. Two more long swallows fired his own stubborn pride.

He wasn't going to beg. Never would he beg her.

It was nearly three hours later that Lacey stood outside the office. She heard Rafe stumble against the furniture, swearing softly in Spanish. The thought of confronting

Rafe, drunk and furious, made her hesitate. She should leave him to drink himself into a stupor and pass out.

Maggie took the decision out of her hands. She came bearing down on Lacey with a covered tray, her mouth set in a grim line, her eyes flashing determination.

"This has gone on long enough, Lacey. Let me by. If you don't care what he's doin' to himself, I do."

"This is between us, Maggie. Don't interfere."

"Someone has got to. You've been ridin' roughshod over all of us this past week. He got himself hurt somehow, and I aim to find out."

"Maggie—"

"Don't be Maggie-in' me. Jus' like his pa. Takin' to the bottle. Shame of it is you could stop it."

"I'm asking you again, Maggie, don't interfere."

"You love him, don't you? You were happier lovin' him than you've ever been. I don't care what happened betwixt the two of you. Ain't nothin' that lovin' can't heal."

Lacey had no choice but to take the tray Maggie shoved into her hands. "Go on, honey," she admonished. "You're a strong woman. The Reina can't heal what's hurtin' you. He can."

She stood for long minutes after Maggie left, uncertain what to do. Her pride demanded she leave Rafe alone. Her heart ached for the loss of what they shared. Her body cried in hunger against the emptiness she fed it.

Lacey juggled the tray and opened the door. Rafe stood with his back toward her in front of the fireplace. One arm rested on the mantel alongside two empty bottles. She was staring so intently at his back that she started when he spoke.

"Come in. I wondered how long it would take you to come to me."

Her heart began to beat rapidly as a shiver of fear snaked its way up her spine.

"Well? Come in and join me," he urged in a deceptively lazy voice. "Or are you afraid?"

He didn't sound drunk, and Lacey couldn't help but respond to the taunt. "I'm certainly not afraid of you."

His harsh laugh grated on her ears as he slowly turned around to face her. "You should be, *bruja*."

The blatant arrogance of his gaze infuriated her. She felt drawn back in time for a suspended moment, to the first day she had met that gaze in this room. Her chin lifted in a challenging manner, but a small warning sounded that she had best not goad him.

He lifted the bottle he held and drank from it, his eyes pinning her where she stood. When he was done, he walked to the sideboard and filled a glass that he held out to her. "Here, princess, take it. You look as if you could use something to put a little warmth back into you."

Lacey set the tray down and went to him. She shoved the glass aside, ignoring the spill of liquor. "You look as if you've had enough for both of us."

"Enough?" His laugh was scornful. "*Por Dios, bruja,* for what's eating me, there would never be enough."

Giving him a disgusted look, Lacey went to the fireplace and began to pick up the broken shards of glass. "Is that why you're getting drunk, Rafe? Something's eating you? Or did you think you'd get away with your scheme to have it all?"

"No, witch," he denied in too soft a voice, watching her as she stood and faced him. "The liquor you sneer at, princess, is only keeping me from acting on what is bothering me."

She paled under his intense gaze, wishing she didn't understand what he was talking about. But she did. All too well she recalled the wildness they could call forth from each other. Earlier in his room she nearly broke her pride's back to answer that desire.

"You really shouldn't have come in here, Lacey," he stated in that same soft, deceptive tone, moving toward her.

Lacey backed away. Rafe was dangerous to her strength of will when he touched her. She refused to let it happen again.

"Maybe," he continued, as if he didn't notice her retreat, "I wanted you to come to me."

"Stop it, Rafe. Go finish drowning in that bottle. I won't let you use me—"

"Use you? Is that what you call it?"

Lacey darted for the door, but he was there first, locking it. She made a grab for the key, but he sent her spinning into the room.

With deliberate moves he came toward her, pulling his shirt from his pants. Lacey flattened herself against the wall. A tiny warning flagged him, telling him not to touch her, not when he was losing control. But all Rafe could hear was her taunting voice saying he used her.

With her hands splayed against the wall, wishing it would somehow open and allow her to escape, Lacey realized her foolishness in listening to Maggie. It was a mistake to have come in here. He stripped off his shirt, tossing it aside. Lacey was intent on running.

Then, like a hunter snagging prey, it was too late. He leaned against her, his hands on either side of her shoulders, blocking her. Lacey swallowed against the constricting dryness in her throat, refusing to look up at him. She was afraid to see him gloating. But she couldn't seem to close her eyes against the sight of his chest, a wall of tautly controlled muscles scored with black hair.

"I'll say this once, Lacey. I haven't touched another

woman. I don't want anyone but you. Stop being so afraid to trust me and what you feel for me."

"I can't trust you," she whispered, drawing a ragged breath. "It almost destroyed me."

"And me. You can . . . you are destroying me." His fingers bit into her shoulders, dragging her into his arms. "You set a fire burning inside me, witch, and it's fast raging out of control. I want you."

The blatant proof pressed against her body, but Lacey tossed out her last desperate gamble.

"Prove it, Rafe. Sign over the Reina to me. Show me how much you want *me*."

"That's your price?"

His eyes were feral and savage glaring down at her. Lacey swallowed. She nodded weakly. Rafe smiled. But there was no softening in his eyes. He stepped back and, with a terrifying jerk, tore her shirt.

He cut off her scream with his lips. A brief, harsh kiss that meant to subdue and punish. When he lifted his head, he continued to rip her shirt."

"Let me see the *puta* worth the Reina," he grated from between clenched teeth.

Lacey's struggles were useless, and she drew on her pride as the cold comfort to stand there when he was done.

With one hand he drew her away from the wall, holding her hand high while he turned her around and around.

"You named your price, and now hear mine. Marriage."

He swept her up into his arms, warning her with his look not to cry out. Lacey knew he had snapped whatever control he had, and she wanted to die when he opened the door to confront Maggie.

"Get out of my way," he ordered, taking grim satisfaction in the way Lacey was forced to cling to him to hide her nudity.

One look at the implacable set of his face, and Maggie had no choice but to step aside. He stalked away from her and in the middle of the courtyard stopped and turned.

"Send someone into San Angela, Maggie. Tell the preacher that the Independence Day celebration tomorrow will mark an end to Lacey's."

Lacey's head jerked up, her hands pounded his back. "No, Maggie! Don't listen to him."

Rafe hurried across the tiles, kicking open the door to his room. Lacey heaved and twisted in his arms as he used his heel to slam it closed.

"You can't do this, Rafe!"

"I can. I did and I meant it. You named your price, and I'm willing to meet it. After you marry me." Swearing softly, he dumped her in the middle of his bed.

Lacey spared one brief thought to Maggie listening to her screams while she fought him. Ruthlessly and silently Rafe subdued her, his face a mask of cold fury as she spit out her hate for him. Panting, her eyes the last storm of resistance, Lacey couldn't move when he threw one powerful leg over both of hers to hold her still, her hands firmly entrenched in his ironclad grip.

"You damn hellcat! Settle down."

"Let me go and I will." Her gaze spoke of vengeance.

"I told you I can't let you go."

Lacey froze as the soft, husky sound of his voice added to the promise blazing in his eyes.

"I'll calm you down, witch. I've let you play wildcat long enough. It's time you learn to sheath your claws."

"So you can hurt me again!" The full throbbing swell of his manhood pressed intimately against her, beating out its own message of need. The fire banked by earlier touches flared to life. She couldn't let him win, she just could not, she groaned inwardly, twisting weakly in his arms.

"Stop fighting me. You want me as badly," he murmured, lifting his head, and with a sudden move of his hand, he forced her to look at him.

The shadowed light lent a sinister cast to his features as she stared up at him. His mouth was taut with repressed anger and seemed cruel to her, or was it only the power his lips had over her that made it appear so? His patience was gone. Lacey felt it leave at a cost she could only imagine. Hadn't loving him proved what a demanding, hungry lover he was? She felt his muscles strain against her body and once more gambled that she was making the right choice. She had to prove she didn't want him.

With her eyes closed she forced herself to remember the sight of April in his arms. His mouth closed over hers. Soft, warm, coaxing. And Lacey felt the insidious heat curl inside her. Her mind was more than willing to fight him, but she couldn't fight the betrayal of her own body.

Her arms rose of their own volition to pull him close. Her mouth opened to the possessive probe of his tongue, and she wanted to hate him for proving that she couldn't deny him.

He ended the kiss too soon, his lips hovering above her mouth. Rafe whispered, "I won't take from you. But before this night is over, you'll give. . . ."

Faint blushes of pink creased the sky when Lacey opened her eyes. She tried to move and found her long hair caught under Rafe's bare shoulder, his arm and leg thrown over her body in a possessive embrace even sleep could not break.

Bittersweet, the thought of her body's betrayal last night flooded her to meld with anger at Rafe for the ease of his conquest and her ultimate surrender. The thoughts brought a renewal of her own humiliation. Her legs ached, her thighs were sore, and overriding these pains was the intense knowledge that he had kept his promise and made her give, all he demanded, all he had wanted, and all she had vehemently sworn to deny him.

Flushing with the memory of the teasing taunts that kept her at a wanton, fever pitch of desire for him in the night hours, she released a small cry of frustration. She was too late to stifle the sound. Rafe began to stir. How could she feel both love and hate for him?

"Impatient so early, bright eyes?" he murmured in a sleep-laden voice as he opened his eyes.

"I'm impatient to get away from you," she whispered with cold desperation. He moved suddenly, pulling the quilt away, and her gasp was sheer outrage. She closed her eyes against the flare of desire glowing in his black ones, their gaze a caress she could almost feel on her bare flesh.

Rafe smiled. "You look like a soft, warm, and uncommonly desirable kitten this morning, Lacey. I admit I thoroughly enjoyed sheathing the cat's claws." He kissed the sweet curve of her shoulder, nipping her, then soothing it with his tongue. Lazily he traced the soft skin exposed to his eyes, smiling deeper when he felt the small ripple that tremored her body. Her eyes, when he looked up, were still heavy-lidded with the little sleep they had had and danced warningly at him. His smile became wicked, his touch firmed, and his mouth found the life pulse in her throat. Her hair, shaded with burnished shadows, was tousled on the pillow beside him. Lacey looked wild, untamed, and his body responded to her silent challenge.

"Rafe. Rafe, don't," she cried out when his hand covered her taut stomach.

"Look at me, Lacey," he coaxed, stilling a flood of need that he couldn't begin to explain. He had made love to her through the night, taking her over and over until she had cried out with a wild hunger and, lastly, with love. And still he wanted her. "Are you determined to fight both of us out of some misplaced need for revenge? How can you deny your own feelings?" He fought to keep calm, but his lips thinned at her move away from him. "Didn't I show you," he stressed, pulling her close, "just how damn foolish that was?"

Yes! she wanted to yell, but bit the word back and faced him. Why did he make her war with herself? The heat was quickening inside her and turning her body traitor once more. She wanted so much to hate him for it, for forcing a response against her stubborn will to his caresses, to his lips that lingered with agonizing madness over the curving side of her breast before lazily claiming the pebbled rose peak as a prize. Her body knew what it wanted, what it needed and craved. Rafe knew, too, he had fed every aching desire from the very first. Just as from the first, her fear of him leaving her nothing of herself had become a reality. It was that thought that made her whisper, "You have nothing more to prove to me. You're the one who had his revenge. Wasn't it enough?"

Rafe's head snapped up, eyes blazing. He captured her mouth, suddenly, savagely, like a hawk swooping for prey. He touched her until she silently pleaded for release.

His lips seared her, branding her his, until she cried out against his mouth. There was no gentle softness now, only a ruthless fire that was Rafe's to fuel until she was shaking and half-fainting beneath him. Lacey knew she was lost, and with a sob torn from inside her, she arched her body up to his. It was an offering, a lover's entreaty to be taken, a woman's surrendering plea of need. In the deepest recess of her mind it was complete capitulation to her lover.

"You're a fire, wild witch that haunts me," he whispered, trailing kisses down her throat. "But you're mine. Only mine."

Before she could move, he slid down the length of her

body, his hands holding her hips still, and Lacey was poised
to receive the plundering manhood that offered a flight to
where only Rafe could take her. She moaned, desperate for
ease from the tight knot that coiled inside her. Under his
marauding lips and hands she now fought him to take her.

"No," he breathed against her skin. Her eyes flew open
at the feel of his lips brushing like hot silk against her thigh.
"Not yet, bright eyes. Not nearly time for you."

She twisted, crying out, and then remained stock still
when he tongued the flesh in a maddening arc along the soft
inner skin.

"Rafe? No, don't . . . please . . . you can't. . . ."
But even to her own ears her protest sounded like a lover's
call for more. She wanted to stop him, needed to regain
some control over her body, which was wild, held on the
edge of precipice. His hands slipped upward slowly, first
cupping her breasts, then teasing both rigid peaks as he
delved into her woman's softness over and over.

Straining against him, fighting the tide that surged inside
her, Lacey cried out, "I hate you! I damn you and hate
you!" Her hands reached for his head, pulling him closer.
She writhed against the fire-tipped tongue that branded her
for his own.

Shaking with throbbing release when it finally laid claim
to her, she offered no protest when he slid his body up and
over hers and entered her with a powerful thrust.

There was self-loathing for the body that so easily
betrayed her, eagerly thrusting rhythmically with him. She
hated the arms that moved across his taut shoulders, her
fingers splayed over the rippling muscles of his back.

She wanted to despise the desire awakening all over
again, hearing him murmur, "Feed me your hate, Lacey.
Show me. Show me how much you hate me."

Mindless now, wildly craving release once more, she

moaned against his mouth while he drove into her, demanding what he gave: everything. They were one in a breathtaking moment, reaching a height on a savage crest that knew no end.

She passed from passion's aftermath into a half-dreaming sleep with the sound of Rafe's husky voice. "Your hate turns to love, Lacey, and someday you'll be woman enough to understand your fear to admit it."

Hours later, when she awoke to the bright, streaming sunlight falling across her flesh in Rafe's bed, Lacey reassured herself with a quick, searching look around the room that she was really alone. Trying to marshal her thoughts into order at the moment was beyond her. She wondered if she had dreamed his last words, then pushed the thought aside. She was afraid that they were true.

Moving gingerly to the edge of the bed, she listened for any sound that would reveal his presence nearby. Silence greeted her.

This time she didn't care that he had left her. She rose, then walked slowly to the connecting door between their rooms. The heat of the wood stove, the steam rising from the deep-sided pan on top of it, made her assume that Rafe had already bathed and left this for her. It was a habit newly formed when they were lovers. And now? a small voice nagged. What are you now?

"Grateful," she murmured, trailing the tips of her fingers through the warm water in the tub. Using a towel, she carefully lifted the pan of steaming water and poured it in. The thought of soaking away some of the aches of her body filled her mind completely. No sooner had she blissfully closed her eyes and leaned back did Rafe's voice behind her make her abruptly sit up.

Chapter 17 ===============

"I WAS COMING in to wake you, bright eyes. You'd better hurry with that bath. We don't have much time."

Glancing behind her, Lacey noticed the tray he held. The sight of eggs, hot biscuits dripping with butter and honey, along with a steaming cup of coffee made her mouth water. She was instantly reminded that she had never eaten yesterday. Rafe's knowing male laugh brought her gaze up to his face. She ignored the appreciative stare that roved over her body.

"If that's for me," she snapped, "just put it down. I fully intend to soak for hours."

Rafe didn't answer. He handed her a biscuit and then the coffee, waiting while she greedily ate it. Her lips were slightly swollen, and a wild stab of desire caught him when she parted them to sip the coffee between delicate bites.

"You didn't forget what today is, did you, princess?"

Frowning under his steady regard, Lacey handed him the cup and slid lower into the water. He set the tray down on the floor, out of her reach, and sat down on the stool next to the tub. He caught her eyeing the platter of fluffy eggs, knew they tempted her, and began, over her protests, to feed her. His eyes grew more somber as she steadily avoided meeting his gaze until she was done.

Turning away, she wished he would leave her some

measure of privacy. Rafe was too attractive, too male, and too damn sure of himself. Remembering her surrender to him, she knew he had reason to be. Ignoring him became a test of will that she had lost before this.

"Well? I'm waiting for an answer, Lacey."

With a soft, resigned sigh she began to soap the cloth only to have him take it from her. "Just what do you think you're doing?"

He hated the note of underlying desperation in her voice that told him how she didn't want his touch. Rafe could not reveal the pain it caused. "I'm going to help you. You seem to have a bit of difficulty moving—"

"And whose fault is that! I don't want or need your help." When he began rubbing her shoulder, she snapped, "Haven't you had enough? Haven't you done enough?"

She made a quick grab for the cloth he held high. Too late she realized by his wicked grin that she had exposed herself to his view. Knowing it was useless to keep fighting with him, she sat down and presented her rigid back to him.

Rafe began a slow circular motion over her skin to ease the tenseness from her body. Reluctantly, he was sure, she relaxed under his soothing massage, and he wondered again at the strength of spirit that made her continue to fight him. "You were planning to go to San Angela with me today, weren't you?"

She froze. "No," came her muffled answer as she bent her head forward to hide beneath the fall of her hair. His fingers flexed with a hint of their power against her neck, but Lacey refused to respond. He had told her enough times during the night what he expected to take place today. She was not about to be badgered again.

Rafe held the slope of her shoulder with one hand and used the other to force her head up. "Lacey," he warned.

"I won't be forced into marrying you. Not today. Not any

day. It was a mistake on my part to demand the Reina as a price."

"And if I'm willing to meet your price?"

"You're not. Don't lie, Rafe."

"You are going to marry me, and it won't be by force."

She jerked her head away, defeated by his flat statement. This time he let her grab the cloth back. She needed time to think and plan, to sort out the confusion of her own emotions, and knew Rafe wasn't about to grant her time.

"You want to keep the Reina, don't you?"

"Don't threaten me, Rafe."

"I'll do more than threaten you, princess. I'll take the Reina, and what's more, you can't stop me. The men already look to me for their orders. Countermand them and you'll find yourself without a hand. You can't run the ranch alone. Most of the men have stayed on because they felt sorry for—"

"I pay top wages, and I'm a damn fair boss."

"You're a damn woman!"

"That doesn't bother you any!"

His grin spread wickedly. "No, it sure as hell doesn't."

The thought burned and rankled. Lacey knew how much she wanted the land, needed it for survival, for it was a part of her, but she could not deny that it had become a part of Rafe, too. Could she have one without the other? No. She could not wrest control away from him. Rafe held the men's respect in a way she never had, but she was the one who had foolishly given him that power.

Watching the play of emotions on her face, Rafe could almost see where her thoughts would take her. She raised one shapely leg high, lingering as she soaped it, ignoring him. He waited with studied patience to hear her answer, already aware of the devious path her mind would take. He didn't wait long.

"Perhaps, just perhaps, you might be right. Marriage might be the answer." She sneaked a glance and saw the teasing smile that lifted the corner of his hard, reckless mouth. Lacey gritted her teeth at the silent challenge. "If I agree to ride into town with you and stand before witnesses to become your wife, would you promise me a few things in return? But before you answer me, Rafe, I mean to have your sworn word that these are promises you'll keep no matter what."

"And just what do you desire for your price?" he asked sarcastically.

Reassured by the calm, thoughtful look he leveled at her, Lacey began. "First, I want us to have separate rooms." His eyes narrowed, and he leaned over the edge of the tub. "You must listen to it all."

"Like the devil I will!"

"If I don't go willingly, what are you going to do? Hold a gun to my head? You'll sit there and hear me out since you have your own reasons for wanting this damn marriage."

Rafe nodded abruptly. He didn't trust himself to speak.

"I will promise to appear the perfect wife—in company, that is—and won't give you cause to complain. But we will share the running of the ranch, Rafe. That means you talk things over with me before you do them. And here in the house you stay clear of me."

Warned by her smug look, Rafe decided to let her think she was calling the shots. She was, as long as it suited him. Lacey was going to grow up and become a woman in all ways. It was more than damned past the time for it to happen. But he wasn't about to let her win easily, and he let her sit in the rapidly cooling water, fuming at his silence.

"And we need to decide what you're going to do about April. I won't have her coming on Reina land. Meet her somewhere else, Rafe, or I swear I'll—"

"You'll do nothing to her! She saved my life. But I forgot, you don't want to hear what happened that day up at the line shack. Don't worry, princess, my lips are sealed."

Saved his life? What was he talking about? But Lacey could be stubborn and refused to ask if it had anything to do with the barely healed wound on his thigh. She flushed, remembering her murmurs over it, the kisses she pressed around the tender flesh, and Rafe's curt dismissal.

She told herself it was the thought of his being in debt to April that made her ask him what had happened. Rafe, without embellishment, answered her. Lacey was swamped with a rush of guilt. She stopped herself from voicing an apology or showing concern, reminding herself that like his father, Rafe used any weakness to his ruthless advantage. And to her surprise, he made no comment about her silence.

He trailed his fingers in the water. "Are you sure that's all of it? If it is, you win. Marriage on those terms." He cut off her beginning smile with his own ruthless one. "Be warned, princess, the door between these rooms didn't stop me before."

"And I warned you to stop threatening me."

"Ah, but, princess, I don't make threats. Remember? I make promises. Ones that I intend to keep. But even if I foolishly made this one, you couldn't hold me to it."

"Then we have no agreement. Hence, no marriage."

Rafe's lips compressed as he ran his hand roughly through his hair. How far did she think to bend his pride? It took him a few minutes to realize the kind of marriage she intended they have. Didn't Lacey know him after all this time? He almost laughed at her resort to such a childish refuge.

"All right. We try it your way. I'll give you my promise that once we are married, I'll never set foot in your room again. Outside of it you're fair game. But answer me this," he demanded over her furious sputtering, his own voice ruffled with anger, "is keeping the Reina worth selling yourself like a *puta*?"

The scorn in his eyes made her breath catch. What was she doing? "Rafe, wait. I need time. I—"

"Answer me. Is it?"

"Yes," she hissed. "Yes, it's worth everything."

"That's what I thought." His grin was deadly. "The promise is made. I won't be the one to break it."

Lacey nodded, but the taste of victory was bitter. She wasn't prepared for his mocking laughter or his abrupt move. Before she realized what he intended to do, Rafe grabbed up two buckets of clean water and dumped them over her.

"Seems to me that you still need cooling, princess." He scooped her up into his arms, grabbed a towel, and ignored her outraged shrieks.

"You arrogant bas—" Lacey stopped at the look of thunderous fury lighting his eyes and muttered sullenly, "You gave me your word just moments ago, and you can't keep it."

"Just remember, Lacey mine, the sweet term of, shall I say *endearment*, that you're so fond of calling me belongs to you as well." Having effectively silenced her, Rafe carried her into her room, set her down in front of him as he sat on the bed, and kept her pinioned between his legs. "Be still," he muttered darkly.

"No. You promised you wouldn't come into my room. I won't go through with it if you can't keep your word. Do you hear me?"

"How can I help but hear you, you're screaming in my ear. But love," he whispered tauntingly, "you will admit you were very clear on the promise you forced from me, weren't you? I am not to set foot in your room once we are married. But we aren't married yet."

Lacey swore under her breath, fighting to ignore the way he lingered over drying her body. She was desperate to reclaim some measure of pride. "Will you stop? Must you glean more satisfaction by punishing me?" When he didn't respond, she demanded, "How can you swear you love me and then threaten me like some—"

His black forbidding look silenced her. An involuntary shudder swept over her, hearing his softly voiced question.

"So, you finally admit that I do love you?"

"I admit nothing of the kind. You proved I can't fight you. But I won't let you continue to humiliate me, Rafe. I won't stand here and let you handle me as if I were a damn possession of yours. And I—"

". . . and I have heard enough!" He tossed aside the towel in a careless heap on the floor and held her captive. "What is it that you think I'm doing to you? You call this humiliation? You were, are, exhausted from last night and this morning," he stated without pride and caught himself before he said he was sorry. Why bother when she wouldn't believe him. "If you let your wild, hot temper simmer down, you would realize that I would never deliberately hurt you. The only one who can do that is you, Lacey. Is it too much to ask you to do a little sensible reasoning?"

Lacey was weary of the arguing. She didn't know her eyes reflected weariness as well as sorrow for what had come to pass.

Rafe ruthlessly cast aside the instant softening he felt. "Lacey, you forced a promise from me that no man who calls himself one would give to a woman he wants for his own. Don't—I'm warning you now—don't dare push me for more."

He released her, and Lacey stared woodenly at him for a

moment before she snatched up the towel and wrapped it around herself. It was a mistake to think she could control him. Rafe was never malleable. This had to stop, now.

"I can't do it, Rafe. I never wanted you to be a part of my life from the first day. You order me around . . . oh," she wailed in despair, gesturing wildly, "why can't you understand what you've done to me?"

His eyes stalked her like a hunter, and his voice coldly rejected her words. "You gave your word to me. I'm holding you to it. The only thing I understand after listening to you is that you're still afraid to be a woman. My woman, Lacey. Last night—"

"Last night! You dare to remind me about that when I want so desperately to forget?"

"I'll dare that and more for what I want!"

Once again he silenced her with a look so coldly forbidding that Lacey backed away from him. Rafe towered over her, following her steps until she was backed up against the edge of the dresser, warning himself not to touch her.

Cornered, the defiance in her eyes shifted to a look of fear when he placed his hands on either side of her.

"You're a liar, Lacey. I've wasted all the time I can trying to reason with you. Willing or not, you're getting dressed and coming with me. I'll warn you again, love," he bit off with rippling fury, "if you don't come peaceably, I'll swear to take you as you are."

"Why do you want to marry me? We can't even talk civilly to each other."

"*Por Dios, bruja*, it should be plain enough. I want you, and if marriage will give me what I want, you and the Reina, I'll risk anything to have it."

How softly he spoke, but she knew he was raging inside. She could feel the tautness of his body, see his nostrils flare before his eyes became hooded, and she knew he had controlled his fury. Lacey felt safe then. She stared contemptuously, taking deep breaths to steady the turmoil churning inside her. The full realization of what she had agreed to hit her.

"You'll end up hating me, Rafe. I'll hold you to every letter of that promise no matter what you try to do. Even if . . ." Her courage deserted her at the sneer twisting his lips, but Lacey forced herself to finish. "Even if I end up killing you."

His laugh was sudden and mocking. "I'll accept the challenge. At least, princess, neither one of us will ever be bored. Will we, sweet witch?" He stepped back from her. "You have fifteen minutes to get dressed."

Lacey shook with repressed anger, but she grabbed a shortened camisole and pulled it on. He was mad! And she was crazy to go through with this! She felt him watching her as she reached for a pair of black twill pants, knowing she was partly to blame for things reaching this impasse. But let him dare say one word about what she chose to wear . . . just let him dare!

When she finally turned around, Rafe was gone. For some inexorable reason she realized the shirt she wore was the one she had on the first time Rafe kissed her. And now there was so much bitterness between them, Lacey didn't believe there could ever be peace.

She had barely finished brushing the tangles from her damp hair when he returned with her boots. He tossed them to her, and she managed to catch them, sitting down on the floor to put them on. She risked a quick glance at him, taking in the sight of his totally black-clad figure, including a leather vest that fitted him snuggly to perfection. She suddenly realized they were Sy's clothes, new ones, but still his. Rafe gave no indication that he heard her soft cry as he stood calmly buckling on his gunbelt.

Lacey sat there, on the floor, watching his strong hands, gentle with insistence to arouse her, tie the rawhide thongs around his muscled thigh. For some reason the sight of the gun made her harden her own faltering resolve to go through with this mockery of a marriage. Her head lowered, and she admitted she couldn't keep the Reina any other way. Whether Rafe used the sight of the gun as a subtle reminder of that fact, Lacey heeded it.

Standing, reconfirming her thought that the Reina was all that mattered, she took a quick look in her mirror. Outwardly she was presentable, if not suitably dressed for a bride. Shrugging her shoulders, she didn't care, yet moisture blurred her eyes. Some wedding day, she thought. All she needed to do was to strap on her own gun. What a loving couple they would appear. Self-mockery brought no smile of satisfaction to her taut mouth.

The house was deserted as she followed him out to the corral. "I suppose you told Maggie what you planned."

"Sure. I told Fletcher and Bo to spread the word to our men when they reached town. I don't want anyone to miss this wedding, Lacey."

She glanced at the saddled bay stallion. "Where's my horse?"

"You're not riding one."

He was already mounted when she faced him, muttering to herself and heading for the barn. "What does he intend for me to do? Walk all the way like some damn trophy of war? If he thinks—"

She never finished, for his arm caught her easily around the waist as he swung her in front of him. "I think it's best if you ride with me. This way, witch, I'll be sure you don't leave me standing at the altar."

"The idea never crossed my mind, Rafe. Marriage may prove to be the sweetest revenge of all."

"There are times when you tempt me sorely to show you whose revenge, as you call it, will be the sweetest."

"You mean you haven't?"

"No," he stated through gritted teeth as she shifted her weight so her buttocks nestled tight against his thighs.

The light but unmistakably deliberate move of his hand brushing her breast made her stiffen. "Stop it. If we must get this done today, Rafe, there's no further need to prove your point."

"A truce, so there's no question in anyone's mind that you're not being forced into this?"

Dispiritedly she nodded. She would go through with the sham. She couldn't forget the terms of Sy's will. If Rafe married someone else, someone like April, she would lose more than her pride. Rafe would have his title to half the ranch. And April would be living right under her nose. Damn Sy for putting those impossible terms in his will!

He would never allow her to buy him out even if she could raise the money. And there were the outstanding notes to be paid. Why had Sy mortgaged the land?

She was getting what she wanted: the Reina. It had to be enough to make her happy. Then why wasn't she?

Lacey ached as the hours passed before the first wooden buildings came into view. Sy's friend, Bartholomew De Witt, had built his trading post here before Permanent Camp was established. He named it after his sister. She could hear the faint sounds of men's voices shouting wildly, punctuated with gunshots. Rafe had gone out of his way to try and talk, as they had so many times before, of his plans for the ranch. Lacey maintained her silence, unable to talk about her growing fear.

"I guess the races aren't over yet," Rafe murmured as a noisy roar came from the far side of town.

"I wonder if Ragweed won. I hope with both of us gone nothing happens with one man short."

"Those aren't thoughts for a lovely bride."

"It's no blushing virgin you roped and tied down. What do you want from me, pretense?"

"Keep your word," he warned. "You did say you would be the perfect wife in company. I guess I forgot to ask or have you spell out whose idea of a wife you'd play."

She tensed at his barb while he guided the horse past the livery. The goading had to stop, but Lacey could not help herself. "I'm not your wife yet."

"But the time draws close. It's like breaking a wild filly. A man knows when to shorten the rope till she moves easy under his hand."

Lacey's neck bent in defeat for a moment. She gazed at the bunting that hung from every available corner of the weathered buildings as they turned onto the main street. Wagons, buckboards, horses of every size and color, mules, and even a few team of oxen crowded this end of town. She knew that people from nearby had used every available means to attend this shindig, one of many held statewide. Ranchers, farmers, shopkeepers, their families and workers— no one would have missed this. The celebrating would go on long into the night, perhaps even until tomorrow, as it had last year, and there would be more than a few fights between men as they drank hard liquor and gambled at the saloons. Lacey wished she could talk Rafe into leaving once the ceremony was over, but she wanted to avoid being alone with him at home.

Rafe continued down the main street. Two saloons and a cantina farther down blared forth tinny music, men's laughter, and the accompanying high-pitched giggles of women. Rafe finally stopped before Rebecca Lynn's restaurant and boardinghouse.

"Why are we stopping here?" she asked as he set her down and dismounted. "The preacher lives down the other way."

"Is that where you thought we would marry? Don't answer. Rebecca was kind enough to offer her home, and Maggie left early to help her." He tied the reins to the hitching post and drew alongside her. "There are people waiting inside who are happy about our marriage. Don't disappoint them out of spite. Give us a chance."

Lacey wished she could believe him. She longed to be able to trust him again. She tried to smile, but her stiff lips wouldn't obey her. Without another attempt to talk Rafe led her directly around to the back of the house, down the dimly lit hall, and into a small, gracefully furnished sitting room. She was reassured to find it empty. She needed a bit of time to herself. The familiar furnishings of Rebecca's room gave her confidence that nothing had changed—only her mind persisted in telling her that everything had.

"Before I leave you, Lacey, I need to know . . ."

The look in his eyes prompted her answer. "I'm not changing my mind, if that's what's worrying you."

He gave her a long, searching look, then said, "I love you, Lacey. Don't ever forget that."

He was gone before she thought what to answer.

Lacey crossed the room, drawn to the whispered voices coming from Rebecca's bedroom behind the closed door. She heard the excitement in Maggie's voice and someone's stifled giggle.

"She'll love it, Sadie! A beautiful gown for a lovely bride. But I do wish they would get here."

Lacey forced herself to take hold of the doorknob. She

plastered a smile on dry lips, and with a deep, steadying breath she walked in.

Warm sunlight, streaming in through the lace-covered windows, surrounded Lacey along with the happy chattering voices of the three women. Maggie's enveloping hugs and Rebecca's good wishes were ended when Sadie Lewis, the town's only dressmaker, stood up, shaking out the folds of the gown she held.

"Goodness, I didn't think I'd get it finished. Rafe will be pleased, but I hope you like his choice as well."

"His choice, Sadie?" Lacey stared at her.

"It was to be a surprise. I guess it is. He asked me to make it for you. Wasn't a bit over a week ago when he came into town. Morning, if I remember right. He's so in love with you, Lacey."

"Yes. Yes, he is. But you were saying . . ."

"Well, I was in a bit of a tizzy. My boy went off and left me to unpack a whole shipment of cloth and trimmings all the way from St. Louis. Rafe stayed to help me, and then we picked out the material and pattern for your gown."

Lacey was struck by the fact that if Rafe was in town helping Sadie, then April lied about his spending the night with her. But she couldn't have known where they made love unless Rafe told her. It was pain she refused to deal with.

Sadie held the gown against her rail-thin form, her eyes expectant for Lacey's approval. She frowned and turned to Maggie when it was not forthcoming.

Coming to her rescue, Maggie took the gown. "Why, I'll bet she's flustered with all the excitement. You do like it, honey, don't you?"

Lacey couldn't look at it. "Sadie's work is always lovely. Maggie's right. I'm excited and overwhelmed that Rafe—

well, it certainly is a surprise to find out he picked my wedding dress." The last was spoken in a lame voice, and her gaze fled to Maggie, begging help.

Rebecca was puzzled. "But, Lacey, what did you expect to wear to get married in?" Her sweeping gesture indicated Lacey's rough clothes. "Surely not those?"

Lacey nervously smoothed her braid. It was a gesture so unlike her that Maggie quickly ushered her toward the washstand and began giving orders.

In a trance Lacey stood while they fussed over her. Maggie guided her at the last to Rebecca's prized possession, a large pier glass.

Lacey couldn't look at herself. She stared at the oval wood frame, at the carved legs of the mirror, and then at Maggie's urging, she forced her gaze upward.

"Oh, Sadie," she whispered. Pale, creamy lace surrounded her throat and softly gathered and delicately etched lawn material made up the tightly fitted bodice. Her skin, she noticed, glowed warmly beneath the open work while a satin camisole barely hid the full curve of her breasts peering enticingly over the top. Long fitted sleeves ended at her wrists with a shirred ruffle. The soft, full folds of the satin skirt swayed over a diminished hoop as she slowly turned to their sighs of admiration. Rebecca had cut blazing stars and woven them into a crown of flowers that perched high on the cascading curls Maggie had coaxed in her glowing chestnut hair.

Sadie came forward, tears glinting in her eyes. "You are a beautiful bride." Her aged hands trembled a bit as she placed a long matching lace veil over the flowers. She adjusted the material to fall over Lacey's shoulders and then handed her a bouquet of the wildflowers tied with long streamers of blue ribbon.

Maggie dismissed the two women to tell everyone that Lacey was ready.

Lacey dreaded being alone with her. Maggie would not be fooled.

"I didn't have anythin' to give you that's mine, but I've saved this silk hankie that belonged to your mother."

"Maggie! I thought Sy had destroyed everything that belonged to her."

"Well he did. All 'cept this. It ain't much, but I've been savin' it for the day you marry."

Maggie surprised her by reaching up to pinch her cheeks. "There, now you've got color. I ain't askin' why your eyes looked terrified when you walked in, but I'm the closest to a mother you've had. Don't sell Rafe short. You've got tempers hot enough to singe hell betwixt you, but he loves you. Be happy with him."

The full enormity of the step Lacey was taking settled along with a cold knot inside her. Maggie kept talking about love and happiness, the dreams that should be hers, just like they were before. But Rafe had betrayed her trust. How could she remind Maggie of that or that this marriage was a business arrangement?

She couldn't love and trust Rafe again . . . could she?

Maggie stood, waiting for an answer.

Fighting the constricting dryness of her throat, Lacey said, "I'll try, Maggie. That is all I can promise even myself right now."

"Use that damn Garrett pride that Sy instilled in you, even if you ain't his. Let your pride make this a day to cherish. Make your own happiness. Yours and Rafe's."

Happiness? Was there a chance that she and Rafe could have that? How could they, when the words they used against each other like knife thrusts still bled? Why was she doing this? No land could be worth selling herself for.

She wanted Rafe as he had been. Joyful and loving, trustworthy. Rafe, who was waiting to make her his wife. Rafe, who said he loved her.

But Sy Garrett had raised her to know the futility of wishes.

Chapter 18 ═══════

LACEY FOLLOWED MAGGIE down the hall to the front parlor. The walls were draped with white bunting gathered into scallops with bunches of greenery and wildflowers. A blur of faces milled about, becoming silent at her entrance.

Rafe commanded her attention. He was dressed in a superbly fitted black broadcloth suit, shirt ruffles crisp and white against the faint tan of his skin. Her gaze dropped at his smile, and she noticed the gleaming boots, his well-muscled legs, and the gold embroidered vest. He had truly taken Sy Garrett's place, for the clothes were Sy's, never worn. Maggie walked ahead of her and joined Rafe at the minister's side.

Lacey felt gentle hands taking her elbows on either side. She looked up to see first Bo, then Fletcher. They, too, wore stiff new suits.

"We both figured it's our right to give the bride away," Bo huskily murmured.

"Yeah," Fletcher agreed with a catch in his gruff voice. "We're the ones that seen you growed."

Lacey touched each of their weathered cheeks, her eyes misty, memories crowding her.

"Sy would've been proud of you, gal," Fletcher added.

Lacey lowered her lashes as someone began to play a soft melody on Rebecca's spinet. Bitterly she thought of how proud Sy would have been that she had put the Reina first. It was what he had taught her to do.

They walked her the few steps to Rafe's side. Lacey braced herself to hear the words that would change her life forever. Listening to Rafe's strong, clear voice answer the minister, she prayed her own voice would not betray her.

The ring he slipped on her finger was warm, but Lacey saw it through a haze. She glanced up at Rafe, saw his lips moving, but no sound reached her. There was a somber set to his features, and she was his, to love, to cherish, to obey, to have and to hold, for now and forever. Was there a forever? Had she responded? She must have, for Rafe's head was descending, his lips lowering to hers.

He stole her breath with that kiss. It was a lingering, tasting caress that told of ecstasy, possession, and satisfaction. It spoke of a satiated hunger that could flame again at the slightest provocation. Lacey trembled under the impact of it, finding his kiss strangely soothing after the morning's chaos.

Catcalls and whistles slowly penetrated Lacey's dazed state. Rafe lifted his lips, and people were suddenly surrounding them, slapping his back, shaking his hand, a few shyly kissing Lacey's cheek with their offered good wishes.

Music blared forth, its tempo lively, and Lacey turned around. Rafe's hand around her waist steadied her. April, Evan, and Tom Darcy stood barring their way. She was never more sure than at this moment how much April hated her.

"Rafe," April murmured, "now you have everything you wanted."

"April, I warned you," Evan grated in a harsh whisper before either Rafe or Lacey responded.

Tom Darcy smiled, ignored his children, and shook

Rafe's hand. "Don't mind my gal. She ain't come out a loser when she sets her mind to havin' somethin'. But I'll admit I'm sorry it worked out this way."

Lacey thought his look at Rafe implied so much more, but she wasn't given a chance to hear their conversation, for Evan drew her from Rafe's side. His body blocked off her view of the three of them.

"Don't let April spoil today for you," he whispered.

Bewildered, Lacey stood on tiptoe to peer over his shoulder. Her heels hit the polished wood floor the second she saw April kissing Rafe. Evan's soft "Let me kiss the bride" added to her dismay, since Rafe did nothing to stop April. The light touch of Evan's lips met her cool, unyielding ones. How could Rafe? She closed her eyes and gave herself almost fiercely, despairingly to the press of Evan's mouth searching her own. She snapped out of the haze that had held her enthralled, for Evan's arms were holding her tight, and she knew he was reading more into this kiss than she meant.

He released her the moment she tensed, and Lacey blindly turned away. She snatched a drink from a tray Rebecca carried and tossed it down, choking on the liquor but needing its warmth. A crowd of well-wishers drew her aside, and she went, desperate to be away from Rafe. She forced herself to nod and smile, hoping that was what people wanted from her, for none of their remarks, none of their insistent questions made sense to her.

She was almost to the double-door archway, thinking only of escaping, when Curt suddenly appeared, barring her way. His usual immaculate appearance showed the ravages of a hard, dusty ride.

"I'm too late. I rode out to the ranch, hoping to stop you, Lacey."

"Why? It's a marriage of convenience. We both wanted

the Reina, and this seemed the only way to settle the matter. Rafe and I agreed on the terms, and you can see for yourself," she stated with an airy wave in Rafe's direction, "he's not letting marriage interfere."

Curt followed her gaze across the room to where Rafe stood off to one side talking with April and several other women. But he also noticed the fierce glitter in Lacey's eyes when April, with a laugh, rested her hand almost possessively on Rafe's arm.

"Are you?" Curt asked, then clarified at her puzzled look. "Prove that marriage doesn't change anything. Prove it to him and perhaps to yourself. I wanted you for my bride."

"I am sorry, Curt. Don't make a scene here. Please."

He took her into his arms, his lips urgent, taking her mouth. The fierceness of his emotions quickly communicated themselves to Lacey. She heard voices rise and then quiet as she firmly pushed Curt away.

And suddenly Rafe was at her side, his voice harsh and sarcastic to her ear. "If you're trying to make me jealous, Lacey, don't bother. But you're making a sorry spectacle of yourself, my too-new wife. Your promise, remember?"

He forced her from Curt's side with a firm arm around her waist that Lacey was sure appeared a loving embrace as she encountered curious gazes. Rafe wore his most forbidding look, which held her quiet, and she wondered if he was jealous. She dismissed the thought. He hadn't stopped Evan from kissing her.

Halfway across the room he deposited her like unwanted baggage beside Sadie and the McCord sisters.

"Our guests need your attention, love." His fingers squeezed in warning. "I'm sure, my dear little wife, these lovely ladies must be dying to hear how you beguiled me till I had no choice but to marry you." With a graceful but most mocking bow and a last warning look at Lacey, he left them.

"My, he certainly is a bold one, isn't he?" Emma McCord remarked with a wishful gleam in her eyes.

"He's dressed the gentleman, but I sense the savage beneath, Emma." With a delicate shiver Lula Mae turned to Lacey. "I almost envy you, but tell me, dear, is it true that his blood is . . . well . . ." She faltered to a stop under Lacey's furious glare.

"My husband's mother was Mexican. That's true. But he is more of a man than any pure-blooded *Anglo* in this room."

"Oh, I'll attest to that."

Lacey spun around, facing the unexpected source of support. April Darcy smiled and fluttered open her lace fan.

"And if you good ladies want to know more about Rafe, I'm sure he'll not only answer your questions, he'll be happy to demonstrate what Mexican blood does for a man."

The McCord sisters went off in a huff, and Sadie gazed after them, uncertain of following. Once again April decided the matter.

"Rebecca would be grateful for your help in the kitchen. Lacey and I have a few things to talk about."

"I suppose I should thank you for defending my husband," Lacey said.

"Don't. I didn't do it for you but for Rafe. And you were right. He is more of a man than any other in this room."

"But you shouldn't have goaded them, April. You only fed them gossip."

"Don't be a fool, Lacey. Married to Rafe, you'd best get accustomed to it." April gathered her pale blue silk skirt in hand and pushed her way through the crowd to one corner. "Come along, Lacey. We haven't finished talking."

More annoyed than curious, Lacey followed her.

"Rafe's a man that invites constant speculation about himself, Lacey. And we both know why he married you. But I wonder if you really know what he gained today?"

"Do you love him, April? Or are you so eaten with jealousy—"

"It doesn't matter." She fanned herself in an agitated manner, looking over Lacey's shoulder. "Think whatever you like. I know Rafe only married you to get his hands—"

". . . on the Reina that much sooner. You're not telling me anything I don't already know." Lacey was a bit shocked to find the words came easily, in a calm, almost bored voice, but inside, she hurt to say them.

"You really are a fool! Rafe only married you to get his hands on the money. A bonus, Lacey. Money that Sy left him," she stressed, relishing the sudden blanching of Lacey's face. "You didn't know, did you?"

Across the room Rafe, who had been watching the two women who seemed to bedevil him no matter what he did, caught the slight sway of Lacey's body. She turned at that moment, her complexion ghostly, scaring him. Mutely and, it seemed, blindly, she searched for him. He was drawn to her, his gut screaming a warning, his steps hurried.

Curt seemed to have the same idea, for he reached Lacey just as Rafe did. There was no effort on Curt's part to hide his animosity for Rafe while his attentions were for Lacey.

Rafe refused to allow him to lead her away, distractedly noticing that Lacey wouldn't even look at him now.

He couldn't know that she did not trust herself to risk meeting his eyes while April's words were still ringing in her ears.

Curt was not about to back down this time. Lacey's silent appeal firmed his purpose. "Surely, Rafe, you don't intend to deny me some time with her. She is obviously upset, but more, I need to talk to her. Be gracious enough to step aside like a gentleman."

Where she found the strength to speak then, Lacey didn't know, she was just grateful that she could. "Goodness, Curt, we are not living in the dark ages. Rafe will not be dictating who I may speak to." She risked a quick glance at Rafe. His eyes lost a bit of their forbidding heat, and his mouth quirked in an odd sort of smile. With a light little laugh, determined that no one, not April, and most of all not Rafe, should see how devastated she was, Lacey placed her arm on Curt's. "We have our little agreement, dear."

"Lacey, I think you should—"

"Come now, my dear husband, you won't deny me a few minutes with Curt?" Her hazel eyes were sparkling with spite. "April will keep you amused, won't she?"

With a jaunty toss of her head she smiled up at Curt. "Shall we find a quiet corner? It's much too crowded."

Curt guided her toward the open doors and out into the hallway. Lacey held on to his arm, refusing to think about what April said. But she really didn't want to be alone with Curt. When she said as much, he stopped.

"Lacey, I·do have to talk to you. I just got back from Austin. You did ask—"

"Not now. I don't want to hear or know any more about Rafe. That damn report was enough."

"No, it couldn't have been. You married him, didn't you?"

Rebecca and Maggie chose that moment to walk by them. Lacey forced a reassuring smile for both women, but Curt spoke to them.

"I was just telling Lacey how pleased Sy would have been with all you have done for her."

"It's no more than she and Rafe deserve," Maggie

answered, noting Lacey's bright eyes and flushed cheeks. Rebecca urged her on, and Maggie reluctantly left them.

"Curt," Lacey began as soon as they were out of earshot, "you knew weeks ago that Rafe and I would marry. I made no secret about it. Fletcher said you were with Spanish Mike the day he told him about it."

"But Fletcher didn't tell you that I gave him a message for you to wait until I came back?" He grabbed her arms and pushed her back against the wall. "I told him I had to go to Austin. Unfortunately, my trip had to be delayed. Did he tell you?"

"No. No, he never said anything. But I still don't—"

"The letter, Lacey. Remember the letter the judge withheld from you? I went crazy when I got to the ranch this morning and found out you were getting married today." Pulling the envelope from his inner jacket pocket, he handed it to her. "Please, when you read this, keep in mind that I tried to warn you."

First April and now Curt making aspersions about Rafe. Lacey knew she had forgotten about the letter. She had forgotten or pushed aside everything but those few glorious weeks when Rafe filled her every thought. She didn't want to cope with this now, but Curt pressed her fingers around the letter.

"Go on," he urged. "I'll make sure you're left undisturbed." Her hesitation made him add, "If you don't read it, you'll never know why Rafe pushed so hard for this marriage."

Lacey once again found herself defending Rafe. "If this is a ploy on your part to hurt either of us—"

"Is this what that bastard has done? Has he managed to destroy your trust in me?"

Her eyes flared darkly, pinning him with a condemning stare. "Rafe never spoke against you."

"I'm not talking about words. That man gave you the Reina. It's what you've always wanted. No one knows that better than I. I just can't believe you would easily forget that I love you."

"I never forgot, Curt. I can't give you the love you want." Tears sparkled wetly in her eyes before she turned away. Clutching the letter, she walked to Rebecca's sitting room, thankful that Curt did not follow. She wanted to read the letter from Sy, and yet something warned her to throw it away. For a wild moment Lacey wished that Rafe were there, holding her, kissing her senseless. Staring at the envelope, Lacey knew she was afraid of what it might reveal. The thought that Sy may have explained the circumstances of her birth and the reason why he called her his daughter gave her the courage to rip the envelope open.

Sy's bold scrawl covered the single page she unfolded. It was dated almost a year before he died.

Lacey,

If you're reading this, I'm gone and can't be asking for forgiveness. I wronged you not telling you the truth all these years. You got to make your own choice about what you feel for me. I raised you hard.

I know it. I'm still asking you to be kind to my boy when the judge finds him. You ain't never had a hungry belly, and I ain't never taken a strap to your back. I know you're wondering what I done with the money I got from mortgaging the Reina. It's only fair that I be the one to tell you.

It's all for Rafe. Not all at once, mind you, I ain't that much of a fool. The boy gets fifteen thousand in gold when he sets foot on the Reina. It ain't much for the years I didn't have him, but if he don't want part of the land, the money gives him a start somewheres else. If he stays and works out his first year and marries you, Lacey, to keep the Reina whole, the judge will give him another ten thousand.

If things don't work out like I want, the boy gets this extra money at the end of his first year. Good beef prices will pay most of the notes. If not, I hope he'll do the right thing by you and the Reina.

Keep the land I loved safe. Your mother was a weak woman. I couldn't raise you to be the same. She never learned to love the land and you did. I ain't got the right, but I'm asking just the same. Give my boy a chance.

                              Seymour Garrett

It was long minutes before Lacey once again heard the music and noise from the front parlor. The letter lay where it had fallen from her nerveless fingers as she was forced to sit down. Her legs were shaking badly, she attempted to draw them together to still the involuntary moves, but it was hopeless. She couldn't seem to make herself believe what she had read. But Rafe's voice came from her memory, asking about the letter. And then, once they had become lovers, he never mentioned it again.

Now she knew why. Blessedly, her mind stopped all thoughts of Rafe. She felt numb, unable to move or feel or think.

But as the minutes went by and Lacey did not return, Rafe grew anxious. Someone had come in with a fiddle, and another man added his harmonica to the lively tune played on the spinet. The doors were open, people milled about, but he couldn't find Lacey. Rafe began to push his way through the crowd, coming out into the hallway. His gut was screaming a warning for him to hurry and find her. He shoved several people aside and began opening the doors, growing desperate when the rooms proved empty.

Fletcher was right behind him, as was Bo and Evan. Rafe opened the door to Rebecca's sitting room, saw Lacey, and shouted for everyone to leave them alone. His look toward them was blackly forbidding as he slammed the door closed. He hesitated before facing her, but when he did, her blank stare had him frantic to find the reason. He spied the paper lying beneath the folds of her gown and had to force himself forward to pick it up. Rafe's curse was swift and sure for Curt's duplicity.

"Lacey?" he whispered as she focused on him. Her eyes glowed with unusual brilliance, her teeth gnawed her bottom lip, and when he reached for her hands, Rafe found them cold. She offered no resistance as he pulled her up into his arms. He found himself searching for a way to evict a response from her, settling on invoking her pride. "You have April believing that you ran from your own wedding because of her. Deserting your husband has caused speculation, Lacey. You did promise to be a proper wife in public."

She weakly pushed against his chest, and Rafe tightened his hold. He was suddenly afraid to let her go. He sensed what a fragile hold she had on herself, and the memory rushed forth of the first day he had held her. Shocked as she had been, Lacey had not appeared this remote and cold. He could feel the chill of her body. "Answer me, Lacey. I can't do anything unless you talk to me." Pressing light, almost desperate kisses against her hair, he murmured incoherently.

Lacey felt the coldness slowly leave her body in Rafe's embrace. She barely managed to tilt her head up to look at him. Searching his features, staring deeply into his eyes, finding them concerned, she tried to deny what April had told her and what she had read for herself. From somewhere she found the courage to speak.

"Did you know what was in the letter, Rafe?"

He closed his eyes for a moment, bitter with the thought of Curt holding on to the letter, waiting until now to show it to her. He had forgotten it, forgotten everything when he had finally claimed her for his own. And afterward, he had believed it wouldn't matter, that she loved him without any questions. First April, now Curt. But why were they enemies bent on destroying what he and Lacey had?

The dark, scowling look he wore, the lips compressed with anger told Lacey she no longer had to hear an answer. Yet a devil nagged her to know the truth even as she wished she could forget. Her lips seemed to form the questions of their own volition. "You knew what Sy wrote to me all this time, didn't you? You knew before the judge ever brought you to the Reina. But why did you lie? Why did you let me believe it was me you wanted?" A dark flush of anger colored his cheeks. She struggled for breath and freedom, both terrified and furious that he wouldn't let her go.

"Don't touch me, Rafe. You're an arrogant sidewinder!"

Attuned to his moods, Lacey knew his control slipped.

"Lower your voice, Lacey. Or are you hoping that someone will come in and make you a widow? Someone like Curt? Let me explain why I never told you. Don't deny me this."

"Deny you?" In disbelief she stared up at him. "I withheld nothing from you. I made it all easy, didn't I? You conniving bas—"

"Stop it!" He released her, fighting the urge to shake her until she would listen to him. "You don't know what you're saying. It wasn't like that."

"What was it like? What excuse lessens the hurt? You

took everything from me!" She took a hurried step back seeing the sudden blaze of fury in his eyes as his hand snaked out to grab hold of her. "Go on, Rafe," she taunted contemptuously. "Use force. You've already proved that brute strength can silence me." There was no rationalizing why she gloated to see him stop. Her pain needed release, and she lashed out at him.

"How does it feel to know he mortgaged the ranch to make you twenty-five thousand dollars richer? Did you think I wouldn't find out? You used those damn notes as a wedge to force me to marry you! Were you afraid that once I knew the terms, I'd kill you before I let you near me? Did you," she grated after a deep shuddering breath, "think I'd come to you willingly, husband mine, knowing that you were paid to marry me? Did you?" she screamed.

She could see the barbs were striking deep by the thunderous rage in his glittering eyes that narrowed to slits. His jaw was clenched tight as if he had to stop himself from uttering a sound. Lacey saw the muscle twitch in his cheek, but she wasn't afraid of him. Not now when she had him at her mercy.

"Nothing to say? Moments ago you were begging me to listen to you. You're so quick with caustic remarks, Rafe." Lacey lifted her chin, her eyes challenging. "You should have told me the truth. I was honest. I told you I only agreed to this marriage to get the Reina."

"Did you?" His voice was softly brutal, and his look denied her solace from her statement.

"You make it easy to hate you, but I'm sure you already know that." Her voice cracked under the rigid constraint she demanded of herself. "You asked me this morning if selling myself for the Reina was worth it. You made me feel like a whore. Tell me, Rafe, since you get the money now, does that make you one, too?"

"Lacey," he warned, tossing the crumpled letter to the floor and almost lunging at her. His hands clenched at his sides, and he turned, grabbing hold of a small side chair.

Lacey stared in horrified silence as his knuckles whitened with his fierce hold. Her gaze flew upward, drawn by the force of the fury that gripped him. Once again she stepped back and away, afraid of what he would do. She stifled her cry with one hand, the other clutched her gown as Rafe lost control.

It was the chair that shattered under the force of his throw, and he cursed her with a despising tone.

"Basta ramera! Por Dios el bruja mi destruir."

More than the chair had shattered. Lacey's frozen state dissolved. Her laughter was brittle before she thanked him for teaching her his dialect. "Whore, yes. But I only wish I was a witch that could destroy you. And you, dearest, are the devil's own bastard." She flinched as his rage once more exploded, a rage that reached out across the room to her before he started toward her and then abruptly stopped.

"Then we make a fine pair, lovely wife. The desirable bitch and her bastard. I won't waste time arguing or explaining. You won't believe me. But I got what I wanted from the first." The set closed expression on her face made his voice hard and flat.

"You're my wife. I don't care why you think I married you. I tried to tell you about the money the night I came back from Austin. But you drove everything from my mind but having you. It's done. We're married. You can't forget it."

"Perhaps not. But I can despise you for destroying any love I had for you. And I can hate you for laughing with April over what you did to me." Determined to prove that she wasn't afraid of him, Lacey stepped closer. "April warned me before Curt ever gave me the letter."

"And you believed her? But of course. You believe everything and anything April or anyone else tells you before me." Rafe couldn't help the incredulous tone of his voice. He was sure the shock of what she told him was written all over his face. He wanted to put his hands on her and silence her the only way he knew how, but even as he desperately tried to think of how April knew about the money, Lacey refused to give him time.

"Once I warned you that if you forced me into doing something desperate again, I would kill you. Don't make the mistake of thinking I didn't mean it."

"Don't you know by now that your threats mean nothing? You want to believe I betrayed you." The words came from behind gritted teeth as he tried once more for a semblance of control and found himself losing the battle.

"That's not true. I can't do anything else," she whispered brokenly.

"Be still! The money wasn't important. Not after I saw you." Dragging his gaze away from her, Rafe pushed his hair back with an impatient move. He was damned if he would beg her to listen to him. He had already made himself a fool over Lacey. And yet, glancing at her again, he couldn't make himself leave.

Lacey heard his impassioned voice replay in her mind. She didn't want to listen, but it nagged her. If the money wasn't important, why had April taunted her about it? And she found herself asking him as much. "If you didn't tell April, then who did, Rafe?"

"Damned if I know." His lowered lashes hid the lie in his eyes. He was sure that Curt was behind it. But why? He couldn't think clearly with her near him. "It doesn't matter. None of this does."

"How can you say that?" She turned her back on him, and he was behind her in an instant, forcing her around.

"Did you think about why Sy made that offer to me?" He held her arms at her sides, shaking her. Lacey tossed her head from side to side as the only way she could answer him. Her throat was closing and her cry was a whimper. Rafe stopped shaking her but he didn't release her.

"He did it to make up for the years he denied me. Besides, you know I would've gotten the money anyway after I took title to the ranch. It didn't matter that I married you."

Her face whitened, but Rafe was beyond caring how he hurt her. "Do you know me so little that you believed any man, dead or alive, could force me or bribe me into doing something I didn't want for myself? Why did you let what happened with Curt destroy all that's soft inside you?"

"No more!"

"Why the hell do I have to be the one to pay for it?" He released her, and she brushed past him, but barely reached the door when the controlled violence in his voice stopped her. "Don't leave, Lacey."

She swung around to face him and knew she should have been warned. He hadn't made a sound, but he was right in front of her. His broad chest filled her sight, the wide, crisp white ruffles of his shirtfront brushed her cheek when she refused to look up. Lacey knew she couldn't last another moment in the same room with him. Not when she felt the heat of his rage. Yet she strained to hear him whisper.

"Your pride bent before. I know I can bend it again. The marriage stands. If you're foolish enough to believe that money drove me, Lacey, you're wrong." She looked up, and he smiled. "I wanted you the moment I saw you standing like a princess, facing them down. I still want you. After last night we both know there's nothing to stop me from having you, is there?"

Chapter 19 ════════════

A STRANGE NEW expression crept into his eyes, leaving Lacey bewildered and distracted. He made no move to touch her, but she felt herself drawn against him even as her mind screamed in denial. Every nerve ending warned her to run, but she refused to listen. His hand shot out, his fingers tangling in her hair, holding her still. She had to close her eyes against the blaze that sprung to life in his. He pulled the lace veil from her head, and Lacey shivered as it barely touched her shoulder.

"Don't . . . touch me," she pleaded, feeling the heat of his breath on her cheek, his lips slanting to press a kiss on her face. "I won't let you do this, Rafe. I can't."

"Why? You're my wife. You were willing enough before we were married. Remember?" he asked cruelly.

How could he steal her strength of will to fight him? Lacey cursed her traitorous body before he kissed her, taking her breath away. She reeled under the demanding onslaught of his lips, feeling the intense, insatiable need searching for an answer. He had taken her deep in a moment's time to the fiercely wild heights he alone had shown her, but never, never like this. She tried to force herself to deny him, but her mouth was already parting in soft surrender. She hated him for the savage hunger that made her reach her arms up to clasp him closer, her fingers threading his hair, wanting more even as she damned herself.

His sudden release stunned her.

Lacey didn't open her eyes. The sounds of their hard breaths mingled and filled her ears along with a roaring sound that left her weak. It was bitter to know that Rafe would always have this power over her. Only in his arms, with his lips sweetly silken or savagely tormenting her until she caught fire, was there any appeasement, and even then, she knew, it was only a short respite.

Controlling himself with difficulty, Rafe cursed her. He hated the pallor of her face, the strained look of her features, but he knew he had reached the end of his patience with her. She was a weakness inside him, heating his blood just by being near. He wanted to strip the gown he'd spent hours choosing for her and take her now. Heat ran like a fever through him, the need so strong he trembled like the woman he held in his arms. But Rafe found himself denying it and in doing so made himself taunt her unmercifully.

"That should prove what I'll do if you dare me. Later my dear wife, I'll begin the lessons in what I expect. Right now you're going to come with me and show yourself before there's more talk of your running off alone. I don't want anyone raising the question of why you want to hide. Or," he added with a sardonic twist to his lips, "we could explain you had a case of bridal-night nerves."

"I don't care what you say, Rafe, just leave me. I can't face anyone now, and I don't care what they think."

"But I do," he answered harshly, impatiently setting her hair into some semblance of order until she pushed him away.

He stood aside, a tiny half smile tugging at the corner of his mouth, and watched her walk unsteadily toward the small mirror hanging on the wall across from him. He had the damnedest urge to kiss her until the dejected, almost sullen look disappeared, but managed to fight it down. He knew how far he could push himself, and he had lost control once. The next time he might not hold himself back at all.

Lacey fumbled with the pins in her hair, thankful she had managed to put distance between them. He was right about them going back to face the others but not for the reasons he mentioned. She was aware of what would happen if she remained alone with him and knew she didn't have the strength to fight him.

Narrow-eyed, she stared at herself. There was later to contend with, and she worried about him keeping his word. His threats clouded her thoughts, and she wished she had a gun. Her hate was strong enough to kill him. No, she would make this marriage her sweet revenge. Rafe wanted her, he had proved it. All she had to do was refuse to yield. That would be the first blow to his pride. She had to dismiss the thought of her own surrender to his kiss. Her mind whirled in turmoil, leaving her unable to concentrate, and she found his implacable face staring at her, his eyes dark, emotionless.

Deliberately she fussed with one curl, chancing another quick look, and saw he grew impatient. She didn't dare risk his coming near her again, and that spurred her to hurry.

Lacey stepped back, realizing that she had done the best she could. While far from the elaborate style that Maggie had arranged, her hair was presentable. Besides, her veil would cover it. Turning, she flushed as she wondered if Rafe had read her thoughts. It unnerved her, for the flimsy lace was draped over his fingertips extended toward her.

Snatching it from him, she jumped just as someone knocked.

Rafe shot her a warning look before slowly moving to open it. She could see over his shoulder that Maggie stood there ready to knock again. In turn Maggie peered around Rafe's shoulder as if to reassure herself that Lacey was there.

"We'll be out in a few minutes, Maggie, just as soon as Lacey finishes fixing her hair."

Maggie's smile died under the hard flatness of his look. She knew Curt had something to do with Lacey's disappearance, but she was worried about the tension she felt. "Well, then, let me by, and I'll help her."

"There's no need. I managed myself." Lacey knew she couldn't handle Maggie's knowing how wrong everything was.

Maggie glanced from one to the other. Lacey's voice was brittle sounding, and Rafe had a forbidding look on his face that stopped her from asking questions.

"I only came lookin' for the two of you 'cause folks are sayin' it's funny you both ain't around. 'Sides, Rebecca brought out the cake she baked, an' we can't cut it without you there. After all," she scolded, "it's your weddin' we're supposed to be celebratin'."

Lacey hurried to Rafe's side, and he took her elbow as he urged her out the door. Maggie glared at them and then preceded them.

"Try and pretend you're enjoying yourself, princess," Rafe leaned close to whisper. "If you don't, you'll have them all wondering if the reason you're being skittish is that you're worried about tonight."

He had, he saw in an instant, pushed her too far.

Beyond caring if Maggie or anyone else heard them or saw them, Lacey jerked her arm free. With a look of smoldering, insolent defiance, she mocked, "Perhaps that is exactly what I want them to think. Or I may, before I'm finished with you, have everyone wondering just who I'll spend my wedding night with!"

His lips curled in a smile, and his voice held a note of

suppressed amusement. "Still making threats? I thought we were finished with them. But I see by the look of you I was wrong. Another attempt to make me jealous? It doesn't matter, Lacey. Before the night is over, we will both know where we stand."

"Don't be ridiculous. I only meant that I don't care for your empty threats, either. And if you think to stand guard over me every instant while you can be free to do as you please, you are the one who is wrong." The blaze in his eyes went through her like a jolt. He slipped his arm casually around her waist, pulling her against him, forcing an unwilling admission. "I don't understand you at all, Rafe."

"Don't you?"

"No. And stop kissing my ear when you lean so close to talk to me. People are staring."

He saw that was true. Heads were turning as they reached the archway.

Lacey forced a smile in acknowledgment. She resented his composure as she risked a quick glance up at him. He tightened his arm warningly around her waist before he leaned down once again.

"I thought you didn't care. I certainly don't. Let them look. Perhaps the tender-hearted among them will think how much in love we are, and some women here might even envy you."

"Envy me? If they knew you the way I do, Rafe, that's the last thing they would feel."

Rafe didn't answer, and Lacey was forced to wonder if it was true. He seemed to go out of his way to be charming to everyone around them. Lacey automatically introduced him to the townfolk crowding them, offering congratulations. She heard the brittle sound of her voice, felt herself smile, and thought of it being someone else.

Yet, as the hours slipped by, she had no chance to carry out her threat, for Rafe refused to be drawn from her side. He wouldn't give anyone a chance to detain them for more than a few minutes, just kept her moving from one group to the next.

Now, as night fell, the brilliant flashes of the fireworks were over, spent shells from the guns that had roared in unison with them lay trampled in the dirt of the street, and Lacey along with Rafe mixed with the crowd outside. She had insisted he take her out there, and she couldn't help but notice that he had been steadily drinking, although he showed no sign of it.

Small bonfires lit the street with a tawdry glow. From the saloons came wild yells and sporadic gunfire that punctured the tinny music from pianos and fiddles. Rafe's whispered innuendos kept her in a fever-pitched state, alternating between anger, despair, and her own rising frustration. To combat the feelings his nearness caused, she began drinking more of the raw whiskey being passed around, disregarding his constant amused stare directed at her while he made no move to stop her.

Loud, boisterous music grated on Lacey's ears. Flushed and feeling slightly dizzy, she was spun from one partner to another. Rafe, after the first few, refused to dance with her again, and she couldn't have been happier with his decision. Her control was strained, having to bear his warm breath fanning her face as he held her far too close.

She caught sight of him now, lounging with a lazy grace that reminded her of a hunting cat, against the wooden post of the hitching rail, arms folded over his chest. His eyes, hooded in the shadowed light, never once left her. She was glad that he made no move to stop her. She was just drunk enough, just reckless enough to cause a scene, and perhaps her mood communicated itself to him, for her eyes taunted and dared him when she was swung past, and his gaze mocked her.

Barely able to grasp the next man's hand held out to her, Lacey swore she didn't care what he did, as long as he left her alone, and forced herself to concentrate on following the wild steps of her partner.

Glancing around, she suddenly realized that not one of the faces were familiar to her. They could have been men from other ranches or farms, but they were definitely men she didn't know. In her reckless state she felt no fear, not then.

Not even minutes later when spinning wildly around until she could not catch her breath, she found to her disgust that she was suddenly locked in an enveloping bear hug that revolted her. Pressed against the soft, paunchy body of a whiskered, drunken cowhand, she tried yelling over the noise for him to release her. Struggling in earnest now against the desperate hold he had on her, Lacey knew her movements were slowed by the amount of liquor she had consumed. She tried to avoid his slobbering lips so determined to capture her own as he crushed her tighter. Her long, full-skirted gown tangled around her legs as if it, too, damned her for being so stubborn to insist on being out here as she twisted her head wildly.

Catching sight of Lacey on the far shadowed side of the rough circle of dancers, Rafe didn't hesitate to move. She was, he knew, drunk and angry enough to get herself in real trouble. The kind, he thought, only a hell-bent witch like Lacey could invite from any man. Already pushing his way through the crowd, he couldn't help thinking what a merry chase this unreasonable, prideful woman would lead him, and at the same time he cursed her for forcing him to make the first move.

Closer now, he saw she barely managed to avoid the

man's lips, her hands caught between their bodies. Another man appeared at her side, both pulling her toward the darkened alley, even as they appeared to be arguing over her.

Rafe was telling himself he should teach her a lesson and let her get herself out of this when he was forced to untangle himself from the two women who were dragging him into the dancing. He hated the thought of any man putting his hands on Lacey, even if he wanted to punish her. In the sudden break of the crowd a flare of light showed her eyes, frantic with fear.

Feeling capable of murder, Rafe shoved his way clear. He swore to himself that he let her get the best of his temper when all he wanted to do was keep her beside him. But this was the last straw. She had taken his carelessly spoken words as a challenge. With a slightly questioning lift to his brow, the mocking smile she hated creasing his lips, he finally stood beside her.

"It seems you are in need of rescuing, princess," he stated pleasantly enough while his gaze warned her to silence.

At the sound of his voice Lacey caught herself from letting the grateful smile spread further. She managed to remove the shocked, almost dazed cowboy's hands from her arm. She glared up at Rafe, hating the grin he returned until the other man stepped between them.

"Go find yore own woman," he drunkenly demanded, weaving on his feet. "This here one is spoke for. Ain't she, Jacob?"

"I am not taken by either of you, or by him." Lacey gestured pointedly at Rafe, knowing she sounded like a belligerent shrew. Through slightly blurred eyes she saw the move Rafe made toward his gun. She tried to remember when he had put it on, but her fuzzy mind wouldn't clear. With one hand she held her head and raised her eyes to his face. Rafe was glaring down with a frightening intensity at the older man, who had also caught his deliberate move.

"Hell. Ain't no cause for that. Silver Lady's got plenty of girls jus' like this one. Prettier, too, iffen you ask me." Yet even as he slurred his speech, he took a step back, his own hand dropping down to his side, where it hung suspended over his holstered gun.

"You're mistaken about the lady. . . . She's my wife."

The deadly calm warning in his voice cut through Lacey's befuddled state. "Rafe?"

"Hold on there. I ain't lookin' for trouble. Ain't no way I coulda known."

Lacey had the grace to blush, knowing what he was thinking, what they all must have thought with the way she was being passed from one man to another out there. Dancing and drinking just like the girls from the saloons, who even now, she saw, were drifting close to hear what was happening.

"Now you both understand," Rafe murmured in that same tone. Without another word or glance he grabbed Lacey's arm and pulled her away, ignoring the crowd and the whispers. "Damn you, woman! Do I have to put you under lock and key? Do you have any idea what could have happened to you just now if I hadn't decided to get you? What's more, do you have any idea of what the hell you look like? I can't even blame them for what they thought."

Her abrupt stop almost made him stumble. Sweetly then, she slurred, "Are you makin' noises like a straitlaced husband already? I was havin' fun. That's right, fun—till you showed up. I wanna go have some more."

"Hush up, Lacey. You're drunk and—"

". . . and I demand to know where you're takin' me."

"Not where I'd like to, that's for damn sure," came his terse reply.

"I'm not done with celebratin'," she insisted, pulling away from him. "Ain't every day I get bought."

Her harping on that made him clench his jaw. The deep slur to her words told him she had had more to drink than he had thought, and she was itching to fight with him again. He refused to answer. But she stood firm when he tried to grab hold of her to force her to walk along with him.

Suddenly so irritably tired of it all, Lacey tried to swing at him with her clenched fist.

Her hand merely grazed his shoulder. He wanted to laugh but instead caught her wrists. "Your hands are like ice. Come inside and I'll find something to warm you."

Lacey stared up at him. She managed to tilt her head, heard his calm tone, felt his almost impersonal hold on her arm while her heart was thudding madly and wanted to push him away. She couldn't quite coordinate her thoughts to make her body obey. She dreaded the thought of being somewhere alone with him. "What's inside? Where? I wanna go home." She hated the note of desperation in her voice but couldn't help it. "Rafe, take me home."

"Stop struggling with me, Lacey. It's no use. You know that. Now, be a good girl and walk along beside me, or I'll be forced to carry you."

"No. I don't want your hands on me." She was afraid of the sudden smile taunting her, and the quick jerk away from him made her aware that he knew it. "Tell me when we're going back to the Reina."

He didn't want to get rough with her and shifted his gaze away, catching sight of the same two men who were ready to fight over Lacey standing off to one side, watching them. He puzzled a moment on their looks, but her darting move brought his full attention back to her. Lacey stilled under his look.

She couldn't know he was realizing her elaborate curls

were streaming wildly down her back or that her eyes glittered with desperation in the blanching face she lifted up toward him. And slowly, so that she would have no trouble understanding his meaning, he answered her.

"We're not going back to the Reina tonight. Rebecca was kind enough to keep one of her rooms free for our use. Sort of a wedding present. Besides," he added roughly, "you, my charming little wife, are in no condition to ride home."

The dawning realization of exactly what he was telling her made Lacey wail. "You can't mean that! You promised me. Oh! Damn you to hell, you devil's spawn! You never . . . What are you doing?" He scooped her up into his arms until she felt her ribs would break. Hitting him, she cried out, "You never intended to keep that damn promise you made me, did you? You liar! You no-good stinking liar!"

They were already in the darkened alley between the boardinghouse and the dressmaker's shop. She hated being held against him, hated the light scent of bay rum whirling about her head, hated the enticing warmth of his breath against her cheek, but most of all, Lacey hated herself for the seeping heat that formed inside her.

"Put me down this instant, Rafe."

The sudden jolt of his doing just that startled her, but no more than the patient tone he addressed her with.

"You're wrong, as usual. I never lied to you this morning. I know you're not thinking clearly now, but I do remember every word. I told you if you married me, I would promise never to set foot in your room on the Reina again. But, Lacey, that is all I promised."

It was said with such cold finality that she felt her head clear. She would never admit that he spoke the truth. "You are a conniving liar. Evan said I couldn't trust you. You know that wasn't the promise I meant to have from you at all."

"And I'm tried of hearing you swear at me. But since," he stated with exaggerated patience, "I can well understand your frustration in being bested, princess, I'm giving you one last warning. Now, stop it."

"I won't. He warned me. They all tried to warn me."

"Then you should have listened to them. And that's enough."

Before she could avoid him, he had grabbed her wrist and half-pulled, half-dragged her around to the back of the building. Someone had thoughtfully left a lantern burning in the small window; its feeble light, Lacey noticed, was barely enough to see with. He pulled her against him with a jerk, her "I don't want—" sharply cut off.

"Behave yourself. At least till we're in our room. Just the way you keep reminding me of broken promises," he stressed in a harsh tone, "I'll thank you to remember your own. I believe you were to appear in public as the perfect wife. So far," he added jeeringly, "you're not doing a very good job of it. If this is the way you keep your word, princess, can you with any honesty ask me to keep mine? Sometimes, Lacey, you leave me to wonder—"

"Wonder all you want." Her thoughts deserted her, refusing, under his glare, to form the caustic words she longed to fling at him. "How can you expect me to keep my word, Rafe, when you obviously intend to break yours?"

Grim amusement twitched the corner of his lips, but that half smile never reached his eyes. "I haven't broken my word, Lacey. At least, not yet."

With that threat hanging between them, he opened the door and pushed her inside, his hand firmly placed in the center of her back. Lacey was surprised to see there were still a few people milling about the long hall.

"Smile, princess, and show me how you keep your word, or I might change my mind."

They started up the stairs, Rafe constantly nudging her upward as he answered a few drunken remarks. Once clear of their sight, he strided down the hall, pulling her along until they were in the back of the house. In the dim light Lacey saw him take the key from his vest pocket and open the door, ignoring her resistance to gently push her into the room.

Silent and sullen, her head aching unbearably, Lacey watched his shadow spring to life when he lit the lamp. He hesitated a moment, and then to her surprise, Rafe returned to the door.

"Where do you think you're going, Rafe?"

"I thought you would be glad to see me go. But if you insist—"

"I don't," she replied scathingly, turning her back on him. She could feel his eyes boring into her and prayed that he would leave—and quickly. The seconds stretched out as they stood there, Lacey holding her breath, not daring to look at him. She admitted to herself she was frightened of what she would see in his eyes.

Chapter 20 ━━━━━━

THE QUIET CLOSING of the door behind her made Lacey spin around and she grabbed hold of a chair to steady herself. Heat flushed her, and she swayed dizzily on her feet. She stifled the urge to run, for she knew that he would come after her. And then what? Thinking made her head pound.

Lacey gazed at the bed, thought of being in it when Rafe returned, if he did, to prove how unconcerned she was, and began to undress.

The thought was easier than her attempts. Struggling with the long line of tiny buttons at the back of her gown, she felt tears of angry frustration start, and with a tug born of rage for Rafe, she tore the back of the gown open. The innate piece of fragile material was the recipient of her despairing fury. Leaving it where she had kicked it away from her, Lacey's unsteady fingers fumbled with the ribbons holding her petticoats in place. Swearing as each was undone, she tossed them behind her, not caring where they landed, until she was exhausted by her efforts and stood clad in soft cotton drawers and a short satin camisole.

She managed to raise her eyes, her head thundering wickedly with the motion, and realized she faced an oval mirror over the dressing table. The sight of herself disheveled, while the soft curves of her body were clearly defined by the lamp's warm glow, made her lean forward.

"A hell of a way to spend your wedding night, my dear. But remember, you did Sy Garrett and the Reina proud today."

She raised her hand to her lips, caught sight of the golden band glinting in the light. She spared a thought of where Rafe had taken the ring from before all her despair focused on that bit of gold.

She pulled it off and threw it across the room. The small act of defiance seemed to drain her, and she stumbled to the bed to remove the counterpane, only to spin dizzily around at the sound of the door opening.

"You!" she gasped at the sight of Rafe framed in the doorway, a bottle held high in one hand. She saw that his string tie was gone and his shirt was opened to the waist, as was his vest. She didn't realize she had grabbed the quilt in a protective move to shield herself until he mentioned it.

"It's rather foolish, you know," he mocked, motioning with his free hand toward her wary pose. "You're hiding nothing I haven't already seen, Lacey."

"Don't remind me. What are you doing here? I thought—"

"I don't give a damn what you thought. I'm tired of hearing what you think and believe. I have no intention of spending my wedding night bedding down with a bunch of drunks in the livery. Besides . . ."

It was the narrowing of his eyes moving slowly over her in a heated caress that freed her tongue. "That's good enough for the likes of you. All right, stay. But I won't spend another minute in this room with you."

"Then don't. There's plenty of men in this town, so I'm sure you can find one to ride roughshod over." He slammed the door closed with his heel and, disregarding her wide-eyed stare, crossed the room and set the bottle down on the small table with a decided bang.

His gunbelt followed, and Lacey irrationally thought of the scar he would leave on the wood. The jacket came off next, and she found herself backing away until she pressed against the wall. He quickly shed the vest and tossed it on the chair. She almost heaved a relieved sigh to see that he had stopped undressing, but frowned when he poured himself a drink.

"Still searching for courage, Rafe?"

"The only . . . 'courage,' as you call it," he stated coldly, facing her, "that I expect to find in this bottle, *bruja*, is the type that will stop me from putting my hands on you." He knew she saw the flare of desire in his eyes, even as his words denied it. He'd made no effort to hide what he felt. She sagged weakly against the wall, and he found himself saying, "Go to sleep, princess. I won't touch you."

The chilled finality in his voice did not invite her to question him. She scurried under the covers, holding her breath, not quite trusting him. But her eyes never left him, and she knew as he turned his back on her when he caught sight of the torn, crumpled gown.

She stifled a gasp of terror as he kicked it aside. Lacey heard the ring roll across the floor. His profile was enough to tell her once again that Rafe was capable of murder. And now that furious, murderous contempt was directed at her.

Lacey longed to whisper she was sorry, but his rage was replaced by a mask of indifference.

"I'm sorry you valued the ring so little, princess. It was all I had of my mother." He leaned down to pick it up and slipped it into his pants pocket. Without another word he pulled out the chair and sat down.

She didn't dare breathe deeply, much less think to speak.

He sat with his back toward her, and the only motion Lacey saw was the refilling of the glass coming more and more frequently, until he pushed it aside and drank deeply from the bottle. She was amazed at the amount of liquor he consumed all night and now this. Rafe didn't appear to be drunk. That convinced her that she really didn't know this man she once believed she loved and had married. Her eyes began to ache, and Lacey never remembered closing them, but she did.

It was the sound of her soft, even breathing that made Rafe finally stop. He stood up, jerking off his shirt, boots, and pants, his eyes never leaving her.

The sudden feel of his weight on the bed made her eyes open. Rafe had left the lamp lit and was leaning over her. She refused to look at him and stared at the dark curling hair on his chest. The line it formed narrowed as she gazed lower, and Lacey closed her eyes. She should have known he was lying! He waited until she relaxed her guard so he could catch her unaware, but her arms and legs felt leaden when she tried to move.

Rafe drew her resisting body against his own, placing her head on his shoulder, his arms holding her securely. "Go back to sleep. I only want to hold you."

She didn't struggle, but as he held her, it was no longer Rafe that she didn't trust. It was herself. His hands seemed to burn her where they held her. The lean hardness of the leg he pressed over her own sent a shiver of warmth through her. She could feel her blood surging, its tempo matching his rapid heartbeat where the soft flesh of her breast pressed against him. She flushed as her own breathing quickened, knowing he had to hear it.

Hoping to lull her back to sleep, Rafe cursed himself. He had thought he had given her enough time to be deeply asleep before he came to lie beside her. He was wrong. Even as he had tried to drown his rage at seeing his mother's ring thrown carelessly on the floor, he knew he couldn't blame her entirely. He could well imagine the fury that prompted Lacey.

The ache inside him grew until his lips flattened against his clenched teeth. He should have stayed in the saloon. At least the women there had been willing for his attention. But he couldn't see any of them for the haunting Lacey left him with. A haunting that churned the desire inside him. A smart man would push her away. But he was never smart about Lacey.

The rapid rise and fall of her breasts made him all too conscious of the fire she stirred unknowingly. A fire that was in the midst of threatening every bit of self-control he ever demanded of himself.

She no longer stirred against him, and his groan of relief was soft. He was a fool and cursed himself for one, to remain here and not take what he wanted. No, not what he alone wanted, what Lacey refused to admit she wanted. Slipping his arms free of her, he moved to the edge of the bed. He knew that even if he left the room, there would be no peace for him this night . . . not with the fire raging inside him, not with Lacey ready to fight him.

Lacey should have been relieved when he moved away, but she wasn't. She couldn't stop the tears that slid silently down her cheeks while questions began to surface as the cloud of liquor-induced stupor lifted. Was this what their marriage would be like? Nights of longing, days of bitter fighting? Neither of them would find any peace until one or the other was driven over the edge. Rafe's impassioned voice haunted her. He wanted her, not the money. He had always wanted her.

For all that had happened, Lacey knew in both mind and heart that she loved him. She wasn't about to lie to herself. Rafe had brought a beauty to life that she would know with no one else.

Like the wild, restless meanderings of a prey escaping the hunter, her thoughts took her on a journey of the day. April's caustic voice gloating, Curt, pretending to help her, reminding her of what they once shared. Curt, who, while professing to love her, made her doubt he knew the meaning of the word. Rafe knew what love was. Rafe had not lied with his kisses or the feelings they shared. Love was what he had offered. Love was what Rafe made her feel and give to him in return.

She felt his restless moves and wondered if he, too, was thinking of the day past. How different it all could have been. Every nerve ending in her body was alive to him. This should have been the beginning of something special for both of us, she painfully acknowledged. Here we lay, inches apart, while miles of deceit separate us in thoughts.

But she didn't want to begin a life of war, and that's all that rose before her. Trust could be rebuilt; she feared it, but she had the courage to try. Would she allow pride to erect a wall that might never be torn down? What if there was a child? Could she bear raising a son or daughter with the coldness that she had been forced to live with?

Lacey turned to her side. There were more questions, but she was tired of not having the answers.

Her hand rested lightly on Rafe's chest, and she felt him tense.

"Don't," he warned. "Don't push your luck," he added in a hoarse whisper.

"My luck hasn't been very good so far, has it, Rafe? And you never let my being angry stop you. We made promises to each other today. I don't want them to be lies, too." She closed her eyes and felt his fingertip brush the tears from her lashes. "Do you want me to beg?"

"No, *por Dios*, no. I just want you to be sure of what

you're saying, Lacey." He shook like a green boy awaiting her answer.

"Loving someone isn't easy, is it, Rafe?"

"Hell, I don't know. I never loved any woman before you."

"Your mother—"

"What a man feels for his mother . . . it's different. I don't know how to explain. She tried to shield me and was good to me, and maybe a man looks for that in the woman he loves. But there's more," he whispered harshly, framing her face with his hands, "so much more that I want and need from you."

The ache in his hard, tense body was reflected in her own, and Lacey knew she feared talking now. "Rafe?" she murmured, opening her eyes to see him watching her. "I want and need you, too."

It seemed that time froze for a few moments as they stared into each other's eyes, doubts and questions clouding them, giving way to the passion flare each so easily called from the other. With a groan that was torn from deep inside him, Rafe slowly lowered his head, his lips hovering over hers.

"Be sure, *mi esposa*."

"*Esposa*?"

"Wife," he grated against her already softening mouth. He breathed into the honey warmth that beckoned. "*My* wife."

The day had begun with lovemaking designed to conquer, but with the first touch of his lips, Lacey prayed that the night would end with the same earth-shattering tenderness of this shared kiss.

She had feared that words would destroy this chance, yet knew that Rafe spoke to her with every delicate touch of his fingertips that she helplessly returned, shaking with passion.

Her senses were alive to his determination that bitterness be cast aside to allow the wonder of a softer, but no less soul-embodied loving to begin. They moved together with the liquid grace of lovers who knew each other well, but with the added newness that here began a commitment for the rest of their lives.

His hand stilled her impatience and fired her need until Lacey desired only to return its full measure. He made short work of ridding her of the camisole and cotton drawers, but when he tossed them aside and turned back, Lacey strung kisses down the side of his corded neck and across the misted swell of his shoulder. When he tried to stop her hands teasing the inner flesh of his thigh, Lacey moved her body against him so that he was forced to pay heed to the fervency of her need to love him.

Rafe slid his hands through her long hair to cup her head when she persisted in trailing kisses over his chest. His breath caught when he realized her intent.

"Come to me, love," he whispered. "Let me love you."

His words fueled the yearning she had to claim him just as he had possessed her beyond herself. She felt his body jerk with a convulsive move as her lips, provocative and warm with moisture, touched his heated flesh. Rafe's soft, almost tormented groan satisfied the womanly instinct that drove her. Lacey let the swirling move of her tongue drive him to the edge of desire, hold him there, and then, slowly entice him back.

She was caught unaware when, with a quick, brutal twist, Rafe had her beneath him, poised and waiting. With a gentle move she offered herself, and just as gently he claimed her.

But their passion was that born of storms, and they were

lost in a fever of emotions that intoxicated their senses, until neither knew where the other began.

The sound of men's excited voices along with the loud banging of doors in the hall made an unwanted intrusion into their world.

Lacey tensed and Rafe quickly soothed her. "It's nothing. They're drunk. Drunk like me, from loving you." His lips stole her cry, just as his need drove him to share again the ecstasy that was theirs alone.

Lacey had no thought for what was past and what was to come. There was only now and Rafe. Rafe who brought her warmth and life. His mouth bit into hers. She made a tiny sound, straining to be closer to him. She could never deny him, not even in her deepest dreams. And never when she needed him so much.

Rafe felt emotions spear through him like lightning in a storm. It changed him in an instant when he thought of the emptiness he faced without Lacey. He felt the bite of her nails raking his back and held her beneath him until the hard, sensual tugging of his mouth made her cry out. He could feel the pleasure that ran through her body in the same rhythms that drove his. And when she was wild from loving torment, crying his name with broken breaths, only then did he come to her, moving inside her, inciting her with a dark savagery of words and even darker caresses. When she tightened around him, he took her mouth to still her scream and give her his own as they rushed to join in passion's endless song.

With a sudden cry of outrage that stunned Lacey, Rafe tore himself away. It took seconds for her to understand that someone was shouting and pounding on their door.

Her initial fright and bewilderment gave way as Lacey thought they were going to be treated to a shivaree. She had never participated in one but had heard stories where friends of the bride and groom had come in the night and stolen one or the other away. There would be a great deal of teasing and laughter, blushing and pleading before the bride and groom were allowed to be rejoined. Rafe cursed softly, and Lacey smiled as he jerked on his pants, muttering for her to cover herself.

"This better not be someone's idea—" He cut off his words as he threw open the door, glaring at the men who stood gathered there.

Leaning forward on the bed, Lacey saw that it was Luke and Matt McCabe with other men from the Reina crowding behind them. She held the quilt up to cover her mouth and stifle her giggles. Rafe was going to be furious when they hauled him out of their room and kept them separated for a good part of the night. She almost felt sorry for the tongue-blistering he was about to deliver.

But he wasn't given a chance. "They took it all," Luke said. "Every damn cow and calf—and the horse remuda."

Lacey's smile died. She heard the sudden babble of their voices as they all tried to talk at once until Rafe's rose above theirs. "I'll be down in a few minutes."

"Got your horse saddled," Matt said. "There was shooting, and we don't know how bad."

Rafe nodded and closed the door before he realized that Lacey was up, fumbling with her underthings to dress.

"Where the hell do you think you're going?"

"With you," she snapped without looking up.

"You heard him say there was shooting," he muttered, finding his boots and cursing the liquor that slowed his movements.

"Rafe, don't leave me here."

Angrily he pulled on his shirt and roughly tucked it, unbuttoned, into his pants before he grabbed his gunbelt.

"Rafe, answer me."

He looked up, despair in his eyes. "I want to keep you safe. Can't you understand that? And while I might enjoy the sight of you half-dressed, since this is our wedding night, I'm not having any man see you like that."

"Then go down to Rebecca and get my clothes. I left them there."

"*Por Dios!* You *were* drunk. You told Maggie to take them home when she left with Fletcher."

Lacey ignored the forbidding frown that marred his face. "I may have been drunk, but I'm sober now. Find me something to wear or . . . or I will go as I am."

Rafe knew he risked breaking their fragile bond if he refused. He wanted to stay and make that belligerent gleam disappear from her eyes, but he flung open the door and headed down the hall.

Using the door as a shield, Lacey thought about his temper as she watched him enter a room, only to emerge a few moments later, empty-handed. He repeated the same with several more before she saw him come out, carrying clothes.

He pulled the door open, tossed the clothes at her. "Put them on. They're all I could find. I do apologize for the lack of a pair of boots, princess, but the cowboy wasn't sleeping all that soundly when I stole these."

"They smell."

Precious time was wasting, and Rafe snapped, "Just where would you like me to find suitable, clean clothes at this hour? You want to come, wear them. If not, stay."

Lacey couldn't tell him about the fear of being apart from him. She hid her revulsion at the strange odor of the shirt and pants. They were of an undeterminable color, caked with travel dust, and way too big, but she used a torn piece of her petticoat for a belt after stoically rolling them up. With a strip of lace she tied back her hair and joined him.

"I offered a bonus to the man who catches and hangs the first rustler. Let's ride, Rafe. I want to be there."

When Lacey saw the men's faces, she knew they had not expected her to ride with them. Rafe swung up onto his saddle while she fumed that there was no horse for her. She didn't bother to ask why. A lone horse tied to the hitching post across the way caught her attention, and without a word she headed for it. Rafe rode up alongside as she readjusted the stirrups.

"What are you—"

"I need a horse, Rafe. Now we have two thieves in the family." Mounting, she thought Rafe was laughing as she followed him out of town. Her head pounded along with the thundering beat of hooves on the hard-packed earth. But the mustang she rode was not going to be able to keep up, and she spared one damning thought for Rafe forcing her to ride with him this morning.

The moon lent its light to guide the group across the open flat plain. Rafe dropped back to ride beside Lacey, worried that she was with him. He signed to Cal to pull up even with them.

"Switch horses with Lacey," he ordered, motioning Lacey to slow her pace. Both cow ponies were well trained, and they accomplished the change in seconds. Cal rode off at a word from Rafe, and Lacey took point position at his side.

To Lacey, she felt this was a true peace offering from Rafe and glanced over at his features etched like granite in the moonlight. With an arcing swing they headed north, steadily covering ground, grim determination guiding them in the darkness.

Rafe began to grow uncomfortable with the nagging that burned his gut. He turned time and again to be certain that Lacey was there. The sky behind them was paling, its grayness tinged with soft rose streaks, and he made out the sharply edged crags of the Blues toward their right. Judging they were still a good hour's ride from where the herd had been quartered, Rafe eased his horse into a canter, shifting his weight in the saddle even as Lacey did the same. They could not afford to tire their horses when no one was sure how long they would need to ride them.

Lacey noticed that the men behind them followed suit. Scrub brush and angled cactus marked their trail now, and she knew they were well past the southernmost boundary of the ranch. The intruding sound of someone groaning made her realize that the men she rode with, on whom her very life would depend in the coming hours, were for the most part still reeling under the effects of the celebration they arrived late for. It was a sobering thought and gave her a feeling of unease. Her hand slid down her side, but there was no reassuring feel of her gun holstered there.

Two miles from the main house Rafe slowed and fired orders. "Half of you men take the north range. Two shots will mean you sighted them. The rest of us will ride south. Just find them."

Automatically taking the lead of the group splitting off to obey him, Lacey pulled up when he shouted at her.

"Stay with me. You don't have a gun."

"If we split up, we have a better chance, Rafe. Let's not waste time by fighting. I won't be coddled."

Against every instinct screaming a warning, Rafe rode back toward her. He leaned over his saddle to roughly catch her chin. Before Lacey could move, he kissed her, hard and fast. "Keep yourself safe for me, princess."

Her whispered promise was lost, for he spurred his horse away. Lacey caught up with the men, riding beside each one, reassuring herself that if he was drunk, he hid it well. The threat to the Reina had sobered her from the effects of the liquor, but she tasted the lingering warmth of Rafe's kiss, which was an intoxication all its own.

Minutes later she called for Scanlon to take the lead. Lacey veered off, knowing she had to get a pair of boots and her gun. Fletcher and Maggie came running from the house as she rode in. Lacey was thankful that only two men had been wounded and not badly. Neither Fletcher nor Maggie wasted time with questions. Fletcher ran off to saddle a fresh horse for her, and Maggie followed her into her room.

Lacey stripped and changed into her own clothes, firing warnings at Maggie. Once her boots were on, Lacey took the gunbelt that Maggie handed her.

For once Maggie was at a loss for words. Lacey looked ready to kill to protect the Reina as she buckled the belt with the ease of long practice, hazel eyes glittering, her jaw clenched.

They both heard the sounds of someone running on the tile bricks and turned toward the door. Maggie was the one who cried out.

"Take it off, Lacey, nice and easy," Curt ordered, motioning to the belt. "Put it on the bed where I can see it. Get near her, Maggie."

Lacey was too stunned not to obey. Curt was no longer dressed in one of his impeccable suits and finely starched shirts, but in coarse fringed buckskins that made him a stranger. "Curt? Why? You can't—"

"Shut up. We'll talk after you tie her up. And don't think your pepper-gut husband will find the cattle. My men have already driven them south."

His eyes blazed with a coldness that frightened Lacey. Yet she refused to accept what he said, what was happening here in her home. The shot he fired splintered the wood at her feet. His face was a mask of violence, and without a word she grabbed the discarded shirt to tie Maggie's hands.

"Gag her and tie her feet."

Lacey went to her dresser and tore apart a drawer looking for a neckerchief. Her hand closed over a small forgotten derringer concealed there, but she was never given the chance to use it. The mirror exploded into a thousand shards of glass as he fired another shot.

She jumped back and spun around.

"No games, Lacey." He shoved Maggie to her knees. "Do it."

Afraid that he would hurt Maggie again, Lacey moved. She didn't dare make the ties loose. She pleaded with a glance for forgiveness as she gagged Maggie.

"Get over here, Lacey."

With a last helpless glance at Maggie, Lacey walked to his side. His arm snaked out, pulling her against him, his hand roughly covering her breast. His jeering laugh grated in her ears as she shuddered with revulsion.

"Tell that Mex bastard that Lacey is mine, old woman. She was mine first."

His voice shook with rage and other emotions that Lacey refused to name. He backed from the room, dragging her with him. Under the tiled archway he changed direction toward Rafe's room. "I'll kill you if Rafe doesn't, Curt." She struggled against his hold, and he spun her around, backhanding her to the floor. Lacey gazed up, refusing to beg as he stood spraddling her prone body.

"I was good enough for you once. That bastard deserves to know his bride spent her wedding in bed with me. Go on," he taunted, "you were willing enough once."

He began to unbuckle his gunbelt, and Lacey judged her moment. He screamed when her boot caught him square in the gut, but before she scrambled out of his reach, his hand tangled in her hair and yanked her face up. His free hand caught her wrist and wrenched it behind her back before his mouth ground down on hers. She trembled with the need to scream. He leaned his body against her until she thought her back would break. A roaring filled her ears along with the sound of a voice calling, and she prayed that someone, anyone from the Reina had come.

Shock registered with a despairing jolt when she realized who it was calling for Curt to answer. It was Evan's voice she heard as Curt seemed to suck the very breath from her.

Evan grabbed Curt away, leaving her kneeling, sick with the thought of how thoroughly they had fooled her.

"You want to blow it all, Curt? There's time later."

"Just so you understand how it's going to be, Evan."

Lacey could not fight them then as she was shoved out to the courtyard. Betrayed. Curt and Evan together. The doubts they planted about Rafe. The trust she had for each of them. But she needed her wits, not self-recrimination.

Why she ever noticed the clarity of the night sky that reminded her of Rafe's eyes, she never knew. She fought free of the painful grip Curt had maintained as they neared the corral and she spotted Fletcher's prone body. He was lying sprawled in the dirt near the hooves of the white mare that Evan had given her.

"Come along quietly, Lacey," Curt ordered. "He isn't dead . . . yet."

The click of the gun hammer made her reassure him. "I won't give you any trouble."

"She won't, Curt, but I sure as hell will."

Lacey half turned to see Bo, his gun drawn, standing to their side. She started forward, but Curt grabbed her and used her as a shield.

"Put it away, Bo."

"This wasn't part of the deal, Curt. Let her go."

Part of the deal? What was Bo talking about? Lacey repeated the words to herself. Bo couldn't be partners with

them. Not Bo. He had been a part of her life. But Evan
made her realize that she wasn't having a nightmare. She
was living one.

"Settle your differences after we ride out. Curt, you're
wrong to take her with us. She'll slow us down, but I can't
blame you. Bo, either shut your mouth and ride with us, or
stay and face Rafe. It might be interesting to hear you
explain your part."

"Bo?" she questioned, but he wouldn't look at her.

Fear for Fletcher's life made Lacey mount up on Curt's
horse. He sat behind her as the four of them rode out into
the night. Lacey clung to the saddle horn, her back rigid,
but the rocking motion of the horse pressed Curt's body to
hers. She blocked out the whispered threats he made and
tried to think clearly.

Rafe would come after her. She had to find a way to leave
a trail for him. And it was thoughts of Rafe that helped her
bury the screams that rose as Curt's voice grew more
gloating with lust.

Chapter 21 ════════════

ANGRY FRUSTRATION WAS clouding Rafe's thoughts as he rode with his men. Why he should persist in thinking of Lacey when his mind should be directed on where else to search for their cattle, he didn't question. He knew that something was wrong. The short hairs on the back of his neck were prickling with alarm.

He was riding point toward the south range near the small canyons where Lacey had been shot when the sounds, like that of rolling thunder, caught his attention. No man who worked cattle needed to be told they were listening to stampeding cattle.

"Sweet Christ!" someone yelled.

They turned as one and spotted the oncoming tide of close-packed bodies that headed directly toward them. Their horses, Rafe knew, were winded, yet they pushed them to a man as the fear of being caught under the onrushing hooves made them lash and spur and curse the tired beasts for speed. Rafe thought of firing his gun to try and turn the cattle to the side, but they were already too close.

The noise was a roar as cattle, lowing with terror, bawled like souls lost in hell when a shot rang out. Someone screamed, and Rafe tried to see in the darkness. The shadow of a man and a horse went down before the sight was blotted by the herd. Riding off to the side, and slightly ahead of his men, he realized he had drawn his gun. Luke gave him a shout of approval, and Rafe knew it was one of the rustlers he had shot in a reflexive gesture. A quick look told him he didn't have a chance in hell of getting off another. He used his reins as a whip on the powerful grulla's neck. The advantage was all the rustlers' now—he and his men had to fight for their lives. Their only hope of not being crushed to death was to reach high ground.

Dust clouds swirled up, coating them, blinding them. Rafe moved to draw his shirt collar up as men used their neckerchiefs to protect their mouths and noses from the stifling grit that made it impossible to draw breath. Men's knees pressed tight against heaving horses' sides, guiding the well-trained horses into blind obedience of their riders. It was the western slope that Rafe headed toward, rising up before him, offering the only hope they had.

Labored breathing marked with swearing filled Rafe's ears. Along with his men he urged the grulla up the graveled slope. He felt the grulla's swerve and saw the rider beside him slide from his saddle as his horse stumbled. Rafe reached out blindly for the man's hand. Clasping the callused palm firmly, he felt the strain he put on his horse and demanded more as the grulla faltered and lost precious moments. Rafe leaned toward his left to give the man purchase as he clung to the saddle and threw the reins aside to give the grulla his head. The horse regained his footing, muscles straining as he carried them to safety.

No one spoke. The silvered profiles of the ragged line of harsh-breathing men hunched over their horses' necks were totally silent as they watched the herd thunder past below them. Bleak eyes turned upward as Rafe watched, whether in prayer or rage, he didn't know, but he was sure they all understood how close they had flirted with death.

The dust clouds below made it foolish to shoot, just as one horse going down made Rafe realize it was foolish to try and follow them without fresh mounts.

"We head back for fresh mounts and grub," he stated, slowly straightening himself in the saddle. Luke was by his side, but Rafe brushed off his thanks for saving his life. "Who's got the freshest horses?"

"Me an' Hank'll trail them," Matt McCabe answered. "But first we need to talk."

Rafe knew they all could do with a few minutes of rest and dismounted. He walked off away from the others. A few curious glances followed him, but no one spoke. He only hoped that this time they had something worthwhile to tell him.

"It ain't much," Matt began. "Back in town Hank here saw Curt and Evan as cozy as peas a bit after you wed. When they left Rebecca's, they were with Bo James."

"So? They know each other. Have for years. Don't waste my time, McCabe."

"Ain't wasting your time. Jus' listen. I followed them to the edge of town, but they were too far away for me to overhear them. That lawyer's got a powerful hate for you."

"Like I said, tell me what I don't know."

"The judge finally answered our wire," Hank cut in. "It seems that Bo James ain't got a past. He's the only one that the judge couldn't trace."

Rafe's gut twisted. Lacey had refused to believe him when he told her his feelings about Bo. Now he'd have proof. Before he could ask any questions, Luke walked over.

"The men are gettin' anxious to go after them."

"Well, do. You don't need me to lead you like—"

"Ain't got a call to yell, Rafe. I'm jus' tryin'—"

"Try doing it, Luke, not talking. I pay your damn wages, don't I?"

They stared at each other until Luke backed down under Rafe's fierce gaze. Without another word he walked away and began firing orders.

Rafe regretted his harshness but couldn't think about it now. "Finish up, Matt."

"You remember me telling you that I ran into a friend in Sonora when I picked up the mail? Well, he was trailing a mean son of a bitch that killed two clerks in a bank robbery in El Paso. Caught him, too, but he runs into Curt there. He did some checking for me and found out that our lawyer has three accounts in that bank, and he handles them for himself, Evan, and Bo James."

"Overheard talk down in San Antonio last week while you were gone, Rafe, that Blaine has a spread the other side of the Rio. It's a friendly place if you're runnin'."

"Why the hell did you wait—"

"Hold on, Rafe," Matt said, grabbing his arm. "You weren't around. I suspect that horses for the army ain't the only thing that Evan's bringing across the border. I'd bet my boots that he's selling guns to the Comanche and that Curt's the one that staked him."

The pieces tumbled into place, and Rafe glanced at both of them. "Find the bastards. We'll be right behind you."

Rafe damned himself for not taking Curt seriously as a threat. It was past time for him to worry about it now. He gained no satisfaction in knowing that he had been right in thinking that someone from the Reina was working with the rustlers. What he didn't understand was why Bo had been shot. Unless it was to simply throw off suspicion. And he couldn't deny that the man loved Lacey like she was his own. But Rafe couldn't ignore what Matt told him. He had to find Lacey and tell her. She had a right to decide how to handle this information. He glanced around and saw that Hank and Matt were mounted and heading down the treacherous slope.

"Be careful, you two!" he called out, but neither man acknowledged his shout as a sudden rising wind carried his voice away. He looked up at a stormy sky. The men were long gone, and he rode out after them, cursing the first splatters of rain. He was filled with a sudden urgency to hold Lacey, and he willed her to be back at the house waiting for him.

Nothing, not even the questions that Matt and Hank raised, could shake the sight of her from his mind. He dug his heels into the grulla's sides, demanding the heart of him in his need to be with Lacey. Blinding sheets of water soaked him as the full fury of the storm broke.

Rafe found himself struggling against an onslaught of bone-weary tiredness even as he struggled against believing that the very fates conspired to keep him from reaching Lacey.

Lacey had sized up her situation and knew she could not escape on her own. The small outcrop of rocks they had sought shelter in minutes before did little to protect her from the driving rain. She huddled beneath the blanket Curt had flung at her while the three of them sat off to one side whispering among themselves.

She did not want to believe that Bo had been in league with them all this time. From the heated remarks they had exchanged as they rode, she gathered that Bo was the one who had approached Curt with the idea of stealing Reina cattle.

But why? The question tormented her. She wanted a chance to ask him, but her hope was dashed when, despite the blinding downpour, they rose and gathered their gear.

Bo walked over to her, silent as he offered her his canteen. Lacey took a long drink of the colorless liquid that burned her throat raw, but she was grateful for its spreading warmth.

"We're moving on," he said.

"Bo, how could—"

"Get away from her, Bo," Curt warned. "I told you not to give her a chance to work on you. Lacey's smart. Too smart for her own good. You want to find yourself swinging at the end of a rope? And you know her, Bo. She'll be the one to slap the horse out from under you. Don't make me tell you again."

Bo walked away, and Curt hauled Lacey to her feet. She ached in every muscle as she followed him. Uncertain as to where they were, Lacey would not chance running. She intercepted the looks Curt exchanged with Bo and Evan. It seemed they both acceded to his right to her. She would, whatever was to come, have only herself to depend upon. Pulling the blanket around her, soaked as it was, she offered no resistance when Curt lifted her up onto his horse, mounted, and settled himself snuggly behind her.

Once more they rode on.

Lacey's fingers worked at the edge of the blanket. She hated the feel of his hand pressing her stomach. He laughed when she tensed. But Lacey smiled, too. It wasn't an idle threat she had made when she swore she would kill him. And it wasn't just for taking her but for the betrayal of her trust.

Rafe would come after her. She had to cling to that thought and conserve her strength for when she would need it. But she was so cold.

"Damn it, Maggie, think! They had to say something about where they were headed."

Maggie once again shook her head in denial at Rafe. She was frightened by the wild look in his eyes. Her hands tremored as she wrapped a bandage around Fletcher's head. She was afraid of what would happen to Lacey. She tried to draw strength from the merciless gaze that was in Rafe's eyes as once again she realized how much he was his father's son.

But even as Maggie thought this, there was not a man present in the warmth of the kitchen that could meet Rafe's despairing glance as he looked at each man in turn. His muscles were knotted tautly beneath the dark brown shirt, and he stood clenching and unclenching his hands at his sides. They couldn't know he cursed and damned himself for letting Lacey ride off without him.

"Rain's almost stopped, Rafe," Luke said softly. "I'd like to ride after them with you."

Rafe directed a level gaze at him. "Ever done any cold-blooded killing?"

Indrawn breaths, then silence greeted Rafe's question. He knew he broke their code to ask it. A man's past was his own, unless he wanted it otherwise. For a long moment they gazed at one another.

"I've done what I've had to do," Luke finally answered.

Rafe nodded, satisfied. "Cal, are you sure you saw only three horses ride out?"

"Yep. Weren't close enough to see who. After I hauled Fletcher inside, I went out with the lantern just before the rain come and saw one was carryin' double."

"It's Darcy, Blaine, and Bo that have Lacey," Rafe stated. "Blewett, you take the men and pick up the trail that Matt followed. Rain or not, he'll have left you sign. See if any of you spot Scanlon and his bunch. They'll have holed up but should be riding soon." Rafe watched as they milled about, drinking down the last of the whiskey-laced coffee

that had warmed them. "I want every man here to understand one last thing before we ride out. No quarter." His
voice reflected the leashed fury in his eyes. One by one they
nodded, and Rafe turned to Maggie. "I'll bring her home.
I swear it."

Blewett watched as they parted to let Rafe pass between
them with Luke following at his heels. He remembered the
stories they had exchanged about Rafe selling his gun to
whoever had the price, some half-wild rumors that he was
as good with his knife as his gun. Rafe's temper had burned
more than one man for misusing a good piece of horseflesh
or for disregarding an order. Blewett knew he wasn't alone
in thinking that he was glad Rafe wasn't riding after him this
night.

Outside, Rafe watched as the men made sure that their
rifles were secure but free enough to be pulled from the
leather when needed. As the last of them rode off, he turned
to Luke.

"You sure? There's no turning back."

"I'm sure."

"Let's ride."

Ride. Lacey was desperate to have an end to it. Dawn had
ebbed its way across the night sky, and Lacey paid close
attention to the changing terrain they were riding through.
Flat land gave way to sandy cropped hills dotted with
twisted, gnarled piñon pines. She judged their direction
north, and north meant Permanent Camp. For a moment she
wondered if Curt and Evan were crazy enough to go there,
but a nagging voice reminded her what lay beyond . . .
Indian territory.

The sight of a red-tailed hawk soaring above them made
her envy its freedom. Indian territory would kill any chance
she had of escaping. They had all been silent. She thought

again of how easily they had fooled her and glanced at Evan riding alongside. There was nothing soft or boyish about his arrogant profile. The implacable stare he offered told her he would not help her. Bo, then, she decided. But she had to get him alone. Her body still felt the chill of the rain, and she trembled.

Sharp, jagged peaks rose in front of them. Lacey thought they were the Bradys. She could see shadows, dark and menacing in the rock crevices, as the sun strengthened. They rode on, bold and careless, almost as if they had nothing to fear.

"We're in Indian territory, Curt. Are you looking to get us killed?"

"Frightened, Lacey?"

"You'd like that, wouldn't you? If it was a choice between you and—"

"It would be me that you'd choose, Lacey. Have you ever seen what Comanche do to white captives, especially the women? Not only the warriors but their women. You remember what Captain Chase told you?"

"Do you think I believed him? He's fresh from a desk job back East where he sat out the war. The Comanche would have taken scalps if they were raiding. That only happened once."

"Maybe they were ordered not to."

"Ordered?" Lacey repeated, horror dawning. "You were a part of those killings?" His soft laughter was enough of an answer. Now she was desperate to hide her fear of him. How could she have ever thought she knew him?

"And don't worry about what will happen to you, Lacey," he whispered with his lips against her neck. "I told you, you're mine."

Lacey didn't move or speak as she swallowed bile. She directed her gaze on Evan as he pulled ahead, his relaxed posture suddenly rigid. They slowed the horses under the serrated peaks. She watched and followed suit as he carefully swept his gaze over the rock walls.

"No safe sign?" Bo asked.

Evan didn't answer, but he did ride out ahead as they kept their horses to a walk.

Lacey, her gaze intent, noticed the slight ease of his seat. Whatever Evan had been looking for, he had found it as he led them to a narrow gorge. She noticed the trail was tortuous and rocky, like an age-old Indian path. The deep cleft with walls that rose so high they almost shut out the sunlight was gloomy and silent. Despair once again filled her. Rafe would never be able to follow them. There was no mud here, and Evan led them over rocky ground so they couldn't leave tracks. Once again she pulled free a bit of her blanket.

The thin threads weren't much and Rafe might never see them, but it was all she had to leave for sign of her passing. She lost track of the miles they covered, pushing deeper and deeper into the rocky bowels of the mountains. They had briefly stopped once to eat jerky and finish the last of the water. Just remembering that made her work her mouth, hoping for a bit of moisture, for she felt hot. Their slow, upward climb allowed the sun to beat down unmercifully on her bare head.

The raucous cry of a piñon jay bird drew her gaze up. The walls were filled with the stunted growth of junipers, their contorted forms clothing the walls with rich, dark foliage. Evan drew rein and cupped his hands over his mouth to repeat the sound. Lacey barely stifled her scream when a tawny-skinned warrior appeared above them. He held his war club in one hand, a rifle in the other, both raised high as a signal to Evan.

"There'll be no escaping, Lacey," Curt warned as they moved forward.

She tried not to dwell on his pronouncement as the scrub brush became thicker before small fires became visible. Lacey heard voices as they neared the edge of the camp. She fought the urge to lower her eyes as they rode to the center of the tipis. Women sat before their cooking fires, silent and watching, but the men began to gather around them. Lacey found her eyes drawn to the man who stepped forward. Only his lined face betrayed his age, for his bare chest rippled with muscles. She was flustered at the sight of several young boys, no more than seven or eight years old, naked as the day they were born.

Evan began to speak in a thick guttural voice to the old man she assumed was their chief. But as she felt their eyes upon her, she straightened and pushed the tangle of her hair from her face.

"Don't think Walks Like Cat will offer for you, Lacey. The only thing he wants is guns."

She didn't bother to answer Curt but kept her attention on Evan. His voice was raised, and the one Curt called Walks Like Cat was gesturing, his black eyes fierce. She wished she knew more of these Indians, who were sometimes called the Snake People. All she could recall were tales of their revenge against soldiers and towns whenever they demanded white captives be returned. She knew they considered white captives as wealth. The tale of an ill-fated meeting with Lone Wolf and a leader of the Texas Rangers came from her memory with startling clarity. The chief had agreed to return the captives he held and offered one white woman. Colonel Karnes, the Ranger, felt tricked and insulted and slaughtered every Indian in the meeting room in San Antonio, then went outside and shot warriors and their women alike as they ran for their ponies.

Lacey shook with a chill as she met the proud black eyes of Walks Like Cat. She would find no mercy here. In revenge for the killing of their people, the Comanche had gathered seven hundred warriors and rode on the town of Linnville. Those who did not manage to escape when the warning came found no quarter given when the Indians attacked.

Yet she had to remember that Sy had given cattle to roving bands when their hunting was poor and salt to help preserve their meats. They had helped themselves to horses on occasion, for they valued the ownership of horses and were masters of riding, but the Reina had been free of destructive trouble.

Bo dismounted at a signal from Evan, and Curt did the same. When he roughly pulled her down, Bo came to them, but Curt shoved him away.

"That's the last time I'll warn you, old man. Stay the hell away from her, or I'll tell Evan to turn you over to them."

"Curt, for God's sake, Bo didn't—" Curt's brutal yank on her hair silenced her. She stumbled against him.

"You don't want anything to happen to the old man, do you, Lacey?"

She could barely shake her head.

"Then you understand I'm the one to be obeyed?"

Lacey nodded, refusing to speak. He would hear the fear in her voice, and she couldn't give this . . . this stranger another weapon to use against her. Weak from lack of food and water, Lacey felt nausea churn in her stomach. She met the staring eyes of men, women, and children alike, black eyes that held no emotion. Curt grabbed her arm, still holding her hair, and began to lead her away. Evan walked alongside them.

"Well? What happened?" Curt asked him.

"He's angry, so hurry up."

"Where are you taking me?" Lacey struggled to stop, something inside her demanding that she resist being meek.

Curt smiled coldly and spoke softly, but he cut through any remaining hope she harbored.

"You're no longer the boss lady of the Reina. Whatever I decide, whatever I want, is all you know. What's more, you will obey me willingly. Here I own you."

Lacey involuntarily trembled to hear the gripping conviction in his voice, to see a wild madness in his eyes.

"Seems to me, Curt," Evan taunted, "you're doing more to convince yourself than Lacey."

"Shut the hell up! I know Lacey and you don't. She still harbors the thought that Rafe or her men will follow us here. This time I will kill the man that tries to take her from me."

Evan backed away, hands held wide from his body. "Take it easy. I'm not looking to get myself killed. Not even for Lacey."

Minutes later at the edge of the camp, Curt showed her through the hide opening of a tipi. "I won't bother to tie you. We both know there is no place for you to run. Be smart and don't test me, Lacey. I won't be responsible for what happens to you outside." He stared at her for long moments before he smiled. "Later I'll come to claim what's mine."

She gagged in reaction and watched the hide covering flap behind him as he left. Thankful that she was alone, Lacey sank down to the hard-packed earth floor. The tipi was bare, and she shivered. Muffled sounds like the yipping cries of coyotes reached her. She was too exhausted to care who made them and huddled her body to stop the sudden chills.

Lacey dozed and had no idea how much time had passed when Bo stealthily entered the tipi, throwing glances over his shoulder.

Forcing herself to sit up, Lacey wasn't surprised when he

refused to meet her direct gaze. She took the small bowl he handed her and using her fingers began to eat. Whatever it was, the taste was savory, and Lacey knew she needed her strength. Bo sat across from her, but whenever she snagged his gaze, he looked away. Finished, she wiped her mouth on her torn sleeve. "I don't suppose you could get me some water. Will Curt allow that?"

"Don't matter if he would. They's parlayin', so you don't have to worry that he's comin' back soon."

When he returned, he had a blanket and kindling for a fire. Lacey wrapped the blanket around herself and watched him build the fire in the center pit. As she sipped from the battered canteen, the chills beset her once more.

Bo hunkered at her side, ignoring her jerky move away from his callused hand as he touched her face. "You got fever."

Lacey raised glazed eyes up to him. She saw him turn away and managed to whisper, "Please, Bo, don't leave me alone." His body wavered in the firelight, but her teeth were chattering with a will of their own, and she had to clamp her lips tight to still them. Racking chills shook her body. She never remembered feeling like this. Cold, then so hot.

Lacey didn't remember lying down, but she felt cool clothes on her face. She was grateful for the liquid someone gave her to drink, but when she tried to move, she couldn't. Words tumbled incoherently from her lips, and she thought she was calling for Maggie, but then she slipped into a restless sleep.

Bo sat and stared at Lacey as two women chanted in their singsong voices while tossing herbs on the fire. A kettle steamed the inside of the tipi, but he felt helpless and was wishing that Maggie were there. He didn't know how long he sat after the two women had left, but he rose the moment Curt and Evan entered.

"Get out. You're to blame that she's sick. Anythin' happens to Lacey, and I swear, Curt, I'll kill you."

"I wanted to see for myself, old man. But don't you think it's a little late for your concern? The time for that—"

"Stop riding him, Curt," Evan cut in. "Let him stay with her. Lacey's strong. She's just got a chill from riding in the rain."

Evan turned his back on the two of them. He wished Curt had never veered off to the Reina that night. He could understand his obsession with Lacey, but now Rafe would follow them. He'd made sure there wasn't much of a trail for him to track, but he didn't relish the thought of confronting him. Pushing aside the hide, he turned to Curt.

"You coming? Or are you figuring on playing nurse?" He couldn't help his anger. Coming here with Lacey was a mistake. It wouldn't have been if the guns he had arranged to have waiting had arrived. But the shipment was late, and Walks Like Cat was angry. "Curt! Let's go."

"Don't get any crazy idea of sneaking off with her, old man."

"Where would I take her, sick as she is? But you won't hurt Lacey. I'm warnin' you that I won't stand aside—"

"Warn me . . . ?" With a growl, Curt sprang at him, only to have Evan's wiry grip jerk his arm back before he slammed his fist into Bo's face.

"What the hell are you letting him rile you for?" Evan demanded. "He ain't going nowhere."

Curt pulled free of his hold and smoothed back his hair before stalking out. Evan shot Bo a last warning look and then left them.

Throughout the night, the long day that followed, and well into the next night, Bo sat beside Lacey, watching the two Indian women care for her. All he could do was bathe

her brow with water and wait. Praying was something he
had given up on.

The camp was quiet tonight, not even a wind stirred. He
glanced up at the young woman who entered with his food,
understanding from her signing that she wished him to
leave. He sat in front of the tipi, thankful that both Curt and
Evan had kept away. Once the woman left, he returned to
his place by the fire. It took him a few minutes to realize
that Lacey was awake.

"Bo? You stayed."

"Couldn't leave you to these savages. Don't be talkin'."
He kneeled beside her and offered his canteen for her to
drink.

"Why . . . with them, Bo?" The effort to hold her head
up taxed her strength, and she lay down.

He met her fever-bright eyes and then looked away. "I
got a story to tell, an' maybe it ain't the right time or place,
but there's things you need to know. I don't know what's
gonna happen here. You got to promise to stay quiet and let
me talk."

Lacey managed a nod and gripped the blanket.

"Ain't gonna start with excuses. Jus' swear it's all true.
Even," he added solemnly, "if my bein' with Curt and Evan
left you without any faith in me." He swallowed and found
that he had to force himself to continue.

"My real name's James Beau Lacey. I'm your father."

Chapter 22

LACEY'S CRY WAS weak. She closed her eyes and then had to look at Bo. Her mouth worked, but she couldn't speak. It couldn't be true, and yet, even as she denied it to herself, Bo began to speak.

"Your mother was a pretty woman, happy and always singin'. She'd stop by my brother's place on her way to bringin' some of the fancy linens she sewed for the plantation owners. We were dirt-poor farmers, Lacey, I ain't makin' no apology for that. But when I tried to court her proper, her brother ran me off. He wanted better for her, and young fool that I was, I left her be. When Garrett come 'round, talkin' 'bout his spread an' all, her brother arranged for them to marry."

His gruff voice caught, and Lacey saw he was lost in his memories, but even as she tried to speak, he continued.

"Her brother sold her to Sy! He wouldn't tell me where she'd gone. An' then five years later she come back. She ran away from Sy. Her body was hurtin' so bad an' her heart was breakin' after seein' her babes die off. She hated him," he ground out in a raw voice.

From somewhere Lacey found the strength to speak. "But how? Later . . . I mean . . . you both . . ."

"I loved her. I didn't have nothin' to give her, but I loved her."

"But Sy followed her. Maggie said—"

"He came after her. She wrote him an' said she wasn't ever goin' back. She was a possession to him. Sy wouldn't let her be. I went lookin' for work up the river, an' when I come back to get her, she was gone."

Exhausted, Lacey pushed herself to sit. "All this time. You never told me. But why did he say I was his?"

"That's why she went back with him. He swore everythin' would belong to you. I had nothin', and he could give you everythin'. She knew she was carryin' my child."

There was pain in his eyes and accusation in his voice, but Lacey found no answering warmth stirring inside her. All her life had been centered on the Reina; for that she had been denied a father and love. For the land she had bartered herself in marriage. And her mother, her mother lost love for . . . for things. It was all a bitter, bitter draught to swallow.

"She never told Sy who your father was." Hanging his head, unable to bear the pain in her eyes, he added, "I know how much you must hate me now that you know."

Hate him? Did she feel that angry emotion? Hating Bo was pointless. Staring at him, she saw him for what he was: a broken man who had lost whatever respect he had once had for himself. The words were the hardest she had ever spoken. "I don't hate you, Bo. You made up for Sy's coldness. . . . Oh, what does it matter! It's all past. But how could you be—"

". . . be with Curt and Evan, rustlin' your cattle an' dealin' guns with savages?" His laugh was harsh. "I hated Sy for takin' her away. I couldn't leave things be without knowin' 'bout you. Workin' for him an' stealin' his cows was small revenge. Didn't use the money. Put it all by for you so's you'd have somethin' from me. Curt saw to it. It's wrong for one man like Garrett to have so much. Curt let slip he felt the same way an' I guess I was fool enough to admit the truth 'bout me to him. He used it. He used me."

"Bo," she gently reminded him, "Sy's dead. Why did you keep on?"

"Yeah, he is. An' he tricked me with that bastard son." He saw how she rubbed her head, weakly bunching the blanket that served as a pillow. "You rest. We'll talk later."

"No. There might not be time. Will you help me? Or are you going to let Curt—"

"Hush! You don't know what you're sayin'. I never meant for things to go this far. Curt's shrewd. When he figured out how I was gettin' money, he wanted in. When Sy died, I wanted to stop, but he figured if you lost enough, you'd give up an' turn to him. Fool don't know you at all."

"And Evan? Where does he fit in?"

As if her question had conjured him up, Evan pushed aside the hide and entered. He glanced from one to the other. "She's better?"

"Fever's broke. She ain't ready to move on."

Move on? Lacey tensed. Bo hadn't said anything about them leaving.

"Curt wants you, old man. I'll stay with her."

Bo glanced over at Lacey, hesitating.

"Go on. I'll watch her. Got my own reasons for wanting nothing to happen to her."

"You let her rest."

"I hear you. She'll be here when you get back."

Only Lacey heard his soft whisper as Bo left.

"If you get back."

Rafe coldly eyed Captain Chase. He cursed and thanked whatever luck had led him and Luke to cross trails with the detachment of soldiers. The thanks were for capturing Evan's men and a wagonload of new Sharps carbines. The cursing was for the two days they lost helping the captain and for the army officer's refusal to see reason.

"Captain, I want the guns. They're the only chance I have to get Lacey."

"And you must understand that I can't let you take these guns to the very savages—"

"Luke!" Rafe drew his gun, grabbed the stunned captain in a choke hold, and used the gun barrel to nudge his chin up. "I didn't want to do it this way, but you left me no choice." Rafe glanced over at Luke, nodded as he saw him gather the reins and release the pole brake. He dragged the officer backward toward his own horse. "I don't want to hurt you, but I will if you come after me."

"You're stealing government—"

"I'm taking pay for helping you out of a tight spot." Rafe clicked back his gun hammer in warning and shouted for Luke to go. In a smooth motion he shoved the captain into a spinning forward turn, leaped onto his horse, and fired two shots into the air. Flattened down in his saddle, Rafe was off at a run.

Captain Chase waved aside the men whose rifles were sighted to fire at Rafe. "Let the fool go." He turned to the ragtag band of men they had captured. At his signal the call went out to mount up. "We'll get the information we need from them," he said to his wounded sergeant. With a glance toward the Bradys, he added, "Send for a full company from the fort. Maybe we can manage to save their fool necks."

It was late afternoon when Rafe and Luke stopped on a flat rise in the shadow of the Bradys. Rafe quartered the area, smiling when he added yet another of the blue-gray threads to the small roll he carried in his shirt pocket. The toe of his boot nudged the overturned rock. "Figure it's three maybe four days since they passed this way?"

"That's what I figure," Luke answered. "Three tired horses, one still carryin' double."

"I found another half print up ahead. Same vee chip in the left hoof. Two tips of brush are broken, same as we found two days ago. Lacey's still with them, still leaving a trail for us."

Luke gazed at Rafe as he looked off toward the craggy peaks of the mountains ahead of them. He knew without asking what was bothering him. They were well into Comanche territory. His own neck hair prickled at the thought.

"Evan's good," Rafe remarked, taking a spare sip from his canteen.

His voice was as flat and hard as the few times he had chosen to speak these last few days. Luke respected him for not pushing on without caution. They had rested their horses for short spans, snatching sleep as soon as dark fell, for Rafe refused to push on and chance missing a sign of their direction. Luke moved to check his horse's cinch strap. They had ditched the wagon in a hidden canyon and loaded the team of horses with a few of the guns, just enough to wet the Indians' interest.

"Mount up, Luke. We've wasted enough time."

"You figure the captain will come after us?"

"I'm not counting on it."

Swinging into his saddle, Rafe urged his horse into an easy canter. He knew where he was going and what would be waiting for him. His worry was for Lacey. Curt and Evan were dead men for taking her, but where Bo James fit in to this, he could only wonder.

Lacey was wondering about Bo, too. Evan had left her last night, and Bo still had not returned to the tipi. Two women had brought her skins of water this morning, showing her how to crush berries by rubbing them against her skin to make a soapy lather. Lacey had shied from them remaining with her but couldn't get them to leave. They had offered her a comb made from animal bone for her hair and left her a worn buckskin shift she now wore with her own pants. And she had been left alone since then.

She couldn't stand the waiting and rose, pushing aside the hide. No one was around, and the tipi was at the edge of the camp. Blinking as she stepped out into the sun, Lacey was struck by the silence. She judged the distance to the edge of the wood and took a deep breath, ready to run, when she was jerked unceremoniously back by her braid.

"Where were you going, Lacey?" Curt asked softly.

"I was hungry."

"Spare me your lies. Get inside, I want to talk to you."

Meekly obeying him and hating herself for it, Lacey did, but stood at the far side.

Curt smiled. "Still the child. But it doesn't matter. Rafe's coming." Her cry deepened his smile. "You're right to be afraid for him. He'll never make it through the pass, but I want you to see for yourself."

"See for myself?" she repeated, realizing what he meant. No, she didn't want to see Rafe die, but she refused to cower again. Away from here might mean a chance of escaping and that was all she could think about.

He held out his hand, and with a shudder of revulsion she took it. "We'll ride to the top of the ridge. The view should be excellent from there." He caressed her hair. "And when it's over, there's no need to wait."

Where she found the courage to shrug his hand off, she didn't know, but it fed her strength to taunt him. "You'll never have a moment's peace with me. Someday I'll kill you for what you've done. And you'll never take Rafe's place. I love him."

Her eyes rich with hate met his. Lacey read nothing in the look he returned. Had she sealed Rafe's fate with her taunts? As she followed him to where two horses waited, she tried to find an answer and couldn't.

Walks Like Cat stood off to one side with three warriors, but Curt stopped short of joining them. He gestured toward the edge of the high ridge, and Lacey moved closer. "Rafe?" Her voice was a mere whisper as she saw him and Luke file into the pass. Lacey glanced again at the Indians. They were armed with only knives and made no move to stop them. Were they luring them in deeper and planning to capture them? The thought of Rafe being tortured made her turn, ready to bargain herself.

"Why are they letting them through?" Curt muttered angrily. "Damn savages! Why don't they kill them?"

It was Evan who rode up and answered him. "Seems you've underestimated your man, Curt. And I know what happened to the guns. Somehow he's got them. They talk stronger than empty promises. That Luke speaks enough Kiowa to get by. You know how they admire bravery, so don't start on me. There was nothing I could do."

"More's the pity I chose you for my partner," came Curt's bitter answer, demanding in the next moment, "Did you tell them there would be no more horses or guns?"

"These savages, Curt, have their own code of honor. Aside from trading the guns, which Luke claims that they have, he demanded Rafe be allowed to fight for his woman. 'Course, if he's lying, he's dead."

"How will they know?"

"They got ways to settle things. Maybe you can fight him for Lacey since you want her so badly."

Lacey refused to look away from Evan's eyes or his grin,

as if that thought amused him. Rafe was good with his
knife, she knew that. He had survived other fights. But she
knew as little as Curt did. Would the Indians give him a fair
chance? Curt took her reins and led her horse back to the
camp. All she hoped for was a chance to see Rafe and found
that Curt was not going to let that happen.

"Tie her, Evan."

Don't beg, she warned herself as she went back into the
tipi. She didn't struggle as Evan made short work of tying
her hands and ankles with rawhide thongs. But she wanted
to give Rafe time without either Evan or Curt there.

"Evan, wait. Why do you let Curt order you around? I
can't believe that you would be a part of this." She felt the
heat of his gaze when he hunkered back on his heels at her
side.

"It won't help, Lacey. No matter what Rafe says to Walks
Like Cat, he ain't taking you."

"You know what they'll do to him, don't you?" His smile
chilled her. "Tell me why, Evan."

"So demanding! Guess you'll never change. I threw in
with Curt to have enough money without having the old
man holding his ranch over my head, forcing me into his
ways." He stood up and looked away from her eyes, which
pleaded with him. "No matter what I did, it wouldn't have
been enough for you."

"You can't hold that against me. Sy wouldn't let me
marry you, Evan. And I never loved you. I never once said
that to you. I thought you—"

"That maybe I forgot? I didn't. You made it clear that I
wasn't man enough for you or the Reina." His eyes glittered
with hate for a moment before the look became one of
desire. "Let Rafe and Curt kill each other. I'll be the only
one that comes back for you."

The chilling promise in his voice left her shaken. She lay

watching the pinpoint of light at the top of the tipi give way to night as the drums began. She only knew that Rafe was still alive, for she was sure that if anything had happened to him, she would know.

Her skin was abraded where the ties cut. She didn't hear anyone approach, but somehow wasn't surprised when one of the Indians came for her. He set his torch in the firepit and with his knife cut her free. She tried not to shrink from the wicked blade he held as he pulled her roughly to her feet. Lacey stood and tried to walk, but the pinpricks in her legs made her falter. "Wait, please," she whispered foolishly.

She couldn't believe he understood her, for he said no word but flung her over his shoulder and lightly ran with his burden as if she weighed nothing. The sounds of voices, the brightened flare of firelight, and the louder drumming told Lacey she was close to where everyone was. Dumped unceremoniously to the hard-packed earth, Lacey sat up and found Luke beside her.

She kept her eyes lowered from the harsh light. Luke didn't move or turn when he asked if she was hurt. Lacey shook her head, trying to get her bearings.

"Rafe's here," he whispered.

Lacey's eyes followed his gesture. She had the presence of mind to stifle the scream that rose in her throat.

Across the circle from her stood Rafe. But it was a Rafe she had never seen. Stripped to the waist, firelight rippling over his muscles, her gaze was drawn to his face. A rawhide band held his hair back, black stripes covered his cheeks, and his eyes, staring back at her, held no emotion. Her eyes drifted lower, and Lacey almost bolted to her feet. There was a rope around his neck, and as he moved to accept a knife, she saw the rope was attached to a post. Slowly then she looked around the circle, and Lacey realized that no one spoke, not one face revealed any expression.

"Luke what's happening?"

"They're goin' to test him. This is a renegade band of Comanche, Kiowa, and Arapaho. Near as I can tell, Rafe's got a chance of saving himself."

Lacey wanted to ask more, but the drums ceased abruptly. One warrior stood and began speaking, calling names, Lacey thought as six men came to stand in the center of the circle. They were young and each held a knife. The motions that were made were toward where Rafe waited, and her heart cried out with the need to touch him, speak to him, but something warned her to keep silent. There were murmurs of dissent from some, but they were silenced quickly.

"He's goin' to play coup with them, Lacey," Luke explained. "I understood some but not all of what they said. I only hope Rafe catches on fast. He's got to kill one of them to go free. If three of them mark him with their knives, he's the one that dies."

Lacey bit down her lip until she tasted blood. Rafe couldn't die without knowing how much she loved him. She couldn't stand another moment.

As if he sensed what she was about to do, Luke grabbed her arm. "Don't move or make a sound. No matter what happens. You try to interfere, and you'll cost him his life."

She swallowed and nodded. Rafe ran his finger along the knife blade, then tested its balance in the palm of his hand. His free hand touched the rope, and then she felt the tension that marked his body. At an unseen signal they were ready; all six young Indians spread themselves in a semicircle.

It sounded as if they egged each other to be the first. Lacey didn't watch their faces. She kept her gaze locked to Rafe's knife. Two men approached him from each side, and she held her breath. One crouched low, the other leaped high, and Rafe's leg shot out, kicking the young warrior's knife hand, spinning quickly to block a thrust. It sounded as if they were all taunting each other, two others moving in, darting and backing away from the swing Rafe made with his weapon. Lacey didn't wish for anyone's death, but she prayed that Rafe would not be the one cut. God wasn't listening. Sweat mixed with blood on his chest. Rafe tripped another man, holding his lithe body down, but two others leaped for his back, and he set him free, jerking aside to avoid another cut.

Lacey covered her mouth with her hand. The rope pulled taut, and Rafe's head snapped as he almost fell to his knees. She heard others begin to yell, insults, encouragement . . . she didn't know. There was a scream of rage, and one Indian backed away, holding his arm.

"Oh, Christ! He's cut twice."

"Luke!" She grabbed his arm as Rafe wiped the sweat from his eyes, yanking at the rope. She wanted him to cut it, was going to yell as much, when he suddenly went down on his knee. She saw the glint of knives as an Indian flung himself on top of Rafe. They were holding each other's wrists away, but after the first roll they made together, Lacey knew the rope held Rafe in place. The firelight played over the strain of his muscles as he held on to the struggling Indian. She did cry out, but the sound was muffled as another Indian swiped at his back. Whatever sense warned Rafe, she was glad, for he stretched out, taking up the slack of the rope and using it to imprison the man he held.

Rafe straddled him for a moment, and it seemed to Lacey that they were locked in a silent combat of wills. She saw the Indian's mouth move and Rafe's flashing grin.

What was he waiting for? Dear God, she prayed, let it end.

With a deliberate downward slash of his knife, Rafe opened the flesh on the Indian's side. With another slashing move he cut the rope that held him and rose. He walked to stand before Walks Like Cat.

Lacey blinked her eyes. The Indian was smiling at Rafe! He was bleeding, and Lacey needed to hold him. She gathered herself to stand when Luke grabbed her and held her tight.

"You stay here until he comes for you. It ain't over."

Rafe made no move to staunch his wounds. There was a flurry of movement among those near him and low-voiced orders. Lacey looked around, trying to understand what was happening, and saw Evan removing his buckskin shirt.

"Luke? Luke, what are they telling them?"

"Evan's goin' to fight him for you." He shoved her face against his shoulder, felt the pain from her fingers digging into his arms, and barely nodded when Rafe faced him. He could see the cut on Rafe's arm bleeding freely and knew he would have to end this fight quickly. Lacey struggled against Luke's hold, her muffled voice begging him to let her see.

When she looked up, her eyes met Curt's across from her. His smile was triumphant, and Lacey felt her stomach churn. Evan tied his hair back and walked to stand beside Rafe. An Indian came to them, and they each held out their left wrist. Lacey saw the rawhide the Indian held, and as firelight played over their bodies, she heard Rafe taunt Evan.

"No running this time, Evan. I warned you about Lacey. And I promise you, I'll make your death slow."

"Will you?" As Evan dared him, he turned to face Rafe, and the brave tied their left wrists together. "You're hurt and you've lost blood. How long will you last? Odds are mine." He gestured around the circle. "Think they'll let you live if you kill me? I'm the one supplyin' what they need."

"But you want trade for those guns, and I offered them for nothing but Lacey," came Rafe's deadly calm answer.

She wanted to scream that she would go with them, do anything to keep him from fighting. Excited grunts made her look around at the hide bags that came forth. Hands were held high, grunted over, and Lacey judged there were agreements made, if nods were any indication.

Luke made her face what was happening. "They're wagerin' on the outcome, Lacey. Most of them favor Evan. Expected that. He supplies guns, horses, and whiskey."

"They're betting on who wins? This is a show to them?"

"Calm down, you're yellin'. Understand that their ways ain't so different from ours. A man's strength is measured by how well he fights and dies."

"Stop it, Luke!"

"I can't. They'd kill me. Rafe wouldn't let me. He has to do it. And you—you need to let him."

Lacey couldn't sit here and watch him again. Galling bile rose in her throat, and nausea rocked her belly. She felt chilled even with the heat of the bonfires. Sweat coated her brow, and she used her sleeve to wipe it.

"Don't be hidin' and shame Rafe," Luke warned. "There's nothin' they respect more'n bravery."

"You think I'm being brave, Luke? I'm not. I'm shaking. I don't want to see anyone die."

"Evan deserves it."

But she saw his eyes drift past her, his lips whistling, and she faced Rafe. Excited voices babbled around her. They were not done with their games. While Rafe and Evan stood, immobile, their hate an almost tangible thing, three Indians scattered brush and firewood in a smaller, tighter circle around them.

The drums began their beat, and the brush was lit in a

ring of fire around Rafe and Evan. Through the haze of
smoke she heard the chanting begin, and she watched
mesmerized as the two men began to move within the
circle.

Crouched low, she knew Rafe had the advantage of
strength against Evan just by his size. But Evan was not
wounded, her mind countered. Evan had not fought one
bloody fight already. Evan had been resting for three days;
Rafe had ridden hard to catch up with them. She didn't want
to think of all that Rafe had against him. She didn't want to
think at all. She didn't want to watch them, either, but it
seemed she had lost her strength of will to turn away.

Evan was lithe and grace, balancing on the balls of his
feet. Time and again Lacey saw how easily he swayed to
avoid the thrust of Rafe's knife. There seemed to be no
hurry to them, yet Lacey sensed that each one was aware of
how much space they had, of how far they could stretch the
rawhide that bound them. The breeze came up, making the
flames dance hideously, but now the smoke haze was gone.

Her gaze locked on the whiteness of their knuckles that
gripped each other's weapon hand. Rafe began to push Evan
to the edge of the firelit circle. Lacey thought the flame
reached out greedily to lick against Evan's pants. Sweat
gleamed on their bare skin. She bit her lip again when Evan
viciously kicked Rafe's leg. Staggering back, Rafe pulled
Evan with him.

There were cries as Evan attacked with his knife, and
only a quick twist of Rafe's body saved him from a slicing
wound.

Lacey wrapped her arms around her knees, shaking and
tense, her fear near to exploding. How much more? She
heard their taunting voices rise and fall above those of the
Indians. She saw their cold smiles, which promised death,

and looked at their eyes, which seemed intent on finding the other's weakness.

Feeling sickened, she couldn't deny in the dark recess of her mind that there was a grace to them both. Their balance and strength had a deathly savageness that held a form of beauty, too. Blood mingled with sweat on their skin. Rafe looked like a devil from hell, and Evan seemed as savage as the Indians that watched.

Rafe was weakening. He staggered again, going down on his knees, but managing to pull Evan with him. The swift arc of Evan's knife descending toward Rafe's chest brought Lacey's scream. Luke clamped his hand over her mouth, and she closed her eyes.

"Damn you, Rafe!" Luke yelled. "Get up. Don't let him win!"

She heard the lust in Luke's voice. Lacey felt as if she were brittle, about to break, and wondered irrationally about the dark side of men and their need to fulfill their clamoring bloodlust. Why? Why did death alone satisfy them? Rafe! she screamed silently over and over. Don't die. Live for me! Live for the dreams we shared. Live . . . oh, please . . . just live.

Her eyes were squeezed shut, but blinding herself to what was happening made it all a nightmare she couldn't cope with. She couldn't stand what her own hellish thoughts were forcing her to imagine.

Chapter 23 ====================

RAFE WAS NO longer on his knees. She could feel, just as if she could reach out and actually touch it, the raging hate that flared between him and Evan. They still circled each other. The knives were slashing, coming together and slipping free at the last moment before steel met flesh in a final blow.

Her pulses drummed along with her blood, which was pumping at an alarming rate, knowing they were toying with each other like two vicious animals, so sure of proving their male prowess.

Lacey didn't feel Luke wiping her tears. She didn't know she was crying. Rafe held every thought, every nerve of her body. He was down again. Evan jumped on top of him, straddling his body, every muscle standing out like twisted cords. Evan's hand held the knife in a grip so tight that even she could see it made the veins stand out on the back.

Her gaze locked to the sight of Evan's hand. She saw it rise, the rawhide tie taut, Evan's eyes glittering like the flames that were reflecting there. He was poised to kill Rafe with that last thrust. Rafe's arm and knife were caught beneath Evan's knee.

It was over. Evan had won and now he would kill Rafe.

Lacey wanted to die. There was no air to drag into her lungs. Her chest was tight, as if someone had bound it.

Helpless, she waited for it to happen. There was no one else that she saw, nothing else that she felt.

Luke was yelling, urging Rafe not to give up, and he turned to hear wild laughter from Lacey.

She never counted on Rafe ever having the strength left to resist death. His body, pinned beneath Evan, gave one heave, strong enough to unsettle Evan so that his descending knife plunged into the earth beside Rafe's neck. There was a wild twist of bodies then, and Lacey strained forward. She heard a grunt of pain and saw Evan fall forward. His body sprawled in a parody of a lover's embrace across Rafe.

But Rafe didn't move.

She stood, ready to run to him. Indians blocked her. Their black eyes held no pity, no mercy, but were warning in their cruelty. Just as she was about to strike one of them, Luke grabbed her hand and pulled her down with a sharp jerk.

"You can't help him! He's got to do it alone, Lacey. I warned you. If he can't get up, then no one won."

"Luke?" she called, not believing him. "Can't you see? He's lost so much blood," she wailed, struggling against his hold. "He can't get up! Have pity, Luke. Help him!" she screamed. "For God's sake, help him. Rafe has nothing left. You can't leave him to die," she begged, clawing at him.

"Shut up!" he ordered, gripping her arms so tight that flesh melded to bone. "Do you think I don't want to help him? I can't. No one can," he repeated harshly, trying to make her listen. "He'll lose face if anyone dares to go to him."

"You cowardly bastard!" Lacey lost control of herself, and she kicked and scratched him wherever she could reach.

Luke held on with one hand and slapped her into stunned silence. Like a bewildered child, Lacey sobbed and looked up at him. Tears streaming down her face, she silently asked why, and all he could do was hold her trembling body close.

"I'm sorry for hittin' you," he murmured, stroking her head. "I can't risk his life and ours. We have to sit and wait." He lifted her head, pity filling his eyes, and he waited for her to regain some control over her hysterical senses. "Show me some of that Garrett pride that made you the boss lady of the Reina. They may be savages, Lacey, but they have pride, too. Rafe is one of them now. He proved himself. You're his woman. Don't shame him."

Dying inside, she forced herself to obey him. Luke released her, and she shoved her hair back. Her hands clawed her thighs when she looked at Rafe struggling to push Evan's body away from him. The fire had been smothered. She barely noticed the exchange going on of the wagers won and lost.

Her gaze was targeted on Rafe's hand as he pushed himself to sit and use a knife to cut the rawhide. His back was toward her, glistening with dirt and sweat, his shoulder muscles bunching and moving. She cried inside, felt his pain with every motion, and let her love silently will him strength.

He rose to his feet, swaying as he turned slowly and met her gaze. If she lived the years with him, Lacey knew she would never bury the look in his eyes deep enough to forget.

His black eyes held a savage possessive pride that seemed to capture her. She couldn't tear her gaze from his. She didn't know when he moved, but he came toward her, kicking aside smoldering pieces of wood to cross to her. And all she saw were his eyes, binding her to him like nothing else had. He stood in front of her, legs braced apart, silent, yet demanding that she rise to meet him.

In a trance Lacey rose, her legs trembling, as was the rest

of her body. She was suddenly frightened of this man she had given herself to in love and then married for all the wrong reasons.

"I told you you're mine, Lacey," he stated in a raspy voice as he pulled her to him. Her head fell back, her tear-filled eyes searched his face, trying desperately to see what was beyond the savage look in his eyes. With a sob torn from unwilling lips, she came against him, crying his name until his arms encircled her and his lips took her mouth.

She felt the tension of his hard thighs pressed against her own, the fierce possessive moves of his hands running down the length of her back as if he could draw her body into his own. She had no breath but that which he gave her, no strength but that which she took from him.

His fingers tunneled beneath her hair, gripping her neck, slanting her head for his mouth. And sounds receded, faces disappeared, time and place were lost to them. He kissed her as if she were a drink of life to him, and Lacey could withhold nothing from him, desperate with the thought of losing him.

Her hands would not be denied the touch of him. His silky black hair was damp to her fingers as she clutched him to bring his head closer. Their lips tore free of each other at the same moment, slanting to touch and taste, wild with need to reconfirm love and life.

"It's over," Rafe whispered, releasing her.

Stunned, Lacey watched him move through the throng of Indians until he stood before Walks Like Cat. When she tried to follow, others blocked her way.

"Luke, make them understand, I have to go with him," she pleaded, bewildered by Rafe's leaving.

"He has to talk and—"

"You're crazy! He'll bleed to death if those wounds aren't tended."

Luke grabbed her chin and forced her to look. "See! He doesn't need you now."

Lacey stared at the two young women who came to wash and bind his wounds. Walks Like Cat was speaking in his guttural voice and held sway over the others.

Were they all insane? Could Rafe sit there and ignore her need to be with him? She glanced around, realizing that Curt was missing.

"Luke, where's Curt?"

Distracted from watching the lithe young girl who was offering Rafe something to drink, he answered her abruptly. "He ain't far. Let it be. Rafe'll take care of him." But he was already being pushed forward, and Lacey stood alone.

Rage filled her, and she, too, walked away. She couldn't stand another moment of watching Rafe sitting with them. Rafe had shown her a raw, savage side to himself that she didn't want to confront now. And no one stopped her.

The drums started up and her head began to pound along with the pulsing rhythm. Stumbling in the darkness as she made her way past empty tipis, Lacey tripped and hung on to the hand that reached out to steady her.

"I waited for you, Lacey. I knew you couldn't stay with him . . . not when you realized what a savage he is."

Curt! Dear God what had she done? In running from Rafe for pride's sake, she had put herself into his hands again.

"You're a fool if you think I'll come with you," she said, trying to brazen it out. "What's more, you can't force me."

"Can't I?"

The press of his gun barrel against her side was enough to silence her.

"Come along. I have horses waiting. No one will miss you. They're too busy celebrating." He laughed as she moved ahead. "We'll ride to Mexico. You didn't know that I have a ranch there. You'll forget that greaser. I promise you that." He gripped her arm and steered her away from the tipis.

"I'm far richer than you know, Lacey. You'll have everything you want, even the Reina. Someday, when I'm sure of you, I'll let you come back."

Lacey stopped abruptly, knowing she couldn't meekly let him take her. "You're the one who bought up the outstanding notes," she accused, realizing that he made no move to push her forward. She cursed the dark that hid his face from her. "Bo said you knew he was my father all this time. He told me that you forced him into helping you steal from me. How could you believe that knowing all this, I'd think of anything but killing you?"

"I know you're not a fool," he replied softly. "I was willing to wait until Rafe showed up. I wanted you for myself. Sy knew how I felt, but he was a stubborn old man. He refused to force you to marry me. I underestimated Sy. He fouled my plans with that damn will. I thought he had forgotten about looking for his son. I know I did my damnedest to make sure that he couldn't be found."

Rafe's tormented voice came to her mind. The times he had tried to find work, honest work, and how he was denied. And all because of Curt's driven desire for her.

"How could you deny a man his son?"

"I told you. I wanted you. I paid to keep Rafe hunted and running."

Lacey wondered if she dared to run. But there was a driving need to know more from him. Desperate enough to gamble, she demanded answers. "How did you find out about Rafe? How could you betray Sy's trust and mine?" Lacey fought not to cringe when his body brushed against hers.

"Sy was drunk and told me about a rumor he heard when he went back to buy stock in Mexico. He asked me to search for his son. And I did look for him. Once I had the confirmation from the village priest, the rest wasn't hard to arrange. It's a shame the Federales didn't kill him before the judge found him. Let's go, Lacey. I want to be away from here before dawn."

He grabbed her arm, and Lacey saw that he holstered his gun. "Curt, wait, please." She pulled back and never expected his swift half turn or the slam of his body against hers.

"You bitch! You think I don't know you're hoping that bastard will come after you?"

Lacey made her choice. Blindly her mouth found his. She swallowed the bile that rose, for his lips devoured hers. Her skin crawled when he pulled her hips tight to his and thrust his tongue into her mouth. She knew he took her whimper as a cry of pleasure and grunted when she leaned back against his arms.

She forced herself to caress his back, knew her touch excited him. He fumbled with the ties on the side of her shift, and she knew he would take her, here in the dirt.

Rational thoughts fled. He was pushing her down. Lacey grabbed at his thigh, panting like a wild thing caught in a trap. She heard the sound of his voice but not his words and pulled his gun free. Her mouth opened on a silent scream. She thrust the gun between their bodies and fired it over and over.

The shots were muffled, and she was suddenly cold. But not her hands. They were hot and wet. She glanced at them and flung the gun aside.

Terror sent her running blindly. Driven by the same desperation that made her kill Curt, animal instinct to survive surfaced. She twisted between looming shapes of tipis, mindless horror lending her strength to keep going until she crashed into the side of a horse.

Snorting and plunging against the staked rope, the horse scented blood on her. Unconsciously she scooped up handfuls of dirt, grinding it between her palms, murmuring incoherently to the horse as she wiped her hands dry on her pants. She could smell fear and didn't know if it was the animal's or her own. Grabbing the rope, she gathered it to shorten its length until her breath mingled with the horse's. She held on to his mane and boosted herself up on his bare back, ripped aside the rope halter, and urged him into a run.

Only the fluid motion of the animal seemed real to her. She reached the safety of trees, but branches slashed her, and she cried out in pain as her hair caught. The twigs and limbs felt like fingers reaching out to capture her. The horse pitched its high whinny into the night, and Lacey tore her hair free. They plunged deeper into the wood when she became aware of a rider behind her.

The horse found footing on a rough trail, and Lacey beat him with her hands as the rider came abreast of her. There was no room to move—she was being crowded against the massive tree trunks. She saw a hand reach out for her and slapped it away, almost losing her seat. No one was going to take her freedom again.

Tears blinded her. She felt the strength of the arm that caught her around the waist, pulling her from her horse to slam her against a hard body.

Nothing mattered but escape. The horse beneath them reared as she sank her heel deep into his side, clawing wildly at the arm that held her.

"Be still! Lacey, stop it or we'll both get hurt!"

The moment she heard Rafe's voice she sagged limply against him. But the horror of these last days had taken its toll. She gathered her strength to run when she felt the slowing motion of the horse.

Rafe didn't give her a chance. He flowed down out of the saddle with the silent grace of a shadow, taking her with him.

"Killed!" Lacey screamed the word, struggling in his arms. "I shot him . . ."

Rafe tried to soothe her with murmurs and his touch. He had found Curt's body, and his guilt weighed heavily for leaving her alone to face him.

"It's over, Lacey. Over," he stressed, pressing her trembling body close to his. He lifted her hand and brought it to his mouth. "You're—"

"Don't! Don't touch me." But Rafe held her in a death grip that she couldn't break. She heard his repeated whispers, but nothing he said made sense to her.

"Let me go. Didn't you hear me? I shot him."

"Never. I'll never let you go," he breathed with a shattering intensity, his eyes as dark and fathomless as the night. She was straining to drag air into her lungs. The savagery of the night had ripped aside his control, and now Rafe fought to leash it. Yet there was a wildness to Lacey that he couldn't still, a wildness that fed his own.

"Hold me," he demanded. "I won't let anyone hurt you." He tried to capture her mouth with his, but Lacey fought him, and they both fell to the ground.

Chapter 24 ================

RAFE ROLLED AND took the brunt of the fall. Lacey shoved free of his hold and scrambled away from him.

Her eyes darted frantically from side to side, and he slowly lifted his hand out to her. "Lacey, no one's going to hurt you. Hold on to my hand."

"They were going to kill you," she raged in a soft voice, backing away. "You left me alone."

Rafe levered himself up, half sitting, and leaned toward her. "I didn't want to leave you alone, and I'm here with you now. Take my hand, bright eyes. You won't ever be alone again." He had never felt such a deep sense of knowing another person, and it was this sense that warned him Lacey was losing her ability to reason. "Talk to me," he coaxed. "Whatever it is, we'll face it together. Come here to me. I need to hold you."

"No. I told you I don't want you to touch me."

Rafe became frightened at the way she was breathing, but was more afraid of sending her into another panic. A twig cracked in the woods behind her, and she cried out.

"They're coming after us!"

"Who, Lacey? Who's coming?"

"Curt. Evan. Those savages."

"Curt and Evan are dead, Lacey. They won't ever come after you again." He measured the distance between them.

"They'll hang you. And me," she added in a broken voice, shaking.

"No, bright eyes. The army was searching for them, and Matt and Hank are Rangers. They were—"

"Rangers! More lies from you."

Rafe spoke softly then, gathering himself to lunge at her while he told of how the judge talked him into letting them work on the Reina while they scouted around.

"No more! I don't care. Just leave me. Walk away."

"I told you I can't do that. And you will listen to me. Matt said they were desperate to stop the sale of guns to the Indians. No one is going to hang us for what we did. I might have to answer to the army for stealing the guns that Captain Chase captured from Evan's men."

Rafe shifted his weight and came to his knees slowly. He breathed deeply, willing Lacey to stay still long enough for him to grab hold of her.

Lacey stared at him without truly seeing him. She had to block the sight of him fighting from her mind. But the images flashed over and over, and then she saw herself with Curt, felt again the hard wooden grip of the gun and the cool metal trigger that she pulled . . . She went rigid.

Rafe made his move. He lunged across the space and gathered her into his arms. Her body was chilled, and he was held in a grip of fear. "What's wrong, Lacey? Tell me. I can't help you if you won't talk to me."

In her mind she ran from his demand and his touch. She didn't want to talk, to remember. Lacey seized on the first sane thing that would make him stop his demands. "Where's Bo? Did you see him? He stayed with me. He wouldn't let them hurt me. I want to go home, Rafe. I need—"

"Hush. Hush. You're safe now. I promise you that."

But Lacey didn't want to hear, she wanted the security

that only the Reina could give her. She twisted away from
him, and he let her go, seeing that she sat up, huddled into
herself.

"We can't go home yet. I need to finish what I started.
And you need to know what I found out about Bo James."
He didn't try to touch her and hoped that talking, telling her
what he knew, would reach through her shield. Rafe had a
nagging suspicion that Lacey already knew who Bo was.
But when he finished and only the night rustlings of small
animals broke the silence, Rafe felt she was miles away
from him.

"You know, don't you?" she asked in a deadened voice.

"He was your father, wasn't he?" Rafe raised his hand to
her shoulder as she nodded, but she shifted away as if she
had sensed his touch.

"It hurts you, bright eyes. I know that. I've lived with the
same bitterness and anger. But we can make it pass, we can
put it all aside with time. You have to want to do it." He
moved to kneel behind her, his arms encircled her body, and
he buried his face against the wild tangle of her hair. She
was withdrawn from him, and he wasn't sure how to reach
her. He knew the unanswered questions that must be
plaguing her. He had lived with them for a long time. But
no matter how much love he offered, Lacey had to face this
her own way.

Her body held no warmth, yet even as he rubbed her
arms, trying to give her his heat, he searched for a way to
break down the wall he felt her reinforcing. Time pressed
down on him. He had to get back and somehow stall the
renegade band about the guns he had promised them, but
Lacey came first.

"Stop thinking about it, Lacey. There's nothing you can
do. Bo made his choices just as Evan and Curt did. They
paid for them. Pity me, wife. I have to find a way to turn
down Painted Red's offer of twenty of his best horses for

you. Luke believes he's a member of the Kiowa *Ko-eet-senko*, one of their elite warrior bands that mustn't be insulted."

"Am I to be honored by that?" What nonsense was he talking? She wanted to be alone with her pain. Why couldn't he understand?

"So Luke said. Only a chief's daughter could command such a high price," he teased, thankful that she was talking to him.

"I want to go home." But when she tried to stand, he held her still, and she cringed at his touch.

"Stop it! We have to go back. But you must understand that you do nothing, say nothing without—"

"No! No more! No man will ever hold any power over me again. Do you know," she raged, scrambling to her knees and facing him, "how helpless I've felt? Do you have any idea of the fear that crawled inside me? You don't know what it was like to be pawed! You didn't care. You didn't even ask what they did to me."

"I know they didn't rape you, Lacey. I wouldn't have killed Evan so quickly if he had dared to touch you. He's the one that saw us together and told April. I made him tell me."

She froze in a crouch, eyes darting between him and the horses. There was a deadly note in his voice that made her afraid. The moon peaked from beneath the clouds like a shy lover and illuminated his face. Lacey caught her breath. Her widened eyes were trapped by his, emitting an almost tangible fury. There was a savage, untamed streak in him that went beyond what she had witnessed this night. She could see it in the arrogant tilt of his dark brows, the curving mockery of his mouth. Lacey shivered and heard the echo of her own heartbeat pound dully in her ears.

"You're like a wild thing with your hair all tangled like

an Indian maid caught unaware and your eyes catching the moonlight." He leaned forward, gathering his legs beneath him. "You make me want you all over again." By inches he moved closer, knowing she was ready to run. Her eyes were glazed, and he waited with bated breath until she focused on him. He willed her from her numbed state, praying he wasn't wrong.

"You've eyes with the power to steal inside me and stir my blood with a look. And your lips, witch, hold a man's breath inside him, find his soul, and demand it in promise of your kiss." His hand covered hers, and he drew her near. "Shall I court you like some half-tamed maid?" He cupped her chin and lifted it, brushing his lips over her mouth.

But it wasn't Rafe who kissed her. Lacey couldn't block the image of him lit by fire, fighting and then walking away from her. She didn't know him. She'd married and loved a man she had never known. When he spoke, he only confirmed her thoughts.

"I want a woman, not a child. Maybe," he grated with a taunting smile, "I should keep you here and show you how the Comanche train their women." She shoved him away, and Rafe hunkered back on his heels. "I didn't think you'd swallow that." He tried to be satisfied that she was angry and turning it on him. It was what he had wanted. At least she had lost that glazed look, but he didn't think it would hurt him to taunt her. "So, you've seen another side of me, and you don't like it."

"Like it?" she repeated, almost spitting the words. "I hate it. I hate what it makes you. I won't stay here. You're no better than those savages!" Her hands clawed the earth, and a fury seemed to erupt. "Next you'll tell me this is all my fault. But it isn't. If you hadn't insisted on staying in—"

"Stop this crazy talk. You sound like a spiteful child."

"You've called me that once too often. You never think I'm a child when you take me."

"Take you?" He came up from the ground slowly, his body taut, and grabbed her shoulders to haul her up in front of him. The thin buckskin shift tore beneath his fingers and fell to her waist. He ripped it off.

"I wasn't going to say a word about that night! But you're right. Only you've got it twisted, Lacey. If you'd've stayed where you were safe, none of this would've happened. But you didn't," he raged, shaking her. "Wishing won't make it all go away. I'm not going away. I killed a man tonight. For you, Lacey. I killed him because he dared to touch you. I'd do it again. But you're not going to drive me over the edge. Do you hear me," he demanded, beginning to shake himself. "Never again!"

"You throw that up to me?" she screamed. "But I killed a man to protect you, too."

He stared down at her, fighting for control that had snapped. "You're always trying to prove—"

"Nothing! I don't want to prove anything to you. I hate you. I'm going home, and if you try to stop me, I'll kill you. I don't want you to touch me!" she cried out, arching away from contact with his body. "You're a savage. Like them. Savage!"

Rafe couldn't let her go. Her eyes were wild, and he knew he'd lost his chance to reason with her. He had wanted her aware and alive, and she was, but it was fury that made her so. Fury directed at him.

His lips silenced her, bruising the mouth he had tenderly worshipped. But she fought his kiss, and his rage against her sharpened so that he attacked her in kind.

With a brutal twist he released her mouth. "Now," he grated from between clenched teeth, "the savage kissed you. Home for you, if you love me, is wherever I am. Or is your loved based on lies? You can't," he warned, "go anywhere till I'm good and ready to take you. And if I was teasing about showing you what an obedient wife is, understand that now . . . now," he ground out furiously, "I mean to do it." He had to stop and take deep, shuddering breaths to still the storm inside himself. If Lacey hated him, it was nothing for what he felt for himself. Her face was white, her eyes horrified.

"Lacey, please. You're my wife—"

"Wife! You mean your bought-and-paid-for whore, don't you? I haven't forgotten about the money or the lies. I despise the thought of being called your wife. I hate the thought of you touching me. I don't want you. I never want you near me. The very thought of you sickens me."

Lacey found herself free. Her hand flew to her mouth to stifle the words already said. His eyes pierced her like daggers. Without a word he shoved her away from him, but when she turned to run from him, he grabbed the waistband of her pants and hauled her back. Tripping her down, he fell heavily on top of her. With her breath knocked from her, Lacey couldn't struggle.

He levered up to turn her around, roughly taking hold of her chin. "Look at me. No shy bridal hiding, Lacey. Show me the whore I bought." With a savage oath he used his knife to slice open her pant leg and tore them away. "You called me a savage. Was I ever that with you? I loved you. You're mine. But you want to feed off hate," he whispered, settling his body tight to hers. "When I'm finished with you, you'll feel enough hate to last a lifetime," he intoned with soft, murderous fury, ripping open his pants.

"Rafe! Don't do this. Don't destroy—"

"You already did that."

He took her mouth as he took her body, plunging them both into hell. She bucked against him like a wild mare being saddle broke for the first time. But the rage that was unleashed, rage he couldn't control, became a punishment for both of them.

"Hate me," he grated. Her silence, her very stillness seemed to enrage him further. His fingers gripped her hips to raise her higher. And his mouth closed over hers.

Lacey twisted her head away. Her throat closed as her body betrayed her, but there was an agony in her soul that would never heal. A rasping sound tore free from her lips, and she found the strength to answer him.

"I can't hate you. I don't feel anything that strong for you, Rafe. There's nothing now."

But there was. There was the violation of her soul and his.

When he rolled away from her in disgust, Rafe slid his hand over her shoulder before he hunkered back on his heels and stared at her.

Lacey believed his face was a mask of her own. She saw the pain reflected in his eyes and felt it was a memory burned forever in time. She lay sprawled where he left her and watched him hitch up his pants. Without a word he walked away.

For long minutes she didn't move. What had happened to them? What triggered this violence between them? Had she driven him to . . . No! She couldn't accept all the blame. She wanted to talk to him, but when he came back, leading the two horses, tersely ordering her to dress, she said nothing.

Her shift was torn in two. He slit the center of one half for a poncho. She ignored his gesture to help her mount.

Aching, she followed him back to the renegade camp.

At the edge he drew rein and dismounted. He made no move toward her. He had hurt her, and the knowledge brought a shiver from his gut to his soul.

His silence was painful. She gazed at his hands clenched at his sides and tried to remember when they held her with tenderness. His black eyes, forbidding as she was drawn to them, seemed to refute her pleading gaze. Lacey turned away, unable to bear the sight of him.

"Wait here, Lacey. I'll get Luke. He'll take you home."

His voice was calm and chilling. She nodded. "Yes. I need to go home. I need Maggie."

She sounded like a wounded child, and it tore into him. "No!" The fury exploded all over again. "You don't need Maggie. You don't need anyone but me. Here is where you belong." Rafe kicked the earth at his feet. "Here by me. Nowhere else. And . . . no one else."

He waited and hoped and offered a prayer for some sign, a cry, a word, some damn thing! But Lacey slumped on the horse's back, staring through him. He turned his back and walked away.

Lacey knew the choice was hers. She could follow him and try to mend this breach. But she wasn't sure that she wanted to try. Shivers racked her body in the fading aftermath of shocked reaction. Would it change anything if she went after him? Somehow she didn't think it would. Neither bent well for another. Pride . . . perhaps that was one reason. The only way they came together was to cool the savage desire between them, and now that, too, was destroyed.

"Luke's waiting for you," Rafe said suddenly at her side, handing her a blanket. "Think before you go, Lacey. You're my wife. Your place is with me. When you decide what you want, I'll be waiting for you. And wherever I am, that's where our home will be."

She had no answer to give him. Weary beyond thinking and shaking with uncontrollable shivers, Lacey reached down inside herself to find strength. She found tattered bits of her pride.

Pride took her in hand, and she looked at Rafe.

She couldn't face his violence again. He had broken her for the last time.

Slowly then, clutching the blanket, she turned the horse away.

Chapter 25 ════════

MORNING SUNLIGHT, BRINGING with it the first sweltering heat of the day, streaked across the golden wood floor of Lacey's bedroom. She lay on her bed, telling herself, as she had for the past two months, that today Rafe would come home.

She didn't want to remember the few days it had taken her and Luke to make their way back to the Reina. Luke had little to say after he told her he had found Bo James dead at the bottom of a ravine. They had taken his body home to Reina and buried him beside her mother. Never once had she looked back. Rafe wasn't going to follow her. Not then. They both needed time apart.

Once she was home, Lacey offered no protest to Maggie's fussing. She made no effort to appease the worry evident in Maggie's eyes each time she looked at her.

The only spark of interest she had managed to show was when Captain Chase had come a few weeks ago, telling her that he had seen Rafe. Some of the renegade band had escaped, but they stopped the guns from going with them. There were other bands that he had to track, and Rafe had offered to help him.

But there was no message for her.

"No," she could still hear him say regretfully, "I'm sorry. Rafe didn't say anything." She had hated to beg, hated to see the pity in the captain's eyes.

But that had been weeks ago, she reminded herself, and still there was no word of him.

Even gruff Matt McCabe, when he returned with news that most of the cattle had been found, couldn't rouse her from the deathlike lethargy settled so snugly around her. She had answered his questions as best she could. When he was done questioning her, she knew he and Hank had returned to Austin.

Restlessly she turned, punching the pillow beneath her head, letting her thoughts drift, hating herself for the crushing weight of pain that tore across her insides when she thought of Rafe. How could she stop herself from thinking about him? She curled tight on the bed, her hands cradling her stomach.

Would he ever come back, or was it, in truth, finally over? Surely, she consoled herself, he would come back for his share of the Reina. And the money? The judge had come and given it all to her. He wouldn't tell her if he had seen Rafe. And Rafe wanted the money, didn't he?

But she was no longer sure of anything that dealt with Rafe, not even if he loved her.

She brushed aside the tears that started, knowing that they came far too easily now. Once she had been strong enough never to cry, but Rafe had changed that from the very first day. Rafe . . . always Rafe . . . haunting her every waking moment and thought.

Even at night her dreams gave her no solace, for the blackness surrounding her brought to mind his eyes. Tender and passionate, gleaming with devilry, sparkling with laughter, even his anger came to haunt her. She missed him desperately. How could she forget him?

Sometimes she was driven in desperation from her bed, unable to sleep. And she stole into his room to touch his things, imagining the still warm scent of him near, and for a little while the ache inside her would ease, and she would find herself in the morning asleep across his bed.

But there was no real peace inside her, and she knew until they faced each other again, there never would be.

It seemed as if all her emotions had been left with him. Except pain.

Berating herself to stop, as she had done a hundred times past, Lacey heard Maggie walking outside in the courtyard. When she didn't come in, Lacey grew curious. She rose and went to her door, but stopped from opening it when she heard Maggie talking to someone.

Lacey's heart began to pound. It couldn't be, she told herself in one breath and in the next thought that maybe Rafe had come back.

But instead of flinging open the door to see, Lacey wearily returned to sit on her bed. She didn't have the strength to face him.

Maggie knocked a few minutes later and opened the door. "Good, you're up an' it's 'bout time, too. You got a visitor, so let's get you dressed without any jawin'." She went to the wardrobe and pulled out a pale green gown that was sprigged with tiny white bows. She shook out the folds and held it up for Lacey's inspection. "Reckon this will do you nicely."

Rousing herself, Lacey looked from the gown back to Maggie. "Who's here that I need to wear a gown?"

"It's not Rafe, honey," she answered quickly, hating to see the flare of hope die in Lacey's eyes. "It's Tom Darcy, and I think you should see him."

"In the trappings of a woman?"

"That's what you are. Can't go an' change things, now, can you?"

Lacey was too beaten to argue. Shrugging her shoulders,

she said softly, "Tell Darcy to wait in the office. I'll get dressed."

"Already done that." Maggie came to her side and gave her a quick hug. "In a few weeks you'll feel more like yourself, honey. Draggin' 'round and wishin' ain't gonna make it happen any different."

Maggie closed her door, muttering to herself. "Damn country ain't the only thin' that ain't been reconstructed yet. Put mules head to head an' it's more'n a body could handle at times. Iffen I had my way . . ." Moments later she was outside, calling for Fletcher.

Lacey knew that Maggie had been angry, but then, she had been for weeks. Dressing was a chore, but she took the time to brush and braid her hair, wondering why Darcy had come. Captain Chase had told her how hard he had taken the news of Evan's death. She felt pity for the prideful old man who had learned what his son had become. Filled with a vague unease, she struggled to dismiss it.

Shock hit Lacey like a hardfisted blow when she stepped into the office and faced the haggard blue eyes of a man suddenly old and beaten. His once broad shoulders sagged, and his voice as he turned to face her, once filled with arrogance and pride, faltered when he spoke.

"It was good of you to see me, Lacey. I hope, well, you don't mind that I helped myself to some of Sy's brandy?"

"No. No, of course not," she answered, coming to sit behind the desk. She didn't want to stare and reveal how upsetting the changes in him were.

"As if he had read her thoughts, he chuckled softly. "Don't hide it, Lacey. I'm gettin' used to it, you know. But then, I didn't come here to talk about me or what happened to Evan."

"Then why did you come?"

"I rode over to give you these." He reached into the

pocket of his somber gray jacket and removed a sheaf of papers, which he tossed on the desk in front of her.

Lacey stared at them but made no move to touch them.

"Go on," he urged. "They ain't gonna bite you. Take a look at them."

Lacey's clumsy fingers tore at the string tied around them. After she opened and read the first one, she looked up at Darcy. A welter of confusion danced across her mind.

"Why are you giving these to me? I thought this was what you always wanted."

"Once, I did," he admitted. "Once the dream of having all of the Reina for my own drove me. But you don't want to hear about an old man's dreams. Let it suffice to say that it doesn't matter anymore. They're yours."

"Curt bought these notes. How did you get hold of them?"

"I didn't mean to rile your temper, young woman, and I know how hot the itch gets to set your tongue to waggin', but you sit and listen to me."

"By what right do you dare come here and order—"

"By the right those notes give me. You can't meet them, can you?" Resentment flared in her eyes as he watched, and she shook her head. "I thought not. But I can call them in anytime I want to."

Anger rose. Vaguely Lacey realized that it was for the first time since she had left Rafe. But there was more at stake than keeping the Reina for herself. "I still have time to meet these notes, Darcy. Are you telling me that you'll deny that?"

He didn't answer, and Lacey nervously played with the edge of the papers. If Rafe were here, she would have the money to pay him off. But he wasn't, and she didn't dare use it. If Rafe came back and demanded what was his and found it gone, Lacey knew if he wanted to, he could make her pay in ways she didn't want to imagine. Her only hope was to convince him to give her time.

"Guess you stewed long enough," he said. "Before your feathers get ruffled any higher, I'll tell you that I don't want the notes. They cost my son his life, and my daughter ran off when she found out what he'd been doin'. Lit out with that no 'count Farel. Evan shamed me. Can't figure his reasonin', even now."

He lapsed into a brooding silence, and Lacey dismissed the thought of telling him why Evan had turned on him or the part she had unknowingly played.

"Why did Curt give you the notes?" Lacey asked.

"They had agreed to it. Him and Evan. They both knew how much I hated Sy for costin' me cattle. An' I don't know why Curt was lookin' to hurt you. Guess we'll never know the truth."

"No, I guess not. But I can't just take these. There must be something you want as a fair exchange."

"Nothin'. Don't matter now."

He was, she noticed, a bit unsteady as he stood, slowly straightening his jacket. She was confused by what he had done and didn't know what else to say.

Darcy turned when he reached the door. "There's one thin' more, young woman. Don't be a fool over what happened with Rafe Parrish. Doc told me some, the rest I can guess. You married the man. The land can't talk to you, girl, or share your pain. I know that now. We were wrong; me and Sy. The land ain't all there is. Let there be an end to the bitterness between us, Lacey. We both lost. Pride cost me my children. Pride, if you let it, will cost you more."

When she looked up again, he was gone. Staring at the door, his lingering words brought a renewal of pain. He was right about the Reina—it had cost her dearly.

But what could she do now? Rafe wasn't here for her to

tell him he was right, too. Home was only with him.
Without him all she had worked for, fought for, and denied
to herself was meaningless. She knew it now that it was too
late.

Leaning her head down, she massaged her aching temples. Eventually Rafe would come home. Until then she had
to stop thinking about him. With an inward cry of despair
she knew it would be easier to ask herself to stop breathing.

When Maggie came looking for her, carrying a lunch
tray, Lacey was still sitting at the desk, finishing a glass of
brandy.

"Didn't you hear me callin'?" she demanded upon
entering. "Land sakes, Lacey, I don't know what's happened to you!"

"Don't you?"

"Right. I do. But you ain't got a lick of sense—"

"You're right, Maggie, I don't. But I already decided that
for myself." She smiled up at Maggie's stunned face and
nibbled on a ham-filled biscuit.

"Well? Ain't you gonna tell me what he wanted?"

"Darcy?"

"Yes, Darcy. You seem mighty slow-witted, Lacey.
What's that paper you're hidin'? How much whiskey did
you drink?"

"Brandy, Maggie. One glass and I didn't quite finish it."
She chewed the last bite of biscuit, swallowed, and moved
the notes so Maggie could see. "Darcy had the notes that
Curt bought up. He gave—"

"Oh, Lord, I knew it! I told Fletcher somethin' bad was
gonna happen. Now you'll be glad that I did. He wants you
to pay them off, don't he? You can't do it."

"Well, I'm glad you stopped long enough to let me
finish. That's not what happened. He gave them to me.
Signed them over, paid in full."

"Jus' like that without askin' for nothin'?"

"He said he'd lost enough." She met Maggie's gaze, and her eyes blurred with tears. "Just the way I've lost Rafe."

"Didn't think he meant all that much to you to begin with," Maggie snapped.

"Maggie! How can you say that? I married him, didn't I? You know I loved him—"

"So! That's jus' what I mean," she calmly interrupted. "Can't say you love him now, can you? You wouldn't sit in Sy's chair an' lie to me 'bout how much you care for him?"

Confused by the way Maggie seemed to be baiting her, Lacey rose to her feet and leaned over the desk. "I do love him, damn you! I even forgive him for what he did to me. I wish to God I had the chance to tell him that!"

"Then do it!"

Maggie's smile as she backed toward the door should have warned her. Following her with her eyes, Lacey saw him. She looked from one to the other.

"Maggie," she whispered, hurt that she had tricked her.

But Maggie shared a long look with Rafe before she gave him a shove and then slipped out the door.

Speechless, Lacey saw that he was leaning against the doorframe, his stance reflecting the wary look in his eyes.

She felt herself thrown back in time to the day he had first stood in this very room, his eyes assessing her and waiting.

Hungrily she drank in every detail of his appearance while they stared at each other in weighted silence.

His body looked leaner than when she had last seen him, and his boots were coated with dust, as if he had ridden long and hard. The fabric of his pants seemed strained by the tenseness of his leg muscles. He wasn't wearing a gun, only a worn belt. A black shirt, open at the neck, emphasized the deeply tanned skin of his face. His hair was longer than she remembered, and the breadth of his shoulders was daunting.

Time and again his dark eyes drew her gaze, and a knot tightened in her chest.

And Rafe, while nothing of his emotions showed in his face, stared as hungrily at her. He had learned long ago to school his features to show no more expression than that of a hawk arrowing out of the sky after prey.

The dark grave look in his eyes was possessive. The first sweet yearnings of desire burned inside her. Every nerve ending screamed out for her to go to him, but she couldn't move. What if he didn't want her? Desperately she found herself thinking that she had to do something, say something to stop him from just looking at her.

All she managed was an imploring whisper. "Why, Rafe?"

"Why what, princess? Why I stayed away or why I'm back?"

"Don't call me that." His voice had been low and harsh, filled with that impatient arrogance she remembered so well. He stood and seemed to radiate power and pride, making no move to take her into his arms and kiss away all the hurt and pain they caused each other.

"Does it matter why you're here, Rafe?"

"I guess not."

She still hadn't moved, nor had he, yet a thousand memories of his lips and arms reached out from his eyes to capture her, to touch her and make her long to be beside him.

"Darcy was here," she whispered and looked down at the desk. "He gave me the notes. Paid in full. And the judge was here. He left your money. And I . . ." She looked up and then away. But she couldn't be denied the sight of him.

As if in answer to her unspoken plea, he sauntered toward her, stopping in front of the desk. She watched his hand reach into the pocket of his vest and remove something. He tossed it on top of the papers. "I came back to see if you still wanted this."

The warm patina of gold glinted against the stark white. His mother's ring . . . her wedding ring. How could she have forgotten it? Lacey stared down at it not trusting herself to meet his gaze. She didn't dare pick it up. It would be too easy. Rafe would say something more, explain why . . . yet she despaired that he might be toying with her. That was a pain she could never live with.

"Lacey."

She glanced up quickly and caught the pleading, almost expectant look in his eyes, but he masked it just as her own softened.

The reckless slant of his mouth tilted into a knowing smile, somehow making his voice all the more insolent. "I guess what I overheard between you and Maggie wasn't true. I had a feeling it was a mistake to come back here. Told Maggie as much, but she's thick-headed. Seems she had this feeling you wanted me back. I guess I had to know for sure."

"And now you think you do?" she asked in a breathless whisper. He was really here. Rafe. She trembled at the thought of it.

"I figured to pack my gear and get out, since I know how you feel."

"Running again, Rafe? You do that very well. And you're wrong. You don't know how I feel." She couldn't let him go. This time she knew it would be for good. "Rafe, where have you been?"

"Around."

"Damn you! That's no answer. I've a right to know. After all, I'm still your—" She stopped and couldn't look at him. The word hung there unspoken between them. The word she denied he had a right to call her. *Wife*.

She sensed his movement and glanced up, but it was not toward the door—he was coming around the desk, and she stepped back.

"Afraid? Don't be. You just reminded me that you're my wife." He cursed himself a thousand times for coming back, yet knew he could never stay away from her. She was a heated, haunted memory that left him without peace, no matter how hard he pushed himself to forget her. He had told her she claimed a man's soul, and he knew she had his.

Backing her into a corner so she couldn't run, he stood before her but did not touch her. The memory of the last time they had been together, the violence, the hate that had raged and its ending was still between them. It was a wound that Rafe knew would not heal, and one he would live with forever.

"Rafe? Why have you really come back?"

"It ended wrong between us," he answered softly, noting the dark shadows beneath her eyes. He tried to still the trembling in his hand as he reached out and brushed one finger under her eye. "You haven't been sleeping, have you? I'm sorry if I caused that."

"Are you?"

"Questions, always questions, Lacey," he snapped as his resolve to be calm disappeared with every frightened look she gave him. "Don't fear me. I swear I won't hurt you."

"No. No, you won't. I've had no peace with you and less without you, Rafe. I don't know what you came back expecting to find."

"Don't you, Lacey?"

She sensed her time was almost gone. "I'm not sure how to answer you. I don't know what you want to hear me say. I love you. I haven't felt alive without you." Such softly whispered words that she never meant to say. But they had been spoken. She cradled his cheeks between her hands and rose on tiptoe to brush her lips against his own. Pride and everything else be damned! She wanted him as he was. This time, this time she would give him her love without reservations, or she would lose him forever.

His kiss was fleeting. "Lacey," he breathed against her mouth, "do you know what you're saying . . . doing? I won't leave you again. I swear that."

Her lashes were dark smudged crescents before she lifted them and looked into his eyes. "We've made so many promises, Rafe. We've broken them, too."

He leaned his forehead against her hair, placing his hands flat on the wall to either side of her. He was afraid to touch her. "You haunted me," he said, his voice hoarse. "I wanted you and needed you. So many times I wanted to come here and found myself knowing fear for the first time in my life that I had lost you."

She brushed his lips, shaking. "I wanted to find you. I didn't know where to look, and the nights were so lonely without you. How will you forgive me for the cruel things I said to you?"

"No! The guilt and the blame are mine for what happened."

She pressed her fingertips against his mouth, silencing him. Slowly Lacey shook her head, her gaze locked to his. "No, Rafe. I won't accept that. I pushed you over the edge that night. I know that now. I pushed you because that's where I was, and I was too frightened of you to admit it. I didn't know you anymore. I wondered if I ever had, and the hold you had over me was too powerful. But it's only in your arms that I find my world begins and ends."

Very gently she placed each of his hands on her shoulders. "I want you to hold me. I need you to do it." She agonized over the seconds that passed before he gathered her into his arms.

"I shared your fear, Lacey. You take everything that I am and leave me with nothing unless I have you." Her eyes were filled with softness, fired with love and desire, but he needed the words to end his torment. "Say that you forgive me." His eyes glittered with pain and the words tremored forth.

"If I forgive you, I need to forgive myself for driving you into hell. I can't do that alone."

"The nights were empty without you," he murmured, kissing away her tears. "I want my wife."

"As she is? I can't promise to be sweet and docile, Rafe. You have a knack of setting my temper to simmer."

"And you don't do that to me?" He pulled back slightly and found laughter in her eyes. Hugging her close, he knew he needed to share this as much as everything else she had to give him. Her kiss of tender promise stole his breath, and he returned it with all the love that welled inside him.

Sweeping her up into his arms, he gently pressed her head to his shoulder. "You'll learn to trust me again. We'll share the Reina the way Sy wanted us to. We have what he lost, Lacey. I swear that I won't make his mistake and lose your love."

She closed her eyes as they walked out into the sunlight, only to open them at his soft laughter. Maggie stood, broom in hand, Fletcher at her side with his shotgun.

"There's no need for that," she chided. "Rafe's come home, and we have promises to cherish." Lacey sealed her words with a kiss, making a vow that the Reina would be home, with all that Rafe dreamed of, all that he wanted. They had love, and soon she would tell him about their coming child.